Dan Fesperman is a reporter for the *Baltimore Sun* and worked in its Berlin bureau during the years of the civil war in former Yugoslavia, as well as in Afghanistan during the recent conflict. His first novel, *Lie in the Dark*, won the CWA John Creasey Award for Best First Crime Novel in 1999 and *The Small Boat of Great Sorrows* won the CWA Steel Dagger for Thriller of the Year in 2003. His new novel, *The Warlord's Son* will shortly be published by Bantam Press.

Acclaim for *The Small Boat Of Great Sorrows*:
'Thoroughly recommended . . . Has the tang of someone writing with conviction, compassion and, above all, an understanding of the Balkans'
Observer

'A dark and morally complex novel that won this year's Crime Writers' Association Ian Fleming Steel Dagger – the top award for a thriller'
Daily Telegraph

'Fesperman's credentials as a reporter covering the war in the former Yugoslavia serve him well as he leads us through 50 years of politics, ethnic hatred and war, while his skill as an observer of familial ties and human nature marks *The Small Boat of Great Sorrows* as another instalment of what should set a new standard for war-based thrillers'
Los Angeles Times

'Engrossing . . . Fesperman tells his atmospheric tale with great elegance. The teasing out of historical elements displays a sharp analytical curiosity'
Guardian

www.booksattransworld.co.uk

Also by Dan Fesperman

LIE IN THE DARK
THE WARLORD'S SON

THE SMALL BOAT OF GREAT SORROWS

Dan Fesperman

BLACK SWAN

THE SMALL BOAT OF GREAT SORROWS
A BLACK SWAN BOOK : 0 552 15023 1

Originally published in Great Britain by Bantam Press,
a division of Transworld Publishers

PRINTING HISTORY
Bantam Press edition published 2003
Black Swan edition published 2004

1 3 5 7 9 10 8 6 4 2

Set in 11/14pt Melior by
Phoenix Typesetting, Auldgirth, Dumfriesshire.

Black Swan Books are published by Transworld Publishers,
61–63 Uxbridge Road, London W5 5SA,
a division of The Random House Group Ltd,
in Australia by Random House Australia (Pty) Ltd,
20 Alfred Street, Milsons Point, Sydney, NSW 2061, Australia,
in New Zealand by Random House New Zealand Ltd,
18 Poland Road, Glenfield, Auckland 10, New Zealand
and in South Africa by Random House (Pty) Ltd,
Endulini, 5a Jubilee Road, Parktown 2193, South Africa.

Printed and bound in Great Britain by
Cox & Wyman Ltd, Reading, Berkshire.

Papers used by Transworld Publishers are natural, recyclable products made
from wood grown in sustainable forests. The manufacturing processes
conform to the environmental regulations of the country of origin.

For Emma and Will,
the chairmen of the board

'Awesome symbols, the Crescent and the Cross;
their kingdoms are the realms of graveyards.
Following them down the bloody river,
sailing in the small boat of great sorrows,
we must honour the one or the other.'

From the Serbian epic poem
The Mountain Wreath
by Petar Petrovic Njegos, 1847

Prologue

Eastern Bosnia

When they came to arrest the general he was polishing his boots, an orderly man to the very end. At least, that's what the soldiers would tell the debriefers and reporters, having found the boots on the bed with a blackened rag, the smell of polish still strong in the air.

Earlier that morning it rained, and when the soldiers first assembled in the trees some two hours before dawn, the general was asleep. Lulled by the wet drumbeat on his bunker roof, he dreamed of marching, watching a nocturnal parade pass before him – his men, their men, everybody's men, it seemed, the dead and the wounded among them. They wore bedclothes, he realized with a start, and their feet stirred clouds of dust that coated their skins in chalky grey. He wanted to look away but couldn't, hypnotized by the tramping feet, row after row of everyone he had ever commanded or fought.

Then the rain on his rooftop slackened. The sleep-walking legions faded. And when the tinny alarm on his watch sounded a few minutes later, at 5 a.m., the general awakened with the taste of dust sticky in his mouth. He climbed from the bed for water, drinking straight from the tap, as if he were bivouacked in the field, crouching at some farmer's spigot.

The grey light of the mirror revealed a drawn face with bags beneath the eyes, deep creases framing loose jowls. Stubble everywhere. With luck it would be a full beard within a week, though he couldn't say for sure, never having grown one. He had a high, jutting forehead, peaking with a thick shock of grey in need of a trim, brushed straight back and smelling of the pomade that forever scented his pillow. But the most striking feature was his grey-blue eyes, as clear and cool as stones in a stream, eyes that could convey either rage or resolve without a word being spoken. 'Command eyes', one colonel had called them, and they had watched dozens of offensives come and go before the guns had fallen silent nearly three years ago. It was only later, in the calm of peacetime, that people in other places had decided that his army had exceeded the rules – rules made in their lands, where no-one knew the fears and histories that ruled his. And somewhere, he knew, in some room with maps and charts and file drawers stuffed with more information than any order of battle, others were still fighting his war. They were still assessing his movements and commands, clucking and shaking their heads, exercising a calm reason that one never had time for in the midst of battle.

He remembered the heat of those five days that were now the subject of such scrutiny, the hardness of the roads on soles worn thin by four years on the move.

Cicadas roared in the spiky underbrush while his men forded the thickets of scrub and low trees, calling out to each other, and to the enemy, too. The town in the eastern valley, so long a problem, had finally fallen, months of stalemate bursting like a worn belt in a tired engine, and during the first night thousands of the panicked foe had broken through to the forest in a long, sinuous column in the darkness. By morning they were running, a herd cut loose with only fear to drive it, and his army joined the chase as if it were a hunt, the rattle of gunfire non-stop.

The cleverness of his men had astonished him, a rustic ingenuity blooming in the elation of pursuit. Some donned blue helmets – the trademark of the UN 'peace-keepers' – luring the skulkers from the trees by shouting through loudspeakers, pledging protection, food, water, a bed to sleep in. Others drove hospital trucks slowly down country lanes past patches of woods, beckoning the wounded out of hiding. We will heal you. We will save you. Give yourselves up and end the struggle. It worked more often than he would have believed.

The roads were dry. There was nowhere to fill your canteen, and the dust was so heavy that by nightfall of the third day he and his men were coated, ghostly in its whiteness. Too weary to wash, they slept where they halted and swallowed dust in their sleep, and by morning it was the taste of death itself, so they rinsed and scoured with shots of brandy, passing bottles down the line. They grew giddy with the flush of alcohol and the promise of another easy chase; more fighting that would bring this war to a close. Destroy a hundred of their sons and you saved a hundred of your own. It was an old formula, closed to debate. With any luck they would shut down the bastards for a generation. So they moved back onto the roads and into the trees, clipping their ammunition into place, a sound to get your blood going.

Late in the final day a messenger arrived with new orders, and the general took fifty of his best men to an empty factory six miles to the rear. The torn innards of its machinery sat rusting on high grass at the front, and the big building echoed with voices, a hollow sound leaking from high windows. Hundreds of the enemy were inside, stragglers and quitters, men and boys, eyes lit by fear and exhaustion. The general strolled indoors and nearly gagged on the stench, the sweat and shit and grime mixed with the factory smells of metal and machine oil. The noise was unbearable, too, like the keening of newborn calves. A cordon of his troops stood on one side of the walls next to large sliding doors while an officer in a black beret walked the general to the opposite end. They climbed a catwalk raised on a steel frame, draped with pulleys and chains, and as the general rose into view the crowd's noise seemed to rise with him, a swell of echoes appealing incoherently for his mercy.

'Listen to them, General Andric,' the officer in the beret shouted above the din. 'They must think you're the lord high executioner.'

The general looked the man over, scanning the pockmarked face. The man stank of brandy, and a belt of ammunition was draped across his torso like a sash, a

12

risky stunt done only for style. The raked beret was smudged brown across one side. Popovic, his name was. Branko Popovic. A freelance, accountable to no-one. The man did know how to fight, after a fashion. He could secure a village, clean it out and keep moving, and you knew that nothing from that quarter would ever threaten your flanks again. But his methods were, at best, unorthodox, and the general kept his distance when he could, although lately that had become difficult. To his way of thinking, their fortunes had become far too enmeshed.

The crowd quietened after a minute or so, the men jostling as they sat or squatted on the oily floor, spent from five days in the heat. Sunburned faces turned towards him as if he were about to deliver a speech, and he looked into the eyes of a few, seeing sons and fathers, the rough hands of ploughmen and hay balers, the flab of shopkeepers. Boys who needed scolding and a firm hand.

For a moment he wavered, and Popovic must have sensed it, for the man was suddenly bobbing at his side, gun at the ready. Colonel Popovic, it was, though God knows where the rank had come from. The deep scars of acne and the croaking voice. Two days earlier the general had seen him in a burning village with a column of laughing men, their arms full of stereos, televisions, bottles of whisky. Some hauled bulging sacks across their backs like Father Christmas, cheeks powdered by the unceasing dust.

'Take them now, sir, and we'll never have to fight them again,' Popovic urged. 'Let us finish it, sir.'

13

The general wanted to laugh at all of the 'sirs', as if suddenly Popovic considered himself a real soldier, and this was their usual way of fighting. For a moment the man's insolence was more distasteful than the thought of the rabble at his feet. But the orders were clear, so he nodded without turning, not giving Popovic the satisfaction of verbal acknowledgement.

The men below must have been watching for a sign, because they began standing, eyes rolling, panic taking hold. Fathers clutched at their boys, and the wailing resumed. The younger men shoved, going nowhere in the crush of bodies. Then an officer shouted, Popovic perhaps, and the shooting began, close and rapid, with no place for the bullets to go but into the meat and the filthy clothes, the shrieking roar and clatter of all that death locked beneath the low metal roof. Most of the general's memory of the moment had gone fuzzy. All that remained sharp was the image of a single face – some farmer or labourer who happened to stand out from the crowd for a split second, his mouth opened as if gasping for breath, then overflowing suddenly with blood, chin covered in red, a gargle of anguished pain. Everything else was unclear, a miasma of sound and stench. But his memory of the dust remained, and he still tasted it every morning as clearly as if he'd swallowed a spoonful each night before bed.

The general ducked beneath the tap for another drink. Then he re-checked his watch – 5:08. Timing was important. He mustn't be late, of course. That would be the end. But acting too early might be fatal as well. He strolled to the high window, the one he always kept

14

open no matter the season, anything to rid the room of the damp concrete smell of a prison. The sky was clearing, moonlight beaming through the tall slender pines like searchlights. Nothing stirred but a cow, slumped low against a dim bank of underbrush. Even his sentries were quiet, their usual buzz of conversation stilled for a change, although he could smell their cigarette smoke, could hear the chirp of a lighter.

He gazed at the stars, seeking omens in the deepness of the sky. There was no light from any of the houses in the valley, yet he sensed their presence, the red rooftops that climbed the gentle slope like a tiled footpath. He inhaled deeply, smelling turned earth, the resinous bite of the pines.

At times like these the general found it easy to imagine these hills were enchanted, a place where mere farmers and peasants slipped their skins by night to become ogres and knights, gliding into the trees to joust and thrust in secret, writing new chapters in the lore of the forbidden. There were treasures in these fields and forests, for those who knew where to look – old bundles in oilcloth, dormant beneath cabbages and pumpkins, or concealed in the darkness of stables. So much that was buried, not just in his valley but in all of them – plots and secrets just beyond the reach of memory. Wait long enough, perhaps, and the moonlight would lay everything bare, melting the cover as if it were snow, at least until morning, when all would again be concealed in the white light of dawn.

But a soldier could grow old and die waiting for the moonlight to do his work. And old soldiers didn't die, he mused, nor did they just fade away, as the arrogant American had so famously insisted. They simply grew slow and fat awaiting the judgement of history, listening alone for the knock of the verdict upon their bunker doors.

Not him, the general thought, as sure of himself as ever. Not him.

1

November 1998

Down in the mud of central Berlin you never knew what
you might find. Last week it had been an American
bomb, as long and fat as a giant bratwurst. A poor fellow
from Poland poked it with a shovel and the whole thing
went up. Five more fatalities for the casualty lists of the
Second World War, courtesy of a B-17 that hadn't flown
for half a century.

Then there was the corpse, or the skeleton, rather,
that rose from the ground on the yellow teeth of a mech-
anical digger. Probably nobody famous. Just a Russian
from 1945 who never made it home, judging by the
buttons, the boots and the rusty helmet. Two efficient
men in sports jackets and ties hauled him away in a
black plastic bag.

Barbed wire turned up too on this landscape of accidental archaeology, but that was of a more recent
vintage, left by the East Germans in the path of their long
and formidable Wall. And sometimes when Vlado
Petric trudged through the ooze he pondered all the
German Shepherds that had patrolled this narrow strip
of land, day after day, year after year. Plenty of their left-
over shit mixed in the mire, he supposed, and for all

these reasons he spent ten minutes at the end of each workday cleaning the waffled soles of his boots with a screwdriver, prying loose the mud. It was the richest sediment of twentieth-century misery the world had to offer, and he had no wish to track it home. He'd tramped enough to his doorstep already, nearly five years earlier, as one of the hundreds of thousands of Bosnians who'd escaped their own war for some quieter venue across Europe's sagging theme park of history.

So, when Vlado and Tomas Petrowski mounted diggers on Monday morning to dig into the muck of Potsdamer Platz, they knew there was always a chance they would unearth some history, even though they were construction workers, not archaeologists. They were the merest of drones, in fact, two among thousands on a landscape that was being billed as the world's largest construction site. Not since Albert Speer unrolled his blueprints for Hitler had Berlin witnessed such architectural hubris, and tourists with nothing better to do could pay a few Deutschmarks to climb the stairs of a red building on stilts at the heart of it all. Inside, there were photos, maps and charts to see. But the real attraction was out in the elements on top of a switchback of corrugated metal stairs. It was a high viewing platform where you could stand in the wind and rain to marvel at it all, to watch the city be transformed from the inside out. It was as if an alien spaceship had uprooted a massive high-rise shard of Dallas and dropped it onto the belly of old Europe.

With a set of binoculars on that particular Monday morning you might have picked out Vlado and Tomas as they went to work, marching towards their diggers, almost emulating a goose-step as they picked their way through the slurping ooze, yellow hard hats bobbing. They were a few hundred yards from the green edge of the Tiergarten, Tomas a short and stubby Pole with the golden hair and beard of a Viking, Vlado of medium build and measured expression, clipped dark hair above deep-set brown eyes, a face that strived mightily to give away nothing. Each wore jeans and flannel shirts bought from the battered metal stalls of outdoor markets on grey Saturday mornings, and each knew how lucky he was to be working for 12 DM an hour, with all the right papers and documents to make it legal.

Neither spoke the other's language, but both spoke enough German to grunt and nod their way through a day on the job. Their task was simple enough. Other men drove stakes and markers into the ground, then Vlado and Tomas dug trenches and holes between them, generally working straight through until lunch. At noon they carried brown bags to benches in some damp birch glade of the Tiergarten, as calm and green as an Alpine meadow, then ate their sandwiches and apples, watching rucksacked legions of young Germans glide past on bicycles.

But this morning, if you'd been patient with your binoculars up there on the viewing platform, you might have noticed an interruption in their routine, shortly before ten, when they shut down their engines and dismounted.

Tomas had found something.

The jagged mouth of his digger had struck a slab of

buried concrete, and out here that meant you'd made a discovery. The rules were clear on what to do next, and both were careful about knowing the rules.

'Who's going to tell them?' Vlado asked in his halting German.

Tomas shrugged. Somewhere in the warren of trailers where the supervisors sat was a keeper of old maps who could put a name to what they'd found. And somewhere in a ministry nearby, in a room with rolled yellowed charts bearing faded swastikas, there was an authority on this subterranean history, an expert in naming and classifying every hibernation chamber where men in grey had once hunkered down for defeat. He was always the one who decided how to proceed, and so far his decisions had never varied: re-bury it and keep building.

'Maybe it is not something to report,' Tomas said, knowing as the words left his mouth that he was wrong.

Vlado's answer seemed to take them both by surprise.

'I think maybe you're right. Let's make sure it's worth reporting. Let's investigate.'

A half-century earlier such disobedience would have earned each of them a bullet in the head. Now, labour rules being what they were, the consequences would scarcely exceed a tongue-lashing as long as everyone's immigration papers were in order. Few Germans would work for these wages any more, no matter how high the unemployment rate, which is why thousands of Poles, Irish, Scots, Russians and others streamed every morning to this grand amphitheatre of mud. Men had become too valuable to spare on this front line, especially with companies like Sony and Daimler waiting anxiously to move in.

So, Vlado and Tomas climbed aboard their machines and went back to work, grinning as they heaved and shoved at the earth to expose more of the slab, fighting down a panicky sense that they might be stopped at any moment. Within an hour they uncovered the top of a door. Within another hour they reached the bottom, and by 1 p.m., having forgotten about lunch altogether, they'd completed a sloping trench that would let them reach it on foot. It was then, with stomachs growling, that they finally shut down their engines and dismounted again, sweating in the cold, stunned by the sudden silence.

They glanced around to make sure no-one was watching, then descended the mud passage and pushed against a heavy steel door – once, twice, then a third time, ready to give up until it began groaning open against the concrete floor. Leaning with their shoulders, they pushed it further ajar, the air issuing from it like the stale breath of a tomb. Then, breathing rapidly, they stepped into the damp chill of May 1945.

Vlado clicked his cigarette lighter to reveal a mural on the opposite wall, as bright and fresh as if it had been painted the day before. The flickering light played across the faces of rugged SS men, dapper in pressed uniforms, standing watch over blonde wives and blue-eyed children, a sunny tableau of Aryan comfort for this grey day in early November.

Vlado and Tomas might well have spoken, but their new language tended to fail them at moments like this, as if they'd misplaced the manual for some particularly unwieldy tool. But both knew they'd gone far enough, and Tomas strode off to fetch the foreman. Vlado waited in silence, wondering what sort of ghosts might yet lurk in a place where the concrete walls still smelled wet and new after half a century underground.

He took a deep breath, then, flicking his lighter again, walked across the floor into a second room, where he found a row of low iron beds with thin mattresses. Steel lockers lined the opposite wall, but Vlado's eyes were drawn to a yellow and black inscription on the door, a lightning-bolt insignia of the SS. Above the door were German words in Gothic script. It took a second for him to translate: 'There are many people, but few good men.'

Vlado stepped slowly, as if there might be someone asleep just round the corner. None of the noise from above made its way down here, and he felt a weight on his chest, a change in air pressure, or perhaps it was all in his head. His flannel shirt was damp with sweat, cooling against his skin.

There was one last room, and he stepped inside. Emptied of furniture, there was a mural here as well, only this one was a detailed map of the Nazi empire at its zenith. Germany lay at the centre in red, her spidery borders encompassing Austria, Czechoslovakia and half of Poland. Beyond it, slanting red stripes covered captured territory – Hungary, Scandinavia, Belgium, the Netherlands, as well as much of France, the Soviet Union and the Balkans. He found his own land, the old name 'Jugoslavia', and, to the upper left, 'Kroatien', the Nazi puppet state of wartime Croatia, its borders encompassing most of what was now Bosnia. His home city of Sarajevo merited a black pinprick, and he touched the careful lettering for 'Sarajewo', the concrete chilly, its surface just bumpy enough to imagine that the mountains themselves were beneath his fingertips. How odd to feel a stab of homesickness from this map of conquest, yet, if he closed his eyes, he knew he would see old women in kerchiefs and long *dimije* skirts scuffing down dirt lanes, bent men in wool caps seated on mule carts piled with hay, wheels creaking. For the most part Vlado had been raised a city boy, but farms and villages were always only a valley away, and they were the places that called to him now. Odd, he knew, especially down here in this well of captive darkness. Enough to make him feel like a homesick old peasant who'd never been five miles beyond the milking shed.

The sound of a voice made him jump, but it came from the entrance, not the past. A column of chattering men was approaching the door down the slope of the muddy trench, and he retraced his steps to the bunker entrance just in time to see a foreman in a hard hat squeezing through the opening, looking hurried and embarrassed, speaking rapidly in German, loud voice going hollow as he entered. Accompanying him was a tall, balding man in a suit, shod in Italian loafers caked with mud. Tomas was behind them, looking scolded, saying nothing. The second man unrolled a blueprint in the beam of the foreman's flashlight, everyone's breath misting in the ancient air. The man needed merely a glance before he found what he was looking for. He poked at an upper corner of the map while shaking his head slowly, as if disappointed in them all.

'*Ja*,' the construction boss said. '*Hier*.' And from their expressions Vlado gathered this was a well-known place.

'*Der Fahrerbunker*,' the man in the suit mumbled.

'Führer*bunker*?' said the foreman, eyebrows raised in panic. He looked ready to flee.

'*Nein, du blöder Idiot! Fahrer*.'

Drivers, in other words. Chauffeurs. This had been the home for the SS men who drove the generals and the chiefs of staff. But with nowhere left to drive in the springtime rubble of 1945 they had mostly stayed here, awaiting the end. Vlado had heard of the place. It had been unearthed a few years ago and re-sealed, lest it become a shrine for neo-Nazis. This was not the sort of tourist attraction the locals wanted in the heart of the new Berlin.

'Bury it,' the man announced in German, rolling up his blueprint with a disdainful flourish. 'And next time,' he said, eyeing Vlado, 'come to me before you go this far. We already knew of this place. There was no need for all this.'

They plodded back to the surface in single file, Vlado reluctantly so. He had wanted to stay a while longer, not just to poke among the relics but to get a handle on the climate, the atmosphere. Such readings seemed important when you had recently lived through two years of a siege, with death dropping from the sky like cinders from a chimney. He and his neighbours had somehow made it through, subsisting on the world's handouts of bread and beans – two winters without heat, two years without electricity or running water or glass for your windows, without coffee for your breakfast, salt for your food, soap for your bath, candles for your darkness. Two years without a wife and child to keep you company. And down there in the bunker he had suddenly seemed very close again to the feel of those lonely nights, to the mood of a city where even a funeral became an invitation to gunfire from snipers who might have once called to you by name.

Surviving that qualified him as something of an expert on manmade disaster, he felt, and what better place to take comparative readings than in that damp hidey-hole. Check the barometric pressure, the relative humidity. Collect the motes of dust. How could you possibly draw such air into your lungs and not be changed in some small way, and who knew where that might lead?

Or maybe this was just the wishful thinking of a man who, for all his joy and relief in escaping a war and rejoining his family, ached to return home, or, at the very least, ached for change. Four years, ten months and counting in this land of flat horizons, doing work that numbed him to the bone. The mountains of home had begun to seem like something out of a dusty old atlas, a fairytale of a place with all its crabbed problems snagged in the creases of the hills.

But as the foreman departed, Vlado felt a giddy sense that perhaps change was in the works at last, that a day already so different from all the others would only become more so.

Within an hour they had re-graded the mud into a neat, level surface above the bunker. Then other workers poured a layer of new concrete, the foundation of yet another high-rise. Vlado and Tomas watched in chastened silence as they belatedly ate their sandwiches, marking the location by other points of reference, mapping it in their heads for posterity. No matter what rose here, they'd always know what lay underneath, like a dormant cell of some once-virulent plague.

So this is what becomes of the ruins of war, Vlado mused, staring at the wet concrete, and he wondered if his home in Sarajevo had already been torn down and rebuilt in his absence. Or his favourite café. The house where he'd grown up. His office? That would be fine, considering the way so many people in it had ultimately betrayed him. Then he thought of friends, some of them dead, and of a woman he had only briefly met, yet whom he felt he knew quite well. And as he sat on a kerb to clean his boots in the gathering dusk, he took extra care in removing the day's mud. Then he brushed off his hands and walked half a mile to the long stone platform of the Unter den Linden S-Bahn station. He boarded a rattling commuter train for a forty-minute ride to the eastern reaches of the city, out to where, if you kept walking, the plains would take you all the way to the forests of Russia.

By the time he reached his stop, it was dark, and it took a brisk twenty-minute stroll to reach a tall, grey high-rise where he took the lift to the eleventh floor. He then opened a door at the end of the corridor to find an American in a suit waiting for him on the living-room couch.

2

'He has been here for an hour,' Jasmina whispered quickly as Vlado shut the door behind him. 'I've made coffee twice. I ran out of things to say twenty minutes ago.'

She was flushed, wiping her hands briskly on a tea towel. Their daughter, Sonja, was nowhere to be seen. Across the room on the couch sat the American visitor, putting down a German magazine and looking towards them expectantly.

'Did he say what he wanted?' Vlado whispered. 'Who he's with?'

'Nothing but small talk. Family and jobs and the lousy German weather. Said he's here on business and left it at that.'

The man's grey suit said government, but nothing else did. He was all elbows and knees, folded into place like a jack-in-the-box, and on closer inspection even his uniform wasn't what it seemed. The suit was wrinkled, the shoes scuffed, the tie knotted with the slapdash skill of a groom late for his wedding. His face was impassive, probably as intended. But the eyes gave him away – an expressive gleaming brown, lively and eager. If he had a tail it would be wagging, and Vlado wondered why. And why an American?

The authorities, both national and international, had long since lost interest in Vlado following his sudden arrival nearly five years ago. He had shown up unannounced at an American military base in Frankfurt on a cargo plane from Sarajevo, spilling from a wooden crate like the misloaded parcel he was. As a police detective who had smuggled himself out of a sealed war zone with a sheaf of incriminating documents, he had been something of a sensation at first. Not the sort that made headlines – just the opposite, in fact, for the results of his work had been an embarrassment for more than a few international agencies. He had attracted various men in grey from miles around, fretting over what secrets might have been blown, who might have been compromised, whose credibility might need to be rebuilt.

Just about everyone had wanted to hear the story he'd unearthed, a tale of theft, smuggling, murder and corruption that might have been impossible to believe if not for the packet of evidence in his satchel.

He'd been debriefed by everyone who seemed to count in this part of the world – the UN, NATO, the Council of Europe, Interpol and half the embassies in Germany. Protocol demanded that the Germans go first. Then came a tag team of Americans and French, arguing loudly over who had precedence. Next came the British, the most polite but somehow the most frightening, with the cool, clipped manner of executioners. The parade seemed never-ending, and everyone spoke the careful language of damage control.

Some played it friendly, offering cigarettes and jokes.

A short jolly American talked Yugoslav basketball for a while, biting off half his questions with inappropriate giggles, lunging forward every time he came to a key point. Vlado, who knew a thing or two about interrogation, thought the man was probably proud of his style. The ones who weren't good at it usually were.

The French and Germans were icy, unyielding, seeming to frown at his every word. An intense chain-smoking German named Rolf kept asking about another German named Karl, who, judging from the line of questioning, must have been a Balkan smuggler of some success. Pleading ignorance of Karl only earned a raised eyebrow from Rolf, followed by an unconvinced smirk and a slow release of cigarette smoke.

The whole thing lasted four days, hours on end in a small windowless room in a cool blaze of fluorescent light. Mornings brought lukewarm coffee in chipped mugs that left sticky rings on white Formica. Cold lunches arrived on a wobbly cart. Then more questions, followed by a bland overcooked dinner and a night of poor sleep in a steel-frame bed down the hall. A guard outside the door turned the pages of newspapers throughout the night while Vlado tossed in his sleep, trapped in dreams of long walks through ravening crowds, awakening exhausted and sweating to the knocking of a radiator before the whole business started again. He could only guess what the fallout had been back in Sarajevo – fewer bureaucrats to worry about, perhaps, but probably little else.

In the end, the Germans deemed him unsuitable for repatriation – too many enemies on both sides, especially in the middle of a war, when it would have been too easy for someone to kill him. Besides, he had a family already living in Berlin. They'd been there for two years, in fact, a wife and daughter who'd been evacuated during the first month of the war. So the authorities did the easy and humane thing by letting him stay, and sent him packing to Berlin with a train ticket, a residence visa and a work permit. He would later discover just how rare and valuable such documents were, when the Germans began sending home every Bosnian refugee they could find.

But for all their care with paperwork, the authorities never bothered to inform his family that he was on his way, or even that he had escaped. For all Jasmina and Sonja knew, Vlado was still back in their besieged apartment, biding his time until his next monthly phone call to Berlin, still braving the bombs and the bullets. Which is why, when he showed up on their doorstep on the eleventh floor, fresh off the train, he'd been something of a shock, making for an awkward moment or two.

Since then, the international authorities had forgotten him. There hadn't been a single visit, letter or phone call, either to thank him or to let him know what had occurred in his wake. It was as if he'd been dropped into one of the holes at Potsdamer Platz.

Until now.

The American looked up, opening his mouth to speak.

'Herr Petric?' he said.

'Vlado Petric. Yes. And please, speak English. Mine

is a little out of practice, but it is still better than my German, Mr . . .'

'Pine. Calvin Pine.'

Pine stood, tall and bony, reminding Vlado of the big construction cranes that loomed above him at work, like praying mantises in search of a meal. Being an American, Pine smiled and held out his hand for a firm shake. The only people who grinned more in this part of the world were Japanese tourists. But the smile had a glimmer of mischief at the corners, a boyishness that made it hard to feel put upon. His light brown hair was as stiff as broomstraw, with various sectors in revolt. And when he spoke, at least he kept his voice down, unlike the noisy Americans you saw rattling down Unter den Linden in bright clothes and running shoes, shooting video of everything that moved, griping about exchange rates and whatever they'd just paid for lunch.

Vlado wished he'd had time to clean up, wished he'd shaved that morning, wished he hadn't just stepped out of a huge, muddy hole in the ground. He wondered at the sort of impression he must be making.

'You're from the embassy?' he asked.

'Actually, no. From The Hague. The International War Crimes Tribunal. I'm an investigator.'

Vlado's curiosity turned to concern. He knew of only one matter, a single name, that could have brought the Tribunal to his door, and it had nothing to do with his work back in Sarajevo, where the criminals he'd dealt with had been smugglers and black marketeers, commonplace murderers intent on money, not ethnic slaughter. All he knew of the Tribunal he'd learned

31

from a Bosnian in Berlin, someone whose name he didn't wish to utter just now – someone, it now appeared, who had got him into deep trouble. If that was why Pine had come, this would be an unpleasant evening indeed, for Jasmina as well as himself.

'Why do you need to speak to me?' Vlado asked, knowing he must already sound like a suspect. Probably looked like one, too, reaching for his cigarettes and staring at his feet.

Pine seemed to note the change. He hesitated. 'Because we need your help. We've got a job we think you might be interested in.'

This answer was a pleasant surprise. Vlado glanced towards Jasmina, as if she might offer a hint of what came next, but she only shrugged.

'I'll make more coffee,' she said. 'And Vlado, why don't you ask our guest to sit. You've both been standing for the past five minutes. You look like gunfighters in an American Western.'

Vlado translated her remark for Pine, who grinned and folded himself back onto the couch. He had that American way of informal amiability, the salesman's knack for banter, for easing into his surroundings. As they sat, Vlado saw Sonja peeping round a corner.

'This is my daughter, Mr Pine. Sonja, who I haven't even said hello to yet.'

He coaxed her out with a smile, but she wasn't yet ready to forgive Pine, who had taken her usual spot on the couch. It was where she and her father always sat at this hour to read, and she held a story book in her right hand.

'We'll do that later,' Vlado whispered, switching to his native tongue. 'Go on now. I'll come and get you.'

She turned, casting a parting glance of cool appraisal towards the couch.

'She's nine?' Pine asked.

'Just turned it.'

Pine had learned that either from Jasmina or from a file, and Vlado wondered uneasily what other information he'd dug up.

'One bit of housekeeping', Pine said, 'before we continue. I have to ask that you keep the details of our meeting entirely confidential, no matter what you might decide to do. For reasons of operational security.'

So here it comes, Vlado thought, worried again. 'I suppose I can agree to that.'

'Good. In that case, how would you like to go back to work? Real work, I mean. Police work, like you used to do. A temporary job only, I'm afraid. But it could lead to something permanent, if you decided that's what you wanted.'

Vlado tried not to show his relief. He lit a cigarette, then offered one to Pine, knowing the American would probably refuse.

'No thanks. Don't smoke.'

'Investigative work? I hadn't heard you were short of help at the Tribunal. And it's not as if I could just pull up and move to The Hague, if that's what you're saying. What exactly are you saying?'

'You wouldn't be working at The Hague. You'd be going back to Bosnia. Only for a few weeks, at the most. Then, later, for good. If you wanted.' Pine glanced towards Jasmina in the kitchen. 'Which you'd have plenty of time to think about, of course. And we'd help with resettlement. Housing. Plus a regular job, doing what you did before. Investigations. In a jurisdiction that would actually be glad to have you.'

'But not working for the Tribunal. That part would only be temporary, as you said.'

'Yes. A one-time job only.'

Vlado wondered which police jurisdiction in Bosnia would be glad to have him; he doubted such a place existed. Pine wore a little smile, as if sharing an inside joke about the way Vlado had left things in Sarajevo. There was no sound from the kitchen, but Vlado sensed Jasmina listening just beyond the doorway. Her mouth would be set firmly and her hands still, wondering what was about to happen to the little world they'd made in Berlin, which, on balance, was comfortable enough. Safe enough, too. If there was going to be a problem about taking this assignment, it would be Jasmina. Like many Bosnian women strewn across Europe by the war, she had somehow blossomed on the barren soil of abandonment, spreading shallow but hardy roots in an unwelcoming land. Vlado had seen it happen in plenty of families, the women picking up confidence while the men, suddenly adrift, wandered and drank, sliding off towards melancholy and dreams of home.

'Maybe we're not too eager to go back,' Vlado said for her benefit. 'And maybe you'd better tell me a little more about this one-time job.'

Jasmina had edged to the kitchen door, her expression letting Pine know she wished he'd never come.

Vlado, however, was transformed. The sagging man of ten minutes ago was now edging forward in his chair.

'Of course you'd be free to stay here, once our work was done,' Pine added, perhaps playing to his audience in the kitchen. 'The Germans have assured us of that. And either way you'd be well compensated. If you took the assignment.'

Vlado blew a cloud of smoke towards the ceiling. He had tried to think as little as possible about his old line of work these past few years. Burning your bridges and nearly getting yourself killed can have that effect. But it wasn't hard to recall the buzz of putting together an investigation, peeling away the wrappings until you found the prize at the centre, or, sometimes, found nothing at all. Guessing and arguing with colleagues as you went, like a scientist waiting for the smoke to clear in a beaker. That sort of business seemed a long way from here, another distant land with its own hills and valleys, and he'd pretty much given up hope of returning.

He sighed. If his life was about to pivot he hoped he had the energy for it, the resolve. He recalled his sense of premonition from earlier in the day, down in the bunker. Walk through a door into 1945 and this is where you came out – into a room where a tall American arrived bearing gifts, offering to usher you through another door to a place you hadn't seen in years.

'Tell me about this assignment.'

Pine looked awkwardly around the room. 'I'm afraid your wife will have to leave first. Some of this isn't supposed to go beyond you and me. Not for now, anyway.'

'It's all right,' Jasmina said briskly, striding past with a tight smile. 'I'll go and read to Sonja.'

They waited until they heard the door of the girl's room shut with a snick. Sonja, who'd been eavesdropping from the hallway, complained noisily at the injustice of it all. Vlado and Pine looked at each other, a hint of conspiracy in the air, leaning forward, forearms propped on knees.

'There's a suspect we want to bring in,' Pine said, almost in a whisper. 'Have wanted to for some time. A Serb general, Andric. Do you know of him?'

'Yes. From the massacre at Srebrenica. His name comes up around here now and then. All their names do, if you talk to the widows. And going after him would only make more widows. He's protected. It would be suicide.'

'Which is why we're letting the French army do it. He's in their sector and they've promised to take care of it. He'll be their first arrest, but at least they'll be starting off with a bang – after two years of letting him drink coffee right under their noses.'

'Getting Andric would be quite an achievement.'

'It won't be easy. Especially when the French like to think Belgrade still has a soft spot for them. The timing's tricky, too. Bad time to go stirring up Serbs, with Kosovo ready to blow sky high next door. But that's where we come in. We provide the consolation prize. A suspect from the other side – a Croat from the American sector – to help balance the scales a little. Unofficially, of course. That way the Serbs don't feel so singled out, which helps keep the French happy, diplomatically speaking. And if the French stay happy, maybe they'll go after more suspects for us, further down the road. But our part of the deal looks a whole lot easier than theirs, because our man's been out of action for fifty-five years.'

Vlado knew what that meant.

'A suspect from the Second World War?'

'Yes. From Jasenovac. Heard of it?'

'I should think so.'

It was like asking a German if he'd heard of Auschwitz. In the Balkans, Jasenovac was the darkest stain of the Second World War, perhaps of any war. It was a concentration camp where, depending on whose history you were reading, 20,000 to as many as 600,000 people had died – Jews, Gypsies and Muslims, plus a few thousand political dissidents and assorted others from Hitler's roster of 'undesirables'. But the great majority of the victims had been Serbs, killed not by the Germans but by their local collaborators, the ultra-nationalist Ustashe, a faction of Croatians ruled by puppet dictator Ante Pavelic. All of which explained why the death toll was still a matter of debate. In that war, the Croats had been the reigning villains. In the latest one, the Serbs had the bloodiest hands. And in both conflicts, bitter ethnic arguments had at times masqueraded as scholarly debate over body counts and degrees of cruelty. Depending on your ethnic stand-point, Jasenovac was either the great blot of Croatian guilt or the overblown lie of Serbian propaganda. The outside world had pretty much settled on the former version.

But if the death toll remained in doubt, there was

nothing ambiguous about methodology. The killings at Jasenovac had been brutal and blunt, a crude Balkan antidote to German industrial precision. The locals had done things their way, using bludgeons, knives, axes, pistols, often taking an inordinate amount of time. It was a genocide of gouging relish that had shocked even the Nazis, whose officers had huffily written to Berlin to complain about the barbarity. Not that their letters did any good. Hitler seemed to like the idea of an ally willing to show some initiative. Besides, even the local Catholic Church had tacitly endorsed aspects of the project, with the priests and bishops of Zagreb lining up in support of the new regime.

'Of course I've heard of it,' Vlado said. 'My mother was Catholic. She was more interested in religion than nationalism, so she was always ready to admit that Jasenovac was something horrible. Her parents were a different story. Her father put me on his knee to tell me all about the lies of the Serbs before I even knew what a Serb was. He'd point to Orthodox priests in their beards and black frocks as if they were vampires who'd just stepped out of a tomb. I used to have nightmares about them snatching me in my sleep. But mostly it sounded like a lot of old people getting too worked up over things that didn't matter any more. Then the shells started falling in ninety-two and I realized maybe I should have paid closer attention.'

'You and everyone else with any sanity. Well, the fellow we're after can tell you all you'd ever want to know about Jasenovac. He ran a guard unit there, right in the thick of things. There's an interesting file on him back at The Hague. You'll be reading it soon enough, I hope.'

'I'd be more interested in finding out how he managed to avoid being caught after the war.'

'That's not a bad tale, either. Up through Austria and into Italy. Hid out in farms and monasteries for a while. Then a DP camp, a big holding pen for displaced persons, before he ended up in Rome. Stayed in Italy more than ten years, with a lot of help from some church people, a bunch of Croatian priests who ran a little operation on the Tiber. Ever heard of the Ratline? Laundered Western money paying for forged documents and freighter rides to Argentina. Seems that the Brits and we were already more worried about Stalin than a few left-over Nazis. We figure he made his way back to Yugoslavia in nineteen sixty-one. Living under a new name and doing OK for himself. These days he's a pretty successful businessman. Gas stations. Beer and liquor. And still pretty active. Lately he's been winning economic-development grants from the European Union. Brokers stolen cars on the side.'

'Then why do you need me?' Vlado said. 'This case seems to be solved. Sounds like what you need is an armed escort. A bodyguard. You've got a name for it in the States, I'm sure.'

'A marshal, you mean, or a process server. Yeah, we could use a few thousand of those. It's generally not our job to pick these guys up anyway. Ever. Then again we're not really supposed to be handling cases from the Second World War either. I guess you might say all of it's a little unorthodox, even off the books. The UN

39

Stabilization Force normally picks up our suspects, but they usually say no thanks whenever we ask. S-FOR likes to keep things quiet, not stir them up. But this guy's in his seventies, off in a backwater. His security's decent, and he's pretty careful, but if our plan works, using force shouldn't even be an issue. And that's where you come in.'

'How?'

'You'd be working undercover. Posing as an expat Bosnian who's just returned, which will be true enough. You'd carry in the bait. Lure him out into the open where we can pick him up with as little fuss as possible. Preferably at his favourite café. That way he comes along nice and quiet so nobody gets hurt, as we like to say.'

'Why an expat? Why not a real local? Buy off somebody from his village who he'd really trust.' Vlado realized he might be talking his way out of the job, but this didn't add up. 'In fact, I'd say you've got a few million locals to choose from without flying me anywhere, or a few thousand even if you're just talking about policemen. One of the local constables would probably do it for a few cartons of cigarettes.'

'The local constable is one of his top cigarette distributors.'

'Which I should have guessed,' Vlado said with a smile. 'You can tell I've been away from home too long.'

'Look,' Pine said, 'let's just say we have our reasons. Good ones. Some of which we can't get into right now because of security considerations.'

It was a line that immediately put Vlado on his guard. But Pine quickly moved on.

'Another reason is the bait. It has to come from an outsider, but one with some local connections, and you're the perfect match.'

'What's the bait?'

'A de-mining concession. Mine removal. He's been wanting a piece of the action for a while.'

'Doesn't sound like the most desirable work in the world.'

'You'd be surprised. It's lucrative business. Everybody and his brother wants a piece of it. Warlords, crime lords, mayors, police chiefs.'

'Which covers at least two people in every municipality.'

'You got it. But this fellow's always stayed out of local politics, unless you count the bribes and the vote-fixing for some of his buddies.'

'Forgive my ignorance, but how much money can you make digging up a few hundred mines? Or even a few thousand?'

'More than you'd guess. There are millions floating around. Some of it's UN money. Some is from the EU. The rest from various international do-gooders. Think of Princess Di. This was her pet cause. That made it glamorous, so now you've got donations from all over, well-meaning people handing it out wherever someone will take it. And if you're the top local contractor for your area you can usually pocket about half the grant for yourself, then pay the rest to a bunch of poor dumb farm boys who'll work for cigarettes and a few D-Marks. They dig 'em out the old way, with sticks and crowbars. Hand tools. Every week or so somebody gets blown to

41

pieces, but so what? The boss has his cut and the locals have a little hard currency and a big funeral with two lambs on a spit. And guess who gets to keep some of the unexploded mines if nobody's paying close enough attention to your demolition programme?'

'Ah. Lots of money, and free weaponry, too.'

'Which is why the UN has been wary about giving our man a piece of the action. But you'll be arriving as his guardian angel, the new EU representative for de-mining operations in his region, with a slick new business card that will knock his socks off. He'll figure that since you're Bosnian he might finally get an even break, because you'll know how to do business the way he likes.'

'With pay-offs and kickbacks, you mean.'

'Something like that. But you'll learn everything you need to know in debriefings at The Hague.'

'What's his name, this suspect?'

'Sorry. Still classified. Everyone and his brother knows we're after General Andric because his indict-ment's four years old. This indictment's sealed. We don't want to risk tipping him off and having our little bargain fall apart at the last minute. But he's no-one you've heard of, that I can guarantee.'

'A location then?'

'A small town in central Bosnia. That's as specific as I can get for now.'

'And you, Mr Pine. You're an investigator yourself?'

'A lawyer, to be exact. I'm what the prosecutor's office calls a legal officer, working with a team of about a dozen investigators, plus a military intelligence guy. I do some interrogations, a little fieldwork, then usually I'm co-counsel when cases hit the courtroom, the one who can connect all the dots. But if you look at the last line of my job description, which my boss did just the other day, there's also something about "undertaking such special assignments as may be required".'

'Which makes it sound as if you'd rather not be here.'

'Let's just say I already had plenty on my plate involving the here and now without spending a few weeks on the Second World War. This could all get kind of tricky if something gets screwed up. Which is why you really can't be talking about this.'

'What did you do back in the States, before the Tribunal?'

'I was an assistant US Attorney. Drug cases mostly. Part of a DEA task force for a while. Mostly young American thugs, with the occasional South American and Nigerian for good measure. Sort of like working on an assembly line. Which is why I volunteered to come over here. A little like you, I guess. Another reclamation project a long way from home.'

But Vlado wasn't sure he wanted to be reclaimed, especially if it meant going back to police work in a country where the economy had gone to hell and half the population was still nursing a grudge. It was the sort of work that tended to turn honesty into a game, a series of bargaining sessions between integrity and expedience. If you weren't careful you soon found your-self slapping backs and buying rounds with all the wrong people.

Nor was he convinced this invitation didn't have at

43

least something to do with what he'd become involved with here, a role that made him feel guiltier by the minute. So much for his reputation as the clean cop. He'd have to check a few things for himself before he could say yes. He would also listen to what Jasmina had to say. They could wait until later to decide whether to move back, because that would be the tough part, the part with the arguments and the tears, no matter who prevailed.

But his gut told him that he wanted the assignment, and if spending a few weeks back in Bosnia cost him his construction job at Potsdamer Platz, well, there would be other holes in the mud to dig, in other parts of town that led to other regions of the past.

Pine stayed for dinner. It went without saying unless Vlado and Jasmina wanted to violate every law of Balkan hospitality. They talked shop for a while, swapping tales of old colleagues and cases, stories full of humour and language that had to be edited for Sonja's ears. Having cleared the dishes, Jasmina put Sonja to bed. The girl had stared sullenly at Pine throughout the meal.

Vlado and Pine were relaxed, both sensing that, even without an official answer yet in hand, their immediate futures were decided, and that it was time to begin getting used to each other's company. Vlado uncorked the obligatory bottle of slivovitz – plum brandy – and the drinks flowed as they spoke of families, friends, and others they remembered on the distant landscapes of home.

Pine said his father was an *advokat*, a lawyer working in a small town in the American South. Vlado's had been a foreman in a machine shop. Metalworking. Could do anything with tools. Made the equipment sing but never said much himself. He'd let his work do the talking.

'Still alive?'

'No. He died fifteen years ago.'

'And your mother?'

'Two years later.'

'Did your father fight in the war? World War Two, I mean.'

'As much as most people did, I think. It was that or hide in a root cellar. He was with some volunteers, although it never came to much. There really wasn't much fighting where he grew up, just lots of digging trenches and guard duty, some marching through the woods at night, and constant hunger. There wasn't much room for a Muslim in that war, which is probably one reason he didn't try to make it more noble than it was. When I was a boy I used to resent that, especially after hearing other fathers brag about what heroes they'd been. Now I realize it was a virtue. It was the lying that got everyone in trouble in the end.'

'Well, good for him, then.' Pine raised his glass. 'He was from Sarajevo too?'

'Further south and west. Podborje. A small village in the hills towards the coast. After the war he couldn't find work so he moved to Sarajevo. We lived in a small valley a few miles from the city until I was about six. After that we were in the middle of the town.'

'Brothers and sisters? Uncles and aunts?'

'I was an only child. My parents had a late start. Either that or I was all they could stand. Some uncles and aunts in Sarajevo, mostly on my mother's side. A few in little places out in the country. We'd go a few times a year, weddings and funerals. Most of my father's people had died by then. I only remember one uncle, down on a farm with goats that were always trying to eat my sleeves. He and my aunt lived like hermits, so we only saw them once or twice. They'd drink brandy all night out in the back. It was about the only way you could get my father talking.'

That was an understatement, Vlado thought, recalling his father's brooding silences. Like a bird on its perch, seeing things below that others didn't, but never bothering to share what they were. His mother had always been the talker of the family.

'Family always seems to make such a difference in your country,' Pine said. 'Families and where you grew up. I'm always amazed. You'll meet people from the tiniest villages who got uprooted in the fighting, maybe had to move twenty miles down the valley, but you'd think they'd had to move to another country, the way they talk. Their village was all that mattered. Hell, if you're from a small town in America the first thing you want to do is get out. Staying is a slow death. I think that's one reason we don't understand half of what's gone on in Bosnia. We had the Civil War, and we drove out a few million Indians along the way, and we've got race and crime and poverty. But history is pretty much, well, history. People are too worried about their jobs and their sports teams and whatever's

46

on cable that night to be shooting each other over something that happened fifty years ago, much less six hundred.'

'That's because you didn't grow up listening to everybody older than you gripe about the last war. Telling you not to believe all that crap about peace and brotherhood because someday those people over in the next house would try to do it to you again. In some places it was the same whether you were a Serb or a Muslim or a Croat. The mistrust never really went away, and once the fighting started – boom. No more peace and brotherhood.'

'We've got plenty of old farts griping at the dinner table too. But I thought part of growing up was to not believe a word your parents tell you. In America nobody listens to the old farts except other old farts. What happened to you guys?'

By now, Pine was drunk. But Vlado, tipsy himself, realized the man had made a pretty good point.

'I suppose we all bought into the "wisdom of the elders" a little too much. Even I did. And look where it got us.'

'But you weren't out there hunting down Serbs during the war, so you couldn't have been too poisoned. What was the wisdom of the elders in your house?'

Another good question. Vlado shrugged, thinking it over.

'My father couldn't have cared less about politics, so maybe that's why I didn't care much either. It was little things, mostly, that he passed along. The way he lived. His work habits. Being trusted, relied upon. Showing that, even when times got difficult, you could bend without having to break.'

'None of the small-mindedness, then. None of the village mentality he must have grown up with.'

'Again, just little things. Old stories about his cousins or aunts. Traditions on holidays. The best way to butcher a lamb for a wedding feast. The best way to mend a broken universal joint. Things you did with your hands. Some fathers passed on their beliefs, their hatreds and passions. Mine gave me his way of looking at life. And a toolbox.'

'A toolbox?'

'It's the main thing he left me when he died. That and some old photos.'

Pine had nothing to say to that. He rubbed his face, slouching towards the table. 'I've had too much to drink.'

Vlado grinned. 'Maybe a little.'

'Guess we drove Jasmina off to bed.'

Vlado's smile broadened. 'Now we're the ones acting like old farts from the village. Drinking late after the womenfolk have gone to bed. This is when we're supposed to get out a deck of cards, or start an argument and push the table over.'

But Jasmina wasn't sleeping. Vlado looked down the hall and saw the crease of light below their door. It made him remember something that had been knocking around in the back of his mind throughout the evening. Before the night was over, he'd have to deal with it, face to face. Pine spoke up from across the table, breaking his reverie.

'Well, give America another six hundred years and maybe we'll be burning each other's houses. Of course, by then everybody will have unlimited channels on his cable system, so nobody will have time to start a war.'

They clinked glasses over that one, laughing.

'Maybe all Bosnia needs is a little collective memory loss,' Pine said. 'A lot of us at the Tribunal figure it's the only real solution. A little electro-shock therapy for everybody and your troubles are over.' Pine laughed again.

Vlado wanted to. But there was something vaguely troubling in the thought of all those Americans and Europeans in their trim Dutch apartments, laughing over cocktails at his country's recurring genocidal folly. Making sport of all the raw country people with their quaint ignorance, as remote to most modern Europeans as the dough-faced peasants of a Breughel painting.

Vlado pulled deeply on his cigarette, blowing a cloud towards Pine. If the man could get used to Balkan history then he could get used to Balkan smoke. Then he leaned across the table, lowering his voice.

'Look, this job you're asking me to take. I'll tell you right now, I'll probably take it. Jasmina won't want to move. She hates the work around here but she likes the peace, the stability, so that's something we'll have to decide later. But I still wonder what the hell I'm getting into. The way I see it, you want my "local expertise" to help you go after an old man I've never heard of from a war I never knew in a town I've maybe never seen. And I'll tell you now I've never done any undercover work. I'm not sure how convincing I'll be posing as some kind of broker for de-mining concessions. So tell me, what part of the picture am I missing? Why me?'

Pine smiled, squinting into the tobacco smoke. Vlado saw him reel slightly, perhaps from the exhaustion of the long train journey, the heavy meal and five shots of brandy. Then Pine straightened in his chair, as if realizing he'd lowered his guard. He was careful when he had to be, Vlado observed. Maybe that was part of his training as a lawyer.

'Good question. But you'll have to save it for my boss. You'll meet him later this week. Just say yes and you'll know soon enough. All I can tell you is that, based on your file, you're what he likes to call "the last honest cop in Bosnia".'

It was good for another laugh, and Vlado poured a final shot. Pine's answer should have sounded an alarm bell, Vlado knew, but he had his own means of answering the questions still troubling him, never mind the lateness of the hour.

For the moment, however, his overriding urge was to pack his bags, sit before a pile of case notes and begin the sort of work he had done before. If pressed, he might even have hopped into a car this very moment to drive south for eighteen hours, cross the border and climb into the green hills, his ears popping, the windows down, feeling the cool air of the beeches, the poplars and the pines against his face. He was ready to go home; the sooner the better.

They said their goodbyes at the door a few minutes later. Jasmina joined them, her arms folded. When the lift doors opened on the ground floor, Pine walked to a pay-phone outside.

All in all, he thought, it had been a productive evening, even if it had taken a while to warm up to the man. He'd read Vlado's file on the long train ride from Amsterdam and had been suitably impressed. His evaluations from his years as a detective had been particularly striking: bright, inquisitive, independent to a fault – which didn't bother Pine because the same sort of words always showed up in his own evaluations. Even better, the man had stayed off the bottle, no small feat when you were an exile working a low-paying job well below your talents.

Nonetheless, Pine's first impression in the flesh had been jarring. Vlado had looked like one of those young tobacco farmers from back home in Lasser County, the kind his father had always evicted for some landlord, or sued for their last penny on behalf of the power company. They struck the pose of the rough and ready but were actually naïve, always believing better times were ahead, until they woke up one morning to find themselves old and poor, realizing too late that hard work alone wouldn't save you.

But Pine had been wrong before when he applied American standards over here, so he reappraised, shifting into European gear – after more than five years abroad he was pretty good at it – and he discerned a face that was classic Balkan, features cut close to the bone, with the dark searching eyes and cropped black hair you saw everywhere down there. Vlado, he surmised, would be slow to smile, slow to trust. There was also

51

something vaguely Germanic in the man, a stolid sense of order, of everything in its proper place. Or maybe he'd drawn that conclusion from the apartment – simple but well-kept furniture with clean lines. No clutter. Floors and walls spotless. Shoes in a neat line by the door.

But it was another, darker part of Vlado's file that had brought Pine halfway across Europe, a piece of grim trivia that made the man oddly perfect for the job at hand. Those revelations would come later, and Pine didn't wish to be the one who delivered them. For now, it was time to call the boss, and he dropped a few Deutschmarks into the coin slot.

It was nearly midnight. Spratt would be asleep, but to hell with him because this had been his idea. Besides, he'd want to know.

'Hello?' said a sleepy voice with a flattened Australian accent.

'It's Pine. The deed is done.'

That seemed to rouse him. 'Good work. So he's come aboard?'

'Not officially. Has to talk it over with his wife. But rest assured, he's hooked.'

'And our secret weapon. Still a secret?'

'Not by my choosing.'

'Understood. But don't worry.'

'I'll let you tell him that.'

A muffled chuckle. 'I'll be happy to when the time comes. Don't worry, the wound won't be mortal. Now get some sleep, Pine. And let me get some sleep. You sound drunk, by the way. Hope you're not driving.'

'On our budget? Mass transit all the way. And it's a forty-minute S-Bahn ride to my cheap hotel.'

'Then don't miss your stop. And make sure to bring Mr Petric back to The Hague with you. An awful lot of people are eager to meet him.'

3

If Pine had stayed on the phone much longer he might have bumped into Vlado, who soon headed out of the building on his own midnight errand.

Vlado and Jasmina looked at each other the moment Pine shut the door. They were exhausted, not just from the lateness of the hour but from the weight of the questions now facing them. Should Vlado take the assignment? If so, what came next? They were too weary to discuss it but too stirred up to sleep, and for Vlado there was a more pressing matter to deal with.

He grabbed his jacket and headed for the door.

'Where are you going?' Jasmina asked.

It wasn't something he could tell her, not now. Maybe never. Not her nor Pine nor anyone else.

'There's something I need to find out before I can give him an answer.' He came up with the closest thing to an explanation he could offer. 'It's . . . a law-enforcement matter.'

'At midnight? In Berlin?' Jasmina frowned, incredulous.

'It's related to the war. Some people from home. You'll just have to trust me. It's their affair, not mine. I just have to make sure it's been dealt with before I can say anything to Pine. Please, that's all I can tell you. But it won't take long.'

'You're running to catch up with him, aren't you? To catch Pine before he changes his mind.'

'Of course not. I wouldn't do that without talking about it with you first.'

She considered that for a second, seemed to accept it. 'How long will you be?'

'No more than an hour. Probably less.' He hoped it was true.

She sighed, still sceptical. 'But you are going to take it, aren't you? This job.'

'Maybe. I don't know. Probably. If you think you and Sonja can handle it.'

'The better question is how we'll handle it if you don't. You'll be in a black mood for the rest of your life. What I'm more worried about is what comes next, when this is over and you want to move back.'

'Maybe I won't feel that way. Maybe it's still as bad there as everyone says. Just knowing I can visit it is good enough for now.'

She shook her head, smiling. 'One walk in the mountains is all it will take. One of your old paths.'

'Until I see a mine on one of my old paths.'

'Right. Then you'll run straight back to your trusty JCB. Let's see, what would Vlado rather do for the next twenty years? Dig holes in the mud or go around asking people nosy questions, and for a better salary, too. I'm sure you'll need a lot of time to decide that. Especially since you already love it here so much. The

55

food you're always raving about. The sunny weather.'

Vlado grinned. 'Don't forget the beautiful flat countryside.'

She smiled back. 'I hate it too. Some of it. Being a stranger all the time. Not understanding half of what people are saying no matter how hard I try. The stares we get from all the people who wish we'd just go home. If it were just the two of us I'd go back tomorrow.' She nodded towards the hallway. 'It's Sonja I worry about. She's spent all but two years of her life here. This is where she learned to speak, to make friends, to read and write. This is her home. She's a German, Vlado, a Berliner, whether you and the Germans want to admit it or not. She likes bratwurst and doner kebab and those little chocolate eggs with toys in the middle. She hums the tune to *"Liebe Sandmann"* every morning at break-fast – excuse me, every *Morgen am Frühstück* or however you're supposed to say it. She probably even likes the idea of schools and playgrounds that haven't been blown up or burned to the ground. And OK, even if half the people on the U-Bahn give her a dirty look when she sits down, at least most of them wouldn't kill her if she wandered into their neighbourhoods without permission, which is more than you can say about our lovely country.'

'I know. All that's true. And we'll talk about it more later. When we've slept on it.'

He pulled her close, and she whispered in his ear.

'It's also nice not worrying about you every day. Even if you do hate the job. At least I always know you're coming home.'

'You wouldn't say that if you knew where I'd been this morning,' he said. 'Ghosts and old Nazis, down under the ground. It's been a strange day.'

And it was about to get stranger, he feared.

Vlado walked briskly from the building. The U-Bahn stopped running in less than an hour, but his destination was only a few blocks away. The man's name was Haris, and Vlado's stomach still did a backflip recalling the first time he'd heard it. He'd noticed the man's presence almost the moment he'd returned to his family five years ago.

He'd knocked on the door of the apartment twice, feeling more like a postman with a package to sign for than a husband and father. Jasmina opened the door and gasped, then smiled, nearly collapsing, while the warm air of the apartment poured into the hallway. Sonja looked up from the floor just as you'd expect a sceptical four-year-old to do when a stranger was on her doorstep. Before her lay a menagerie of toy zebras and lions on a carpeted plain. She'd gathered them to her with a frown, then gasped when her mother actually embraced the stranger, sobbing and pulling him into their home.

To her, Daddy had become a voice on the phone that called once a month from a place called Sarajevo, a private radio show broadcasting only for her, a novelty that had grown old over time. This man stepping into the house was something else altogether.

It took only a few minutes before Vlado noticed the sports magazine on the table, the one in his native tongue with the names of football stars he had once cheered for. Not long after that he found two beers in the refrigerator. Jasmina hated the stuff.

Once she had recovered from her initial surprise she dashed about tidying, snapping up the magazine as she collected assorted clutter, her cheeks rosy, and not just from the excitement, he supposed. She headed first to the bedroom, carrying his suitcase, and as he looked down the hall from the couch, he saw her quickly stuff some items into a plastic bag. He sat exhausted, overwhelmed by the realization that the last two years had finally come to an end. His war really was over. The idea of another man here shouldn't have surprised him, he supposed, and for the moment he was too dazed and weary to feel angry, or even hurt. He had been sealed away for so long, with no prospect of escape, and suddenly here he was, watching his daughter eye him from the kitchen door. He knew from his own experience that lonely people in unfamiliar places either made friends or went crazy, and sometimes friends became something more. Beyond that, he was too drained by the interrogation, the long trip back to his family. It was less than a week since he had left Sarajevo. The emotions of the years under fire still clung to him like wet clothing.

Jasmina never once mentioned anyone, or offered a hint, although there were times when she seemed to hesitate, to hold back in conversation, whether out of reluctance to hurt him or in sorrow for some loss he couldn't say, and wasn't sure he wanted to know.

Fortunately they had Sonja to distract them. She took

to Vlado quickly, some old bond taking hold, as if she had encoded his smell, his voice, the way he felt when she snuggled up to him with a book, asking to be read to, and within a week she had latched on and wasn't letting go. He developed an afternoon routine of reading her a story in German. It was good practice for both of them, although it was a toss-up as to who was doing the teaching. He proceeded down the pages like a man on stilts while she gently corrected his pronunciation, her little hand darting to the page while she deftly enunciated the throat-clearing sounds. Her Bosnian – if that's what they called his language now, Serbo-Croatian having become a contradiction in terms – faded more by the day. He and Jasmina used it around the house, but breaking into their native tongue began to seem like shuttling to another era on a tram that had become creaky and outmoded.

Their marriage felt that way too for a while. They'd lost their feel for each other's rhythms, their comfortable give and take with its catchphrases and gestures. It was like re-learning a language, but with each day more words came back to them.

Vlado never wanted to ask about any man, though he was tempted to broach the subject with Sonja. It would have been so easy to enquire about 'Mummy's friends'. But in trying to form the words he'd feel the policeman in him coming out, interrogating his daughter, so he'd push the thought away. Besides, Jasmina showed no sign that anything had continued. No lengthy unexplained absences, no furtive moments on the phone – and, yes, he listened for them, with an attentiveness that made him ashamed. The only clues she offered were those moments of emptiness, when she would gaze into corners where there was nothing to see. Whose face was still over there? he wondered.

After a few months it had all surfaced anyway, while Jasmina was out shopping. Sonja was playing on the floor with a small plush giraffe with orange yarn for its mane.

'That's a nice toy,' Vlado said from the couch, just making conversation.

'Haris gave it to me,' she answered, and at first it didn't register. He assumed Haris was a playmate, some generous boy from the *Spielplatz*.

'When he brought Mummy the smell-good.'

Now she had his attention.

'The smell-good?'

'Yes.'

'Show me,' he said, dropping slowly to the floor, sidling up to his daughter like a conspirator, but keeping his voice light. 'Show me Mummy's smell-good.'

'You knowww.' She crinkled her nose with a smile, shaming his ignorance.

'No. I don't know.' He smiled back. 'Bring it to me.'

And like a good little informant she hustled off down the hallway with the wobbly walk of a four-year-old. He watched through the open door as she rose on her tiptoes in their bedroom, rummaging in the top drawer of Jasmina's dresser.

'Here it is,' she said sweetly, approaching with the prize in her outstretched hand.

It was a bottle of Chanel.

Vlado unscrewed the cap, sniffing. Jasmina hadn't worn this since he'd been home, but the bottle had been used. He held it to the light, feeling the coolness of the glass, admiring the amber colour. Even the bootleg versions of such items fetched quite a price on the streets. At their income something like this would be a real sacrifice. He pulled Sonja to him in a tight hug, blinking back tears.

'Isn't it nice?' she said, her voice muffled against his shirt.

He summoned another smile. 'Yes, sweetie. It's very nice.'

So now he had a name. Haris. And he mentally flipped through a catalogue of faces from their building, from the bar, the sausage stand, the market, trying to remember a Haris. There was the Bosnian Cultural Centre in Kreuzberg, a place where his countrymen sometimes met, celebrated holidays, held weddings. But the only Haris there was an old man, soup on his shirt-front, always muttering about his lost sons and the crimes of the Serbs.

The front door opened and Jasmina, soaking wet, stood with two cloth bags overflowing with groceries. She stared at the bottle of perfume in his hand, then at Sonja, who was back on the floor with her giraffe, oblivious to the sudden charge in the air.

The colour rose in Vlado's cheeks, and he gently set the bottle on a table by the couch. Jasmina walked to the kitchen without a word, not bothering to remove her shoes, trailing wet footprints across the carpet. He heard keys clattering on the counter, the opening click of the refrigerator, then a bustle of slamming cabinet doors, clanking bottles, rustling bags. He wanted to be angry but felt only coldness, a dull, deep pain.

He looked again at the bottle. Now was his chance to return it to the drawer, any drawer. The move would save face for both of them, buy time, a gesture to build on. They could talk about it later. But instead he switched on the television and returned to the couch, leaving the bottle in full view, an open accusation. Exhibit A for the prosecution.

They waited until after dinner, when Sonja was asleep. Then Jasmina made tea for herself and opened a beer for him, bringing it in a glass. That had seemed a first step towards accommodation, and he seized the opening, speaking slowly.

'Sonja told me about someone called Haris.'

Jasmina folded her legs beneath her at the opposite end of the couch, the mug steaming in her hands.

'Haris', she said, pausing, 'is a friend. Or was a friend. A friend and sometimes . . .' She faltered, looking into Vlado's eyes with an expression of care and concern. 'Sometimes something more. A companion. More for warmth against the loneliness than anything. The days without you just went on and on. Between calls I would think you were dead. I'd be sure of it sometimes, knowing that no-one would find you in the apartment for days, and that even when they did, no-one would know who to reach, or how. And it was on one of those days that I first met Haris.'

He didn't need to hear more. He only needed to hear

that the man was gone, finished in her life. Otherwise the conversation would veer towards the stalemate they'd often reached since his return. Both seemed intent on proving to the other that they'd suffered the most during their two years apart. And it was true that neither could fully appreciate what the other had endured. He'd never known the fierceness of life alone in an unwelcoming place with nothing but your child and your wits for company, swept along in a cold stream of indecipherable babble and officials who always wanted to see your documents, papers and more papers. She, on the other hand, could not fathom the fear and exhaustion of two years inside a claustrophobic little war, where shells and bullets were part of the weather, flakes of ash in a stale atmosphere that stank of backed-up plumbing, burning rubbish and death.

But the mention of the man's name – hearing 'Haris' pass from her lips – seemed to prod Vlado out of his accustomed trench, and she out of hers, and from that day on neither was quite as insistent about documenting their two years apart. Gradually, those discussions faded, and with them the name of Haris.

It was not the last time Vlado would hear the name, however, and he regretted that all the more now that the American, Pine, had arrived on his doorstep.

He had met Haris more than four years later – a mere month ago – in a place called Noski's. It was a bar, one of the few where a Bosnian could hang out and not worry about being beaten within an inch of his life by the neighbourhood pack of young toughs. Vlado went there sometimes to read outdated newspapers and magazines from Zagreb and even from Belgrade, piled at the end of the bar. Sometimes there was a fairly recent copy of the Sarajevo daily, *Oslobodjene*. The manager, an old barman from Prijedor, never seemed to mind that Vlado seldom bought a drink. He knew most of his customers couldn't afford it, and the few who could more than made up for the others by drinking themselves to oblivion, day after day.

Vlado was sitting at his customary roost when a voice hailed him from behind.

'You're Vlado.'

He turned to see a thin, grizzled man in jeans and a scuffed black leather jacket, hair unkempt, eyes that would have been a nice calming blue if they hadn't been bloodshot. But they were eyes that wouldn't let you look away, and Vlado knew exactly who this must be.

'And you're Haris.'

The man nodded. 'I'll buy you a drink. Then I'll tell you a story.'

He sat down at the next stool, smelling of whisky. But he seemed sober enough, neither swaying nor slurring his words.

'I don't want a drink,' Vlado said. 'And I definitely don't want a story.'

'It's a story for a policeman, and you're the only one I know. And, OK, it's a story for a husband, too. A husband who only wants to read his newspaper and go home to his wife and daughter.' He turned to the bartender. 'One beer, please. And a whisky.' Then, turning back to Vlado, 'Just hear me this once. That's all I ask.'

His eyes pleaded from some far and distant hill in his past.

'OK. Just this once.'

Haris put a crumpled note on the bar for the drinks and waited for his whisky. Then he began.

'I came here with my sister in late ninety-two. My sister Saliha. From Bijeljina. We grew up there. Went to school there, got jobs, made friends. Most of our friends were Serbs. When the war started, I knew we would all be fine, because everyone knew us. No-one would let anything happen.'

He took a long swallow of the whisky, wincing, then wiped his mouth on his sleeve.

'Saliha was raped in the first month of the war. Five times by a group of men in a room where they kept her for two days. I was put in the concentration camp at Keraterm. They loaded fifty of us on a bus and put us behind a fence. Nothing to eat for four days while they took us out, two at a time, beat us around the head, chained us to trucks. A few of us they shot. Me they just beat. Legs and face. Left us behind the wire for five weeks until one day a commander drives up and sets us loose. All the ones who hadn't died, anyway. But they took our papers, our money, then put us on trucks and drove us up to the front lines, where they dumped us and told us never to come back.

'Snipers shot two of us while we were walking to the other side, stumbling across the lines. Another one stepped on a mine. The UN was there and everything, but there was nothing they could do. I think someone filed a protest later.' He sipped his whisky, gestured

65

towards the foaming mug of beer. 'Please. You will need to drink if you're going to hear all this.'

He watched as Vlado lifted the mug and drank.

'I found my sister three weeks later in a school gym where she was sleeping on the floor. The place was full of refugees. Hundreds. Whole families on towels and blankets, laundry hanging between the basketball hoops.

'Lice, bad food, every smell you can imagine. That was life in the gym. My sister wouldn't talk to anyone. Just lay there all day on a cot, eyes open. I slept on the floor next to her for a week. Then on the eighth day she finally stands up and decides to take a walk outside. It is snowing and she is barefoot, but she just keeps walking while I follow her, afraid to say a word. Two blocks and she stops and looks down at her feet and begins to cry. I carry her back and on the way she tells me what happened, whispers it into my ear like a child telling her father she's done something bad. She knew the men, three of them anyway. Knew their faces and names. One taught our nephew at school. One grew up on the farm next to our uncle's. I used to play football with him at school. The other man was from the village, a baker.' He paused, shaking his head. 'Five months later we came here. This was late ninety-two. For three years she was pretty much the same, not going anywhere, just lying around the apartment, watching TV.

'Then one day it was sunny and warm, a spring morning after some rain, so I took her for a walk, almost had to push her out of the door and carry her down the steps. But she started looking around. We stopped to sit on a bench awhile, across from a bus stop. Then we decided to catch a bus, to go for a ride. We crossed the street and she looked at the crowd, seven or eight people waiting for the bus. And that's when she saw him, one of the men, not one of the three she knew but their leader, the main one, the one who had the scar and wore a black beret, leaning into her face with brandy on his breath, sweating onto her for twenty minutes. She tried to scream, tried to tell me who it was, but nothing came out of her mouth until the bus had gone with the man on it. She told me his name was Popovic, and I'd seen him, too.

'So the next day I go to the bus stop again and wait for him. Nine hours I'm there. Then the next day, and then the day after that. I decide I will go every day until he comes back, as if it's my job, because I didn't have a real job anyway. Just construction work without papers, tearing out old walls and plaster, and half the time we didn't get paid. So I kept going to the same corner. And that is how I met Jasmina.'

Hearing him say her name was a jolt. But Vlado kept quiet, waiting for Haris to continue. He'd stopped for another swallow of whisky.

'She'd seen me, I guess, seen me on that corner day after day, like someone obsessed. And I *was* obsessed. Crazy and dirty. Same coat, rain or shine. Same little water bottle tucked under my arm with a newspaper.

'She came up to me one day, curious more than anything, and asked who I was looking for. After days of being ignored by almost everyone in Berlin it seemed like some kind of revelation, as if I'd been invisible to everyone but her. And when you're feeling like I was, so focused on something that you can't see anything else, when someone actually notices what you're up to it seems like magic. As if they have powers no-one else has. So we talked. And I relaxed a little. I felt almost normal for those few minutes before her bus came. And the next day we talked again, and I still hadn't told her why I was there, or who I was after. But she told me she was waiting for someone too. I think that morning I might even have shaved. Changed my shirt. Given my coat a wipe. I don't really remember now. But on the fifth day she brought me an apple. I must have looked pretty pale. And in a few more days I stopped going there altogether. We met instead in other places, more normal places, and we became friends.'

That was all Vlado cared to hear on the subject. He started to speak, but Haris raised his hand.

'Please. Another beer. I pay, you listen. I am through with the part about your wife, but I had to tell you that much, so you would know.'

The bartender put down another round, Haris another crumpled note.

'Later I heard more about this man, Popovic. It wasn't the name he used here, and people who knew him said he had gone back, back to Bosnia and the fighting. He had his own unit, his own men with their own black uniforms and a nickname: Popi's Lions. But by then I had a life again. I was working in old buildings. Painting, or stripping out insulation. Paid in cash at the end of every day, or sometimes not paid. My sister didn't care. She stayed at home, quieter than ever, the TV on. After seeing Popovic that time she wouldn't leave the house again. But I kept working. And, yes, sometimes I saw Jasmina.'

It was the only time Haris came close to raising his voice, a brief note of defiance.

'Then, in early ninety-four, the person she'd been waiting for came home. And, for me, that was the end of Jasmina. She called me, only once, and said goodbye, said good luck. And for a while it seemed that was the end of life. So I went back to work. Tried to find jobs. Made a little more money. And forgot about women, even forgot about Popovic. Until three weeks ago, when I saw him again. I'd heard a bit about him, like lots of people. Someone had told me that in the last year of the war he'd been at Srebrenica when the city fell, leading his unit again, helping round up men and boys. Looting, killing, doing whatever it is he did. Other people said later he must have gone to Belgrade, or even to Kosovo.

'But now it was peacetime and there he was near the same bus stop as before, this time walking across the street towards the U-Bahn. He was in a hurry. I'd always worried I might not recognize him if I saw him again, that his face might have gone out of my head for good, just to torment me, but even after more than four years I knew him right away, and knew that he hadn't seen me watching him. So I followed him, got on the U-Bahn a car behind his. Watched him through the windows and got off at the same stop. A long ride, a couple of changes. Then half an hour of walking and he's on the

Ku-Damm. And by now he was looking out of place, I'm sure, a grimy Bosnian on this nice street of shops and theatres and West Berliners with all their money and bored expressions. I was half a block behind him, trying not to lose him. He went into the Ka De We, the big department store, and for a few minutes I couldn't see him. I thought I'd start crying right there in the store if I lost him after all that. Then I saw his head across the counters, heading towards an escalator. He went to the café, upstairs at the top of the store, all those plants under a glass roof. He sat down. He was waiting for someone, so I went to another table. I had to buy something or they would have kicked me out. I took five Marks out of my pocket for a coffee and it drained me for the rest of the week.'

Vlado couldn't help but think of the bottle of Chanel, which must have drained him for a good month.

'I watched him enjoy his schnitzel, his pastry, his Coke and his coffee. He spent what must have been twenty Marks just having a snack, and he kept looking at his watch until finally a woman came and sat down with him. Nice looking. Probably a Bosnian but I couldn't be sure because I couldn't hear what they were saying. But she was done up. A nice dress and black stockings. Lipstick. Very nice and she was his. She belonged to the rapist, the killer. She gave him a little kiss, then they talked for a while, a lot of smiling with his little smirk. And later she said goodbye. I think she must have worked there. Then he walked back, same way he'd come. Same U-Bahn stations. Same stop at the end, and now I was excited. Because now I knew he was going home. He walked into a house. A building like yours. And I was almost in a panic because I didn't know what to do about the lift. If I got on it with him he would recognize me, I was sure, or would see something in my eyes and know I was crazy enough to kill him. I thought I was about to lose him after all this. And then, my lucky day. Movers were using one lift. Loading some big piece of furniture. The other one was broken. *Kaput.* So he took the stairs, and I stayed one flight behind, tiptoeing so I didn't make a noise. I heard the door open on the fourth floor and I ran up behind as it shut. I looked down the hall in time to see a door closing behind him, and I got the number and checked the name on the door and the mailbox. It was fake, of course, because I knew his real name. I had heard it many times, had even read it in the newspapers.

'So, then. What to do next? First I told my friend Huso, because he was from Srebrenica. He'd run through the woods for four days, trying to get away from there. And he had seen this man Popovic with the crowds of Chetniks, putting people onto buses, calling men and boys out of the woods. Both his brothers went, but he kept running. He made it to Tuzla, but they never did. They got on the buses. No-one ever saw them again.

'Huso said all we needed to do was tell the police. He said we tell them, then they tell the War Crimes Tribunal, then someone will come and arrest him. So we did that, the very next day. We waited two hours at the police station and you would have thought we were thieves the way they acted, as if we were dirty and they just wanted to put us in jail or send us home, all the way

71

back to Bosnia. But finally they took our information. They said they'd make a phone call.'

'And then?' Vlado asked. By now the policeman in him was hooked. He swallowed some beer, not taking his eyes off Haris.

'And then, nothing. Two weeks go by and I check on him every day, just to make sure he's still here. Every day he goes to see the same woman, but in different places. Sometimes he spends the night with her. Sometimes she comes back with him. He wears the same nice clothes and spends his Marks as if they mean nothing at all. But no-one has come to arrest him, or take him away. And Huso and I, we've started to think that no-one ever will.' Haris paused, as if reluctant to continue. He asked for another whisky then looked straight at Vlado.

'So now you want me to do something about it,' Vlado said. 'Because I used to be a policeman.'

'Because you know how these things are done. Making arrests. Bringing people to justice. You've been a part of that.'

But it wasn't the policeman in Vlado that answered. It was the husband, suddenly and irrationally angry that this man who'd taken comfort from his wife wanted comfort from him as well.

The policeman in him would have said, 'Let matters take their course. Report him again if you want to feel better. Make yourself a nuisance if you have to, or telephone The Hague directly, and definitely offer yourself as a witness, but otherwise stay out of the matter. You'll only be asking for trouble.'

The husband in him shouldered aside such practicalities.

'If the police were going to do something, they would have done it by now. Someone like Popovic must not rate very high on their list. The Germans are more worried about Asians selling tax-free cigarettes, or Turks dealing heroin. All they want from Bosnians is an exit visa and a quick wave goodbye. The only way to get them interested in someone like Popovic is to bring him to their doorstep. If you and Huso want something done about Popovic, you'll have to do it yourself.' As soon as he'd said it, Vlado felt ashamed, even a little nervous, like a kid who has lit the fuse of a huge firework and now must throw it, not knowing where it might land. An absurd image flashed into his mind, of Haris and Huso tying up Popovic with yards of rope then dumping the man at a police station with a gag in his mouth and a note pinned to his shirt, scribbled in ungrammatical Bosnian.

Haris was still staring at him, as if awaiting further instructions.

Vlado obliged, unable to resist the temptation to coax the flame a little further along the fuse.

'Look, if Popovic is living here as another person, under another name, then who do you think would miss the real Popovic? No-one. They would miss this other man. But the other man doesn't exist, except on fake papers. Which the authorities would discover as soon as they searched his house or looked into his background. Assuming they even bothered.'

He sipped his beer, the foam cold on his lips.

'And if you've heard nothing from the Tribunal, how much does that say about their interest? Sounds like you and Huso are the only two worried about it. It's possible he hasn't even been indicted, and if that's the case, it might never happen.'

'But Huso saw him, saw what he was doing in Srebrenica. My sister saw him too. There must be plenty of witnesses who've mentioned his name.'

'Maybe investigators have never talked to any of them. And are you sure that's what you want to put your sister through? Have her up in the dock, answering questions from some attorney for Popovic, who'll keep telling her how much she wanted it, how much she'd been asking for it. He'll ask her what kind of dresses she wore, what kind of perfume she used, how many men she'd slept with. Is that what you want?'

Haris had no answer. He just swallowed more whisky and set his glass heavily on the table, nodding once, a look of resolve in his eyes, and for a moment Vlado wanted to take it all back, to tell him, 'Take it easy. I'll make some calls. Let me handle this.'

But the moment passed, and Haris stood, laying a last crumpled note on the bar.

It wasn't long before Haris took his advice. Four nights later the phone rang. Luckily Vlado was the one who answered.

'It's Haris.'

The anger rose up in Vlado almost immediately, but Jasmina and Sonja were in the next room, so he didn't shout.

'I don't want to hear any more about your problems,' he muttered. 'I want you out of our lives.'

'Then come downstairs and you'll have your wish. I promise. Huso and I are down here.'

'What have you done?' he said tersely.

'Just come. There isn't much time.'

He found them standing in a dimly lit corner of the entrance, by a payphone next to the mailboxes, trying not to attract attention and therefore doing exactly that, a sweating and nervous-looking pair who stank of effort and exhaustion, their eyes glazed with a barely contained wildness and more than a little drink.

'Outside,' Haris whispered. 'Follow us.'

They walked to a far corner of the parking lot, which backed onto a small grove of trees. Both street lights in that corner were burned out. Broken glass crunched underfoot. Their car was the only one within a twenty-yard radius, and Vlado almost laughed to see it was a brown Yugo, like the punchline to some elaborate and clumsy joke – two bumbling expats and their expat excuse for a car.

They stopped by the rear of the car, a nervous huddle, Haris looking at Huso, who fumbled for the keys. Vlado felt his stomach sink as the boot clicked open, swinging up into the darkness with a high creak. A man was curled into place, presumably Popovic, hands bound behind his back. Vlado desperately hoped he was still alive, but the mouth was open, not gagged, and the smell boiling up out of the cramped dark space was of blood, blood gone cold and stiff on clothing and skin.

'He's dead,' Haris said.

Huso looked at Vlado. It was the first time Vlado had met him. Broad flat face and squat body, and the brown frightened eyes of a dog that has just chewed the morning paper. What did they want? For him to arrest them? This was hopeless, and he sagged with the enormity of what they had done, of what *he* had done. Headlight beams crossed them briefly as a car swerved into the opposite end of the lot.

'For God's sakes, shut it,' Vlado said. He was dealing with idiots. Why was he dealing with them at all? What was he doing out in this lot with these two men and this body?

'I want to tell you how it happened,' Haris said. 'We didn't want to kill him. And now we don't know what to do.'

'Get in the car,' Vlado said. 'Tell me while you drive. But don't just stand here attracting attention. If a policeman were to pull in now, this is the first part of the lot he'd check. Come on. Get in.'

They obeyed, tame and tired. Huso sat at the wheel, revving the whining engine, the works tooled in some far corner of home, years ago, before the war – back when owning a Yugo wasn't such a bad thing, and living in a mountain village was a poor but tranquil existence. You were forgotten and so was your country. But now their problems were scattered everywhere, a diaspora of feud and vengeance. They had brought the war to the *Spielplatz* and the *wurst* stand, little Bosnias everywhere.

'Head for a busier street,' Vlado said from the back

seat, the policeman taking control. 'And don't speed, don't do anything that will get you pulled over.'

Huso was rigid at the wheel, the posture of a student driver afraid to do anything other than what the teacher told him.

'How the hell did it happen?'

Haris turned from the front passenger seat. 'We followed him home this afternoon. He'd gone to the Ka De We. To see that woman. On his way back he stopped in a park for a walk. He went into some bushes to take a leak, and Huso grabbed him. Huso had a knife.'

'Where's the knife?'

Haris looked blank. Huso shook his head.

'I'm not sure,' he said. 'Maybe in the trunk. I don't know.'

It was how amateurs always screwed up. Some major detail left unattended. Vlado had seen all the signs before in his work. Now here he was driving along with a pair of such fools, inextricably linked to them.

'We got on either side of him and told him to come with us,' Haris went on. 'Huso showed him the knife. We told him it was about money. That if he came with us and just heard our offer we could all make a lot of money. He wasn't happy but he came with us. I think he thought the knife was something he could deal with. So we walked to the car. Huso had borrowed one, and it was only a block away. Huso kept the knife under his jacket.'

'So this isn't even Huso's car?'

'No.'

'What's he lying on back there. A blanket? Anything?'

'There's a big sheet of plastic.'

Sometimes amateurs got it right, in spite of themselves. Vlado wondered how much blood they had on their clothes. He remembered how grimy they'd seemed in the dim light of the apartment building. Not a good sign.

'Keep going. Then what?'

'We drove out to a construction site. A new shopping centre where Huso has been doing some work, painting. We pulled in at the back. Huso got the knife out and told him to turn round. I tied his wrists. We told him we were going to take him to our stash of drugs.'

Vlado was amazed Popovic had gone along with it. Either too stupid or too greedy. Probably both. Or maybe just frightened. People used to giving orders rarely knew how to act when receiving them.

'We weren't going to kill him,' Huso said from the front. 'All we wanted was a confession. Then we were going to turn him in to the police.'

'A confession?'

'Of all he'd done,' Haris said. 'I was going to take a statement.' He reached beneath the seat and pulled out a spiral notebook with two pens slid into the loops of the binding. As if he were a policeman making out a report. Haris really had thought they were going to take care of it themselves, the stupid bastard. Mostly because a real policeman had been careless enough to tell him they could.

'Go on,' Vlado said, his voice barely a whisper.

'He laughed at us. He said, "This is all you want? Some confession? No business to do? Just some crap

78

about the war?" So Huso hit him. Hit him across the face and asked about his brothers. I told him he'd raped my sister. He went quiet, wouldn't say anything. I think he was beginning to get a little scared, but he wasn't going to admit it, wasn't going to say anything. So we told him we were taking him to the police, that we knew his real name and that they would arrest him.'

'And he told you to go ahead.'

'Yes. How did you know?'

'Why wouldn't he? The police wouldn't know what to make of him, other than that he was some Bosnian with bad papers. They'd deport him and he'd be away from both of you, and he'd know better than to ever come back to Berlin. I just can't believe he was stupid enough to dare you. Or to laugh.'

'We decided it was pointless. Or I did. I told Huso we couldn't take him in. We began arguing in the car. That's when Popovic knocked open the door with his knee. He got out and ran, up towards the street. We caught him and tackled him, dragged him back to the car. Pushed him up against one of the back walls of the building. Then he spat in Huso's face. Said, "Fuck your brothers, they deserved to die." And that's when Huso stabbed him. He stabbed him once then he couldn't stop.' Haris paused. Huso sighed deeply in the driver's seat, as if recalling some distant unpleasantness.

'It was over fast. Like killing an animal. All the thrashing and the breathing, the air and the blood coming out of him, the knife going in and out with that sound, like stabbing a sandbag.'

'Then you put him in the boot.'

'And came to see you. We didn't know what to do next. Where to take him. What to do with his body.'

Vlado took his bearings. They were on a four-lane road heading east, out of the city, the buildings growing sparser.

'Keep going,' he said. 'I know a place. Somewhere I did some work when I first got here. Another mile or so, then go north. I'll tell you when.'

It was too late to back out now. Too late to do anything but keep driving and do the best with what they had. The man in the boot was dead, and he'd always be in the back of Vlado's mind as a casualty he'd inflicted, his first. It would be something to hide from his wife and daughter and anyone else he ever met. There would always be this man's body, riding behind him.

It took another twenty minutes to reach the site. Vlado had unloaded old pipes there, the innards of some building he'd helped gut during his first month in Berlin, before the construction job had opened up. The lot was closed, just as it had been then, with broken padlocks on all the fences, which made it an ideal place for illegal dumping. There was an old waste lagoon in the back, sludge and chemicals and abandoned supermarket trolleys jutting from the ooze.

They looped some of Huso's rope through cinderblocks and a discarded section of heavy iron scaffolding, then tied Popovic to it, knotting the rope round his chest. It took all three of them to heave the body and all the weight over the lip of the lagoon. Popovic sank slowly into the dark bubbling mess. For a moment they stood, wiping their hands on their

80

trousers, staring at the spot as if the body might bob back to the surface at any moment. Then, without a word, they climbed into the car.

No-one spoke on the way back, and Vlado hadn't mentioned a word of it to anyone in the few weeks since then. But now, with Pine waiting for an answer, Vlado had to see Haris one last time. Had to ask him if anyone had come poking around with questions, or if anyone had ever responded to his initial report to the police. He especially wanted to know if Haris had ever heard from anyone at the Tribunal. For all Vlado knew, this assignment might yet have something to do with Popovic. Or maybe that was just the convoluted thinking of a guilty conscience.

He took the lift to the sixth floor. The building was quiet at this hour. It was a carbon copy of his own, one of those grey slabs the East Germans had built in their haste to replace the wreckage of the Second World War. Vlado knocked, not looking forward to the moment of confrontation, worried about what he'd learn. And even with everything that had happened, he still wasn't used to the idea of speaking to someone who'd slept with his wife. He knocked a second time, worried no-one was home. But finally there was a scraping sound, and the door opened narrowly against a security chain. A woman's drawn, thin face stared back at him, her body stooped before its time. This would be Saliha, Haris's sister.

'I've come to see Haris,' he said. 'Tell him it's Vlado. Vlado Petric.'

His name seemed to flip a switch, and a smile

81

flickered slowly to life, although it was hard to recall any smile that was more mirthless.

'Then I know why you must be here,' she said, not budging from the door. 'What do you want with him?'

'To speak to him. Only a minute or two. Is he home?'

'Yes, he's home.' That glint in her eyes again. 'Home in Bosnia. He and Huso both. They should have come and killed you instead, but Haris said no, he'd had enough of killing. They went back a few days ago. And now I'm here by myself, alone, because I won't go back. He has deserted me, thanks to what you made him do.'

'Well,' he said, feeling a need to redeem himself, to excuse his visit at this late hour. 'I just wanted to make sure that he was safely out of things. To make sure the authorities hadn't caught up with him. But I suppose they haven't.'

'There was one,' she said, with a questioning look which slowly turned to a smile as she watched Vlado's alarmed reaction.

'One?'

'One man. Three days ago. The day after Haris left. He came looking for Haris.' She paused. 'He asked about Popovic too. The devil himself.'

'Who was he, this man? Where was he from?'

'He didn't say.'

'The War Crimes Tribunal?'

'He didn't say. I told you.' By now her smile was full. She probably hadn't enjoyed anything like this in ages.

'Was he German? In a uniform?'

'No. Not in a uniform. And not German. Not Bosnian either. A foreigner.'

'American?'

'I don't know. He spoke our language. A few words of it, anyway, and not like a German would. But he spoke it. Enough to tell me he wanted to see Haris. To ask him about Popovic.'

'What else did he say?'

'Nothing. When I told him Haris was gone he left.'

'Was he tall? Short? Fat? Thin? Old or young?'

'About your age, but maybe not. It was dark. Taller than you, but maybe only a little. And he wore a big coat, so I can't say if he was thin.'

So it might be Pine or it might not. Vlado had no idea if Pine spoke any Bosnian. He must have picked up a little if he'd been travelling there for four years.

'What else did he want to know?'

'If Haris was coming back. Where he could find him. If I'd seen Popovic.'

'And?'

'I told him I knew nothing about any of that. I said that Haris had gone back because he was homesick. That he had been in love but that his girlfriend's husband had returned.' Her smile widened again. 'But that was all, and he didn't ask any more.'

'Did he leave his name, give you a contact number? A business card, maybe?'

'None of that. He just left. And I haven't seen him since.'

And I hope to God I haven't, either, Vlado thought as she shut the door, the deadbolt sliding with a heavy click.

4

In the grey light of morning, Vlado's fears seemed unfounded. He woke in a swelter of dry heat. The apartment building's furnaces had run full throttle through the night, and the air smelled of baking metal. Vlado sat up in bed, mouth dry, eyelids glued, hair poking stiffly in all directions. Jasmina's side of the bed was empty with the sheets thrown back. He got up to crank open a window. Cool air flowed in like a balm, pooling around his bare feet, though it tweaked his nose with the smell of burning coal. The sun was up, and he knew by the light that he was already at least an hour late for work. Jasmina stepped into the doorway.

'I decided to let you sleep,' she said. 'You'll need your strength for the trip.'

So it would be that easy. He met her at the foot of the bed, slid his arms round her waist, pulling her closer. Her hair smelled of shampoo, her breath of coffee.

'Just promise me two things,' she said.

He nodded, chin brushing the top of her head. 'That you won't do anything stupid. And by that I mean dangerous, or anything as dangerous as it was for you before, in Sarajevo.'

'OK. That should be easy enough.'

'That's what you always say. And what makes it worse, I think you really believe it.'

'Relax. He did his last fighting before we were even born. He's an old man.'

'And a war criminal. People who learn to kill when they're young don't forget just because they're going senile. It's like learning to swim, or ride a bike. It's part of their muscle memory.'

Vlado laughed. 'Fair enough. I promise not to turn my back on him, especially when he's just had his prune juice. So what's the second promise?'

'That you won't make up your mind about moving before we talk.' She looked up, straight into his eyes. 'Don't get swept off your feet by the hills and a few old friends. By a few glasses of *rakija* or a few bites of *cevapi*. Give us a chance to talk it out rationally, thinking of everything. While you're here, not there.'

He nodded again. 'OK. I promise.'

'Sure you do.' She smiled, shaking her head lightly. 'I can already see it in your eyes, all that eagerness to go back.' Her own eyes shone. 'I wish I could, too. I woke up in the middle of the night, just aching to be home. I wanted to look out of the window this morning and see everything I used to see, then take Sonja around her old city to meet her new playmates, and talk to her without feeling as if we were speaking some special language that only the three of us know, like some sort of family code. That's the way she thinks of it, you know. As if it's our private language, nothing to do with anybody's country or anyone but us.'

'I know. She told me. She heard a boy on the U-Bahn speaking Bosnian one morning and said, "Listen, Daddy. He's talking *our* language." She didn't like it. I think she thought the boy had broken into our house and stolen all the words.'

'Hi, Daddy.'

Sonja was at the door, clutching her Sandmann doll with his peaked red cap and wisp of a beard. His confident little girl who rode the U-Bahn with the bored authority of an old commuter, who knew all the tricks on handling crowds and grabbing the best seats. Knew the best stands for *wurst*, too. It was true, she was a little German, comfortable here.

He beckoned to her, and they all climbed into bed for half an hour, chatty and cosy, with the draught from the window coiling on top of them like a cool velvet snake. Down in his chest, he felt the excitement of the journey building. Jasmina looked in his eyes, seeing the faraway fires, and said, 'Go. Get up and call him before he leaves or changes his mind.'

Vlado stepped barefoot across the floor to telephone Pine from the kitchen, suddenly needing reassurance that the night before had even taken place, all those hours now mixed in a swirl of ghosts – spirits from the dank bunker, dreams of Haris and the body in the trunk. Just the thought of that was a dead weight sinking through the lightness of the morning. He wondered how long it would haunt him. For ever, perhaps. He had a fleeting vision of Haris's sister from only eight hours ago – could that be possible? – her doorstep still darkened by the shadow of whoever had visited a week ago.

But if Pine knew about any of those events, he wasn't saying so this morning. And his voice on the phone seemed real enough, bubbling with excitement when Vlado accepted the job. Within an hour Pine was back at Vlado's door, holding a train ticket, wearing his puppy-dog face and talking a mile a minute. He handed over a small stuffed envelope.

'Maps and directions,' he said. 'Nothing in here you'll have to eat or burn afterwards. But remember, don't speak about the details with anyone before you leave. I'll be heading back to The Hague in an hour. You'll follow later this morning. I know that's short notice, but it's six hours by train, which will barely leave us enough time to get you up to speed before leaving for Bosnia the next day.'

'The next day?'

'Yes. It's moving fast, I know. But they put this together in a hurry. Apparently there isn't a big window for action, especially on the Serb general, Andric. He's the French army's problem, not ours. But their operation impacts on our timing, and they seem to be worried he'll head off to Kosovo soon. There have been a lot of reports on troop build-ups, so you never know. Sorry I can't book you a flight, but that's our budget. I'd hate to tell you how many trips into the field I've cancelled or cut short. That's what happens when your bean-counters are across the ocean and your crime scene's a thousand miles away.

'You'll arrive late afternoon. Take the number seven tram to Churchillplein. You're staying at the Hotel Dorint. It's right next door to the Tribunal, so just walk on over when you've checked in. Security will be expecting you. Then we can get started with the backgrounders. And I'm sure Contreras will want to meet you.'

'Contreras?'

'The new head man at the Tribunal – his official title is chief prosecutor. Took over last month. He's a judge from Peru who made his name putting drug lords in gaol. Survived two car bombings and got his house burned out. Big hero down there. He figures Bosnians are little lambs after dealing with the Shining Path; he can't understand why we don't just go out and haul everybody in. NATO's already sick of hearing from him. They figure he's threatening to upset the status quo just as things are coming to a boil in Kosovo.'

'What does Kosovo have to do with us? If they start bombing, do we cancel?'

'If a war starts there we'll be the last things on anyone's mind, so we just keep going like nothing happened. It might complicate the Andric case, though. With the French as cosy as they are with the Serbs, maybe they won't feel like co-operating if the Americans are bombing Belgrade. But our guy will still be in business, and we'll have an offer he can't refuse. Contreras is a full-speed-ahead kind of guy, so far anyway. He's also as political as they come. Always seems to have a few diplomatic types over at the office, touring them around. So we're a little on edge these days, wondering who'll be the first to screw up under his "new aggressiveness" mandate.'

'Like us, you mean.'

'Only if we find some way to become an embarrassment. But you need to be ready to roll as soon as you arrive. If our man is going to do business with us we'll know pretty soon.'

'And if he decides not to?'

'Then we go to Plan B.'

'Which is?'

'Classified.'

He smiled, patting Vlado's shoulders, then reached into his pocket for a business card. His name and title were embossed above a blue UN globe and the Tribunal's long official title.

'My phone number, just in case. Plus the address of the Tribunal. If you end up on the wrong tram just hail a cab and show him this. Most of the cabbies speak English. Don't try any Bosnian on them. The Dutch aren't too thrilled with refugees these days. Even less than the Germans, in their own repressed little way.' He held out his hand. 'Welcome aboard, Vlado. It's a strong team we've got. Definitely the underdogs, but we play hard.'

All this American slang was going to take some getting used to, but Vlado took Pine's hand firmly – 'sealing the deal', he did know that one – while searching Pine's beaming face. The man's enthusiasm was infectious.

'It should be fun,' Pine said before throttling back a notch, the smile turning almost sheepish. 'Or interesting, anyway. Oh, and hang on to your receipts if you ever want to get reimbursed. Contreras is just as tight with the dollar as his predecessors.'

Vlado smiled. Some things about police work were the same no matter who you worked for.

The train journey was the perfect decompression chamber for travelling from one life to another. By the time they'd crawled through Berlin into the pines of the countryside Vlado felt as if old circuits were springing to life after years of idleness. He bought a Coke and a bag of crisps from a vendor pushing a cart down the rocking corridor, then dozed for half an hour, waking refreshed, and thinking of his family. Jasmina had been excited for him, and a little jealous. It was Sonja who'd remained dead set against the whole thing, tugging at his coat as he'd stepped through the door. The memory cooled his elation. It was still too easy to recall the emptiness of his two years alone, the time and energy he'd spent mending fences. Now he was bolting off on his own again, leaving them behind for who knew how many days, even weeks. But when it was over they'd have new possibilities. Easy, he warned himself. Don't start making up your mind. Just enjoy the adventure.

He stood to stretch in the corridor, swaying with the motion of the train as the bleached November landscape passed at 120 mph. He thought for a moment about Tomas. He must be piloting the JCB through the clay and rubble about now.

In the afternoon they crossed the border into the Netherlands, and the view gradually changed. Canals separated fields, with boats seemingly parked in the middle of nowhere until you realized that the water led everywhere. There were even a few windmills. Vlado stood at the window, elbows propped against the glass. Phalanxes of school kids on bicycles waited at rail crossings, headed home. Rainwater pooled in low spots and creases. That plus the canals left the impression of a countryside afloat like an earthen raft, which the slightest shift might send sliding beneath the waves.

The Hague was a typical European act of concealment – a medieval village wrapped inside centuries of construction. You could chart the rapid pace of recent development in the built-up outermost suburbs, and even towards the centre a new section of steel and glass loomed above old parks and canals.

But the ageing heart of the city was still hunched on narrow cobbled lanes of low brick buildings. Statues of grave old Dutchmen stared from manicured parks. Orderly columns of black bicycles dominated the traffic. The air carried a damp briny touch of the North Sea, with a raw cold that crept into your skin as if prepared to linger until spring.

A brief tram ride took Vlado to his hotel and from there he walked to Tribunal headquarters, a curving four-storey building of steel and glass. It looked like the insurance office which it had once been. At the front a collection of abstract sculptures sprawled from a concrete pond – hulks of metal like wreckage dropped from a helicopter.

Vlado spotted his first Bosnian while security men scanned his trousers with a metal detector. It was a woman, bustling past, speaking his native tongue to a guard, who answered in kind. The guards directed

Vlado to the second-floor canteen to wait for Pine. Men and women sat at small tables over coffee cups and full ashtrays, voices buzzing in English, Bosnian, German, French. Being foreign was just part of the scenery here, not something to hide. A man strolled by with the dark hair and narrow-set eyes that could only come from home, and Vlado was tempted to hail him with a familiar greeting. Then Pine burst through a nearby set of doors, walking at double time.

'Welcome to the big cop shop,' he said. 'Trip go OK?'

'Sure. Everything was fine.'

'Hope you're rested and ready to work. Let's go upstairs and I'll start introducing you.'

They went up to the third floor and along blue carpeted hallways to a partitioned cluster of cubicles where several men sat at desks, each of them on the telephone.

'This is my team of investigators,' Pine said. 'A little crowded as you can see, about a dozen in all when everybody's here. Let's see if Benny's got a minute. Hey, you'd probably like some coffee, wouldn't you?'

'That would be great.'

'I'll run downstairs. Take your coat off and get comfortable. Looks like everybody's on the phone now anyway. Don't worry, none of them bite.'

Vlado draped his overcoat across a spare seat. Three of the nearest cubicles were occupied. A man with a buzz cut and a stylish shirt in electric blue spoke what sounded like Italian as he scribbled in a small notebook. Opposite him was a spidery bald fellow who loomed well above his desktop, dark brown skin drawn tight round a narrow head, giving his forehead the hardened look of a coffee bean. He spoke a language Vlado couldn't place, like the sound of running water, then slipped suddenly into English without missing a beat.

Closest to Vlado was the one Pine had called Benny, the noisiest of the bunch. He was an American, but much shorter than Pine, belly spilling over his belt, tie askew. He leaned back in his chair while talking on the phone, feet propped on a messy desk. A torn newspaper photo of Madonna was tacked to a corner of his partition, next to a bumper sticker in Cyrillic lettering that said, 'Fuck S-FOR.' The back of the chair groaned as he shifted. The phone cord was twisted and knotted in a dozen places, and he'd jammed his left foot against his phone to keep it from sliding off the desk. He was muttering, nodding quickly, and seemed to be growing impatient with whoever was at the other end. He glanced towards Vlado, rolling his eyes. Then the show began.

'Yeah,' he said. 'Yeah, I know. But it's because he's a criminal, OK?' His accent was heavy. Vlado had seen enough American movies to place it somewhere near New York. 'I said *criminal*,' shouting now, then a mutter of, 'Christ, these phones,' followed by another shout: 'A goddamn *war* criminal, OK? Why else would we wanna bring him in? You've heard of us down there, right?' Glancing at Vlado again, rolling his whites.

Squad-room humour. Break out the cigarettes and the naughty calendars. This, too, felt like a sort of home, and Vlado felt a warm flush of energy.

He pulled his cigarette pack from his pocket. Benny saw it and swivelled in his chair, leaning towards Vlado, who braced for a wagging finger or a shake of the head. But Benny only rolled closer, chair wheels squealing. As if by magic, he produced a lighter, raising it towards Vlado as he leaned from the groaning chair. The lighter chirped and Vlado bent forward, inhaling, nearly brushing the man's fingers with his own as his breath pulled the flame into the cigarette.

An absurd vision of the scene sprang to Vlado's mind, a twisted parody of Michelangelo's 'Creation' – outstretched hands meeting in mid-air – and the thought made him laugh, dragon smoke bursting from his nostrils as the New Yorker receded, grinning as if he understood and approved.

'I'm Benny,' he whispered, cupping a hand over the mouthpiece. 'Welcome to the zoo.'

Then he resumed his verbal assault.

'Yeah, yeah. Yeahhh. Well, if that's the case, you tell your boss . . .' A pause, shaking his head impatiently. 'Then you tell your captain, you tell him we're not just a bunch of scared-shitless bureaucrats who roll over at the first sign of more paperwork or every time some local warlord waves a gun at us, and that we're coming after this little shit down in your sector whether you're with us or not.'

By now, sweat was beading on Benny's forehead, reminding Vlado of condensation on an overworked refrigerator, which seemed appropriate enough because, for all his bluster, Benny struck him as a cool customer, someone who'd be imperturbable in the field.

He would love to see how Benny dealt with stubborn checkpoints or paper-stamping officials who tried to slow him down.

Pinned on Benny's desk under his right elbow was a thick document with a bright blue cover. The bold-faced word 'INDICTMENT' stood at the top. He folded open a page and Vlado scooted closer for a look. He was able to read a paragraph at the bottom:

The accused, often assisted by camp guards, usually shot detainees at close range in the head or back. Often, the accused and camp guards forced the detainees who were to be shot to put their heads on a metal grate that drained into the Sava River, so that there would be minimal clean-up after the shootings. The accused and guards then ordered other detainees to move the bodies to one of two disposal areas where the bodies were piled until they were later loaded onto trucks and taken to mass graves.

Benny saw Vlado looking and slid more papers his way, with a quick nod that said, 'Get a load of this.'

'WHEREABOUTS' was the heading. It was a list of indicted suspects not yet in custody, a sort of score card put together by a group calling itself Balkan Watch. There were six pages in all, covering about forty men. Vlado read the first one:

CESIC, Nenad. Crimes against humanity, murder, rape. Frequents the 'Club Markala' restaurant in Zvornik. Lives at home, works for local reserve police. Shares red

Honda motorbike with cousin, also under indictment. Both often seen riding through town.

He flipped to another page:

GOJKO, Dragan. Crimes against humanity, torture. In June 1998 was working as a police trainer in school in Prijedor. Owns the 'Express' bar, where Momcilo Zaric (also indicted, see below) often drinks.

He found Zaric a few paragraphs later:

Crimes against humanity, murder, rape. Nicknamed 'Juka'. Drinks rakija every morning around 10 o'clock at 'Krsma' bar. Can be seen in town driving blue VW Golf. Passes local International Police headquarters every day on his way home.

Vlado glanced at Benny to make sure he wasn't watching, then scanned the pages until he found the entry he sought. Just reading the name made his pulse quicken:

POPOVIC, Branko. Genocide, crimes against humanity, torture. Commander 'Popi's Lions' paramilitary unit. Believed in Kosovo. Often seen at bar of Hotel Grand, or driving black Toyota Land Cruiser. May live in military barracks in Pristina, but also has home in Belgrade. Frequently travels in Europe. Confirmed sightings since January '98 in Zurich, Augsburg. Unconfirmed sightings in Vienna, Berlin.

The Berlin reference made him flinch. But there was nothing more. No mention of witnesses, addresses or a possible disappearance. He checked the date on the front. Two weeks old, only a few days after Haris, Huso and he had dropped the body into the industrial dump. Who knew what anyone might have heard in the meantime? Whoever had visited Haris's apartment had done so about a week after this report had been updated.

Benny was raising his voice again, seemingly working himself towards the finale.

'You wanna be at his house? Then be at his fuckin' house. You wanna sit on your ass at a checkpoint and listen for gunshots? Then you do that. 'Cause we're coming, S-FOR or no S-FOR, and all the military-industrial ass draggin' in the world ain't gonna stop us, OK? . . . I said, OK?' Pause. 'Hello?' He squeezed his eyes shut, then roared, 'Christ! These fuckin' phones! How these people ever gonna have a country if they don't have decent phones? Man!' He slammed down the receiver, shaking his head. 'Five minutes of prime reaming out wasted. I think I even had the guy on the verge of ordering up an operation for us. Or at least thinking about it.' He sighed. 'Either way, I feel a helluva lot better than I did five minutes ago.'

Then he looked up with an exasperated grin that said he'd loved every minute.

'Benny Hampton,' he said, stretching out his right hand. 'You must be Pine's Bosnian. Not that I'm supposed to know or anything. But, hey, I *am* team leader, so I guess I ought to be able to find out a few things around here. Although if Spratt hears about that last conversation I may not be team leader much longer.'

Pine returned. He placed two steaming cups of coffee on the desk and threw his jacket on the back of a chair.

'Benny, Benny, Benny,' he said with some affection, the accent sounding soft after two minutes from the New Yorker. 'How many times do you have to be told? S-FOR is our friend. Just like I-FOR was our friend, and UN-PROFOR before them.'

'Yeah, the army of a thousand names,' Benny muttered. 'Give 'em another year and they'll change it again. They oughta call 'em WHAT-FOR, then maybe somebody'll figure they've been doin' nothin' all along. Sitting around all day watching our suspects have a beer.'

Vlado knew the acronyms well. During the war the troops wore blue helmets and drove white armoured vehicles, and were known as UN-PROFOR, the UN Protection Force. After the peace agreement they painted their helmets and vehicles green and were joined by twenty-four thousand better armed Americans, re-naming themselves I-FOR, the Implementation Force, which in a year or so shrunk by a few thousand soldiers and became S-FOR, the Stabilization Force.

'You know how it goes, Benny,' Pine said. 'We're just not a vital part of the mission statement. Oh, and Vlado, sorry, but no smokes up here. This is World Health Organization territory, not the Balkans. You'll have to snuff it out or take it to the canteen.'

'Fuckin' S-FOR.' Benny was still muttering. 'Fuckin'

NATO. Biggest and baddest army in Bosnia and they can't even get it up to roust a hungover old Serb in his pyjamas. The guy hasn't had a bodyguard for two years and he's still listed as "at large". He must pass through a couple of their checkpoints a day and all they do is wave.'

'Then you go roust him, Benny.'

'Hey, I aim to. That's what I was telling them I'm gonna do. He probably knew I was bluffing, but with this new mandate from Contreras, who knows, maybe I'll even get the chance. Can't be any worse than goin' into some project in the Bronx. I'll handcuff him and drag him halfway to Budapest if they let me.'

'Which they won't. Contreras talks a good game but he's no more likely to run a cowboy operation than the others. If he starts a firefight where S-FOR's got to ride to the rescue they'll never lift a finger for us again.'

'Lotta difference that would make.'

'But never mind that, Benny. Say hello to Vlado Petric. Vlado, meet Benny Hampton, who thinks he's still banging heads back in Brooklyn.'

'The Bronx, for Chrissakes. Yeah, we sorta met, but this makes it official.'

Vlado grasped his outstretched hand. It was hot and springy, like poking your hand into a warm ball of dough.

'So you're the guy who pissed off half of Sarajevo on your way out the door. And you let this backwoods yahoo Pine talk you into going back?'

'Thanks for making my life easier, Benny.'

'Well, if you need help while you're down there, give

me a shout on the cellphone. I'll be in the field for the next week or so if you end up anywhere near Vitez.'

'That's Benny's little way of trying to find out what we're up to and where we're going. But we'll keep your offer in mind, Benny.'

Pine steered Vlado towards his own office, in an opposite corner.

'Yeah, yeah,' Benny called after them. 'Get out the secret decoder ring and I'll just move on. What are you guys up to anyway that even the team leader can't know? I've been hearing all week that something hinky was in the works.'

'Hinky?' Vlado asked.

'Screwball,' Benny clarified. 'Something that's not quite right. For one thing, I hear even the French are involved. Those lovely guys who let Mr Karadzic get away last year.'

'Is that true?' Vlado asked, amazed to hear that one of the biggest suspects of all, the wartime president of the Bosnian Serbs, had even come close to capture.

'Maybe,' Pine said, glaring at Benny. 'But we're really not supposed to talk about it, are we?'

'But we will anyway, now that you're one of us,' Benny muttered. 'There was a raid planned, late summer of ninety-seven, but it never came off 'cause some French major tipped off Karadzic. Talk about the shit hitting the fan.'

'*May* have tipped him off,' Pine said. 'And there *may* have been a raid planned.'

'The French were supposed to court-martial the major. Instead they posted him to a desk in Paris. Not bad, huh? And now I hear you guys are actually going to work with them. Can't wait to see how that turns out.'

'Loose lips sink ships, Benny.'

'Tell that to the French major. Sounds like his ship made it home OK.'

Pine shot Benny another look that said he'd been talking out of school long enough.

'The file you need to see is on my desk,' Pine said, steering Vlado towards his door. 'Use my office. We won't be here long enough to get you a desk of your own. Suspect's name is still confidential as far as anyone else is concerned.' He glanced significantly at Benny, who grinned and offered a parting shot.

'Don't worry, Pine. I get the message. Good to meet you, Vlado. If we don't have time for a cold one before you hit the road, maybe we'll meet up in-country.'

Vlado stepped through the door. Like Benny's desk, Pine's was a jumble of files and papers. Pine had a window, with a view of tram tracks and a narrow brick street. Posted next to the window was a bright blue calendar with pictures of smiling young men above a basketball schedule for the University of North Carolina. The grinning players faced directly across the room to an opposite wall, where a row of unsmiling men from Bosnia stared back in black and white. It was a wanted poster of five suspects, enough to form their own basketball team. Pine noticed Vlado looking at it.

'My biggest case,' he said. 'Massacre in the Lasva Valley in April ninety-three. Two in custody, three at large. He opened a manila folder on the desk, revealing a few single-spaced sheets. 'Here's our man. This is just the summary. There will be more to read later. Army intelligence files, old diplomatic cables. Some of it's still beyond even my security clearance for the moment. But this will get you started.' He checked his watch. 'You've probably got half an hour.'

Vlado eased into Pine's chair and relaxed. Reading case files used to be drudgery. Now it seemed like a privilege. He'd never much cared for paperwork, as if anyone did, but he had always enjoyed spreading the facts before him late at night as an investigation unfolded, watching characters and plots take shape by the light of a single lamp in an empty office, looking for patterns and anomalies, feeling the excitement of moving towards a solution while the city around him slept.

He took the sheets of paper in his hands and eased back into his past as if he were seated at his old desk, up on the fourth floor, a brown glass building on the south bank of the Miljacka River, a cup of Husayn's terrible coffee steaming at the ready. He looked up, glancing at Pine's calendars and notepads, as if to re-assure himself he hadn't really slipped through some time warp. Then, smiling to himself, a little giddy, he began reading, happily back at work.

5

The suspect's name was Pero Matek, and his recent history sounded all too familiar. He was a wartime thug and profiteer, quick to recognize opportunity amid war and chaos. Vlado had seen them by the dozen in Sarajevo during the siege, so he already viewed this one with weary distaste.

It was the man's earlier history that fascinated him. Vlado, like most of his generation, had been taught the history of the Second World War in a series of broadbrush treatments, set pieces of Titoist heroism and selfless sacrifice by the People and the Partisans, a united front of communist rebels battling Nazis and a few scattered traitors, mostly local fascists and royalists, the Ustashe and the Chetniks. If the recent war had taught him anything it was that the truth was usually a lot more complicated.

Matek was born Pero Rudec in a remote region of Herzegovina in March 1923. That would make him seventy-five. He grew up on a farm, attended state schools, and at the age of sixteen enrolled in a military academy training officers for the federal army.

Matek was a Croat, and during his teens he joined the nationalist Ustashe movement, the tinpot fascists who eventually threw in their lot with the Nazis. Hitler was their ticket to statehood, and at the age of eighteen Matek was among the thousands of cheering people on hand in Zagreb on 10 April 1941 to welcome the declaration of Croatian independence under puppet dictator Ante Pavelic. By then Matek had joined Croatia's Home Defence Army. He was soon promoted to lieutenant during action in early 1942 in the Kosarev Mountains, a brutal campaign of killing and burning in northern Bosnia, notorious for its forced conversions of thousands of Muslims and Orthodox Christian Serbs to Catholicism. On a few occasions, Serbs who remained unconvinced had been burned alive in their churches.

In the spring of 1942 he was wounded in the right shoulder, putting him out of commission for a month and resulting in a transfer to lighter duty at Jasenovac, the infamous concentration camp on the Sava River. There he commanded a squadron of guards who distinguished themselves, if that was the word for it, as particularly brutal and efficient, not only in their duties at the camp but in raids on nearby towns and villages, looting and killing and rounding up the usual suspects. In 1945 he was promoted to major. His trail became murky in April, the last month of the war.

One report said he'd headed north with several thousand other fleeing soldiers and civilians, a group that suffered heavy losses to ambushes and outright massacres by Partisans and Soviet troops. Other reports placed him in a convoy of trucks that left Zagreb with weapons and certain 'assets of the State'. This version branched into three further trails, like a legend that has grown and become embroidered in years of re-telling.

One variation had him and a pair of others making it safely to Wolfsberg, Austria, with their cargo, sheltering in a monastery before being taken into custody by the British. The second said they abandoned their vehicles at a mountain pass near the Austrian town of Liezen. The third said Matek had been one of the few to survive a Partisan ambush near the Slovenian town of Maribor.

Whatever the case, after four months on the run he ended up in Austria, where the British sent him to a displaced persons' camp in Italy near the town of Fermo. With him were some twenty thousand other temporarily stateless people, mostly from Croatia, Bulgaria and Hungary. The DP camps were way stations for the millions of Europe's homeless, people who'd been shoved aside by armies or freed from concentration camps, and the living conditions were notoriously bad. The camps were also popular hiding places for war criminals – officers and administrators who shed their uniforms and identities to try and blend in with the masses.

The risk to this strategy was that you might be lost and forgotten for months at a time, susceptible to disease and malnutrition. Or someone might recognize you, or discover something among your papers that would give you away, unless you had friends who could come up with new documents or a way out.

Matek apparently had spent nine months at Fermo before being released to Rome, into the custody of the Pontifical Relief Commission for Refugees. In Rome he took a job working in the offices of the Confraternity di San Girolamo di Illirici, where a Croatian brotherhood of Franciscan priests ran efforts to assist their wandering countrymen, with a headquarters on the right bank of the Tiber, only a mile or so from the walls of the Vatican.

The priests there were anti-Tito, anti-communist, anti-anyone who might want to dig up old secrets about their friends. They secured a new set of identity papers for the newly named Matek, who shed his old name of Rudec.

He stayed in Italy until 1961, a few years after Pope Pius XII died. Afterwards, it seemed, many of the more questionable Croatian émigrés began to wear out their welcome. Matek repatriated to Yugoslavia under his new name. He apparently made it across the border without incident, resettling in the central Bosnian town of Travnik, quite a distance from where he'd grown up, and well away from anywhere he'd served during the war. And that's where he remained, having done quite well for himself in the interim. There was no reference to how his true identity had suddenly surfaced after all these years, but apparently his neighbours were still none the wiser.

The recent war had afforded him unprecedented opportunities for expansion of his various enterprises, and he now owned a string of petrol stations and had managed to win several UN and EU reconstruction grants – around $200,000 worth to date – with some of it actually going towards the rebuilding of homes. A Norwegian grant intended to help rebuild a local soft-drink distributorship had somehow been diverted to help rebuild a local beer and liquor distributorship –

the largest in the region, in fact, owned by Pero Matek. And practically none of a year-old World Bank economic development loan of $100,000 to stimulate local employment had yet been spent on its intended purpose. World Bank officials were now convinced that the borrower would default. Too much overhead and red tape, it seemed. Too many unrealistic expectations. Though the borrower was doing all he could, of course.

Vlado shook his head at the waste and folly. He was nearly as outraged by Matek's recent behaviour as he was by the man's past. Otherwise you might chalk him up as another bent old man playing chess and trying to forget, wanting to be left alone with his grandchildren. This one had never married, never raised a family, and had stayed up to his elbows in the rough work of making money from hardship and corruption. And now Vlado was going to meet him, was going to dangle before him the carrot that he apparently craved most – entrée into the lucrative business of de-mining.

Vlado flipped to the last page, an update from only a week ago. Matek seemed to be in excellent health, based on the account of a World Bank official who'd paid him a call to enquire uneasily about the state of the grant. It now seemed he was internet ready, if still a bit rough around the edges in his countrified manner, offering great quantities of charred meat and strong drink. Glass after glass of *rakija*. His security people seemed to have made quite an impression – several men with large guns, a guardhouse at the gated entrance – and he was seldom seen in Travnik without a bodyguard, unless he was meeting women. One woman in particular, the wife of the mayor from a neighbouring village, seemed to be the focus of his recent attentions.

Vlado stretched, checking his watch. The half-hour had come and gone, and through the glass he saw Pine with Benny, deep in discussion. He put the report back in its folder, left it on Pine's desktop and opened the office door.

Benny saw him first, looking up with that glint of mischief that Vlado had already decided he liked.

'So, ready to join up?'

Before Vlado could answer, a commanding voice interrupted from another direction.

'Pay no attention to him. He'll have you believing we're nothing but a bunch of misfits. Welcome aboard, Vlado. I'm Phillip Spratt, head of investigations.'

Another hand to shake, but Vlado was still trying to puzzle out the accent.

'From Australia,' Spratt said without prompting. 'Volunteered. Like pretty much everyone in the building. Fifty-six countries and most every wart and flaw of their legal systems, all under one roof. And, yes, I know the rest of you have heard this little speech, but Vlado hasn't.'

Spratt had a wide face that looked hard enough to cause mortal injury if you were to run up against it, a grooved oaken forehead beneath a widow's peak of coppery bristle. Pine had told Vlado that the only reliable indicator of Spratt's mood was the patch of skin beneath his ears – tiny thermometers where the colour rose whenever he was building to a boil. For the moment they seemed to be at mid-level red. The crowd around him had gone silent.

'Has Pine given you the grand tour yet?' Spratt asked.

'Haven't had time,' Pine answered.

'You should take a look at our courtrooms while you're here. Quite impressive.'

'And both of them look like the bridge of the Starship fucking Enterprise,' Benny piped up, 'only with wood panelling.'

Everyone laughed uneasily. Benny seemed to be the only one who could get away with such an interruption. But before Spratt could respond, another voice rang out, a sharp fluting sound like the most reckless sort of music. Vlado spotted the rising flush below Spratt's ears and correctly surmised that the big boss must have arrived.

'Ah, there you are, Mr Petric. I'm Hector Contreras, the chief prosecutor. Almost as new to this place as you.'

Vlado's immediate impression was that Contreras was a gentleman of means, yet also a gossip and an intriguer. He would have been hard pressed to say exactly why. There was something of the rake in the man's glance, which came at you from an angle, a slight tilt of the head, as if he'd been looking at something to your left and swivelled his eyes just in time to catch you red-handed. He couldn't have been dressed any snappier, a tailored navy suit with lapels and pockets cut like racing stripes, set off by a red handkerchief peeping from the breast pocket. He wore a small moustache – a gigolo's moustache seemed to be the only way to describe it, again for reasons Vlado couldn't name. By now a few others had drifted over from their desks for the show, and ten faces were turned towards Vlado, awaiting his response – hardly what he'd been used to at the construction site.

He blushed, then blurted a muffled, 'Honoured, sir,' feeling self-conscious, as if his English had suddenly stiffened into the worst sort of Balkan caricature.

Contreras responded with quick grace and warmth. 'The honour is mine. A good man in a tight spot, and incorruptible into the bargain, that's what I've heard about you so far, and I'm only expecting to hear more of the same. You'll be coming to dinner tonight, of course?'

'Of course.' Vlado tried to hide his surprise. Pine looked shocked. Then Spratt, whose ears had gone tomato red, spoke up.

'Sir, I was just about to invite them. I only got word myself in the past hour.'

Vlado saw Benny smirking.

'No matter,' Contreras said. 'All's well now, and I trust I'll see the three of you at seven for cocktails. Drinks will be an open affair, with assorted members of the diplomatic community, the sort of people we have to keep happy if we're to pay the electricity bill. Then we'll shoo them away and shut the doors for the need-to-know crowd, everything off the record. Sort of a combination debriefing and get-acquainted session. I decided it would be just the right atmosphere for kicking off, well, such a grand event.'

'Grand event, huh?' said Benny, who apparently would cut in on anyone's conversation. 'Tell us more.'

Contreras beamed his rake's smile while Spratt glared at Benny. 'All will become clear soon enough. It will be part of the new order around here, and down there as well. But for the moment, I'm sure the rest of you know enough to say nothing of these matters outside this building. Understood?'

There was a round of small nods and muttered assents.

'Very well.' Contreras turned on his heel and walked away, in the manner of a particularly flamboyant butler. It was no surprise he'd been a judge, for he obviously enjoyed performance. Vlado could easily imagine him playing to a jury, or a press gallery.

The investigators straggled back to their desks, but Pine was in a panic.

'Did you bring a suit?'

Vlado shook his head. 'I thought we'd be travelling light.'

'You figured right, but we'd better get you one.' He scanned the room for possible donors, then checked his watch. 'C'mon. We'll hop on a tram into town. We'll expense-account it. Contreras can put it on his goddamn party budget. Got a white shirt?'

'One.'

'One's enough. Let's roll.'

They headed for the heart of town. Every seat on the tram was taken, so they held the overhead straps, swaying with the turns and bumps while Vlado stooped to look out of the windows. It was charming, in its way, this toytown layout of bricks and bicycles. There were cheese shops brimming with red waxen wheels the size of bus tyres, greengrocers with taut bright awnings, and the curtains of every home were thrown open boldly to the evening, lamplight pooling on the pavement out front. But the sense of order was almost unnerving – every brick in place, all those black bicycles wheeling in synch. Most of the faces in the street seemed as humourless as the statues in the park, which seemed to disapprove of all they beheld. He wondered how Pine fitted in here, a sprawling American with his unruly hair.

They reached their stop, walking a few blocks to a men's shop where Pine said he sometimes bought shirts. Pine employed his halting Dutch to explain their shortage of time, and a high-strung assistant quickly measured Vlado, while fretting that this was no way to buy a fine suit. He laid out a few choices on a counter while Pine thumbed through a rack of ties.

'I better get you up to speed on what to expect at this cocktail hour,' Pine said. 'Haven't seen the guest list but it will probably be a minefield. Here, this tie ought to do.'

It was a bold red with gold paisley. Vlado frowned.

'Trust me. Go with red. Power colour. Half the people there will want to pigeon-hole your politics within the first five minutes, and the ones who disagree will try to eat you alive. How much have you been keeping up with the state of play back home?'

'In Bosnia?'

'Not Germany, that's for sure.'

'A little. Sounds like it hasn't changed much since I left. Same parties with the same stupid views.'

'I was talking more about the people really running

the show. The High Representative's office. The EU. NATO. All the NGOs and internationals. You know?'

Vlado didn't.

'I'll give you the short version. At the top you've got the High Representative. Mostly a Euro perspective and bureaucratic as hell. He's supposedly just overseeing things, letting the national governments and parties do their stuff. But his people control a lot of hard currency and tell the NGOs and aid agencies what they can and can't do. Here, try the blue one.' He grabbed a dark blue suit from the rack, tossing it onto the other three.

The old salesman blanched at the brisk treatment of his merchandise but he bit his tongue. Guilders were guilders.

'Then there's S-FOR. Benny's feelings are pretty representative on that topic but they're still the biggest army. The international police force is around too. Powerless. Might as well not be there. Then you've got local police, your old employers, but with three separate ethnic breakdowns, and with the civil side and the Interior Ministry side, the old MUP people who will still lock you up for your politics if you're not careful.'

Vlado glanced up, shaking out his sleeves. This one would do. He nodded to the salesman while Pine continued.

'Somewhere at the margins of all this you've got the private investors, all trying to make a buck while looking as altruistic as possible, and yes I know I'm going fast. Here's a tie you can live with. Red and boring, perfect. Strap it on. What's that one cost, sir, sixty guilders?'

The salesman nodded without a word, not wanting to interrupt the flow of commerce.

'Nationality matters too. The French don't trust the Americans, the Americans don't trust the French, and any Yank will run like hell at the slightest whiff of *anyone* from Iran, Afghanistan or Morocco, the old suppliers of the Mujahideen forces who technically aren't supposed to be there any more, even if everyone knows the holy warriors never went away completely. The Scans are pretty much everywhere, doing good and keeping quiet in the usual Scan way. All the Germans want is to get in and out without having any soldiers caught painting swastikas, which has already happened, so too bad for them. The French want to give the Serbs an even break but without upsetting the balance next door in Kosovo. The Brits want to make it look like they're independent from the Americans, only without pissing off the Americans.'

'And the Americans?'

'Oh, the Americans ask very little. We only want the greatest amount of influence for the least amount of money and aggravation. Anything complicated is the High Representative's problem, and the lower you go down that food chain the more likely you'll find one of his people hanging out with local bureaucrats, the kind who always have their hands in somebody else's pockets. So things get murky. Sometimes even dangerous. Three people dead behind a gas station and you don't know why. Then a week later ownership papers change hands on a dozen local storefronts. And one of the new owners is somebody like our guy Matek.

Throw in a few dozen leftover warlords with various cuts of the black market, plus some rabble-rousers who didn't get quite enough of the war, then overlay that with the usual thieves and drug barons, including a few radical Muslims and some interlopers from the Albanian heroin trade, and that pretty well sums up the state of play. Homesick yet?'

'Sounds like business as usual in the Balkans.'

'Pretty much.'

Vlado pulled his trousers back on. The shopkeeper had pinned the new pair and handed them to a tailor in the back, where the thrum of a sewing machine could be heard. A few minutes later the tailor, pins in his mouth, hustled the suit back up front, where the dizzied assistant waited to be rewarded with a Tribunal credit card.

'OK,' Pine said. 'We're cutting it kind of close. Better catch our tram. You can change at the hotel and I'll swing by and get you at a quarter to seven.'

'That should give me just enough time to check in with Jasmina.'

'Which reminds me,' Pine said, suddenly looking sheepish. 'No outside calls. They've put a stop order on the phone in your room. Operational security. Which I know must sound pretty lame with all the blabbing you've already heard. But no calls home till we're done.' Then, in a softer tone, 'I really am sorry.'

Vlado felt a flush of anger. The last thing he wanted to do was make Jasmina worry.

'You might have told me earlier. Jasmina will assume the worst.'

'Spratt told me not to, until now. I can have one of the secretaries call. She'll tell Jasmina everything's OK, but that she won't hear from you for a while.'

'What else haven't you told me?'

Pine frowned. 'Not much. But by late tomorrow you'll know everything.'

Vlado, holding the new clothes across his arm like a valet, knew that this should set off alarms. He'd heard these kinds of assurances before. Nothing good ever came of them. But he felt powerless to protest.

'Look, I'm not happy with this part of it either,' Pine said. 'If it were up to me I'd have outlined the whole thing for you back in Berlin. You'll just have to trust me.'

Vlado had taken that kind of advice before, too. The last time it nearly got him killed.

6

Contreras had found himself a big brick home on the edge of a park, the grandest residence to date of any of the chief prosecutors, and he liked to show it off. This would be Pine's third visit. The first two were for staff cocktail parties, where the investigators and prosecutors turned themselves into genteel drunks, padding about on oriental rugs while immigrant waiters replenished their drinks. No-one seemed to know quite how to react to these events with their crystal glasses and bottomless booze, but with every sip they uneasily hoped the Tribunal wasn't footing the bill. The smart money said the Peruvian Embassy was paying the freight, gratified to have their man in such a high-profile position. But some believed it was Contreras himself.

The story on Contreras was that he'd married into a rich family, a wealth that not only bought him into the Peruvian judiciary but also kept him living in grand style. The tale had assumed enough heft and substance to keep the staff drinking without guilt. But for most of them the novelty had worn off.

Vlado would rather have spent the evening locked in a room with files and briefing papers, reading more about their suspect. Instead he was strolling up a brick walkway in his new suit, smelling the resin of the tall pines in the raw November evening.

The red and white flag of Peru was hanging at the front, as if this were a consular home and Contreras its resident pooh-bah. A waiter opened the door, bowing slightly and gesturing towards a large room to the side, with white tablecloths and silver platters. Already there was a buzz of conversation, the tinkle of ice cubes in glasses. Brushed and bald heads gathered beneath the shimmer of a grand chandelier.

Vlado felt calm enough, considering. He gave a final tug at the knot of his tie. The suit did wonders for the general impression he made, it seemed. Already people reacted as if his IQ was forty points higher than when he wore the mud and denim of Berlin.

'If anyone asks who you are, say staff unless I introduce you,' Pine muttered. 'Try to stay close by. And if the waters get too deep, just smile a lot and laugh at their jokes.'

Vlado doubted one could get into much trouble here. The scene struck him more as an overly stuffy reception, something that an archbishop might put on, or some government official who'd just been promoted beyond his capabilities.

A deep voice came at them from behind.

'Calvin, you're starting to look bored at these things already.'

Pine stiffened, and Vlado turned to see Spratt, who seemed just as stiff as he had in the office. Unwinding didn't seem to be part of the man's make-up.

'So, all squared away for tomorrow?'

'More or less,' Pine said. 'A little more time to prepare Vlado might have been nice.'

'I suspect he'll do fine. And you'll have more time to bring him up to speed once you're in Sarajevo.'

An odd look seemed to pass between them, and Vlado wondered what it was all about. Having missed lunch, he grabbed a handful of peanuts from a nearby bowl. A waiter swooped in to pour a glass of wine. Spratt waited for the waiter to depart, then glanced around for eavesdroppers and lowered his voice.

'Now if the French will just hold up their end with Andric, we'll be in business. You boys can do your bit and be back in a matter of days.'

'So you really think it will be that easy?'

'The way we've got it sketched it would seem to be a foolproof operation.'

'I just hope we're not underestimating the old man.'

'Not as long as we get him away from the bodyguards. Which is where you come in, Vlado. That's what makes you indispensable. I'm more worried about rounding up all our witnesses on Andric. We're still holding out for Popovic as the star, but apparently nobody has seen the man in more than a month.'

Vlado nearly choked on a peanut at the mention of Popovic. He half expected Spratt and Pine to turn towards him to spring the trap, demanding an explanation. But if this exchange was for his benefit, they were disguising it well.

'I thought they'd tracked him down,' Pine said. 'Lounging at the Grand Hotel in Pristina.'

'You must be thinking of some other thug. No trace of

Popovic. No recent sightings. He could be anywhere. Vienna. Kosovo.' A brief pause. 'Berlin. Belgrade. You might want to ask LeBlanc, our friend from France.' Spratt gestured towards a far corner. 'Apparently he's been making some noise about it.'

Vlado tried to see whom Spratt was referring to, but there were six or seven people where he'd pointed.

'He's apparently the one who helped link these two cases together, he and Harkness.'

'Who's Harkness?' Vlado asked.

'A meddlesome blowhard,' Pine said. 'Paul Harkness. Officially he's the State Department's special liaison to the Tribunal. Used to be posted to the embassy in Belgrade, then to Sarajevo. But damned if I know what he really does other than stick his nose into everybody else's business.'

'Now don't be too nasty about Paul,' Spratt said in a scolding tone. 'He's done a lot for us down there. And none of this would be happening if it weren't for him.'

'Which should tell us something about the whole operation.'

'How did he get interested in Matek?' Vlado asked.

Spratt looked towards Pine, as if to ask how much Vlado knew.

'I can't say with any authority,' Spratt offered hesitantly, 'but apparently either he or his French counterpart LeBlanc turned up something in an old file. They're an unlikely alliance, I must say. Those two have spent the past five years trying to tear each other's liver out and now they're getting along like Ginger Rogers and Fred Astaire.'

120

'More like Jekyll and Hyde,' Pine said. 'Now if you could only tell which was which.'

'Apt enough. But it's the jurisdictional problem that worries me more than any of the personalities. We've got no business going after some old Ustashe. We're only authorized for crimes committed since nineteen ninety-one.'

'So our part of this operation is illegal?' Vlado said.

Pine smiled ruefully, while Spratt rattled the ice in his drink. His ears were red again.

'Technically,' Spratt said the word with evident distaste, 'no. But for *official* purposes, all you're doing is arranging a meeting with Matek for interrogation of a potential witness. Then, while he happens to be under our control, a unit of S-FOR troops will take him into custody on behalf of the Croatians, who are supposedly putting together an indictment as we speak.'

'And unofficially?'

Spratt grimaced, so Pine picked up the thread.

'We're rounding him up, plain and simple. Jurisdiction be damned.'

'If it works, Contreras will be the toast of the town, and our international sponsors will be happy as clams.'

'So here's to Hector Contreras, then,' Pine said, raising his glass. 'The founder of the feast.'

'He's an Ebenezer Scrooge?' Vlado asked.

Spratt looked up with a glint of astonishment. 'Looks like you've got a sharp one, Calvin,' he said, sounding like the headmaster speaking to the hall proctor. 'It's not every Bosnian who could have nailed that reference.'

'I read a lot of English at school,' Vlado said, nettled

121

by the condescension. 'I suppose if I want to stay in character I should say "God bless us every one" and let Pine carry me on his shoulders.'

'Sorry,' Spratt said, rattling his ice again. 'Running low here. Better get another.'

Vlado watched him head for the bar in the corner. 'Sounds like a popular case we're on.'

'Well, anything that puts Andric in the bag can't be all bad. Who knows, maybe you'll even learn a little of your history.'

'Nobody ever said much about the war growing up. Just the heroic stuff.'

'Not even that cranky old uncle you mentioned?'

'Uncle Tomislav,' he said. 'I must have been ten or eleven the last time we went to visit him. Off in the middle of nowhere. Big dry hills where nothing grew but goats and rattlesnakes. I slept in a back room upstairs while my uncle and father sat in the back garden, playing cards and drinking brandy. I woke up in the middle of the night and they were shouting, going back and forth like drunken debaters. And my sense of it was that they were arguing about the war. Nothing specific, just a lot of old grudges about who started it, who did what, all the things no-one ever talked about. It was probably the only time I ever heard my father talking politics, so I went to the window to watch. They were panting like bulls, as mad as hell. It was almost funny, but frightening too. My aunt and my mother went out and pulled them off to bed. The next morning we left without even having coffee, which is about as rude as running off with the silver.' He looked at Pine. 'What about your family? What's your father like?'

'Oh.' Pine snorted, smiling. 'Atticus Finch. That's what he always looked like anyway. Or dressed like. Another literary reference for you.'

'Atticus? A Roman name?'

'I guess you read mostly Brit lit. Atticus Finch is from *To Kill a Mockingbird*. Hero lawyer of the South. He was for civil rights before civil rights was cool. And every morning my dad went off to work looking just like him. Linen suits and seersucker. A wardrobe made for mopping your brow on the courthouse steps, right next to the statue to Our Confederate Dead.'

'So your father was a crusader?'

Pine shook his head. 'Not exactly. I doubt any of his clients ever ran from a lynch mob, although to their credit I guess none of them ever led one. They'd have been on their porches a few blocks away, sipping drinks and wondering what the ruckus was. Doctors, bankers, real estate developers.' He swirled his wine, a faraway look in his eyes. 'Jaycee glad-handers wanting to dispose of one little problem or another. A wife past her prime or a tenant behind on his rent. The kinds of things you didn't want people talking about at the country club. And with my father you got discretion with a capital D. For a nice hourly fee, of course. I guess that's why he could never stomach the idea of his son slumming with thugs and gumshoes. On a government salary, no less.'

Vlado wondered at the tone of disappointment. It all sounded perfectly respectable to him. But now Pine's expression was transforming from disappointment to worry, and Vlado turned to see a woman approaching from across the room, a grim look on her face and a purposeful stride in her high heels. She drew up close to Pine, then, noticing Vlado, turned to accommodate them both.

'Hello, Calvin.'

'Janet.'

'So, guess who drew the short straw on helping the Croatians prosecute Matek?'

'You?'

'Don't sound so disappointed.'

'It's not that. It's just, well . . .'

Vlado watched their body language with interest. The woman eased even closer, as if challenging Pine's right to his spot on the floor. Pine leaned away, but without moving his feet, making him look stiff and off balance. They made a curious pair. It occurred to Vlado that if you were to breed from them you might produce a new species of wading bird, a little tottery on long thin legs and bony frames. Or perhaps the woman was just uncomfortable in high heels. She had large hazel eyes and light brown hair that swept round an oval face. Her small prim mouth seemed barely to move when she spoke, as if she was used to imparting secrets.

For the moment she was zeroed in on Pine. When she moved, her hair nearly brushed against his face, and Vlado could have sworn Pine flinched, ever so slightly, while holding his wineglass before him in a defensive position.

'Well, look on the bright side,' she said. 'It probably means they never found out. Otherwise, they never would have paired us on anything this sensitive.'

Vlado cleared his throat, as much to remind them of his presence as to pierce the bubble of their conversation. She turned without missing a beat.

'You must be the Bosnian. Vlado, is it?'

Somehow he didn't mind it from her, maybe because her offhand nature seemed directed more at Pine than at him. Or perhaps it was the trace of irony in her tone, as if she was saying she knew exactly what it was like trying to prove yourself to this crowd.

'Yes. Vlado Petric. And you are?'

'She's Janet Ecker,' Pine said. 'An attorney on loan from the NSA. That's the National Security Agency. Code-breakers and official snoops, basically, so she's usually the one who gets to handle information when it starts to get touchy.'

'Which is probably why they put me on Matek,' she said. 'To make sure nothing too sensitive is handed over to the Croatians. Or the French. They've got me working overtime with the black marker.'

'And you two are friends of some sort?'

Pine winced, but a smile flickered briefly on Ecker's face, as if sharing in Vlado's minor insurrection. Vlado wondered how much she'd had to drink.

'You could say that,' she said. 'Just don't say it around the office. And if you were going to be here for long I wouldn't say it around you. You see, Calvin spent months looking for a good Dutch girl but settled for an American. Until he got something going down

125

in your part of the world. Doing his part for better diplomatic relations.'

Pine reddened. Vlado considered sauntering off for another drink, but Ecker mercifully changed course.

'So what do you make of his file?' she asked Vlado. 'Matek's, I mean.'

It was pleasing suddenly to be treated as an equal, even if only as part of her fencing with Pine.

'I haven't seen much. Just the summary. But he seems like standard-issue Ustashe.'

'So far we've only gotten the sanitized stuff,' Pine said.

'If I have my way you'll be entitled to as much as you want. It's amazing material.'

'That's what Spratt said the other day.'

'Spratt doesn't know the half of it. And without some of my connections I'm not sure I would.'

'Meaning what?'

'Meaning there's been some strange information management going on. Someone trying to keep too many stray pieces from adding up to anything beyond the specific charges. There are a lot of old State Department cables and CIC reports that make interesting reading. But some of it has been deemed a little too interesting.'

'CIC?' Vlado asked.

'Army Counterintelligence Corps. From the US of A, which doesn't come out of this looking too good, even though most of this stuff is fifty years old.'

'What could be so embarrassing, after all that time?' Vlado asked.

'Details, mostly. And names. James Angleton for one.

126

Dead now, but once quite a wheel at the CIA. The ultimate cold warrior. And just after the war he and plenty of others were ready to make nice with an awful lot of Nazis. Nothing new about that, but the conventional wisdom was always that we only helped a few actual war criminals escape. Klaus Barbie, one or two rocket scientists. This stuff makes you wonder. And that's before you even read about the so-called "missing assets". At the worst it looks like Matek might have helped loot the State Bank of Croatia as the war was winding down. Beyond that I'd better keep my mouth shut.'

'Maybe we should get you another drink and find out more,' Pine said, seeming to regret his words the moment he spoke them.

'That's his idea of a little joke,' Ecker said to Vlado. 'A drink or two always worked pretty well for him where I was concerned. In fact, maybe that's all it was.'

'That's not what I meant.'

'Pleasure meeting you,' she said, again turning abruptly towards Vlado. 'I think I'll go for a refill.' She walked away as briskly as she'd arrived.

'Sorry about that,' Pine said after an awkward pause.

'No problem.'

'Big mistake on my part.'

'She doesn't look like a big mistake.'

'Not in that way. I mean, I was kind of a jerk about the whole thing. Fortunately for both of us nobody found out.'

'These things happen.'

'Yeah. But if anybody asks . . .'

'Don't worry.'

'Thanks. Trouble is, she's very good, so I still like working with her. And she's a Balkan linguist on top of everything, so nothing gets lost in translation.'

Pine scanned the room, perhaps looking for Janet Ecker. Seemingly satisfied that the coast was clear, he said, 'Excuse me, but I could use something a little stiffer than wine. Interested?'

'No thanks.'

Pine headed for the bar, leaving Vlado momentarily isolated in the growing sea of people; the volume of conversation was rising to a roar. He felt a tap on his shoulder, and turned to see a pale, composed face with shimmering brown eyes.

'You must be Monsieur Petric,' the man said.

'And you must be Monsieur LeBlanc.'

'So Pine has already warned you about me.'

'Afraid so.'

LeBlanc was trim and alert, eyes always moving. He spoke with his hands, making little touches here and there, darting and quick. In his dress he carried off the sort of flourishes that only Frenchmen seem able to manage, and although he wore a dark suit like every other man, he somehow looked a cut above them all. His skin was of a pallor that said he didn't spend much time outdoors, but Vlado knew looks could be deceiving. So many of these supposed diplomatic types who'd come to his country during the war had fancied themselves as men of action, and this seemed also the case with LeBlanc who, Vlado would learn later, had been fond of following close in the wake of major offensives by

128

both sides, driving nothing more imposing than a blue Renault while shells burst within a few hundred yards. He eschewed the flak jackets favoured by so many photographers and aid workers, dressing for war as if he might suddenly be invited to Paris for lunch.

'I have great respect for Monsieur Pine,' LeBlanc said. 'One of the few who isn't so partisan, to risk a Yugoslav pun. And in the interests of equal treatment, I hope he at least warned you about Monsieur Harkness, of the American State Department.'

'He did.'

'So tell me, then. How many people have you met tonight who claim to understand your country? Quite a few, I'd think. All it takes for an American is about a week and he thinks he's got the answer to six hundred years of Balkan problems.' LeBlanc heaved with a light laugh. Vlado couldn't help but join in.

'An Englishman's worse,' LeBlanc continued. 'He reads a few books and thinks he has it worked out, but at least he usually has the good grace to keep it to himself. None of this hanging on your shoulder with a drink in his hand to confide his secret knowledge in your ear, waiting on your approval. Always remember, there's nothing an American craves more than approval.'

'And you say that from how much time in America?'

'Touché. But I am sorry to disappoint you. I was posted to Washington for five years in the eighties. And you'll find that need among all of them. Pine as well. Forgive an American for the sins of his country and he'll be your friend for life. But I suppose I should be glad of their bluster and ignorance. It's the ones like Harkness who create difficulties. He actually knows the Balkans. Lives it and breathes it. Knowledge like his turns the comic element into something dangerous.'

'I thought you were partners on this?'

'Oh, we are. Willing partners. Perhaps I just can't help being suspicious now that we finally agree on something. But the more important question for the moment, Monsieur Petric, is what do you know of us? What do you know of America, for instance?'

'Music, mostly. Rock 'n' roll. We listened to all we could in high school. The Eagles, Talking Heads. And books. Hemingway, Fitzgerald.'

'And what did those songs and stories tell you about Americans?'

Vlado wondered. The songs had mostly meant a good time, offering some place to dream about. But that seemed too shallow an answer for LeBlanc, and he realized he'd let himself be intimidated.

'It told me about their generosity. And optimism.'

'When you've got that much to spread around it's not so much generous as indiscriminate. Everyone gets a little something if you hang around Americans long enough. Just don't mistake it for trust. But enough of that. Your escort has returned. Cheers.' He tipped his glass of red wine towards Vlado's.

'Cheers.'

Pine arrived with a bourbon in hand, looking perturbed that he'd left Vlado at the mercy of Guy LeBlanc.

'Hello, Guy. Hope he hasn't been interrogating you too much, Vlado.'

'He did most of the talking actually.'

'About what?'

'Americans.'

Pine chuckled, with LeBlanc joining in, not seeming the least embarrassed.

'It's one of his favourite subjects.'

'But the important thing, Monsieur Petric,' LeBlanc cut in, 'is that soon you will be heading home at last. And no doubt a few surprises will be in store.'

Pine cast LeBlanc a tight-lipped glance.

'In seeing what has become of your country, I mean. A lot happens in five years.'

'Most of the damage was done by the time I left. I doubt I'll be too shocked.'

'I was referring more to the psychological sense. It is a conquered nation, run by dollars and Deutschmarks. I hope you will not be too disillusioned.'

A waiter glided up with more wine.

'Monsieur seems to have had enough already,' Pine said, not smiling.

LeBlanc laughed lightly and nodded for a refill. 'Surely you aren't suggesting that a Frenchman cannot hold his wine? Don't worry, Calvin, your secrets are safe with me.'

Once again, a small alarm sounded in the back of Vlado's mind.

'On the subject of secrets,' Pine said, 'what's the latest on Popovic? We haven't heard a word in weeks, and you're supposedly the man with the plan.'

LeBlanc's smile faded. Vlado gripped his wineglass tightly.

'No need to worry. He is still, as you Americans like to say, our ace in the hole.'

He was in a hole, all right, Vlado thought, stifling a sudden urge to come clean.

'Just as long as you decide to play him someday,' Pine said.

LeBlanc turned towards Vlado. 'It has been a pleasure, Monsieur Petric. And only the first of many meetings, I hope.'

'My pleasure as well.'

They watched him disappear into the crowd.

'Kind of a prick, isn't he?' Pine said. 'But for some reason I like him anyway. Not that I'd trust him as far as I could throw him.'

'I don't think he trusts you either.'

Pine laughed. 'Which I guess you wouldn't be telling me if you didn't trust me a little. Or maybe you're just too tired to care.'

It was a curious thing to say, Vlado thought. Pine's expression seemed almost wistful. Vlado sipped his drink, and felt his face flush as the alcohol worked deeper into his system. He told himself to slow down. The weight of the day was settling into his legs, and there was still plenty to do, plus an early departure in the morning. In little more than twelve hours they would be landing in Sarajevo. He would be home. Home with uncertain company and a strange job to do, but home nonetheless.

'Christ,' Pine said. 'Now Harkness is heading this way.'

'The one in the little bow tie?'

'Yes. Likes to think he's virtually British after all his years abroad. Says things like "chap" and "old boy", "petrol" instead of gasoline. When he's in tweeds you'd think he'd just been shooting birds on a country estate. He's no dandy, though. He'll walk right into a firefight in eight-inch boots, like the great white hunter on safari.'

Vlado watched Harkness approach. He would guess that the man was in his late forties, a little older than LeBlanc. His cheeks were red, and he tilted his nose into the air as if he were the most perspicacious of bloodhounds.

'Hello, Calvin. Good to see you, old boy.'

'Hello, Paul. Meet Vlado Petric.'

'Yes, the last honest man in the Balkans. How does it feel?'

'As if you're having a little fun with me.'

'Well parried. But merely my hyperbolic way of opening with a compliment.'

By now Vlado was feeling a burst of spark and spite, having been under inspection for nearly an hour.

'At least you haven't given me the ancient hatreds lecture about what's gone wrong in my country.'

'Oh, ancient hatred is quite passé these days, old boy. Now it's all economic opportunism and the wrath of Milosevic. We Americans like to personalize our conflicts. Makes it easier to sell them to the *vox populi*. Stalin. Saddam. Slobodan. They all have a certain ring to them, don't you think? And if old Slobo is ever in the dock I'm sure we'll come up with a new one. We're gradually making the transition from Marx to

Mohammed, which makes Bosnia all the more interesting seeing as how we've thrown in our lot with the Muslims.' He had a good laugh at himself, going red in the face, then said, 'You'll have to get used to a more rustic sense of humour if you're going to be hanging around Pine much. North Carolina boy. Surprised you can even understand him through the accent.'

'What Mr Harkness is trying to say is that I'm not Ivy League. I'm public school, just not in the British sense.'

'Easy, Calvin. LeBlanc must have got things off on the wrong foot.'

Someone across the room began banging a fork against a glass. It was Contreras, resplendent in a dark suit with a red buttonhole, beaming at his audience.

'If our dinner guests will please begin making their way to the dining room. And may I wish the rest of you a very pleasant evening.'

The milling crowd split like an amoeba, one part shuffling towards their coats, the rest pulling slowly towards two sliding doors which opened onto another chandeliered room, longer and narrower, with floor-to-ceiling windows looking onto a garden gone dim in the night. As Vlado began scanning the table for his place card, a voice whispered into his ear from behind. It was Harkness, still hovering.

'I'd like a moment with you later, if you get a chance. It's about a mutual friend of ours.' His breath reeked of gin. 'No need for Calvin to listen in, if it's all the same to you. Enjoy your dinner.'

The remarks were unsettling, and it was a relief to finally tuck himself into a chair, where no-one could corner him for further conversation. He'd spent the past hour being reminded of what it was about his old job he hadn't missed. The office politics and manoeuvring. Trying to say the right things while pondering the deeper meaning of offhand comments. Two days ago he'd only had to worry about getting his German right while ordering a *wurst* and fries, now he was answering to lawyers and diplomats. He checked his flanks – the head of operations to his right, a prosecutor he hadn't met to his left. The only person who could ambush him from the rear would be a waiter.

The meal was excellent – roast lamb with potatoes, salad and string beans – although Vlado appeared to be the only one eating with relish. The others seemed bored with such fare, but they hadn't been living on a ditch-digger's salary. But for all the billing as a working meal, the dinner was largely ceremonial, filled more with toasts than operational detail. The names Andric and Matek weren't mentioned once, although the subject of 'the mission at hand' came up repeatedly.

Every time Vlado looked around, it seemed that LeBlanc or Harkness or Ecker was staring at him, although only Ecker would break into a smile when he returned the gaze. Pine, Vlado noticed, seemed focused on LeBlanc, Harkness or Ecker. A curious bunch, to say the least.

Contreras concluded his role with a ponderous speech, flowery waffle about the common enemies of hatred and intolerance. It was his closing line that got everyone's attention, when he remarked on what a pleasure it was to know that the genesis of the current mission had been in the diplomatic corridors of Paris and Washington.

Tribunal lawyers looked down or shuffled their feet in apparent embarrassment, but Contreras either didn't notice or didn't care.

The evening's final toast was to Pine and Vlado. Janet Ecker proposed it. Her words seemed appropriate enough as long as you ignored the line about Pine's 'great rapport with the Bosnian people'.

As the gathering emptied into the raw night air, Vlado emerged into the darkness with the relief of a student who has completed his finals. A poke here, a prod there, but overall not so bad. Then a cloud of gin materialized at his left shoulder, and the voice of Harkness rumbled up out of the gloom like a premonition.

'Tell me, old boy. Something I've wanted to ask you all evening.' His tone was pitched low, conspiratorial. 'How does a clever fellow who's reduced to digging ditches get mixed up in the business of a shady operator like Branko Popovic?'

Vlado was thankful for the darkness, because the shock surely must have shown in his face. He didn't know what to say.

'Perfectly understandable', Harkness ploughed on, 'if you're not up to discussing this just now. But he's a friend of mine, you know. Or, more to the point, a valuable source. So give him a message when you get a chance.' He hesitated. 'Or do you even understand a word of what I'm talking about?'

Harkness was now facing him, studying him carefully. His right hand grasped Vlado's forearm with a squeeze that seemed to tighten by the second. They'd reached the end of the pavement, and others were walking past, hailing cabs and stepping into limousines.

'I don't think I do,' Vlado said in a low voice, surprised at the steadiness with which he could lie.

'Just as well,' Harkness said, his expression unreadable. 'But if you happen to be lying, or worse, if you happen to be working for the man, then you can count on seeing me again soon, and in more places than you'd like.'

With a final squeeze, Harkness released himself into the current of the crowd. Vlado realized that he had never said what his message was for Popovic. Vlado looked around for Pine, needing a familiar face. Suddenly he wondered if going back home was such a good idea. Peace treaty or not, he'd just been reminded that it was still a dangerous place, a landscape of mines, of grief, and of well-hidden interests.

7

Pine and Vlado watched Europe float distantly beneath them out of the window of the jet. Even from the air the land seemed gridded and plotted, the countries backed up against each other like too many children in the same bedroom. Except now they'd all grown old, harbouring their fears and grudges in the same, stale space.

A question from Vlado broke the silence.

'Tell me about this operation. How does it compare to your others?'

'How do you mean?'

'In organization, preparation.' He paused. 'It's just that this one seems sort of . . .'

'Half-assed?'

'Yes. Half-assed.' Vlado smiled. Even he could sense how funny the words sounded in his careful accent.

'That's because it is. I'd never heard of Matek until last Tuesday. I'd never heard of you until the day before I came to Berlin. Spratt called me and said go get this guy, we need him.'

'Which I still don't understand.'

'Oh, it all makes a certain sense, I guess, when you consider that for our first couple years all we had was one Serb in the dock and two waiting. If you can't do better than that, you might as well not be in business.

Lately the pace has picked up, but it's still not exactly what you'd call an overload on the courtroom side. So, we'll take whatever we can get, especially when it's somebody as big as Andric, no matter who puts the deal together or how they offer it up.'

Meaning Harkness and LeBlanc, Vlado supposed, which reminded him uneasily of Harkness's parting remarks the night before.

'And you think their motives are strictly diplomatic. Tit for tat. Keep both sides of the fight happy while still showing that the West means business.'

'Something like that. But with guys like them you never really know.'

'What do you mean, guys like them?'

'You met them. What did you think? Did you get a sense that maybe they operate on other agendas they never tell us about.'

'To say the least.' He wanted to say more but was too worried about where it might lead. The last thing he wanted was another discussion of Popovic.

'Then there you go. They've got their agendas, for whatever reason, and we have ours. And this time, at least, our interests coincide. So if we have to rush things a little bit more than we'd like – the half-assed part of it – then at least we're getting what we want. Or that's what Contreras would argue.'

'You wouldn't?'

'Hard to say. I'm leery of ever letting the political side get involved. Whether it's a federal drug investigation or sending in a hundred French troops to arrest Andric.'

'That's how many they're using?'

Pine turned in his seat, glancing around to make sure no-one was listening. 'So I've heard. He's out in the woods, near some cow town in the east. And if hauling in some old fart that the US helped repatriate is what it takes to get the French to flush out Andric, so be it. The more you stay focused on that, the better you'll feel about what we're doing.' Pine spoke with true conviction. He seemed to believe in the Tribunal's mission. It had been true for just about everyone Vlado had met in The Hague.

'You like this job, don't you?'

'Beats what I was doing before.'

'A federal prosecutor?'

'Assistant US Attorney for the district of Maryland. Narcotics, mostly. Sometimes it seemed like we were locking up half the high schools of Baltimore.'

'Baltimore. I know Baltimore. *Homicide*. The TV show. You can see it in Sarajevo. Dubbed, of course.'

Pine laughed. He liked the idea of Bosnians getting their first look at Baltimore in a TV show about murder.

'Maybe they should film a show in Sarajevo,' Pine said. 'Call it *Genocide*.'

Now it was Vlado's turn to laugh. 'So what made you want to quit to come over here?'

Pine shrugged. 'Burn-out. Office politics. A few other things not worth mentioning. Maybe I was just looking for a better class of criminal – a little more adult, a little more conscious of what he was doing. Seemed like a good way to get back my sense of mission.'

'A strange cure for burn-out, isn't it? Investigating genocide to make yourself feel better about the world?'

Pine smiled. 'When you put it that way. But I've learned a lot. I mean, look at this.' He nodded towards the window. 'Europeans don't realize how small and cramped everything looks to an American. Even in the middle of the Alps you can't go more than a mile or two without running into a Gasthaus and a busload of Japanese tourists. No wonder the Germans like vacations in Texas. All that wide open space.'

But Vlado had to wonder about the trade-off Pine had made. The way he saw it, evil here was just like evil there. Only the motives were different. In America they killed you for your money, your car, maybe the way you looked. Over here, for the sound of your name, the church your father went to, the sins of your grand-father. And sometimes, in both places, they killed simply because they had nothing better to do, nothing but the grim boredom of a hopeless, hardened life in the middle of nowhere. So they were easily swept up in moments of collective passion, neighbours rising in common cause against a single household or an entire village. The call to arms could be seductive. Once a war was in progress, few bothered to ask who started it, or why.

An hour later their flight left the snowy Alps and approached Bosnian airspace.

'Not much longer now,' Pine said, and Vlado leaned across for a better look. 'Christ, what am I thinking? Let's switch. You haven't seen home in what, five years?'

They shifted awkwardly, crushing against the

forward seats. Vlado settled in and gazed down at Bosnia's mountains. Some were dusted with snow, but mostly the scenery was grey with leafless forests. Tiny streams of smoke poured from chimneys into valleys scattered with red-tiled rooftops.

Within half an hour the plane began its descent. They approached Sarajevo from the northwest, the suburbs of Ilidza zooming below. From the air the placed looked considerably better than when he'd last seen it. Houses had been patched, people were in the streets. A glint of sunlight flashed from the river, the cold water that he could still taste from his last day in the city.

As the plane dropped lower, they seemed to descend into a huge bowl, sheltered by the hills, a comforting feeling he hadn't experienced for far too long. The wheels bounced, the pilot throttled back, and they taxied to the small airport that had once been fortified by high walls of sandbags. Now it looked like any other terminal of eastern Europe.

Pine had arranged for a white European Union car to be waiting for them at the airport as part of their cover. A woman at the airline counter had the keys, and they found the saloon parked out front, next to where UN sentries used to be posted in case of sniper fire.

Vlado got an odd feeling in the pit of his stomach when Pine opened the boot to stow their bags. This was the first time he'd been in a car since the night with Haris and Huso. It was as if he expected to see Popovic's body curled in the dark space below, still locked in his foetal embrace with death. It must have showed on his face.

'Don't look so stunned,' Pine joked. 'You really are home. It's not a mirage.'

'Yes,' Vlado said, forcing a smile. 'I suppose it just hasn't hit me yet.'

He slid into the front seat, taking in the surroundings, but for the first few blocks it was as if Popovic was still riding behind him with their luggage, awaiting disposal.

Gradually the sights of the city stole back his attention. Vlado was dismayed to see so much that was still destroyed or abandoned. Some buildings were missing altogether, the rubble pushed aside by bulldozers. Others had been haphazardly repaired. But the trams were running and the shops were full. The city was alive again, and the blank expressions of people in the streets suggested they'd even grown a bit bored with peacetime. Or maybe they were still worn out. He could understand that.

They arrived at the bright yellow façade of the Holiday Inn, camped on the main boulevard that had once been known as Sniper Alley. It was odd to be back at this building that had marked so many important times in his life. It had been a proud place during the Olympic Games in 1984, with its disco and its restaurants and its high atrium draped with plants, a shining wonder from the West. But now it wore its scars openly, still defiantly facing the river where the siege lines had stared back from a mere three hundred yards. Shell holes had been patched and repaired. And now the place again had uninterrupted heat, water, electricity and phone service, with real windows instead of

143

the sheets of plastic that had been taped over the shattered frames during the fighting.

Yet the lobby still smelled faintly of leaks and damp, mildew and smoke, an enduring desolation that clung like rot. Or perhaps that, too, was Vlado's imagination. The place was clear of all the journalists who'd stayed here during the war. They'd moved on to more active venues, and most guests now seemed to be business people. The man behind him spoke German on a cellphone. Two Japanese stood by the lifts, next to an American.

He and Pine checked into adjoining rooms. After unpacking, Pine dropped in. He looked ready to launch into a discussion of the job ahead, then seemed to think better of it and said, 'You could probably use a walk first, before we begin. Get re-acquainted with the place. I wouldn't mind a little break either. And there's someone I want to meet.'

'Ah. Your friend. The one Janet is so jealous of.'

Pine reddened. 'Why don't we meet back here in an hour and a half. Then we'll get down to business.'

Vlado was surprised at how soon he felt at home in the streets, although every corner brought a rush of powerful memories, some from well before the war but most of them from the siege. Places where he'd seen bodies crumpled in the streets. Alleys once piled with cars as a barrier against sniper fire. Some of the steel and glass towers that had been burned out and shelled still stood empty, but no-one paid them the slightest attention. New trees sprouted near the stumps of old ones that had been chopped down for firewood.

Sunlight washed the streets, and everyone seemed to be out. And after a few minutes of working the stiffness out of his stride, Vlado felt a joy he hadn't experienced in years. He again had the freedom simply to walk without a care or worry in this place he knew so well. No-one was looking down from the hills at him through the scope of a gun, and everyone spoke his language. He gazed up at the hills, which again seemed beautiful and benign, dusted by a snowfall which, down in the city, had been shovelled to the kerb in great sooty piles.

He listened to passing snatches of conversation.

'Come here, they've got one now,' said a man by a shop window.

'Mummy, I'm hungry, can we get just one?'

'That idiot, he wouldn't know his backside from a hole in the ground!'

He thought about stopping by his old apartment, but by now it must have been parcelled out, confiscated, given to some refugee family or a returnee whose own home had been destroyed. If it was standing at all. He wondered how much of his furniture or his clothes were still there. And what had become of the little lead soldiers that he'd painted by candlelight? In his sudden departure he'd left behind stacks of old bills, family records. There were some photos he wouldn't mind having back. But he wasn't sure he was up to shouldering all those memories right now. For the moment, just being back was enough.

The cold was raw and moist, and he shoved his hands deep in his pockets. But, as in the hotel, a faint ghost of

145

the wartime smells remained – a hint of rubbish being burned, the stench of drains and pipes still not yet back to normal. Through the windows of stores and cafés he noticed that the same sort of clientele seemed to be dominant, men in shiny leather jackets with cellphones in hand, women in fine clothes who wore plenty of jewellery – in other words, the same hard-currency crowd of mobsters and hangers-on that had held sway during the war.

A block later a familiar voice called out his name. It was Marko, an engineer. He'd lived in a remote suburb and Vlado had hardly seen him after the beginning of the siege, but here he was, all in one piece, even if his smile seemed fixed, a trifle programmed.

'Where have you been?' Marko exclaimed. 'It's been years.'

'Berlin. We live there now. I'm just here for a visit. I don't think I've seen you since ninety-three. Glad to see you made it. Are you working again?'

'Oh, sometimes. Contract jobs that never last. Restoring the water system. The electrical grid. But lately not so much. We lost Dario, you know. During the war. He was killed by a sniper.'

'No. I hadn't heard. I'm sorry.'

'Yes. In late ninety-four, just when things were getting quiet. He was up on a hill on his bicycle and, well . . .' Marko flicked away his cigarette.

'I was gone by then.'

'So were a lot of other people.' Marko shrugged. 'After the war we finally gave him a proper burial. Before he was not in a good place. So we moved him last spring.

The flowers were out and it was all very pretty. Your family, they're all well? Sonja must be growing up by now. I don't think she was even walking the last time I saw her.'

'Walking and reading, too. In German. She's nine. Speaks the language better than we do. We might end up back here, though. Who knows? Everything is sort of up in the air.'

Marko smiled. 'I'm surprised to see you here at all, really. I'd heard maybe you weren't so welcome any more. It spoke well for you. A lot of crooks in the government.'

It was nice to know that was the word around town, that the judgement on the streets was positive. It mattered more than Vlado would have expected.

'True enough. But I'm not a policeman any more. I'm working for some internationals now. Nobody important.'

'Oh, and you can't talk about it. Even better. And more impressive too. Maybe you can clean this place up.'

'It's not like that,' Vlado said, realizing he was sounding too mysterious for his own good. 'Just some aid work. No big deal. Is the place still full of racketeers?'

'Same as during the war. You just don't notice them as much because they can't carry their guns around now. They lost their cover when the fighting stopped. Now you can only tell them by their cellphones, and even that's getting harder, because now it seems like everyone's got a phone.'

'But things look good. Or a whole lot better anyway.'

147

Marko shrugged. 'I guess. Maybe I haven't noticed because the changes have come so gradually. Or because I never go into any of the new stores. Versace. Benetton. There's even a McDonald's coming. But who can afford it? If you don't have mob money, or work for the internationals, then you probably don't have any hard currency. And it's the internationals who run everything.'

'So I've heard.'

'It's better that way, believe me. Our own people would only fuck it up and start another war. The new parliament couldn't even agree on a flag, or a licence plate. Phoning Banja Luka is an international call, just because a bunch of Serb idiots can't accept they're no longer part of Serbia. But do we really need fourteen thousand foreigners here?'

'That many?'

'Maybe more. They're the only ones paying real wages, but even then you're usually just an interpreter or a driver. Not much call for engineers. The outside contractors usually bring their own. But what about you? An aid agency, you said?'

Vlado remembered his cover and decided he'd better start using it. He wondered if Marko was fishing for a job, already hustling him at some level, not that he blamed him. In that way the war was still on.

'The European Union,' he said sheepishly. 'A few grants and programmes I'm involved with. Mostly with de-mining.'

'No need to be ashamed,' Marko said with a laugh. 'It's not like you have a choice. Impressive, in fact. And you think your family might be coming back?'

'I don't know. We'll see.'

Marko nodded. 'I understand. Believe me, if my family was in Germany, I'd stay until the Germans kicked me out. Well, good to see you. But bring them for a visit at least.'

Poor Marko, Vlado thought. And suddenly it didn't seem so bad to be stuck in Berlin. Maybe things would feel different out in the countryside.

A block later he contemplated stopping for coffee. He had some Deutschmarks and a little local currency in his pocket, courtesy of the Tribunal, and felt like treating himself before heading back to meet Pine. There was a new café nearby, and he gazed through the big windows, checking the scene. He noticed a familiar face.

It excited him more than he would have wished. It was Amira Hodzic. Without her he never would have escaped Sarajevo, would probably be buried somewhere out in the soccer field with all the other casualties, listed as a sniper victim but actually done in by the mob. Her role hadn't involved much risk, but she'd provided him with shelter just long enough for him to plot his final escape, having been pursued halfway across the city. Amira and her two small children had tended to him as if he was a member of the family, though he'd barely known them. She had been a prostitute then, forced into the work by hardship. With her husband dead on some battlefront far to the east, she and her children had been herded into the city along with tens of thousands of others from the surrounding valleys.

Vlado had turned to her when he had had nowhere else to go, and the way he remembered it now it seemed he had sought her out as much for her warmth and spirit as for the knowledge that she would be a safe harbour.

In the café she was talking to someone at her table, keenly interested. From the look of her clothes and make-up, she was one of the lucky ones.

As if she sensed his presence through the glass, she suddenly looked his way. She reacted first with astonishment, then with a slow but wide smile and a glint in her eyes that almost looked like tears.

Now he had no choice but to say hello, a thought more pleasing than he cared to admit. As he entered, her companion turned, and for a fleeting moment of panic he was sure it was Calvin Pine.

But, no, the man was some other foreigner. A European, perhaps an American. Amira spoke a few hasty words of introduction in English and the man rose in greeting and stood by the table as if he didn't know quite what to say, seeming as flustered as Vlado. His name was Henrik, and he had the presence of mind to realize that this reunion deserved a few moments of privacy, or as much as you could muster in a crowded café. He graciously pulled an empty chair from another table.

'Here. Join us.' The accent was German. 'I'll get a wait-ress, or else you might be waiting an hour. The service is notoriously slow.'

Vlado was impressed with the way Henrik handled the moment, keeping things more comfortable than they might have been. But why should it be awkward at all, when nothing had happened between himself and Amira?

He remembered the warmth of her apartment, heated by a wood stove in a high-rise that had otherwise been as cold as a slab of granite. He recalled the faces of her two young children gazing at him as he'd bathed and towelled, then as he'd eaten an orange, his first fresh fruit in months.

Amira, too, was standing now. She reached for Vlado across the table, but with a certain reserve. and not just due to her friend Henrik, he sensed.

Vlado settled into the chair, not sure where to begin. 'How did you two . . . ?'

'I'm an interpreter. For the Red Cross. And sometimes, when they don't need me, for other people. I once did some work for Henrik. He's an assistant to the High Commissioner. It seems the only people I work for these days are foreigners. So, still whoring, as you can see.' She smiled but Vlado grimaced, colouring slightly, and looked down at the table. She touched his hand. 'Please, don't be embarrassed. It's just the way I feel sometimes.'

Vlado hoped for Henrik's sake she was referring to her job, not to her relationship with the German. She reddened, as if realizing how the remark might be taken.

'I'm speaking of my work, of course. You sell your ability with the language to the rest of the world and it's all they want. Not your ideas or any thoughts on whether they're doing things right. Henrik was the only one who ever asked about any of that. The only one. Everyone else just wants a mouthpiece, although lately they've started to let me do a little more. I think they've

151

realized I'm not going to crash their computers if I log on now and then. And it's a living, with lots of hard currency, which is more than you can say for almost everybody else.'

Vlado wondered at the undertone of bitterness from one who was doing so well.

'And you?' she said. 'Are you living here again?'

He shook his head. 'Just visiting. A small assignment for the War Crimes Tribunal.' He caught his mistake too late, realizing he should have said the European Union. So much for his cover story, at least with Amira.

'Nice to hear you're still fighting for the right side,' she said. 'But I never thought I'd see you in Sarajevo again. So many memories from that time when you left.'

Now he was sure of it. There *were* tears in her eyes. Something was wrong here, and Vlado couldn't place it.

'Amira, what's wrong?'

She paused, reaching into her purse for a tissue. She dabbed her eyes, then checked her face in a compact, before looking at Vlado again.

'Do you remember my children?'

'Yes. Your daughter, Mirza. She must be what, nine by now?'

'Ten.'

'And your son. What was his name?'

She lowered her face, speaking into her plate. 'Hamid.' She looked around quickly, almost furtively, but Henrik was still across the room, leaning into a doorway in the back, no help from the kitchen in sight.

Had she not told Henrik about her children? Vlado

found that unimaginable. But perhaps that was the sort of thing that would scare a man off.

'The day after you left my house, the authorities came,' she said. 'As you'd said they might. They were looking for you. Your partner had remembered me coming into the office to answer questions. He knew I was one of the whores from the French barracks, and they got my name from one of the others. So they came for me. You must have been on the plane by then, but I didn't know, so I told them nothing. They didn't believe that, of course. They thought I was your lover. They wanted to know what you'd been doing, what you'd been saying, where you'd gone. Fortunately I'd already given the things you left to a neighbour for safe keeping, so they didn't find them. But they did find your clothes, the ones I'd washed. Some colleague of yours recognized them. They took me away for more questions, for more time to let me think about what might happen to me if I didn't co-operate. I asked them to let me call a neighbour to take care of Hamid and Mirza, but they wouldn't. They said they'd take care of them.'

She looked around again. Still no Henrik. Vlado had a bad feeling about where this was heading.

'I hope they didn't mistreat you too badly, or the children.'

'Not really. They kept me overnight, but nothing much actually happened. Just a lot of the same questions over and over. I think by then they must have realized you'd got away and they were starting to panic, were starting to worry more about saving their own skins than about me. So they let me go in the morning.

153

They'd taken the children to the orphanage, the one near Kosevo Hospital. I walked there to pick them up. It was a terrible place. Pickpockets and thieves, children running everywhere in the halls. Dirty. Loud. They'd been separated, Hamid to the boys' side, Mirza to the girls' side. Both of them were terrified. They thought I'd abandoned them, that they'd never see me again. But I managed to calm them soon enough.'

Vlado began to breathe easier. 'I'm glad they were OK.'

A tear rolled down her cheek, and he realized she wasn't finished.

'Two nights later Hamid began coughing, and by the next morning he couldn't stop. I boiled water to make steam. I went and found a doctor. I asked my neighbours, but no-one could help, and Hamid couldn't stop coughing. I wanted to take him to the hospital, but it was too full and there weren't enough doctors. They told me to keep him at home. The next day he got a fever. He was so hot to the touch, and sputtering like a kettle with his cough. There was whooping cough and scarlet fever in the orphanage – it was a miracle that Mirza didn't catch them. I heard later that five of the boys there died. I think it was especially bad on the boys' side, and Hamid had caught both. In four days he was dead. Lying there in his own bed, not breathing. I had fallen asleep in a chair next to him and didn't even know when it happened. I bought every medicine I could get my hands on with my whore's money. But he was dead. I knew as soon as I woke up and saw his face. The strangest part was that I had just had the most beautiful dream, and my first thought coming out of it was how thankful I was that I had finally been able to sleep, and all that time he'd been dead. I carried him downstairs, across town, all the way to the morgue, the whole place stinking with all the bodies from the war. All the shooting we had come through, the shellfire that I'd worried about every day whenever they were outside. Then my son is killed by a cough and a fever.'

Vlado was horrified. 'Oh my God,' he whispered. 'I am so sorry. I am so . . .'

'Responsible?' She wiped her face with the tissue, then snapped it inside her bag. There were no more tears. She looked at him, her face rigid, and he teetered on the edge of the moment, hoping desperately that she didn't blame him, even though he blamed himself.

'No,' she said finally. 'You're not responsible. It's all those other people. The ones who were after you, the ones who started the war. The ones who were supposed to take care of us. The UN. All of them. And it was luck, too, of course. The same luck that used to decide if you would be shot or not when you walked across town. But I didn't always think this way. Just be glad you didn't come back a few years ago. I probably would have killed you.' She fished a lighter from her bag and lit a cigarette, inhaling deeply.

Vlado didn't know what to say. But Amira seemed to recover quickly.

'I shouldn't smoke,' she said. 'But I have to have one right now. Henrik hates cigarettes. Unusual for a German, don't you think?' She offered Vlado a grim smile, biting her lower lip, placing her hand for just a

155

moment on his, squeezing lightly then withdrawing. She wore another face now.

'And so now I have a real job, and a man. A good man. Henrik is sweet. And he doesn't know what I used to do to make a living, so I hope you won't tell him.'

'Of course not. And you still have . . .' Vlado almost couldn't say the name. 'Mirza?'

'Yes,' Amira said, showing her old self for a moment. 'And most of the time that's enough. It's only because of Mirza that I kept going at all. But I did stop trying to get us out of the city on any aid convoys. My whoring suffered too, sad to say.' She laughed briefly.

A woman at the next table who had overheard her remark frowned and ostentatiously shook her head.

'Stupid cow,' Amira muttered. 'Her lover is a cigarette smuggler, so she should know all about whoring.' She paused. 'I think having Henrik is even better for Mirza than for me. Sometimes I think Mirza gets tired of me. I spent all my time for a while hovering over her. For years, if she sniffled or coughed even once I put her straight to bed.'

Amira looked out of the café window, as if gazing at something in the distance.

'Even now there are mornings when I wake up and the first thing I think of is Hamid. And then I remember that he's dead. Hamid is dead. I have to say it out loud to stop thinking it. The days that start like that are my busiest, my most efficient, because I never want to stop for even a second. Grief as a job skill. They ought to teach it in training.' She stubbed out her cigarette. 'It would be a nice slogan for the government, just like one of Tito's. "Peace, brotherhood and sorrow, for a better tomorrow".'

'Success at last.' Henrik appeared with a china cup of steaming coffee in his hand. He placed it with a rattle in front of Vlado. 'Finding a waitress was one thing. Finding one who would actually help was something else altogether.'

Amira looked up at Henrik with a smile that, while warm enough, came from some other place, some other woman, and Vlado was chilled by the transformation, though he wasn't sure if it was on her behalf or Henrik's. Perhaps both. Somehow Vlado doubted she'd told Henrik about her son. She seemed to confirm this suspicion with a quick glance, a look that sealed a tacit understanding. Henrik re-started the conversation, and a few moments later Vlado stood to leave. He was due to meet Pine back at the hotel in fifteen minutes.

'You will phone me before you leave?' Amira asked.

Vlado couldn't think of a decent answer, other than to say, 'Yes. I'll try.'

'Take one of my cards.' She fished one from her handbag, then scribbled her home number across the bottom. As she handed him the card she clasped his hand, briefly but tightly, and once again he thought he saw the beginnings of tears.

'You're working for the right people,' she said, voice lowered. 'Put a few of those bastards away for me, will you?'

Vlado nodded, glad he didn't have to tell her about the suspect from 1945, although he supposed that

Matek had played his own role in lighting the fire that had consumed them.

He took a roundabout route back to the hotel, completing his circuit of the city with a stroll through the old Turkish town, with its low tiled rooftops and wattle and daub masonry. As he looked at the faces in the streets he wondered how anyone who'd survived the war could ever move beyond it as long as they stayed here. Say what he would about Berlin, it at least gave him some distance from the grief. He thought of Hamid and his heart sank, and he wondered uneasily who else might have been destroyed in his wake. He remembered the boy's face peeping at him round a door, staring with wide eyes while he had stood in a tentative embrace, his first and only, with Hamid's mother. Vlado's stomach knotted, and he stopped to lean against a signpost that was still tattooed with slugs from sniper fire. He wanted to vomit, but couldn't. Then the wave of nausea passed and he walked on, face covered in sweat. How long could one survive in this sea of loss, he wondered, without drowning?

8

When Vlado reached the hotel a few minutes later, Pine was waiting outside his door, arms folded, smiling tightly, a file in one hand. He followed Vlado into the room, tossing the folder onto the bed and shutting the door.

'One last thing you need to see before we get started.'

There was a strangeness to his voice, a quieter note, a hint of strain.

'It won't be easy reading, I'm afraid. I would have let you see it sooner but, well, orders from upstairs.'

Vlado sank onto the bed. His earlier excitement at being home was gone, extinguished by Amira's story and now replaced by rising apprehension. Here came the revelation he'd been dreading; the name of Popovic was about to catch up with him at last. But what Vlado still couldn't work out was how it all tied in with Matek. Or perhaps everything had been an elaborate pretence to lure him here for some other, more dangerous task, with Popovic as leverage.

'Tell me,' Vlado said, gesturing towards the folder. 'Once I've read it, are you going to arrest me? Or hold some sort of charges over my head?'

Pine squinted at him, genuinely puzzled. 'Arrest you? I think the better question is whether you'll arrest me.

For withholding evidence. More likely you'll just want to punch me out. And if you do, you'll find me in the hotel bar.'

Pine shut the door behind him, leaving Vlado more confused than ever. He opened the folder, still expecting to see some sort of report on his own recent whereabouts. But when he began to read, his first reaction was puzzlement, followed by relief.

The name at the top was 'Iskric, Josip'.

It meant nothing to him. And from the dates it seemed clear this was another tale from the Second World War. Iskric had been born in 1922, a year before Matek but in the same remote corner of the country. Vlado skimmed the lines below, looking for something to jump out at him, something to solve the mystery Pine had suddenly dropped in his lap, but there was nothing extraordinary. It seemed to be a mirror image of Matek's dossier: officer academy education in the Yugoslav army. Joined the Ustashe movement. Disciplined by the army for nationalist activities. Joined the Croatian Home Defence Army after declaration of Ustashe dictatorship. Served in the same unit as Matek. Involved in Kosarev Mountains offensive in early 1942. Twice decorated for bravery. Reassigned to Jasenovac concentration camp, May 1942. Promoted to lieutenant. Placed in charge of guard squadrons. That would have made Iskric Matek's equal. Vlado kept reading.

Fled Croatia April 1945. Captured by British forces in Wolfsberg, Austria, along with two others. Interned at Fermo DP Camp, Italy, released June 1946 into custody of Pontifical Relief Commission. Yes, it was the same track, with only a few minor variations. Perhaps Iskric was a potential witness, and maybe they were going to pick him up as well, an extra bit of work that Pine had waited until now to spring on him. In fact, maybe there were even more suspects he didn't yet know about, and they were destined to be here for weeks instead of days. The thought was troubling, but not insurmountable.

From 1946, Iskric's career continued to track Matek's. The two must have worked together in Rome. They even repatriated the same year, 1961. But by then Josip Iskric, like Matek, had a new identity.

His new name was Enver Petric.

Vlado stared in disbelief. He calculated the man's age. It fitted. He continued reading, dazed, knowing exactly what would come next. Enver Petric had relocated to Klanac, a village south of Sarajevo. He'd married the following year, and in 1963 his wife had given birth to their only child, a son, Vladimir, called Vlado.

Vlado could have filled in the rest, but kept reading anyway in numb fascination. Moved the family to Sarajevo in 1968. Employed by a machine shop, promoted to foreman in 1974. Died 1983, survived by wife and son. Son graduated Sarajevo University 1982. At the outbreak of hostilities in spring 1992 was employed as a detective inspector with the municipal police force, assigned to murder investigations. Wife and child evacuated to Berlin, where he joined them in early 1994 following investigation of local corruption.

Vlado closed the folder, feeling sick. He needed to stand, to pace, to wail like an animal, but all he could do for the moment was stare at the folder, and at the name typed so neatly at the top: Josip Iskric.

So this was what happened when you didn't return home on your own terms, he thought, temples throbbing. You learned of the death of a friend's son, and your role in it. Then you learned of your father's genocidal past. And what did that make him, other than the blundering son of a murderer, a man whose actions resulted in the death of children, as well as a man who helped killers hide and bury their victims, as he had done with Haris and Huso.

He felt haunted by a strange sense that his personal history had suddenly been altered as punishment for his own recent crimes, as if Pine were some cosmic messenger who would now disappear into the ether, along with the assignment and the entire Tribunal. Stepping into that old bunker in Berlin had made him slip into some uncharted place where old scores are settled and justice is absolute.

The radiator below the window kicked into action with a hiss of steam, and he jumped, startled. He re-opened the folder, touching the papers as if they might somehow prove fake, a forgery. The policeman in him cried out for details, facts, witnesses. He drew his right hand across the ribbed bedspread and looked to the window, into a blue sky where the sun shone and grey hills stood in the distance.

Everything was real, all right. So much for his worries about Popovic. This was the great secret they'd held out on him, their leverage to lure Matek into the open. Hire the son of the man's old comrade, then throw in a de-mining concession for good measure. If that was even really part of the operation. Maybe all they had was the family connection. They'd found his name in some file and thanked their lucky stars that he was available, this outcast in Berlin who so desperately wanted to go home. And a detective into the bargain.

Then he remembered his conversation with Pine only two days ago. He had spoken glibly of his father's basic goodness and honesty while Pine did nothing but nod, the smiling American, letting him rattle on like a fool. And with that thought his panic simmered quickly to a boiling anger – at Pine, the Tribunal, anyone who might be handy.

Breathing rapidly he stood, volcanic, wanting to smash a wall, slam a face. He would burst down the stairs two at a time, find Pine in the hotel bar and fall on him like a predator. Ram his head onto the table until the teeth of his smile rattled to the floor.

He took only one step towards the door, then stopped, turning, compelled instead by some deeper, nameless emotion that he knew he couldn't fight. He stepped to the window and gazed at the blushing horizon and the mountains he knew so well. Out there was his father, buried, beyond reach and accountable to no-one, speechless against these monstrous charges.

Vlado raised his right fist high, like a hammer, then cried out, a gurgling roar that ended with a pounding blow on the tinted brown glass. There was a dull crunch, the entire room seeming to shake, and suddenly the window was cross-hatched by a thousand tiny cracks, radiating like a map grid from the point of impact. Just like the war, he thought, staring with odd fascination, when every window was smashed and gone, covered by sheets of plastic. And for an eerie instant he was transported back into the siege, alone in a single room, cut off from his wife and child, with nothing but shellfire for company.

The detonation of his anger complete, the implosion now began. How could he have let his father fool him all those years? he wondered. Shouldn't there have been a sign, some telling moment? He thought of every cut-throat or killer he'd ever arrested, and the smug certainty with which he'd always approached them, fancying at times that he could actually see the guilt in their eyes. He thought he'd even detected that quality in Haris. Yet in the guiltiest one of all he'd missed everything.

He groped for a memory of his father, the calm man who'd always seemed so rational. As a boy Vlado had visited the workshop every day, to accompany his father on the walk home for dinner. He remembered sparks flying from a grinder, the hum of the motors and the whirling leather belts, the smell of hot oil, and his father, a tranquil and solid presence, intent on his work. He commanded respect; it was evident in the way others approached him, deferred to him, and you sensed his quiet pride. Those moments had spoken to Vlado far more than his father ever had, and they had remained as his final judgement on his father's basic values and common sense. Good with his hands, everyone had said. But now that phrase was twisted into something terrible by this new knowledge.

Vlado sat on the bed, spent, watching the horizon darken through the cracked glass. He felt as if he'd just run ten miles. He lay on his back, folding his hands across his stomach, laid out for viewing. Then he shut his eyes. They were dry, yet as strained as if he'd sobbed all afternoon. Listening to the everyday sounds of the traffic from the streets below, he felt a bereft numbness descending like a heavy blanket, and he eased himself into a troubled antechamber of sleep, seeking whatever refuge was available.

He dreamed. Nothing coherent at first. Just faces and sites from his past. Friends he hasn't seen in years, making their way through the city. And now he is in the crowd with them, walking purposefully towards a soccer game, one he must have actually seen long ago, because he already knows the score, hoarding it from the others. He knows the outcome of each move even as it unfolds. The field is emerald green, a thrilling surface onto which red and green shirts pour, the players taking their places, excitement high in his throat as he shouts. The ball pings from foot to head with the springy tap of leather, the crowd rising so that for a moment he can't see the pitch; nothing before his eyes but a wool over-coat and someone's hat, the smell of their cigarettes and cheap beer. He is a child now, too short to see over anyone, and his friends are gone, but strong and able hands take hold under his armpits from behind, lifting, thrusting him into the sunlight. It is his father, he knows, although he cannot see the face, doesn't want to look. He lands easily on top of the big shoulders, staring down now at all the hats and bald heads afloat on this sea of excitement.

'Look, Vlado. Look!'

It is his father's voice, years younger than he last remembers it, excited, calling his attention back to the game.

'We're going to win!'

Vlado turns his eyes to the field and sees a hundred or more people in kerchiefs and dark rags, long coats, flat caps. It is an army of peasants, all facing the far end of the stadium. Shepherding the rabble are helmeted soldiers in creased grey uniforms, men carrying long rifles with bayonets that gleam in the sunlight. And down at the front, ordering them hurriedly, hands moving briskly, is Vlado's father, whose face is now plainly visible. He looks impatient, shouting commands that Vlado can't hear above the din of the crowd.

The people move towards the goal at the far end, herding towards the white posts and yellow netting, where now the head of the procession is descending into the earth, into a great brown opening of turned soil, marked at the edges with crosses and crescents, and even from his perch in the stands Vlado feels the chill and dampness of that opening, as if the earth is exhaling from deep below the surface.

A thumping noise begins, the beating of a drum, steady and insistent, and a voice calls his name.

'Vlado. Vlado, are you in there? Vlado?'

Vlado rolled over on the bed, blinking in the darkness of the hotel room. It was Pine, pounding on the door.

'I was asleep,' he croaked in reply.

He stepped sluggishly to his feet, feeling as if he'd been asleep for hours, then opened the door to a face creased with concern, even alarm.

166

'Sorry,' Pine said, speaking fast, running his words together. 'I was worried that you . . . that you might have left or something. I thought maybe, I don't know. I also came to apologize. I've been trying to figure out for the last three days exactly what I would say to you when this moment came. The best I could come up with was that I was only following orders, which told me all I needed to know about what I've been a party to.'

'Don't waste your breath,' Vlado said, coming more fully awake.

'Fair enough.'

'And don't try to explain yourself.'

Pine nodded, saying nothing.

'I can't do this, you know. Not after the way it was handled.'

Pine nodded again, biting his lip, still standing awkwardly in the open doorway, Vlado blocking his way.

'OK. I guess I figured that might happen. OK.' He paused, as if waiting for Vlado to say more, or at least to step aside. When neither happened he continued, if only to fill the silence. 'I'll see if there's a flight back to Berlin tomorrow. I won't try to talk you out of it. You'll be paid for the last two days, of course.'

Vlado scowled.

'But do one thing for me, will you? Or do it for yourself.'

Vlado said nothing, but nodded, as if granting permission to speak.

'Try and think about how you're going to feel about all this in a week. It's horrible, especially to learn it like this. But it can't be undone, and I just want you to think about whether or not you might feel differently later. Because if you change your mind, well . . . By then, the whole operation will be over. It will be too late.'

'You'll go after him anyway, you mean. This man, Matek. This . . . *friend* of my father's.'

'We've got no choice. I'll just pose as the de-mining guy myself. I've already got the fake business cards, just in case this happened.'

'Your classified Plan B,' Vlado said with derision. It wouldn't work, and they both knew it. Not with someone as wise to schemes and ruses as Matek. Deception was how he made a living.

So let it fail, Vlado thought. Let the old bastard keep being an old bastard a while longer. In a few years he'd be dead anyway.

'What about Andric?' he asked. 'They'll carry out the raid anyway, right?'

'I guess. Assuming I can grease the skids at this end.'

Vlado sighed. Already he could see what was coming. The arrangement would fall apart, Andric would remain free, and he'd have played a role. Living up to his father's good name.

And what of Matek, for that matter? The man would die on his own terms. Worse, he would die with his secrets, which Vlado now wanted to know more than anything. Telling the Tribunal to go to hell would be throwing away his only chance to find out more about what had really happened, and why.

Then why not keep working, he asked himself. Not as

a good soldier or even as an opportunist seeking re-settlement and a new job, but as a son seeking vital leads to his family's past. He would participate in Matek's debriefing whether the others liked it or not. Pine would probably let him, if only out of guilt. If his questions annoyed the others, they could fire him. His career with the Tribunal was going to be short anyway. And for the moment he didn't wish to consider bringing his family back to Bosnia. The information in the file had changed everything. He didn't want his daughter growing up anywhere in the path of his father's boot prints.

He turned towards Pine, angrily resigned. 'You already know what I'm going to do, don't you?'

'No, I don't. Tell me.'

'When were we supposed to make contact with Matek?'

Pine frowned, looking away. 'They just changed that part, as it happens. Tonight, they say now. The French were getting antsy, so they've moved the Andric raid up a day. They want us to adjust our schedule accordingly.'

'So whenever I'm ready, in other words.'

Pine nodded grimly. 'That's about the size of it.'

'I want a drink first.'

'No problem. Have two. As many as you want, as long as you can still say the man's name. We'll go down to the bar.'

'No,' Vlado said, now deciding on a different approach. 'No drinks. Just the phone call to Matek. Let's do it now. Then I'll have the drink, but not with you. By myself.'

'Look, if you want to—'

'Just give me the phone number, OK? Tell me what I need to say. Then leave me alone. I'll tell you when it's over.'

'Whatever you say.' Pine held out his hands as if pleading for calm. 'It's your show.'

My show, Vlado thought mordantly. It certainly was. A macabre cabaret from his father's past, and he was about to take the stage. Lights, please. Then the script. Let the entertainment begin.

9

Pero Matek loved the internet, loved the whole idea that you could sit in a dump like Travnik and still command a world of contacts and information. At moments like this it always made him smile to look around his office. In recent years he'd taken particular pains to portray himself to outsiders as a provincial king on his rustic throne, barely schooled and barely presentable, a backwoods potentate who could be kept happy with a pat on the head and a generous cut of the action.

So when UN people and aid delegations came calling he always gave them the best show possible, from the decor to the drinks to his pose as a hick who simply aimed to please. The charade began with the herd of goats wandering the grounds, animals that almost invariably crowded around the cars of guests as they parked, trying to chew anything that moved, bleating and pawing at the scuffed grass as the visitors stepped daintily through the droppings. Inside, brown linoleum covered the floor in the entrance hall, and fluorescent tubes popped overhead. The visitors were shown down the hall to his office, to be seated on bulky brown couches left over from communist times. The windows were heavily draped with awful patterned curtains in orange and brown, and the wall-to-wall carpeting was threadbare and burned by cigarettes.

The real show, however, was Matek himself, seated behind a varnished desk the size of a battleship. He was invariably clad in an oversized brown polyester jacket. His trousers featured busy patterns chosen to clash with the ones on his open-necked shirts, where chest hairs proclaimed his enduring virility and reminded his visitors that along with the oafish charm came sterner stuff – this was his turf, and a false step could leave them stranded in God knows what sort of valley or village. The highlight of Matek's ensemble, however, was his salt-and-pepper hair, a full head of it styled in the pompadour wave customary among self-made Balkan lords.

His office was in the back room of a farmhouse on a few acres of sloping land, cleared of everything but a few plum trees on a grassy scatter of slate and granite. The goats did the mowing. His compound – he always loved to hear the reports describe it as such – sat at the end of a twisting gravel road, halfway up the mountains that towered above the town of Travnik like a six-thousand-foot iron gate, shutting the north side of the valley tight. The view from his upstairs bedroom encompassed not only the glittering Lasva River far below but also long stretches of the main road into town, as well as the track leading to his property. He liked seeing visitors before they saw him. Most of his enemies would never have the initiative, much less the stamina, to approach on foot through the trees. And while the internationals might not know it, his local reputation was that of someone who never let anyone take him by surprise, either in a business deal or in more rudimentary forms of confrontation. Those who tried tended to disappear.

At seventy-five, Matek had kept most of his vitality, and he liked to show that off, too. He looked remarkably well for his age, still trim except for the slight poke of his belly, his face creased but not crinkled, and he was still handy with the women when necessary, which in his case was about once a week. One or two were always hovering nearby when he visited his favourite café, and they weren't averse to a few moments with him later in more private quarters, so long as there was time first for a few shots from his bottle. He wasn't so vain that he discounted the power of wealth in this equation, or of the bottle in steeling their resolve. He considered his bankroll merely another mark of his manhood, of his ability to beat the competition.

Not counting his bodyguards, Matek lived alone. Long ago he had briefly tried marriage, a well-kept secret, but he hadn't found it to his liking, and nowadays the occasional mistress suited him fine. No womanly clutter around the house. No voice at his shoulder telling him what to do and when to do it. He believed that was why the laugh lines around his eyes had remained jolly, not careworn. And he was still quick with a noisy joke or a belly laugh, the brown eyes still prone to twinkle at a good comeback or a savoured memory. All of which came in handy when it was time to play the garrulous host for the outsiders who came grinding up the mountain with their money and their contracts. He found that meeting their expectations left them resigned to a certain level of waste, slippage and overruns, and even some fraud, but not in the sense that an accountant might understand it in Brussels or New York. When they inevitably returned six months later with their bar graphs and flow charts, there was always an atmosphere of the parent–teacher conference, a sighing inevitability that they'd known all along this would be part of the bargain. So instead of yanking the rug, they would merely tug and whisk at its corners, letting him know they could still see his few signs of progress. And by then, of course, they'd taken note of his firm grasp on local needs and conditions, and the ways his enforcement could turn severe, even brutal, if necessary. So they tended to tread lightly, even in admonishment, and would gasp through their sips of his fiery home-brew, always served on a Turkish tray of hammered brass, the glasses smudged just so.

The great joke of this was that what Pero Matek really would have preferred was a calm sip or two of a Chianti Classico in shining crystal stemware. But those bottles were kept locked in the cellar, with humidity and temperature controls. Kept out of sight just like his Dell desktop computer with its 21-inch Sony monitor.

On the rare occasions when company could be coaxed to stay for dinner he would order up a big mixed grill just to set their teeth on edge and their stomachs into a roll – quivering Balkan meatfests of lamb, veal and sausage, piled on platters oozing with grease and char. Load their plates like troughs and watch them grin woodenly, knowing they'd compare notes later in their Range Rovers and Mercedes SLs, laughing at the hopeless peasant. An assistant from the High Representative's office, perhaps his most important visitor ever, had later called him 'Pero the Barbarian', and when Matek received the report from one of his secretarial spies he laughed about it for days, spreading the nickname through the village as if it were a promotional pamphlet, cementing his reputation for putting a not so fine edge on things. One American investor who'd nosed about the valley for a week, an Oklahoman with tall boots and a big voice, had compared him to an Ozark moonshiner, albeit one who could be leashed and trained as long as he got his ration of skim.

So he let them believe he was trainable, and housebroken, and kept getting his share, time after time, from just about any financier or do-gooder with currency to burn.

The irony of this dynamic was that it had begun to make him legitimate, even in the eyes of some of the more naïve locals. The back-channel thuggery of his wartime markets was slowly turning into a well-documented realm of signed contracts and foundation grants. His participation in the stolen car operation, regrettably, had been a necessary casualty of the transformation. Too much law-enforcement attention had begun to zero in, so he had quietly transferred control to a few obliging lesser rivals, who were thrilled at their sudden windfall of rolling stock from Germany and Switzerland via Poland and Ukraine, only to be dismayed when it all came apart a few weeks later with a well-informed bust of their open-air distribution market. By the time they suspected Matek's role in the

175

matter, several were in gaol, others were dead and the car market was gone. It would be back, of course, an option that would always be available if Matek ever needed it. But for now the international spigot was running full, and he was content to paddle in the lucrative broth of Europe's alphabet soup, the NGOs and EU sub-agencies who ran this country in a manner befitting the Hapsburgs and Ottomans.

In the case of his other illegal operations, why sell bootleg petrol in wine bottles and plastic milk cartons when you could run six INA stations, supplied straight from Zagreb at subsidized prices? Why keep selling booze in back alleys when your distributorship in spirits and beer was now the largest in five surrounding municipalities? It had been so ever since the previous spring, when his biggest competitor drove across an anti-tank mine. Never mind that the man's neighbours still wondered why he'd been driving off-road in that particular patch of woods. Out hunting, perhaps, for that was his hobby, although no-one ever found out who might have invited him. And never mind that the property in question had supposedly been cleared of mines, or that it was owned by Pero Matek, although the deed had percolated through so many proxies and riders and silent partners that you could spend weeks poring over papers at the municipality's hopeless little archives and not make head or tail of it.

Not that Matek ever worried about establishing his provenance, if need be. All the original documents were filed neatly in his safe, the hulking one in the corner of his office, behind the cabinet with the Dell, where he now sat hammering at the keyboard with his farmer's hands, the pockety-pock rhythm putting him in a fine mood, as soothing as the ringing of a cash register must be for a village shopkeeper. This was the sound of commerce today, he thought to himself. 'Even for a Barbarian,' he muttered aloud, breaking into a laugh. . You could check commodity prices and shipping rates, then plug them into your budgets and your cost schedules. Type in a few serial numbers, plus a password or two, and your orders were updated, the status flashing at you from six different locations. Send an email to Emilio in Trieste, a duplicate to Francisco in Madrid, a confirmation with a bonus porn photo attachment, just for fun, to a supplier in Bulgaria he knew only as Christo.

All of them were people he had never met because, frankly, it was still a risk to travel abroad, and perhaps always would be. It was his one great regret in life. Crossing the border would probably never be a sure thing, considering what they'd done with his papers and his passport all those years ago. He had others, of course, two different sets that were best kept out of sight, and neither carried his old name, his real name. There was no safe or strongbox yet built secure enough for that knowledge, so he kept it only in his head, well towards the back lest it show itself at an inopportune moment.

Rational judgement told him that he should be able to travel wherever he pleased, given the passage of time. Who could possibly recognize him now, all these years later? Nonetheless, he had stayed put, even if he still longed for those days of Italian villas and small towns in the hills, a sunny landscape where everyone sipped wine at midday with big bowls of pasta and platefuls of fish, then napped until three.

A knock on the door interrupted his reverie.

It was his assistant, Edin Azudin.

'Yes, Azudin. Come in.'

Azudin was pale and thin. Matek was always telling him to eat more, then laughing when the man blushed and squirmed. Matek had decided long ago, simply by appearances, that Azudin must be homosexual. It was just as well. Fewer temptations, at least around this valley. You'd as soon be caught sleeping with a goat as another man, given the local attitudes, so Matek never worried about his quiet little assistant causing trouble. It was almost like having his own eunuch at court. Had Matek known the truth he would have laughed aloud: the meek, undersized Azudin kept two mistresses in Travnik, not so surprising when one considered the ready supply of hard currency he earned from Matek. But it was also his manner, a calm mouselike obeisance, practised daily, that placated the women in its quiet way, and he was discreet enough in his comings and goings to ensure that the affairs never got complicated. If you had secrets, they were safe with Azudin, which was why Matek valued his services.

'There is a caller for you,' Azudin said. 'He says it's about a new de-mining contract for the municipality. He believes you may be the right man for it.'

Matek perked up. 'Does he now? Well, leave him on

hold then. For . . .' He mulled the timing. 'For exactly ninety seconds. Then get back on the line and tell him I won't be available for a while. But take his number. And an hour later you're to call and arrange a meeting for tomorrow. In the morning. Ten, if possible. If he can't do it then, you're to check with me. And the meeting is to be here. Understand?'

'Yes, sir, but . . .' Azudin halted, uncertain whether to exceed his usual responsibilities.

'Go on.'

'He insisted that I make sure you knew who you were doing business with. Vlado Petric, the son of Enver Petric.'

And for the first time for as long as Azudin could remember, Pero Matek was speechless. Matek knew he must look a sight, sitting there with his mouth agape, wondering at this strange and sudden shout from so deep in his past.

Matek had known about Vlado, of course. Had known that Enver, whom he still thought of as Josip, had married, had a son, and had died without ever having made much of himself − not surprising, considering their past. Enver had always been too earnest for his taste. His talents were effective only if you knew how to channel them; otherwise he had been too inflexible to be of much use. Enver's son, Matek had heard, had become some sort of policeman, had even had to leave the country, something to do with smuggling and corruption. Had he been a dirty cop, or too idealistic? Probably an amateur, either way, like his father. But he, too, might be useful if channelled. Matek had heard rumours that a change was in the works in the management of the de-mining concessions, but the selection of a Bosnian seemed almost too good to be true. Suddenly he sensed new possibilities, even if the boy's name made him uneasy. What vexed him most of all was how Vlado could have found out about him, or his past connection to Enver. Enver and he had agreed long ago to go their separate ways, vowing no further contact. Yet here was Enver's son on the phone. It was puzzling, and more than a little worrying. Had Enver blabbed something on his deathbed long ago, some father–son confession, complete with names and bodies? He doubted it. And at least the boy hadn't referred to his father as 'Josip'.

'Shall I put him on hold, sir?' Azudin was still waiting for an answer, looking far too curious for Matek's taste.

'No. Put the call through. And why don't you go down to see Silovic and pick up this week's take? If he grumbles about doing it a day early, tell him this is a test. That I'm making sure he isn't raking the till and juggling the books at the last minute, or taking mid-week loans at my expense. Tell him it's a pop quiz. Tell him whatever you like. And take your cellphone in case I need you.'

There, Matek thought. Azudin hated chores like this. It would take his mind off this phone call. No sense piquing Azudin's interest in anyone named Petric.

'Go now. And put the call through.'

'Yes, sir,' Azudin said, departing with the helpless expression of a driver of a tiny car about to be crushed between two careening trucks.

Matek leaned back in his chair, anticipation building to a boil and, he had to admit, his merchant's sense of an impending bargain prickling as well. If the son of an old colleague was in charge of a new de-mining contract, well, that was good news on a front he'd been trying to make gains in for months. But the very fact that Enver's name had been spoken over his telephone was alarming. Although, why worry? Azudin wasn't in the habit of reading anti-Ustashe tracts that named names and dug up old history. He was twenty-six and about as interested in history as any young man on the make, meaning not at all. Even if he had been, the most detailed published accounts available never mentioned young officers who'd been so far down the pecking order. Matek had checked the books and pamphlets himself, looking always for the names Rudec and Iskric, just in case, scanning with a frantic thump in his heart that was always pacified in the end.

He could probably resume using his old name tomorrow without turning a single head, if he wanted. Well, maybe not. There were always the old heads to consider, the grey women in the streets or the men leaning on their canes. Funny how he thought of them as old when they were his contemporaries, and once or twice in his travels around the country he thought he'd noticed some of them eyeing him strangely – probably nothing but idle curiosity, but you could never tell for sure. He remembered that American movie about the old Jews stumbling through the streets of New York, bony fingers outstretched, calling the name of some ageing Nazi who tried to race away. A horror to have it end that way, which was one reason he seldom strayed beyond his region, and almost never journeyed to places where lots of Serbs lived. The war had made that easier, thank goodness, sending each side streaming for its own ghettoes and enclaves, the crescents and the crosses once again penned in their own cantons. Now he could drive for miles without fear of meeting some unwelcome face from his past.

Azudin transferred the call. Matek lifted the receiver, wondering if he might begin to tremble, either with worry or anticipation. But his hand was steady, his voice calm.

'Matek,' he said.

His caller was the one who was tremulous – from anger, from nerves, from dismay. Vlado had dialled quickly, as soon as he and Pine had reviewed the approach he should take, but he realized when he heard Matek's voice that he should have waited, if only for an hour, to give his emotions time to subside.

Hearing the man speak his name he wanted to shout, 'Who are you?' if only to calm the flutter in his stomach, the pressure in his fingertips. Instead he stuck to the formalities, working to keep the quaver out of his voice.

'Mr Matek?'

'Yes. And you're Enver's boy?'

'Undeniably.'

Curious choice of word, Matek thought.

'But I'm not calling to re-live old times, because frankly my father never told me much about those. I've only recently learned that he knew you, that the two of you grew up together. But we can discuss that more

182

when we meet. It's business that brings me to your doorstep.'

'You're hooked up with the EU, I take it?'

'Yes. De-mining contracts. You're in the market for one, and I'm the new regional administrator.'

'I thought the EU was convinced I didn't measure up.'

'That was under the previous management. Now I'm in charge.'

'Glad to hear it. And with a name I can trust. You should visit.'

'The sooner the better.'

'Tomorrow, then. Early, if you can make it. Eight o'clock? We can have breakfast.'

'I'll be driving up from Sarajevo.'

'Make it ten then. A more civilized hour. We'll have coffee, maybe a glass of wine.' Matek was momentarily at a loss as to what to say next. He wouldn't be laying on the usual spread, not for a local, much less one who was practically family. No need for any grand poses with this one, yet he'd still need to do some acting, given the circumstances. 'We'll have more to talk about than just business, of course. So plan on staying a while.'

'I'll look forward to it.'

I'll have to play this one carefully, Matek thought. He needed to gauge exactly what the boy knew before committing himself to one truth or another. He'd need to do some thinking between now and tomorrow morning.

He gave Vlado directions, then they said goodbye. Tomorrow would be interesting indeed.

10

Pine and Vlado drove north on the highway out of Sarajevo, up through Kiseljak, Busovaca and Vitez. During the war the road had criss-crossed territory held by all three warring factions, with sandbagged checkpoints and scattered mines. Travnik was about sixty miles away, but they'd allowed an extra hour for bad roads and slow traffic, saying little to fill the awkward silence as the miles passed. The mountains shouldered the route as the pale winter sun climbed the sky to their right.

Vlado had a slight hangover, less from three shots of the hotel's plum brandy than from the evening's revelations, which had called to him throughout the restless night, a gruff whisper through the pillow.

'Guess we ought to review some of the details,' Pine said, clearing his throat. Their hope was that Matek would want to sign the contract the following morning, a Friday, the day of the Andric raid, co-ordinating the timing to please all sides. The key would be luring him onto neutral ground at the Café Skorpio.

'It's a little rat hole near the Suleiman mosque,' Pine said. 'Cheap *rakija* that will melt the paint off a wall. Matek supposedly has a stash of Italian wines they keep in the back. They don't even need to lock it up. That's what a reputation will do for you. Nobody would dare touch it. There's a *cevapi* grill where he usually likes to stop, too, up an alley round the corner. Then he usually meets one of his mistresses at the Skorpio. Fills her up with Chianti or something stronger before they go upstairs for an hour of fun.'

At one level Vlado was listening. At another he was wondering what he might be able to learn from Matek about his father without revealing the true nature of his visit. Pine probably had more information worth knowing, too. But he was still talking, still reviewing every possible detail of the day ahead. Maybe it was his clumsy way of softening the blow. Or maybe he was just embarrassed about having strung Vlado along.

'Pull over,' Vlado interrupted. 'I need to check something.'

'We'll be late,' Pine said.

'Which would make me like every other Bosnian,' Vlado said icily. 'It's you and the Germans who are obsessed with punctuality. We're way ahead of schedule. Pull over.'

Pine complied with a frown, yanking the wheel, and the car shuddered to a stop on the gravel shoulder.

'I want to see anything else you might have with you about my father,' Vlado said. 'Even if I only have time for a glance.'

'You've seen the file.'

'But there's more, isn't there? Someone must have wondered what would happen if I needed more convincing. That was pretty thin stuff, really. Just a few dates and assignments. If I'd demanded more proof, what would you have shown me?'

Pine sighed, but to his credit never took his eyes off Vlado.

'It's in my briefcase,' he said. 'Just a few pages. There's more back at The Hague, but we figured this would do it. If you really want to see, that is. If I was you, I wouldn't.'

'You're not me. Get it, please.'

Pine nodded, reaching for his briefcase. He snapped it open, foraged a moment, then pulled out a thin, stapled report stamped 'Eyes only' below the Tribunal letterhead. It was an old report from a US Army counter-intelligence officer.

'It's a witness report,' Pine said. 'From Jasenovac. Taken at a DP camp in Italy in nineteen forty-six.'

Vlado had second thoughts as he scanned the cover page. How much did he really need this? He decided to plunge in before losing his nerve.

'I'll take a little walk,' Pine said, opening the door. 'If you don't mind.'

'Watch for mines,' Vlado said absently.

The name of the witness was Dragan Bobinac. He was a musician, a cellist from the Serb village of Crveni Bok on the banks of the Sava River, not far from Jasenovac. His account began with the day he was rounded up near his home along with several hundred of his neighbours, and he had plenty to say about the man known as Josip Iskric, who later became Enver Petric:

186

The soldiers came into our village in early morning, about a hundred of them, led by two lieutenants. I later learned their names were Rudec and Iskric. Iskric was the one giving orders, shouting at his men to keep anyone from escaping into the river. Some of his men shot people as they ran from their homes. Anyone who resisted was clubbed or stabbed on the spot. Children who didn't come fast enough were shot or struck in the face with sticks or bayonets. Some were dumped immediately into the river, still bleeding and alive. As we were marching I saw the naked body of a woman on the riverbank. Her eyes had been gouged out and a metal rod was shoved in her genitals. Iskric ordered me and another man to throw her into the river. The other man's name was Cedomir, he was a baker in the village. When Cedomir saw the woman he fell to his knees and said she was his niece. Iskric took a side arm from a holster and ordered Cedomir to get up or he would be killed, but he stayed on the ground crying. Iskric walked in front of him and shot him in the face, then rolled the body over with his boot. He ordered me to push both bodies into the river. I got them into the water, but the woman snagged on a branch after floating a few feet downstream, and Iskric ordered me into the river to pull her free. All of this time the entire column was halted, watching everything. Some of the children were crying. I waded into the river up to my knees and pulled away the branch, then I watch the woman float towards the main current, which carried her downstream.

Vlado couldn't bear the scene any longer. He skipped ahead to an account from inside Jasenovac itself.

I was one of ten people employed in the carpentry shop in the main camp. We were marching to the shop from our barracks when we were ordered to halt to allow a large column to pass in the opposite direction. They were young women – 150, maybe 200 – led by several guards and Lieutenant Iskric. Someone shouted an order for the women to stop as well, and we looked at each other. Tears were falling from their eyes, and Iskric made a speech, telling our column to look closely because in an hour all of these women would be dead, and that the next morning perhaps we would be killed as well unless we worked hard enough that day. We were forced to watch while the women were marched to the river. They were loaded onto rafts that took them to the other side, where the current was stronger. As they stepped onto the bank they were pulled aside by guards, who stabbed them with bayonets, and cut their throats and stomachs with knives. We could hear their screams and groans very clearly when they were stabbed or clubbed. Their bodies were then thrown or pushed into the current, sometimes while they were still alive and screaming.

Bobinac's account ended a few pages later with his escape the following month. He too had finally been ferried across the river with a hundred others. He got away when one of the guards hastily shoved him into the current with only a superficial wound, from a bayonet to the stomach.

There was more, but Vlado had seen enough. He gingerly placed the pages back into Pine's briefcase. Then he rolled down the window, the air cool and damp on his face, which seemed hot and tight, boiling with shame and revulsion. How much more of this sort of material was on file at The Hague? he wondered. How many chapters of such unbearable tales? He would need to see each and every one, no matter how agonizing.

'All done,' he shouted in a quavering voice. What he needed was a brisk walk to collect himself, but he didn't think he deserved it. Better to take it like this, stewing and guilty in a seat next to someone whose hands were clean, while driving across this tired landscape where armies had marched for generations, from one war to the next.

Pine was about twenty feet in front of the car when Vlado called out. For a moment Pine paused, facing the other way like a forlorn hitch-hiker. Then he turned and slowly walked back, rubbing his hands together for warmth as he slid into the driver's seat. He started the engine without a word.

It was a mile or so before either of them spoke.

'You OK?' Pine said softly.

Vlado nodded. 'No worse than yesterday.' Then he shrugged, exasperated. 'Don't expect me to be OK. Just expect me to do my job. Just get me to the meeting. At least now I know the sort of person I'm dealing with.'

'Sure.' Pine kept his eyes on the road.

Vlado waited a moment, then asked, 'This witness, Bobinac. Is he still alive?'

'Living in Novi Sad, I think. He's prepared to testify in Matek's trial.'

After a few minutes of silence, Pine tentatively resumed his impromptu briefing.

'There's a wide street in front of the Skorpio,' he said, 'and no way to exit through the back without having to go through the kitchen. They keep the kitchen door padlocked. It's a fire trap but perfect for us because he has to come out the front even if he decides to bolt. Try to let the Skorpio be his idea. But if he starts making noises about another meeting at the house, insist that your boss never meets the locals on their own turf, that the meeting has to be in town. That should steer him where we want him.'

'Plus, I'm his old friend's son, and his new partner in crime. So how can he possibly say no?'

'Yes. That too.'

Vlado wouldn't let it go. Not yet. 'So tell me. What would you have done if you hadn't found me? Or if I didn't exist. Would this deal still have been arranged? And don't give me any of that Plan B business.'

'Probably. Just would have been harder. We might have waited until he went to the café on his own, then jumped. But S-FOR doesn't like doing business that way. You have to get paid informants involved, and once you've done that the whole thing tends to leak like an old pirate ship. So we were looking for something to simplify this, and that's when we found you.'

'How did my name turn up?'

'Harkness or LeBlanc, apparently.'

The names chilled him, especially Harkness, remembering the man's face in the dark as he'd muttered about Popovic. For all he knew, LeBlanc had been poking around in his affairs as well. Either of them might have been the man who'd shown up on Haris's doorstep in Berlin. LeBlanc was too clever to have asked him directly about Popovic, the way Harkness had. But none of that should matter to this operation.

'I heard they came across your name while researching Matek,' Pine continued. 'I guess through your father's file. We checked records for any living relatives of either. We couldn't believe our luck. They had me on a train to Berlin within a week. Contreras wanted to move fast. The French did too. Didn't know how long they could hold together the political momentum in the defence and foreign ministries. That was LeBlanc's doing. The French still aren't exactly keen on the idea of picking up Andric. It'll be the first arrest in their sector since the Dayton Agreement. But the main reason you made the pieces fit is because S-FOR loved the idea. There's nothing they like better than ordering up a time, a date and a secure location for bringing in a suspect. I'm not even sure we could have talked them into this one without the kind of assurance you provide. If you can provide it.'

'And if I can't? What if Matek says we close the deal at his place or no place?'

'I can't imagine he would, given the stakes. He's wanted this contract a long time.'

'But say that he does.'

191

Pine turned towards him for the first time, the tyres thrumming on the road. 'I don't know. You tell me. We're flying by the seat of our pants as it is.'

'Like you said, half-assed.'

'Sometimes that's as good as it gets down here.'

Vlado wished Pine would quit saying 'down here', as if it was some quaint corner of Hell.

'How many S-FOR people will be involved?'

'Soldiers? Hard to say. We're never privy to that. I'd guess at least twenty. Two APCs and maybe a Humvee with a big gun mounted on the back. It'll look like they're coming after Genghis Khan by the time they're in place.'

'Won't that be kind of . . .'

'Stupid? Ridiculous? Noisy? Enough to panic everyone in the neighbourhood and maybe him, too? Sure. You ever seen cops or soldiers do it any other way?'

Vlado smiled ruefully. 'I guess not.'

He wondered how many other people back in The Hague must have known about his father when they'd met him. Harkness and LeBlanc had, of course. Contreras and Spratt had presumably known as well, smiling and chatting as if none the wiser. Perhaps Janet Ecker too. All of them looking him in the eye and not wavering a bit. And these were the good guys. No wonder Pine had been so irritated when LeBlanc had made the crack about 'surprises' awaiting him in Sarajevo. Maybe the Frenchman had been trying to warn him in some oblique way, although it struck him more as a clumsy joke, something to get under Pine's skin.

Everyone had fooled him, and now he was about to fool Matek, all in the name of family. He wondered how he'd feel when the moment of truth came, and the old man – his father's friend, for better or worse – looked into his eyes, realizing what was happening. Just what Vlado needed this morning. Another reason to feel rotten. At least after tomorrow he'd be able to call Jasmina. Who knew what she and Sonja were thinking by now? More than two days without a word, except from some Tribunal secretary. And so much to tell her, so much that would be difficult and embarrassing. She'd never met his father, had only seen his picture.

'Here's the turn-off to Travnik,' Pine said. 'Nine twenty. We're in good shape.'

Travnik was long past its prime, worn down by cataclysmic fires, and more recently by wearying tides of refugees. A century ago it had been a hub for the Ottoman viziers who ran Bosnia for the Sultan. European diplomats came and went, observed by the young Serbian novelist Ivo Andric, who sceptically recorded their doings in his *Chronicles of Travnik*. His home there, once a popular museum, was now largely ignored. Never mind his Nobel Prize. He was the Serb who'd portrayed the Turks and their local Islamic converts as bloodthirsty tyrants, deserving of vengeance.

All that was left of those days now were a few old mosques, like the Suleiman, and the fifteenth-century castle overlooking the town from Mount Vlasic, the one-time stronghold of Bosnian kings.

They wove through the crowded narrow streets until they found the small hotel. Vlado left his bag with Pine in the lobby and took the car keys. Pine wished him luck. He was on his own now, could drive the Volvo off into the hills and never come back if he wanted. But Matek was waiting up on his mountain, the only one left who could escort him into the past. As awkward and uncomfortable as the meeting promised to be, there was no way Vlado could refuse the invitation.

He easily found the turn-off to Mount Vlasic and climbed several miles before swerving onto a dirt road where the Volvo's underbelly bottomed out in the deeper ruts. Higher up the bare trees were coated with ice. On some curves Vlado looked back down onto Travnik, and he remembered Pine mentioning that Matek could see much of the road from his house, and always knew when a visitor was approaching. Vlado thought he caught a glimpse of a red rooftop looming high up ahead, but the road was too twisting and narrow to allow the luxury of a longer look. Meanwhile, some rear chamber of his brain was still sorting through every retrievable memory of his father, looking for missed signs, gathering little threads from the past to see if they added up to anything meaningful. His father had passed himself off as a Muslim who never went to the mosque, a Muslim who drank. Neither characteristic was un-usual 'down here', as Pine would have said, but Vlado remembered that his father had also attended Mass on occasion with his wife and son, and those Sundays now seemed significant. In addition, he had given his son a good Christian name, Vladimir. He must have sneaked off at times to confession, Vlado supposed, if he was any sort of Catholic. The parish priest had probably been happy to conspire with him, hearing his petty sins but probably never the big ones.

And what about that trip long ago to see his Uncle Tomislav? That night out in the back with all the shouting and drinking. What had that been about? Had his uncle fought in the war as well?

Vlado remembered a wooden crucifix hanging in his aunt and uncle's bedroom, the bleeding Jesus with the agonized upturned face that had always seemed to be staring at a crack in the ceiling. Of course. His father's family had all been Catholics. The stupid son could have added it up as simply as the beads on a rosary if he'd ever bothered to think. But such details had run together when he was a boy. Tito had asked that crosses and crescents be considered little more than quaint symbols of their past, and Vlado had obediently obliged, never pausing to note their significance.

Vlado glimpsed the tiled roof again, much closer now. Matek was probably watching his car, the engine rumbling like something tunnelling towards him through the mountain. The Volvo's springs creaked through another set of curves and there it was, a small guardhouse with a rusted iron pole barring the way. A man with a Kalashnikov slung on his back emerged from the guardhouse in a cloud of grey smoke. No uniform, just blue jeans and a dark sweater, cigarette drooping from his lips. He sauntered to the car and checked Vlado's papers. Vlado had an EU identification card plus some other documents. If there was one thing the EU people had plenty of, it was paper. The guard pulled a cellphone from his back pocket and punched in a number. Then he tugged at a rope to haul the pole into the air, clearing the way.

Waving Vlado through, he shouted, 'The big house at the top. Go in through the front. Azudin will take you to Mr Matek.'

Mr Matek. How long had it taken to train this one to say 'Mister'? Vlado wondered. If he wasn't working here he'd probably be pulling up turnips and cabbages, or drinking in the loft of a barn, falling asleep and setting the hay on fire with his smokes. Instead he was waving an automatic weapon, empowered to kill by the man Vlado was about to visit.

It never hurt to remind yourself of exactly who you were dealing with.

11

Matek watched Vlado approach from his window, unsure how to greet the boy. He'd been irritable all morning, shouting at Azudin when the coffee hadn't been hot enough, griping about the bread, although it was the same bread as every morning.

When he saw the face emerge from the car he knew there was no doubting the bloodlines. Sometimes, he knew, you saw the father in the son because you went looking for him. But in this one the resemblance was obvious, not so much in the features as in the way he carried himself, purposeful, head held high. This was not the sort of person who would ever apologize for what he believed in. Just like his father. But what did this one believe in? That was the morning's top question, and he intended to find the answer.

Then he chuckled in spite of himself at the idea that they might actually do business together, and he was still smiling when Azudin shepherded the boy – he had to stop thinking of him as a boy, the man was in his thirties – into the room. The smile broadened as he saw the uncomfortable look on Vlado's face. Good God, the boy was embarrassed. So Matek stepped quickly across the room and, without a word, gave Vlado a bear-hug like some Russian grandfather, feeling the young man's sinew and bone beneath his wool sleeves. And in spite of himself he felt tears spring to his eyes. He pulled Vlado closer and spoke into his ear, silently reminding himself not to use any of the wrong words from the past.

'Ah, Vlado, your father and I. Your father and I. Such times we had together. But too long ago now.'

Then the wave of nostalgia crested and broke, and Matek let go, stepping back to look into Vlado's face, inspecting the cool reserve in the eyes that he knew so well.

Vlado had feebly attempted to return Matek's warmth, although it was hard while the big arms gripped him so tightly. Now at least he could offer a smile, not a grand one but enough to do his familial duty. Then the big man withdrew and, in a rolling gait, eased behind the bulwark of his desk.

He had opened a bottle of red wine and set aside two glasses, polished to a sparkle. None of the usual smudges today.

'I know it is early, but please.' He poured Vlado a glass. 'We must drink to your father.'

A Chianti, Vlado noticed, deciding he'd be better off trying to act as an observant detective than as some sort of unofficial nephew. Look for details. Concentrate on the business at hand. But his father's presence was unavoidable, as if he were looming in a corner, nodding sternly, reminding Vlado to be respectful and polite.

The decor was not what he'd expected. It looked standard issue for some small-town mayor or party hack. Nor did it go with this wine.

Matek must have noticed the glances of assessment.

'For the Europeans and Americans it is usually only *rakija*, because they expect it of me. For you, something I really like.' Matek raised his glass. 'To your father.'

Vlado raised his own, and drank.

'And also to his son,' Matek said.

Vlado knew it was his turn, but it took an effort.

'And to his friend,' he finally said, pleasing Matek.

Neither spoke for a moment. Vlado decided to let Matek take the lead; his own mind was still darting into too many places at once.

'Yes, you are your father's son,' Matek said eventually. 'He is the only other person I know who would sit there for so long without a word, determined to make me speak first, even with important business to be done.'

Vlado blushed.

'I'm sorry, but there is one thing I must ask you straight away,' Matek said. 'How did you know about me? From your father?'

Vlado had strict instructions on this point. He was to answer that he wasn't at liberty to say. It was a vague approach that had troubled him all morning, because it seemed obvious that Matek would smell a rat. Why would the son of Enver Petric not be able to answer such a simple question, especially when he was empowered to offer a contract to a man whom the EU had deemed unsuitable only a month ago? He also preferred not to begin their conversation with a lie, feeling it might throw him off balance for the duration. And this first question, at least, he could answer honestly enough without revealing a thing. So he broke with the plan.

'My father never said a word,' Vlado replied, looking Matek in the eye, feeling as if he'd been hooked up to a polygraph. 'I didn't know you existed until years after he died.'

Matek had also vowed to take care with his words. But he, too, seemed caught up in the moment, perhaps seeing his own youth reflected in what remained of Vlado's.

'Then it must have been your Uncle Tomislav. He's the only other one who knew me from those days.' Matek then seemed to snap back to attention, and Vlado sensed that he had momentarily dropped his guard, letting the name slip.

'Yes,' Vlado answered, going with his instincts. 'It was Uncle Tomislav. He mentioned you in a letter, not long before he died. Then when I took this job last month it wasn't long before I saw your name on a list. I couldn't be sure it was the same Pero Matek. But when I found out how old you were . . . Well, it all seemed to fit.'

'He must have told you many stories in that letter, your uncle.' There was a change in Matek's tone, all business now, and it put Vlado on his guard.

'No stories. He just said that you and my father were old friends, and that was all. I wrote back to him, asking for more information, because my father had never talked about the past, the years during the war. He wasn't one of those men who went round claiming to have parachuted into every valley and cave in Yugoslavia, fighting with the Partisans. But by the time my letter reached him, Tomislav had died. My aunt sent me a reply. And she didn't remember much.'

'But if Tomislav was dying, surely he must have told you more than just my name?' Matek poured more wine, and it suddenly struck Vlado that he was like an old lecher trying to get his young date drunk. Outside, a tractor lumbered into motion, the diesel chug stroking like a jackhammer.

'No,' Vlado said. 'Nothing.'

Matek nodded, not wanting to betray any sense of relief. Vlado decided this was a good time to get down to business, but he couldn't resist the opening Matek had just offered.

'In fact, I was hoping you'd be able to fill in all those blanks my father left behind. To tell me what he was like when he was growing up. What he did later. You know how quiet he was. He hardly told me anything.' Vlado knew he'd just veered dangerously from the script. Pine had been explicit on the point. If Matek wanted to talk about the past, fine. Just don't bring it up yourself. But to hell with them. They'd opened this box, and he'd be damned if he'd shut it before pawing through the contents.

'Oh,' Matek said, picking up the bottle to pour again, then setting it down when he saw both glasses were still full. 'Well, we did the usual things you do in a small village. Played sports together, went to school. Then there was the war, which changed everything. There was very little fighting for us, of course. I wouldn't even call it that. Just marching, mostly. Moving people or supplies from one place to another. And always in the rain, it seemed. Always in the rain and cold. Marching and waiting and digging. Very little action. Just grunt work. The sort of things that never make it into the history books. We left the country after the war, you know. For a few years. Surely your father told you that?'

'No. He didn't.'

'He never told you that we crossed the border?'

'My father never said anything about those years, no matter how much my mother and I asked. So we stopped asking.' Vlado felt free to take a good, long swallow of his wine. This was going more smoothly than he'd expected. 'Where did you go?'

'To Austria first. Marching with thousands.' Vlado remembered the tale about trucks. A convoy heading north from Zagreb. 'The roads into Austria were jammed for miles, everyone trying to get out before the Russians arrived from the east. We hadn't been with Tito's men, you know. Just some local militia. And by the end everyone was fighting everyone else. There was mass confusion, and we knew there would be retribution, no matter who we'd been fighting for. So the best thing to do was leave, and we finally made it across the border. We worked on a farm for a few months, in Austria. Finally some British soldiers came along and asked for our papers. They took us off to a DP camp in Italy. In Fermo. Awful place, but your father and I were still together. Thousands of people there. Food was terrible. Lice. Disease. Terrible. Then they finally sent us home. Through the Red Cross. It was not a good time to admit you'd been in the "wrong" army, even if you'd only been privates digging ditches. So we returned the way we'd left, on foot. Crossing the border through the hills at night, and settling in places far from where we'd grown up.'

After this stream of lies, Vlado was unable to resist a little test.

'And this was when?' he asked.

'Nineteen forty-six.'

A full fifteen years earlier than what Vlado knew to be the truth. Now what would be the point of this lie, other than to erase the years in Rome?

'I came here. Your father went to a village near Sarajevo, each of us with nothing. We thought it was better not to stay with each other, or even to stay in touch, the political situation being what it was. So we drifted apart as the years passed. I think I only heard from him once, maybe twice, though I did learn he had a wife and son. As you can see, I don't have a family. Never had a son, though I wanted one. I envied him that when I heard.'

It was clear Matek was finished with the subject of the past. But Vlado was unable to resist a final question.

'My father, what was he like then? As a young man.'

'An idealist. Always too much of one, I thought. You might even have called him a zealot.'

Vlado's heart sank. He'd seen the handiwork of zealotry in the last war.

'He was always more of a patriot than me. I was only along for the adventure and, later, for the opportunity. Because I learned something about war. And I'm sure it's no secret to you, with the business you're in now. War is a terrible thing, but it comes with built-in opportunities, and you either seize them or you're swept

203

along with everyone else who has given up all control of their lives. Your father never liked that in me.'

Soon afterwards they began discussing business, the supposedly crucial part of their conversation. It turned out to be the easiest part. Matek confessed he'd been eager for a piece of the de-mining action for some time, and agreed to a meeting in Travnik the next morning with Vlado's 'boss', ostensibly the one who would have to approve Vlado's choice. Matek even volunteered the name of the Skorpio.

Vlado brought out a sheaf of papers for Matek to peruse and sign. It was an agreement in principle, which Matek was to read and then bring to their meeting the next morning. It was from the EU office, the real thing. No sense risking the operation with fakes.

They said farewell at the door, their parting more subdued than their introduction, with Vlado insisting that tomorrow the food and drink would be his treat. Then he was on his way back to Travnik, grinding down the hill while Matek watched the white car descend the switchback curves, beetling through the dust.

Already Matek was working over their conversation like a piece of gristle, rolling it in his mouth, wondering what it was that just didn't taste quite right. There was no doubting Vlado's provenance. He was Enver's son all right. Maybe that was the problem. Earnest to a fault, just like his father. Wanting to do things for the right reasons, not because of how they'd serve his interests. But what would the right reasons be for a young man like Vlado?

Matek decided he needed a walk to think it over. He threw on a coat and left the house, passing the staring Azudin without a word. He walked past the goats towards a high rocky knoll up in the trees, where the views of the valley were best. He listened to the few birds that had remained here for the winter, faint chipping noises in the icy grey brush.

What stuck in his craw, refusing to be digested, was that bit about Uncle Tomislav. Now when the hell would Vlado's father have told Tomislav his new name, Matek? And why would he have taken the risk? It was possible, he supposed. But Enver was a careful man, he knew the consequences as well as anyone of leaking sensitive details. The boy had to have learned it from somebody, though, and if not Tomislav, then who?

Matek cut short his walk and returned to his office. He dialled the number of the Skorpio.

'Yes?'

'It's Matek. Is Osman around?'

'Isn't he always?'

'Is he still sober?'

'As much as he ever is at this time of day. He won't be completely worthless for a few more hours.'

'Put him on.'

There was a pause, then the sound of a chair scraping the floor, a clatter of glasses, followed by another voice.

'Osman.'

'This is Matek. Listen carefully because I have some work for you. There is a man staying at the Hotel Orijent who I'd like you to check for me. Discreetly, please. His name is Vlado Petric, and I'd like to know what he's up to. If he's travelling with anyone. If so, how they're registered, who's paying the bills. What their business is. Follow him, and ask around. Learn what you can. But you're not to approach him, not to speak to him. Understand?'

'Sure.'

'And no talking about this. Not with anyone. Not if you ever want another drink in this town.'

'Understood.'

Osman was a drunk, but he wasn't a fool, and he'd always kept his mouth shut before.

'I want to hear back from you by the end of the day. Six o'clock at the latest, and before you've had anything else to drink. If you're successful, your bar tab will be paid up for a week.'

'Yes, sir.'

Matek didn't need to add that his instructions were an order. Orders were the only way he dealt with people, and it was well known that disobedience was often followed closely by terrible accidents.

Osman wasted no time. The staff of the Hotel Orijent were always an easy mark, and a few phone calls did the rest. By 5 p.m. he was thirsty and back on the phone.

Matek had just returned from another walk when the call came. He'd been too restless to get much work done. This time he'd walked straight up the goat path to the summit, motivated by the day's events to check on a place he hadn't visited in years.

Azudin appeared at the front door, out of breath. 'The telephone, sir.'

It was still ringing.

206

'Well answer it, idiot!'

'I just thought that since you had returned . . . Yes, sir.'

He disappeared down the hall while Matek knocked mud from his boots, recalling his first walk up that hill so long ago, on a summer night of fireflies and the distant barking of farm dogs. It was 1961. The house had only been a single storey then, and he'd made the one-mile walk at midnight, barefoot in the dew and a little drunk, serenaded by crickets as his trousers rasped in the high grass. It had been an easy walk then, even for someone foolish enough to be traversing a stony hillside without shoes. He'd done too much drinking alone in those days, spent too much time going through his papers and his passports, wondering where to keep them all, knowing they were a sort of dynamite but also a sort of insurance, a retirement plan, even. He'd resolved the matter by climbing the hill with a shovel in one hand and a box in the other, and inside the box was an oiled leather pouch. By now the leather was probably mildewed and stiff; perhaps he would know for sure soon enough, depending on what Osman had to say.

He reached his office, shouting down the hallway to Azudin, 'I'll take the call in here. You go home early today. I'll take care of any loose ends.'

Then he picked up the receiver, listening closely for a few moments, saying little. The news was unexpected, but he tried not to betray his shock to Osman. No sense letting the village drunk know he was disturbed, or soon everyone would know it. So he kept his voice even, but as he replaced the receiver Matek realized that his hands were shaking. It was partly out of anger, partly out of fear as well – fear of the unknown. Because for the first time in more years than Matek cared to remember, his future was in doubt, and this time none of the usual remedies would work. Extraordinary measures were called for. But which ones? On this point he foundered, again uncertain, until it dawned on him that the answer might be as nearby as another walk up the hill, back to that place where he'd buried an unspoken shred of his life. If the road to your future was blocked, he mused, who was to say you couldn't flee instead into the past? After carefully disposing of a few impediments, of course. But that would be the easy part. That sort of business always was.

12

On another hillside some two hundred miles to the east, another former soldier answered a ringing telephone. He was a general, a Serb, and he was in a bunker. He, too, had just been for a walk, and was about to go on another. He instantly recognized the caller, who spoke accented Bosnian with a habitual conspiratorial tone. This time, at least, the tone was warranted.

Andric answered in a low voice. He always kept a window open, and you never knew how close one of the sentries might be. A bored man can be a dangerous eavesdropper.

'It begins tomorrow,' the caller said.

'So. They really mean to do it.'

'Yes. And it will be early.'

'How early?'

'Six. Maybe six thirty. About an hour before sunrise. You still have your plans?'

'Of course. And you're certain of the route?'

'Yes. Just avoid the village. No goodbye fucks with the barmaid. Not even tonight. And don't move too soon. They have to practically be at your door. Risky, I know, but don't panic.'

'I'm not the type.'

The caller chuckled lightly. 'Let's hope so.'

'You're sure of the time?'

'Positive. Any changes and you'll be notified. Just don't forget our terms. Or our schedule.'

'As discussed. But there could be delays. This isn't the sort of work I'm used to.'

'Understood. But I've allowed plenty of time. And you remember the name of the place, of course.'

'Of course.'

Both knew not to utter any names, not with the possibility that others might either intercept or overhear their conversation.

'Good. As long as I know where to find you, neither of us should have any problems. Good luck.'

'Yes. For both of us.'

They hung up without a further word. Andric checked out of the window. The sentry was twenty feet away, seated on a barrel, blowing smoke rings and reading a porn magazine. The poor stupid bastard should've have stayed in the army, but Andric paid on time, and with hard currency. Not that he got much for his money. What a waste of time and expense this had all been, three years of wages for these ignorant boys who talked of nothing but sports, women and booze. Nothing else left to talk about in this ruined land that produced only cigarettes, bread and whatever you could grow with your hands.

He checked his wardrobe for what must have been the twentieth time that week. Everything was in place. The small backpack with a change of clothes. A compass. A filled canteen. Knife. Flashlight. Holstered pistol, loaded, plus a box of extra rounds. He didn't think he would need it tomorrow, but he would kill if he had to. Then, or any other time in the days to come. There were two maps, one of this country and one of another. Lastly, the most valuable item of all, the small pouch with passport and visas, plus the packet of privileged information that it had nearly cost him his job to obtain, and inside it a small key, such as you might have used to open a door long ago. Perhaps it would finally prove its worth.

There was still mud on the pouch, the slightest bit at the edges. He had dug it up late last week at the first word of possible trouble, trudging through the grove of plum trees and over the rail fence, down the path and past the stump, next to the field where, years ago, old Jelisic had grown his pumpkins. Two feet deep, but just as he'd left it. Now he'd see how far it could take him, how good the man's word had been, all those years ago.

There was a pile of old clothes at the bottom of the wardrobe. They were part of the plan, too. Beneath them was a handle that pulled up a small trapdoor. The door opened onto a shaft, with laddered rungs down the side, and the shaft dropped fifteen feet to a tunnel, an old route from Tito's darkest days of paranoia as he prepared to repel a Red Army invasion that never came.

Thank goodness for that paranoia, Andric thought, and he felt like celebrating with a drink, driving into the village for a final toast to his good fortune. But he was not the type to take unnecessary risks. You never knew when some young French officer might decide to jump the gun.

He reviewed the route in his head. A hundred yards beneath the forest floor to the back of the hillside, then up out of the ground through another lost and forgotten trapdoor that opened into a tangle of weeds. Then down the hill through the trees to a farm, where a truck lay parked in the underbrush, looking abandoned and worthless, but he knew better. He'd rechecked the engine and ignition three days ago. New battery and cables. Petrol in the tank and two full jerrycans in the back. A new set of plates in the glove compartment, plus a Croatian pair for further down the road. He'd have to move fast, quietly, and without fear. But he had no doubt he could pull it off. He hadn't been boasting to the caller when the subject of panic had come up.

He simply wasn't the type.

13

The phone was ringing, muffled, seemingly miles away. But when Vlado opened his eyes he realized the sound was coming through the wall from Pine's room. It was 7 a.m. so he decided he might as well get moving. They'd be closing the deal with Matek today, and it made him nervous just thinking about it.

Pine knocked at the door before he was even dressed, and the news wasn't good.

'Spratt just called.' Pine looked flustered, hair in every direction and shirt unbuttoned. 'The raid was a disaster. Andric got away.'

'From a hundred soldiers? What happened?'

'Who knows? His sentries – the ones who lived, the damn French killed three of them – said he'd been asleep in his bunker. They were sure of it. But when they checked there wasn't a soul inside.'

Vlado's heart sank. All the planning, deception and revelations about his past had supposedly been part of the larger, higher motive of bringing Andric to justice. All that remained was the chore of arresting the old man, if that was even still part of the Tribunal's plans.

'Where does that leave us?' he asked.

'Spratt said to go ahead. For the moment Matek is the only thing in the pipeline, and we could use a little face-saving. Our sponsors apparently want it too.'

'Sponsors?'

'Harkness and LeBlanc. It's probably all tied in with budget stuff. The Tribunal needs a win, in other words, and we're it. So let's get it over with. Pick up the old bastard, let Harkness and LeBlanc have the debriefing we promised, then turn him over to the Croatians and get the hell out of here.'

Vlado was too stunned to speak.

'Jesus!' Pine exclaimed angrily. 'We finally get the French to make a move and this happens. Now they'll never lift a finger again. Never. And the press will kill us. S-FOR or no S-FOR, the Tribunal will get the blame.'

He sat down on the bed. He seemed to realize for the first time that he was barefoot and in need of a shave.

'I better get dressed,' he said, collecting himself. 'And I could use some coffee. We need to go over everything again before we head out. Make sure we don't fuck it up.'

They arrived at the Skorpio ten minutes ahead of schedule, just to be on the safe side, which meant they would be sitting at their table for forty minutes before Matek was due. The place was virtually empty. Only the bartender and a single customer sipping coffee towards the back. A Humvee and an APC were parked about thirty yards round the corner, in the opposite direction to the one from which Matek was expected. The vehicles were a fairly common sight around the valley, and had been since the Dayton Agreement, so no-one was likely to be alarmed.

214

When Matek arrived, Pine was supposed to make sure he wasn't accompanied by bodyguards. Neither Pine nor Vlado was carrying weapons or a radio, in case Matek had a notion to search them. As soon as everything seemed in order, Pine would excuse himself to the men's room, where he would call the S-FOR unit from a cellphone and retrieve a .45 calibre pistol from a towel box.

Vlado thought the entire set-up was full of holes. What if bodyguards arrived first? What if Matek himself had a gun? Would anyone else in the bar be armed? They were counting on the shock value of a few M-16s to keep matters in hand.

The door to the bar swung open, and Vlado looked up. But it was just some drunk, squinting into the dimness, getting his bearings. He glanced at their table and seemed to smile. He looked vaguely familiar from the day before in the hotel, but Vlado found it hard to imagine the man had been a guest. Probably an employee. The man strolled to the bar, where he rapped the counter once with his right hand. The bartender produced a bottle and a glass without a word, and the man began to drink.

'Local character,' Pine muttered. 'Shouldn't be a problem.'

Vlado checked his watch. Matek was five minutes late.

The delay stretched to ten minutes. Then fifteen.

'He's not coming,' Pine said.

'He's probably on Bosnian time,' Vlado said, wanting to believe it. 'Or he's just making us wait. Relax.'

'No. He's not coming. This whole operation has been

215

fucked from the start, and this is the perfect finish. He's a no-show.'

Ten more minutes passed, and Vlado knew Pine was right. He saw Pine looking at him, and didn't like the expression.

'What did you tell him?' Pine asked, not accusingly or sharply, but not in a friendly way either.

'Nothing,' Vlado said, with some heat. 'You think I warned him off? Told him this was all a big trap? As a favour to an old friend of the family?'

'Of course not. But what did you ask him about your father? What did you talk about? Something must have tipped him off. Something you said or did. Your body language. Your embarrassment. Hell, what did you say to him?'

Vlado might have been angrier if he hadn't just been wondering the same thing. Matek had seemed eager to meet again, so what the hell had gone wrong?

'I don't know,' Vlado said at last. 'I really don't.'

'We're screwed. And there are twenty soldiers outside to break the news to. Their CO will leak it across the chain of command, and within a couple of days we'll be right there in the headlines with Andric.' He shook his head. 'A flying start for Contreras and the "new aggressiveness". He'll end up as tame as any of them now, and God knows what will become of our budget.'

They decided to wait until Matek was an hour late, but both knew it was an empty gesture. At noon Pine went to the men's room to retrieve the .45. Then he dropped some money on the table and stood to leave.

'C'mon,' he said wearily. 'Let's find the officer in charge. Who knows, maybe they'll give us an armed escort up the mountain to Matek's compound. Stranger things have happened.'

The soldiers were loitering around the Humvee, a few of them stamping their feet in the cold. Pine was directed to a tall American lieutenant with the name 'Hundley' on his uniform.

'We've had a change in plans,' Pine began optimistically, explaining that he wanted an escort up the mountain.

The officer saw right through it. 'What you're saying is that the operation's a bust. Which means we'll be pulling out. Our orders pertained to the town only. Nobody said anything about going up a mountain road that we haven't reconned. It could still be mined for all I know.'

'This man was just up there yesterday,' Pine said, nodding towards Vlado. 'All by himself. So it's not mined. There's only one guard at the gate. Maybe two more inside, plus a suspect who's seventy-five. There's your recon.'

'Sorry, sir,' the lieutenant said, with no change in inflection. 'No go. But you're welcome to speak to my colonel.' He offered Pine a radio handset.

'He'd tell me more of the same, wouldn't he?'

'Can't speak for my colonel, sir. But that would be my guess. Unless he offers to let you speak to *his* CO.'

'I could spend the whole day climbing the chain of command. Think I could reach the Oval Office by sundown?'

This finally got a smile out of Hundley, but nothing else.

'Yeah. I know,' Pine said. 'Just following orders. Have a nice day, Lieutenant.'

'Will do, sir,' the officer deadpanned. 'Let's move out, men.'

And with a rumble of engines and a wintry swirl of dust, the soldiers left, stranding Pine and Vlado at the kerb like hosts of a failed dinner party.

After four cups of the Skorpio's coffee, Vlado was edgy and irritated. He had half a mind to drive the white Volvo up the hill to find out for himself. Maybe Matek was testing them, playing hard to get. But he doubted it.

'What we need is back-up,' Pine said, 'at least enough to go take a look. Didn't Benny say he'd be in Vitez?'

'For the rest of the week.'

'Worth a try then. That's only twenty miles. And if anybody would enjoy mixing it up after an S-FOR bail, it's Benny.'

Pine punched in a number and waited.

'Benny? Calvin Pine. We've just had a major fuck-up, and if you're anywhere near Travnik we could sure use some help. Yeah? Perfect.'

Pine filled him in on their morning, and Vlado could hear nearly every word of Benny's requisite tirade on the impotence of S-FOR. He had an interview to finish, then he'd meet them at the hotel in an hour.

'He's the only one with the balls for something like this,' Pine said.

Benny's other advantage was that he regularly carried a gun. It was against Tribunal policy – Pine's

218

borrowed .45 had been sanctioned only for the arrest and had already been returned to S-FOR – but just about everyone below Spratt at The Hague knew that Benny's local interpreter kept a Beretta pistol for him, hidden in his cellar.

'You think one gun is enough?' Vlado asked. To him the operation was degenerating from half-assed to hare-brained.

'It's not like we're going to storm the place. I just want a peek at the front gate.'

'He'll see us approaching.'

'Which is why I want Benny along. He's got that street-cop mentality from Brooklyn.'

'The Bronx.'

'Whatever. We can get the lay of the land, see if Matek's taking visitors. Maybe we'll even get lucky and bump into him on his way down the hill.'

'If he's still around.'

'Yeah.' Pine frowned. 'There's that possibility, too.'

Benny arrived every bit as eager and gung-ho as he had been at his desk, which made Vlado wary. Still jittery from the caffeine, he envisioned barrelling up the mountain into a phalanx of bodyguards with orders to fire on any EU car. A pistol wouldn't be much good against a few Kalashnikovs.

'Have you ever used it?' Vlado asked.

'Only once. Waved it at a nasty checkpoint a few years ago. Drunken Croats who wanted a "toll" and maybe my car. Changed their tune in a hurry when they saw the barrel. Tried to act like it had all been a big joke. But that was years ago, right after Dayton. Now you never really need to be armed unless you're going after somebody like Andric. Who escaped this morning, by the way. It's all over the radio. But I guess you guys already knew that, huh?'

Pine nodded.

'So it really was a two-for-one, then?'

'Only now it's a none-for-two. Unless we get lucky.'

'Fuckin' French.' Benny shook his head. 'Wonder who the loose lip was on this one. LeBlanc, maybe? I never thought this deal would go through from the moment I heard about it.'

'You weren't supposed to hear about it at all.'

'The names were making the rounds the day before Vlado showed up.'

'Great.'

'What do you expect when you let Harkness and LeBlanc call the shots. Lie down with dogs, get up with fleas.'

Pine explained the likely set-up awaiting them up on the mountain. They agreed to err on the side of caution, vowing to reverse tracks at the first sign of a hostile reception.

The trip seemed longer to Vlado than it had the day before, but with Pine driving he was able to watch the view ahead. They got their first glimpse of the house about fifteen minutes after the turn-off. Benny pulled out a small pair of binoculars.

'Here. Somebody else take a look. Seems quiet to me, but I've never been there.'

Vlado focused on the big upstairs window at the back,

looking down the mountain from Matek's bedroom. Below was his office. The curtains were drawn on both.

'He's either not expecting us or doesn't care,' Vlado said, not sure whether to feel relieved or disappointed. The place looked dead. Not even the goats were out.

They nosed around the final curve and slowed to a crawl as they approached the guardhouse. A door was open on the side. The bar across the driveway was raised, and a dust-covered BMW was parked on the shoulder. Inside the guardhouse, someone stood up. Benny pulled the Beretta from a shoulder holster.

'Know him?'

Vlado saw sunlight glinting off glasses. The man didn't seem to be armed.

'Yes. It's Azudin. His assistant.'

Azudin stepped outside, squinting into the pale sunlight. He looked helpless, out of place. He wasn't even wearing an overcoat.

'It's OK,' Vlado said. 'This one doesn't bite.'

'They all bite,' Benny said.

'And something's wrong if he's on guard duty. The others must have gone.'

Azudin walked uncertainly towards the car as Vlado rolled down a window.

'He's gone,' Azudin said, the plaintive bleat of a lost lamb.

Vlado translated for Pine, who shut off the engine. The three of them climbed from the car while Azudin stood at the side of the track, barely paying attention, as if pondering what to do next.

'Where's everyone else?' Vlado asked.

221

'I paid them for the month and sent them home.'

'What about Matek?'

'He left last night. He sent me home around five, so it could have been any time after that. When I got here this morning he'd cleared out. The overnight sentry must have been asleep, because he didn't see a thing.'

'Is that his car?' Vlado pointed to the BMW.

Azudin shook his head. 'Mine. His is gone. So are his guns, and most of his money. He left this.' Azudin held out a scrap of paper. Stepping closer, Vlado saw that Azudin was pale and drawn, clearly shaken. Vlado took the note from his hand.

'What's he saying?' Pine asked.

'Matek took off last night. I'm translating the note he left.'

Vlado squinted at the cramped handwriting of a man used to bashing a keyboard. Once he had the gist, he translated it aloud in English to Pine and Benny.

'Edin, there was always a possibility this day would come, and now I must go. All of the keys are in my upper desk drawer. The combination to the safe follows. I have signed the necessary documents, which you will also find on the desk. Sendic will notarize them in town. My businesses now belong to you. My bank accounts do not. There is enough cash in this envelope to pay the staff for a month. The rest is up to you. You will not be able to reach me, so do not try. When the son of Enver Petric comes calling, give him and his American friend from The Hague my best. They should be able to answer the rest of your questions. Good luck. Pero.'

'Sounds like he knew all about you guys,' Benny said

quietly, rubbing his hands to stay warm. He'd holstered the Beretta.

Vlado and Pine were silent. The mountain suddenly seemed a vast and empty place.

'This safe,' Pine said. 'Has he opened it yet?'

Vlado translated.

'He says no. He's hardly touched a thing.'

'Tell him we'd like a look around, if he doesn't mind. And we'd like to use his phone.'

Surprisingly, Azudin agreed, but as he turned to lead them up the lane it finally seemed to dawn on him to ask for an explanation. He stopped and turned robotically.

'Why are you after him?'

'Matek is a suspected war criminal.'

Azudin frowned. 'But he was here throughout the war. He did nothing, except make a little money. I know, I was with him.'

'Not this war. The last one. Your boss was an Ustashe officer. At Jasenovac.'

Azudin was unimpressed. 'And because of this he is running? Because of something fifty years ago?' He shook his head, more baffled than angry. 'I thought the world wanted us to forget all that. Come this way.' He continued to lead them with the air of a funeral director.

'Christ,' Benny muttered. 'You'd think he'd lost his father.'

A black look from Pine and Vlado made him realize it was a poor choice of words, but he was the only one who didn't understand why.

'Relax, guys,' Benny said. 'The hard part's over. Just your Ichabod Crane here and a bunch of file drawers. Tell him we'll be out of his hair in a few hours.'

Vlado wondered vaguely who Ichabod Crane was. It did seem that the worst of the danger had vanished along with Matek and his thugs, but he couldn't escape the sense that they were overlooking something in their blithe stroll towards the house. Jasmina's words of warning flitted through his head, and he tensed as they entered the front door, half expecting Matek to lunge at them from the darkened hallway, Kalashnikov in hand. But all was quiet save for the humming of a computer from a room down the hall.

When they reached the office, Pine picked up the phone.

'Might as well get the dirty work over with.'

'Hope you don't mind if I listen in,' Vlado said, heading to Azudin's phone in the adjoining room before Pine could say no. There was no way they were keeping him in the dark on any more operational details.

Spratt deflated like a punctured tyre when he heard the news, emitting a long despairing sigh that even the static couldn't disguise. It was clear he was still in anguish over the Andric fiasco.

'What the hell's going on?' he said tiredly. 'First two moves we make in months and it all goes to shit.'

'We're searching his place,' Pine said. 'I guess we should notify the borders, the airports and rail stations. As if that will do any good.'

'Leave that to the field offices. I'll make some calls. You see what you can come up with. Then we'll

224

plan our next move, if we've even got one.'

'Still no sign of Andric?'

'It's like he never existed. The idiots searching his bunker didn't find the trapdoor for four hours. Four bloody hours! Can you believe that?'

'Trapdoor?'

'Under a pile of clothes in a closet. Down an air shaft to some old tunnel that led through the hillside to the woods.'

'Tito,' Vlado said without thinking, startling Spratt who hadn't known he was on the line.

'What do you mean, Tito?'

'One of his old escape bunkers. So he and his officers could get away when the Russians came. All of them had tunnels.'

'Well, hell, that's what we get for not consulting locals enough. We finally got some dogs in to trace a scent. They spent an hour leading us to an abandoned farm. Fresh tyre tracks, probably a truck. It's beginning to look like he'd planned it pretty well. Now the question is whether he knew we were coming or if he was always this prepared, and just got lucky.'

'What do we do next?' Pine said.

'I'll have to phone LeBlanc and Harkness,' Spratt said. 'They're both waiting in Sarajevo for you and the suspect. We'd promised them a private debriefing with Matek. Now they may want to debrief you.'

'And we'd allow that?' Pine said.

'You'll also need to speak to Janet,' Spratt said, ignoring the question.

'Why?'

'She'll tell you. Sit tight until you've heard from her. Where are you anyway?'

'Matek's office. Up in the hills.'

'Give me the number. I've just been summoned upstairs. Third time today, and this time I've got more bad news to deliver. Stay there until you've heard from Janet.'

'No problem. We'll be searching the place. His little assistant's been pretty co-operative.'

Pine turned to Benny after hanging up. 'Sorry, but it looks like we might be stuck here a while. You game for helping us look around?'

'Got nothing else to do. Where do you want me to start?'

'Well, you're guest of honour. Why don't you take the safe? Matek wrote the combination on the note – as long as our host doesn't mind.' Pine looked around for Azudin, but he had apparently wandered off in a daze, so he handed the note to Benny. 'I'll take the file drawers in the back room. Vlado, why don't you check the rooms upstairs.'

They nodded, glum but resigned to the slow hours ahead. So much for their three-man commando action, or any hope of catching Matek on his way out of the back door. The old man had been cagier than they'd thought.

Vlado was curious to see what his living quarters were like, especially in comparison with the set-piece decor of the downstairs. But as he reached the top of the stairs, a movement through the window caught his eye.

It was Azudin, walking briskly across the barren grounds to the front gate, no longer looking either lost

226

or confused. A small bag was in his right hand, and he glanced furtively over his shoulder towards the house, quickening his pace. In stride and demeanour he was nothing at all like the meek man who had seemed on the verge of tears just a moment ago, and Vlado's nagging worries converged into full-blown fear. A rambling and incautious search suddenly struck him as a very bad idea, and he spun to head back downstairs, taking the steps two at a time and lifting his voice to shout a warning.

His first words were swallowed by a heaving blast that lifted him in the air, as if a gust of pressure had bolted up the stairs. The next thing he knew he was sitting at the bottom, head hurting and ears ringing, his left knee twisted and wrenched. A fine white dust drifted from the ceiling like mist, already coating the hair on his arms. The house was dreadfully still.

'You all right?' It was Pine, in a croaking call from the back room. 'Benny? Vlado?'

'I'm at the bottom of the stairs,' Vlado shouted, finding his voice. He stood, quivering like a fawn. 'I think I'm OK.'

'Benny?' Pine said. There was no reply. Then louder, more frantic. 'Benny?'

Vlado limped into the ruin of Matek's office. Benny's legs protruded from beneath shards of varnished wood and a jumble of paper and plaster. They weren't moving. The ceiling above him was cratered. The door of the small safe in the wall above was open, but the grey metal was twisted and marked with a starburst of black scorch marks, as if a small meteorite had struck. The computer screen was shattered, and the big desk was splintered, the top heaved up like the deck of an ice-bound frigate. But the worst sight was the red spatter across every wall, some of it just beginning to drip and ooze across pockmarked fields of white plaster.

'Jesus!' It was Pine, who'd just staggered to the door, covered head to toe in white dust that made him look like the walking dead. Vlado guessed he must look the same. But it was the silent Benny who drew their attention, and they converged on the motionless legs. They crouched and began pulling away pieces of the desk and chunks of the ceiling, working gingerly, as if worried they'd do him further damage.

It was soon clear that matters could get no worse for Benny. They pulled back a chunk of the desk and revealed that from the waist up he was a shredded welter of cloth, pulp and flesh. Ragged shards of bone poked through in one or two places. He was face down, black hair matted and splayed. It was all Vlado could do to keep from gagging, and neither of them had the nerve to turn his head to look at his face.

'My God,' Pine gasped. 'Oh my God.'

He stood, stumbling backwards and nearly falling on a bloodied pile of debris. Vlado had seen bodies in this sort of shape during the war, and the culprit had always been the same: an anti-personnel mine that sent hundreds of pieces of metal flying into the victim. This was no home-made explosive of nails and fuel oil. This was military-grade hardware, the same sort Matek had been hoping to acquire more of with a de-mining contract.

Vlado remembered Azudin hurrying across the grounds, and the thought made him turn quickly towards the door. Maybe there was still time to catch him. But Pine shouted.

'Don't move!'

When Vlado took another step Pine shouted again.

'Don't move, damn it! For all we know there are more, and we don't even know what that one looked like, or what triggered it. Look for any wires. Any kind of metal box. Hell, it could be anything.' Pine looked around, glaring like a cornered street fighter, a sight made surreal by the coating of dust. Vlado wanted to sit but didn't dare, not with all the rubble around him that might conceal something.

'Where's Azudin?' Pine asked, the volume down a notch.

'I saw him through the window, leaving in a hurry. I started to shout something but that's when the mine went off.'

'Weaselly bastard. Probably halfway down the mountain in his BMW, counting his inheritance. For all we know he wired the front door behind him. We may have to crawl through a window.'

'Or maybe he's sending the bodyguards back up the mountain to finish us off.'

'Possibly.'

They paused, as if listening for intruders or the approach of a truck. But the only sound was a car engine cranking to life, then a purr as the gears engaged, followed by the crunch of gravel. Azudin was leaving, and from the sound of it he was in no hurry, having heard the blast. The quiet little man had fooled them all, and so had Matek.

Pine gingerly reached down beside Benny, poking around in the bloody rubble.

'I'd look for the gun, but . . .'

'Don't bother. I've seen what these things do. It'll be destroyed. Besides . . .'

'I know.' Pine was transfixed by Benny. 'My God. Of all the people. We go the whole goddamn war without a scratch. Then some old man, not even from the right war, gets him. Some fucking profiteer.' Pine glared at Vlado, as if he was somehow complicit. Vlado thought he knew why, because even he felt a bit of the same emotion. His father's old pal had done this, the bloodlines ran straight to him, his country and his people, in a cycle that never stopped. But what was there to say or do, other than nod slightly, as if he understood completely.

Then he shook his head in the manner of a wet dog, trying to clear his head. Tears were snaking through the dust on his cheeks. He sagged into a crouch, still not daring to test his weight on any of this mess but feeling bone weary. He glanced at Benny's legs. The great and glib blusterer, a generous man, so zealous about his work. Vlado had barely met him but had liked him right away, and now he was gone. Just like that. Jasmina had been right to worry. So much for their 'foolproof operation', as Spratt had so cavalierly described it while rattling the ice in his cocktail. The evening of suits and chandeliers at The Hague now seemed a year in the past, and it was certainly a world removed from here.

'OK,' Pine said, calming. 'Let's start moving, just be

careful where you step. Don't open any drawers, cabinets, doors, or anything. Maybe one of the phones still works in another room. We need to get a UN de-mining team up here before we even try leaving the building. Otherwise it's Russian roulette.' He paused. 'Then I'll have to call Spratt. This will change everything. Jesus, Benny. Jesus.' He shook his head. 'I guess we better get an ambulance up here, too. To take the body away.'

The phone rang in Azudin's office. For a moment Vlado and Pine just stared in that direction, as if Matek himself were calling to taunt them into another fatal blunder. On the fourth ring Pine collected himself and began hopping slowly through the mess like a man negotiating an ice floe, looking for safe places to step.

'Maybe it's Janet,' he muttered hoarsely. Even then he hesitated before lifting the receiver. Now every object seemed poisoned, a potential booby trap.

'Hello?'

Vlado made his way to the phone, and without any prompting Pine angled the earpiece outward so he could listen in. The awkwardness and secrecy that had held them at arm's length was gone. For better or worse, they'd become a team, united for the moment by their grief and their edgy suspicion of everyone and everything.

'Well. All hell has broken loose here,' Janet Ecker said breezily.

'Benny's dead,' Pine answered bluntly, putting a stop to everything. 'He was with us, and he's been killed by a mine explosion. It was a booby trap. Matek had mined his office.'

231

For a moment Janet said nothing. They heard the creak of her chair, office sounds in the background. The connection was startlingly clear. Vlado looked through the doorway and could see Benny's black shoes, covered in dust.

Pine filled her in on the morning's details, and their plans of what to do next.

'We were searching the place,' he said. 'But I think it's best now if we don't touch a thing.'

'Is Vlado all right?'

'I'm fine,' he answered.

'Your wife called this morning. She was worried. I told her you were alive and well. Glad I don't have to call her back for a correction. My Lord. I can't believe it's Benny. What the hell were you doing calling him in anyway?'

'Let's sort out the blame and the screw-ups later, OK? Right now we've got a body and no mission. We're a little out of it, as you might guess. Some sense of direction from whoever's in charge these days might be welcome.'

'I'll call back. Stay put.'

'Believe me, we're not moving.'

Pine then phoned the UN's local de-mining office, an irony lost on neither of them. Matek's Rolodex, if he'd had one, was gone, and the file drawers in the back – Pine had only had time to open one – now seemed likely to be wired for destruction.

Vlado headed back upstairs, watching carefully for tripwires, if only to take a quick look and give himself something to do. His suspicions about the decor proved to be correct. Upstairs was all chrome and leather. Cool marble floors with bright throw rugs in modern geometric designs. Just as tasteless as the downstairs in its way, but with a more Mediterranean flavour. Matek had deemed his own culture beneath him and gone in for a garish imitation of Italian. And why not? If Vlado had spent an entire war trying to wipe out a major part of that culture, then he, too, might have sought some way to figuratively shed his skin. But if that was so, then what had his father been up to for all those years, returning home simply to resume the life of a Balkan peasant, acting as if he were still a naïve and innocent toolmaker hovering reluctantly at the fringes of the twentieth century?

Downstairs the phone rang again. Pine waited for Vlado to return before answering, and they again shared the earpiece. It was Spratt, and both of them braced for a chewing out. But Spratt swallowed his belligerent instincts.

'The first thing you need to do is get the hell out of there,' he said. 'Let a de-mining unit do the rest.'

'I've already called one,' Pine said.

'Go back to Sarajevo and await further instructions. From here it's going to depend on how Contreras reacts. My call would be to drop the thing entirely. Let international law enforcement pick up the chase and get the hell out of the way. But from what I've seen of him so far he's liable to take this personally.'

'I sure as hell do,' Pine said.

'I'm not saying you shouldn't. So do I. But operationally you know our limits. The other bit of news, unfortunately, is that our sponsors still want a meeting, and they're waiting at the Holiday Inn.'

It took Vlado a moment to realize that Spratt was talking about Harkness and LeBlanc, the last people he wanted to see right now. He just wanted to board a plane and go home.

'Why?' Pine asked.

'They're trying to pick up the pieces, too.' Vlado winced at the wording. 'This was their baby, and they'll have something to say about what happens next.'

'Just what we need. When do we meet?'

'I put them off until this evening. Seven. That should give you time to collect yourselves.'

'What about arrangements for Benny? Getting his body home?'

'Let me worry about that. You just get back to Sarajevo. I'm sending reinforcements for the meeting.'

'Reinforcements?'

'Janet Ecker. She's catching a two p.m. flight. She's the only one who has seen the whole file. Depending on what's decided in the meantime, you may need to know more. Either way she can help fend off Harkness and LeBlanc.'

'What makes you think we'll have to fend them off?'

'Previous experience. Plus the entire way this operation has gone. Why should things get any easier?'

'Fair enough.'

'For now, get yourselves down the mountain safely. One casualty is more than enough, God knows.'

But after hanging up they were momentarily unable to leave. Neither said a word, both unwilling to simply walk out while Benny's body still lay in the next room.

'Doesn't seem right, does it?' Pine said.

Vlado shook his head. 'None of this has seemed right from the beginning.'

For him that included the past two weeks, all the way back to when Haris and Huso had arrived on his doorstep, bloody and grimy in the darkness. Now all the events seemed part of the same awful package, and he questioned his own role at every turn. The trail of bodies could even include a small boy from Sarajevo, dying of whooping cough and scarlet fever; then a young thug in Berlin; and now a loud, likeable cop from New York. Yet he remained standing, like a man walking unscathed from a plane crash, a freak of fate. A sudden wave of nostalgia for his old life – the one before the war, before everyone had become either a casualty or a refugee – rolled over him heavily, and he averted his face from Pine.

But Pine's attention was elsewhere. He walked slowly into Matek's ruined office and knelt by the legs. The smell of blood was stronger now. Vlado watched as Pine placed his right hand gently on the back of Benny's leg, then bowed his head with his eyes shut tightly. He mouthed a few words, too quietly for Vlado to hear, then paused, still in a crouch. Finally he exhaled deeply and rose slowly. The UN vehicles were just pulling up outside.

'OK,' Pine said calmly. 'Nothing more we can do here.'

They left without another word.

14

They were jittery for the entire ride to Sarajevo, flinching whenever another vehicle approached from behind or slowed down in front of them. Even a creaking farm wagon blocking the road seemed suspicious, part of a possible ambush, given Matek's reach and connections along the valley road from Travnik.

As a result, they said little along the way, giving Vlado plenty of time to think. He decided on a plan for the afternoon, announcing his intentions as they finally reached the outskirts of the city.

'I was thinking I might visit my old apartment,' he said softly, breaking a long silence. 'To look for some old photos and family papers. Things my mother left me when she died. Not much. I just sort of glanced through them after the funeral and put them away in a cupboard.'

'Names and addresses?'

'That's what I was wondering. If any of my father's relatives are mentioned, maybe some of them knew Matek.'

'Like the uncle you mentioned?'

'Uncle Tomislav. His wife was my father's sister. Maybe Aunt Melania is still alive. But for all I know our old apartment is either gone or cleaned out.'

'Would somebody have moved in?'

'I can't imagine it would have stayed empty. With all the refugees coming in, the government took back a lot of housing. Or else people just took things for themselves. Whoever took our place probably assumed we were dead. Maybe they sold everything. It's worth checking, though.'

Pine shrugged. 'Better than doing nothing, I guess.'

Vlado wondered how long it would take them to recover from the shock of the morning's events. They hadn't even had time to wash off the plaster dust and Pine's right sleeve was still stained with Benny's blood. An hour earlier, Vlado had been ready to give up and go home. But now he was itching to do something, anything that might help track down Matek. He was still curious about the link to his own past, and now there was Benny, making Matek's crimes more fresh and personal than ever, whether the Tribunal was ready to drop the case or not. Pine had been silent on the subject so far, but Vlado was certain he felt the same. Both felt foolish, even guilty, for having underestimated Matek, a miscalculation that had cost a friend his life. A visit to Vlado's old apartment might not uncover a thing. But, as Pine said, it was better than doing nothing.

They checked into the Holiday Inn once again. After a shower and a change of clothes, and with a few hours remaining before Janet Ecker's flight was due, Vlado set out on foot, retracing one of his familiar routes through the city, the old apartment key in his pocket. Jasmina had insisted that he bring it, hoping he'd have time for a look. He wondered what she and Sonja were up to, back in Berlin. A fleeting thought of Haris crossed his mind like a small cloud, but the name troubled him more for its association with Popovic than with Jasmina.

The apartment squatted in a block of fairly new buildings on a slight rise, overlooking the fields that led to the Olympic stadium. The fields had once been playgrounds, but during the war they'd been pressed into duty as a cemetery, offering Vlado a daily census of the body count from the front window. The area had been vulnerable to shellfire from three sides, and Vlado had lived mostly in the living room, next to the kitchen, sleeping on a couch. With neither running water nor electricity for much of the siege, he'd tapped into a natural gas line, bootlegging a supply into his house through a garden hose that he'd tacked to the wall. There had been a nozzle on the stove and another spouting from the wall, for light.

He supposed all that was gone now, but he had no trouble recalling the mood of the lonely nights, when there had been little to do but paint a set of tiny lead soldiers arrayed before him on a bench – tedious work that made the hours pass until he was weary enough to retreat into sleep.

Rounding the last corner he was pleasantly surprised to see the building still standing. The windows had been repaired. So had a small hole in the roof. New tiles marked the spot with a brighter shade of red.

He knocked, still not sure what to say, then was surprised to recognize the face of the man who answered. The last time he had seen it, the man's beard had been powdered with plaster, his eyes dazed. It had been five years ago, a snowy morning when a shell had fallen on an apartment next door, scattering the refugee family that had moved in a week earlier. Vlado had been jolted awake by the explosion. Then he had invited all six of them inside to recover from the shock.

That had been shortly before Vlado smuggled himself out of the city in the cargo plane. Now, here they were again, this time on the other side of the door, if he could only recall their names.

'Konjic,' the man said, smiling as he refreshed Vlado's memory. 'Alijah Konjic. And you are Vlado Petric.'

'Yes,' Vlado said, hoping his sudden arrival wouldn't be seen as a threat. Through the doorway he could already see the old couch, the one that had been his bed for two years. The Konjics had arrived in Sarajevo without furniture, so his abandoned house must have seemed like a godsend.

'Please come in,' Konjic said with genuine warmth. He made a sweeping gesture with his arm to usher Vlado across the threshold. 'My wife, Nela. My children. Everyone is here, and we owe you so much.'

'Hello,' a woman's voice piped from the kitchen, and Vlado turned to see Nela in an apron, a wooden spoon in hand. Two children sat on the couch, riveted to a small black and white television propped on an end table. A third, older child sat on the floor doing his lessons. Konjic had said everyone was here, but Vlado remembered six of them. The fourth and smallest child was missing, and he readied himself for more bad news.

Then to Vlado's immense relief the boy came into the room, a good foot taller by now, carrying one of the tiny soldiers Vlado had left behind. Vlado smiled, and Konjic seemed to realize why.

'Ah, your soldiers. He played with them the first time we met. After the shell landed. It was the first thing he went looking for when we came back.'

And here Konjic's enthusiasm faltered, as if he suddenly realized the implications of Vlado's return. Pretty much everything in the room, except the small TV, had belonged to Jasmina and him before the war. By rights everything still did, even if they now seemed like items from a museum – the couch, the chairs, the small oval rug that had been a wedding gift from Jasmina's mother, the old photo of the Mostar bridge on the wall. It was like entering a time capsule, and Vlado moved quickly to put Konjic's fears at rest.

'I am only here for a few days,' he said, and he saw Nela relax. 'We live in Germany now. My wife was able to take the most valuable items when she and my daughter left, two years before I did. I'm not here to claim anything. But I did want to look for something. An old box with photos and papers. Old family records. Some personal things that I left behind.'

'Yes,' Konjic said, effusive in his relief. 'Yes. I know that box. We've kept it. We've kept everything, you know. Some things because we've used them, of course, but all of your clothes and everything else, it's all still here.'

'It's just the one box I'm interested in,' Vlado said. 'Keep the other things. Sell them if you want. The rest of the personal items I may come for later, if I bring my family back. But today there isn't time.'

'Yes. Yes, of course. Come. It's back here.'

They walked to the rear bedroom. Vlado was spooked by the familiar hallway, the smells of the place, the rugs on the floor. Konjic opened a wardrobe and tugged at a cardboard box on the top shelf. It was the one he remembered.

'We thought you had been killed,' Konjic said. 'Someone told us you were a policeman, and we heard a policeman had been shot down by the river on the night after we met you. Later we heard that it wasn't you, that maybe you had got away. There was nothing in the newspaper, and no-one seemed to know much. So we decided to keep everything. In case you ever came back.'

Konjic seemed like a good man. Vlado was glad they'd ended up with the apartment, but he did wonder what his old neighbours – if any were left – must think of this tribe of peasants from a faraway village, bringing their country ways to the middle of the city.

'Some people did try to kill me,' he told Konjic. 'Smugglers. They took a few shots, but they missed. It's a very long story.' And one that keeps repeating, he thought, thinking of the morning. 'But we're in Berlin now. Maybe we'll come back, maybe not. But not here. The apartment is yours.'

As if to seal the deal, he reached into his pocket for the key. He solemnly handed it over, the closest thing to a deed available. With that, Konjic's relief was complete, and Vlado wondered how often the family must have dreaded this sort of visit. If the trip accomplished nothing else, at least it would leave these people at peace.

Konjic set the box on the bed.

'Take as long as you want,' he said. 'I'll be with the children.'

He shut the bedroom door behind him, giving Vlado privacy. Only the muffled noise of the television leaked beneath the door, a faint sound of gunshots and squealing tyres.

Vlado opened the box. On top were old bills and receipts, instruction manuals for radios, a television, a small hand drill. There were photos, a few infant shots of Sonja. He set those aside, knowing he shouldn't slow down until he found what he was looking for, but unable to resist the occasional detour of memories. Their marriage licence. Some photos of friends at a party, from 1989. A stack of handwritten compositions from his childhood that his mother had saved, then given to Jasmina just before they were married. He remembered sitting up in bed late one night – this bed – reading them while she laughed, a strand of her hair fallen across her face. Old magazines that he'd saved for one obscure reason or another. And then, about halfway down, there it was, a large brown envelope with his mother's handwriting on top: 'For Vlado.'

He remembered the short woman who'd been a friend of hers bringing it to him the day after his mother's funeral, after he'd helped move the furniture out of his mother's apartment. It had been a big Catholic service, the priest swinging a censer as he marched slowly down the aisle. He wondered what his mother had known about his father's past. Had she, too, kept his secrets, or had she been fooled along with him, believing in her husband's essential goodness and honesty, the quiet virtuous worker who made a living with his strong but gentle hands?

His mother hadn't come from the same village or even the same part of the country. They'd married only a year after Enver returned from Italy. She'd been a devout Catholic. He wondered now if she had known all along that his father was secretly a Catholic as well. Perhaps she, too, had been a sort of ethnic nationalist in her own quiet way, which would explain why she had later become so frustrated with her son, the non-believer who worshipped only soccer stars and his own future.

There wasn't much inside the envelope, maybe twenty or thirty pages in all, which was pretty much the way Vlado remembered it. Part of it was a technical manual, old instructions for the equipment in the machine shop where his father had worked. There was a diagram of a metalworking lathe, with all the moving parts numbered, and Vlado could picture his father behind the machine, hard at work, the bright curly shavings collecting in the hair of his forearms.

There was an old football programme – perhaps from the game in his dream. He scanned the photos of players, most of whose names he'd forgotten although they'd once meant so much to him. At the bottom of the pile were a few more photographs.

One in particular drew his attention. It was of four men in uniform. On the far right, propped against a giant oak, was his father. Who were the other three, and where were they when this was taken? The fellow on the left looked familiar, and Vlado realized it must be Uncle Tomislav. Yes, that long face with the jug ears. Definitely. Vlado closely scanned the other two faces, looking for any sign of the man he'd met yesterday. But neither of the men was Matek. He turned the photo over, looking for an inscription, but there was only the stamp of the studio that made the print, with an address in Mostar, down in the southwest, the city closest to his father's home village of Podborje.

The topography made it clear the photo hadn't been taken anywhere near Jasenovac, where the landscape was flat and green. In the background were hills and more hills, and the men looked relaxed, at peace with themselves. There was no date, but he surmised it must have been taken early in the war, perhaps before anyone had even fired a shot.

Maybe Aunt Melania in Podborje would know a little more about his father's movements during the war. Vlado placed the other papers back into the box, slipped the photo inside the envelope and placed it in the inside pocket of his jacket. He heard the door opening behind him, the noise from the television rising in volume.

'Find anything good?'

It was Konjic, looming over his shoulder, curiosity having got the better of him. Vlado looked up from the old, familiar bed, clearing his throat.

'Not much. A few memories of my parents.'

Konjic beamed, as if personally gratified that Vlado's mission had been a success.

'Please, when you are finished, I came to tell you that my wife has made coffee. My sons have gone out for cake. In honour of your return.'

Vlado could have sworn that Konjic then made a slight bow, an oddly touching gesture by this man he barely knew. In the larger scheme of things these people owed him nothing. They could just as easily have found a vacant apartment elsewhere. But if they wished to show their gratitude, he would accept it, even though he had little time to spare. Or maybe he simply felt like being among a family right now, with sons and daughters and their parents, crowded together around a table to eat and drink.

'Thank you. I'd like that,' he said.

They gathered in the kitchen, the children elbowing each other for position as everyone made way for their guest. The table was new, rough-hewn but sturdy, with clean lines and well-fitted joints. The one Vlado and Jasmina had owned wouldn't have been large enough. Vlado rubbed his hands along the sanded, polished top.

'I made it,' Konjic said proudly. 'All with hand tools. Wooden dowels and my own joining. You can't get things like screws and power tools any more. Not without a lot of hard currency.'

'It's very nice work.'

Konjic's expression suddenly lit up, and he leaped to his feet.

'I almost forgot,' he said.

He disappeared down the hallway. Following a brief metallic clatter he returned holding a battered tool-box which Vlado recognized as his father's – his lone inheritance. It made him quail slightly to see it now, and he couldn't help contemplating the destructive power of the hammers, the screwdrivers, the wrenches, even though he doubted the toolbox had belonged to his father until well after the war.

'It was my father's,' he said faintly as Konjic set the box heavily on the end of the table.

'Then you must have it,' Konjic said, beaming yet again, although the toolbox was undoubtedly one of his most prized and valuable possessions. Whatever those tools symbolized of Vlado's father's past, they had at least built this sturdy and beautiful table.

'No,' Vlado said, mustering a smile and shaking his head. 'It's yours now. I have no use for it. Please. You keep it.'

Konjic nodded, not saying a word, as if sensing that there might be more attached to these objects than function and utility. He didn't open it, and Vlado did not want to look inside. Instead he looked round the table and noticed the smallest boy watching him from the end, the one who'd played with his soldiers. Vlado smiled at him.

'I hope you're enjoying those soldiers,' he said, wanting to change the subject. 'I painted them all. But it was only a hobby to pass the time. I don't want them back. Too many memories of the war. So I'm glad if you can make some use of them.'

'Tell him the story, Daddy,' the boy said. 'Tell him about the soldier.'

The father's eyes were sparkling. 'Do you remember that morning, when you invited us in?'

'Yes. The explosion woke me up. I wasn't sure you were all OK, and I was worried there might be more shells.'

'We went from here to the hospital, just to be checked out, like you told us. Everything was fine. Then we decided to get our food for the day. Bread, water and rice. You know, the usual. We divided up the chores. Nela and Mirela would stand in line for the rice, the two older boys would wait for bread. Me and this one here,' he rumpled the small boy's hair, 'we would get in line for water. That was when I looked down and saw Hisham playing with one of your soldiers. He had picked it up off the table when I wasn't looking. I'd asked him to put it back and I thought that he had.'

Vlado remembered that he had thought so too, even recalling that he'd been disappointed that the boy hadn't kept it.

'I almost said something about letting him keep one,' Vlado said, 'but you seemed pretty stern about it, and I know how it is when you're trying to discipline your children. You don't want somebody else contradicting you. So I held my tongue.'

'Which was the right thing for you to do. But little Hisham here, when no-one was looking he took one anyway. And as soon as I saw it I said, "No. You must return it now." So Hisham and I walked back to your apartment. You were gone, but the door was unlocked, so he put the soldier back on the table with the others. I saw to it myself. By then of course we were a good ten minutes late for getting in line for water. And then what do you suppose happened?'

Vlado shook his head.

'We arrived at the water line to find that a shell had landed only five minutes earlier. Four people were killed, including two boys. So you see, if it had not been for your soldier, well, that might have been us standing there. Your little man in blue, Mr Petric, he saved our lives. So whenever Hisham plays with them, they remind us of the war, but they remind us of you, too, and all of the memories are good ones.' Konjic nodded curtly, as if that was his final word on the matter.

Vlado felt that the scales had finally begun to re-balance in his favour. In the wake of his departure one child had died. This morning a colleague had died as well. But now, at least, there was this child who had lived, sitting at the end of a table built with his father's tools, grinning, icing on his cheeks.

'Thank you for telling me that,' Vlado said quietly, placing his empty cup on the saucer. 'And thank you for all of this, too.'

They didn't talk much after that. Mostly a lot of smiling and laughter over silly things the children did. Half an hour later Vlado rose from the table.

'I'd better be going. I've got a lot to do while I'm in Sarajevo.'

The family escorted him to the door, waving goodbye as if he were an old friend who'd come bearing wondrous gifts. It was a better homecoming than he ever would have expected, and not until he was halfway down the hill to the Holiday Inn did he remember the photo stuffed in his pocket. He quickened his pace, rubbing the edge of the envelope with his fingertips, wondering what might be waiting for him, if anything, at Uncle Tomislav's house in Podborje. Perhaps the Tribunal was finished looking for Pero Matek – he'd know for sure this evening – but he wasn't finished, and Podborje now seemed worth a visit.

15

Janet Ecker's flight was nearly an hour late, which left them barely enough time to make the scheduled meeting with Harkness and LeBlanc at the Holiday Inn. Janet had to brief Vlado and Pine on the ride from the airport.

'First things first,' she said. 'Contreras wants you to stay on the case.'

This was a surprise, but a good one.

'Officially, of course, we're not calling it a manhunt. For the record you're pursuing leads on the where-abouts of a material witness. One who just happens to have murdered a colleague. But with that in mind . . .' She pulled an envelope from her briefcase. 'You're ticketed on a noon flight tomorrow.'

'To where?' Pine asked, still sounding on edge.

'Rome. Both of you.' She looked at Vlado. 'As long as you're still along for the ride.'

Vlado nodded. Anything to keep him in pursuit of Matek.

'Why Rome?' Pine asked, a stirring of interest in his voice.

'Someone there you need to see. Robert Fordham. Army counterintelligence. Or used to be. He was Matek's handler in post-war Rome. Vlado will need a visa, of course. The Italians promise to have one ready by tomorrow morning.'

'What about Andric?' Pine asked.

'We've got a dozen people on it. Chances are he's in Serbia by now anyway. As for the rest, Spratt's got somebody flying down to handle arrangements for Benny. He's got family back in New York. They're going to fly the body home. There will be a memorial service this Friday in The Hague.'

That silenced them for a moment. Then Pine spoke up.

'I still don't understand our priorities, though. Personally, I'm all for it. After what happened to Benny, there's no-one I'd rather pursue more than Matek. But if I were some Tribunal bean-counter I'd be saying, wait a minute, we're throwing an awful lot of limited resources after some old guy who's not ours to try. Even for murder.'

'Somebody may yet say that. But for the moment the only one who wants us off the case is Harkness. That's the word, anyway. So be prepared for a lecture.'

'I thought this was all his idea. His and LeBlanc's. And now we lose a good man and he expects us to just drop it? What the hell's up with that?'

'Maybe you should ask him. But something about this seems to have him spooked.'

'What do we say when he asks what we're doing next?'

'We mention Rome, and that's it. And we don't back down on anything.'

They arrived at the Holiday Inn with only minutes to

spare, hustling upstairs to a small conference room where the two envoys were waiting. LeBlanc sat calmly to one side, with a prim smile that was almost a smirk. Harkness wore tweeds. He really did bring to mind a British country gentleman, Vlado thought, hoping there would be no further asides about Popovic. They seated themselves round an oval table, Harkness striding to one end as if he were the master of ceremonies.

'Something to drink, gentlemen?' he asked. 'And lady, of course.'

Vlado half expected gin and tonic to be in the offing, given the man's bearing, but a bottle of mineral water was the only drink in sight.

'I'd like to begin by expressing my sympathy. I suppose we've all learned a sad and costly lesson this morning.'

'And what lesson would that be?' Pine asked sharply.

'That this is still a very dangerous place, and also that the Tribunal, for all the growing up it's done, really isn't equipped for the manhunt business. We never should have pushed you into that role. Our apologies. And our deepest condolences on Benny. He was a splendid fellow.'

Presumably he was also speaking for LeBlanc, although it wasn't clear from the Frenchman's expression if he shared Harkness's willingness to accept blame. Janet and Pine were tight-lipped, and Vlado couldn't help but contrast the chilly atmosphere with the warmth of the home he'd visited – his own home, he had to remind himself – only a few hours ago. He also wondered at the way Harkness had taken charge, as if the operation were his to run.

'Obviously,' he continued, 'our main priority now is Andric, despite the personal stakes involved. I plan on having a word with Contreras first thing to make sure he's on the same page. State has been informed, of course, and that's their position as well. If we're going to have police searching half the rail stations and airports of Europe, we might as well focus on the bigger prize, notwithstanding this morning's events in Travnik. And not to mention the obvious problems of jurisdiction and authorization.'

'Actually,' Pine said, colour rising, 'this meeting is only a courtesy, and our orders from the Tribunal make it clear that Vlado and I are to keep pursuing leads on Matek. Janet will back me up on that.'

' "Jurisdiction be damned",' she said. 'Contreras' own words, as of an hour ago.'

'He'll come to his senses soon enough,' Harkness said, polishing his glasses with a handkerchief. 'Either once the sting has worn off or when he's got another dead operative to answer for. Let's just hope it's the former, not the latter.'

'We're not operatives,' Pine said, redder still. 'That's your world. We're just investigators and prosecutors. And if I didn't know better I'd say you'd just threatened us.'

Now it was Harkness's turn to get angry. He slapped his glasses on the table almost hard enough to break them, then levelled a pink finger at Pine.

'Not a threat. Not in the least. Benny Hampton was a

good man. No-one here disputes that. But lurching into matters that are none of the Tribunal's damn business is hardly a fitting memorial, and can only create more problems. Pursue this if you want. Just don't expect the same enthusiasm from the State Department when it's time to pony up for another Tribunal budget. And that *is* a threat. At this point anything that drains resources from apprehending Andric is a waste and a hindrance.'

'As if none of us knows where Andric has gone,' Janet said.

'To Serbia, you mean,' said LeBlanc, who up to now had been content to watch the Americans rip into each other. 'It would make sense. Milosevic is taking everyone he can and sending them towards Kosovo. A cable this morning – and I'm sure that Monsieur Harkness has received the same information – says they've just moved another twenty thousand.'

'I thought the Serbs were your friends, Guy,' Harkness said, affecting a bluff manner. 'And while we're on the subject, you're not going to tell us someone on your side didn't tip off General Andric, are you? I wasn't going to bring that up out of politeness, but with you so certain about his current destination it seems appropriate.'

An awkward silence followed. From the beginning of this operation, Vlado had wondered about the exact nature of the work done by Harkness and LeBlanc. When he was a teenager it had been popular to label all visiting Americans as CIA agents. Every Briton was MI-5, and all stray Russians were of course KGB. It had been more of a game than a belief, to the point of becoming a silly cliché. When the Olympics had come to Sarajevo in 1984 his friends had made a game out of 'tailing' certain athletes and tourists through the evening bar scene, pretending they'd actually identified an operative. But with LeBlanc and Harkness, Vlado sensed, the parlour trick was far more sophisticated. On the one hand, they seemed to do everything but nudge and wink to convince him that their connections ran deeper than the mere diplomatic world. Yet they prattled on with a straight face about their bosses at the 'State Department' or the 'foreign ministry'. It was unnerving, mostly because he wasn't sure whom he was dealing with – the representative of a nation, or of some agency with a more secretive agenda. Or perhaps with these two, he thought, the stakes were personal.

'Maybe you guys could argue later,' Janet said. 'But until we hear otherwise – from The Hague, not from Washington or Paris – we're still on the Matek case. This is a briefing for your benefit, not a planning session for you to direct.'

'All right,' Harkness said. 'I'll play along. And what might your next move be in this vital pursuit of Matek? As a courtesy only, of course.'

'We're thinking Rome as a possible destination.'

Harkness chuckled, then sipped his water with a satisfied slurp. 'You're not really going to waste your time talking to that old windbag Bob Fordham, I hope?'

Janet flinched, but said nothing.

'I know he's on all those old cables. But the man has proven notoriously unreliable. It's why he washed out, you know. No-one could believe a word he said. The priority for all of us should still be Andric. And if I may add my two cents — merely in an advisory role, of course — I'd say the key to finding Andric is finding Branko Popovic.'

Vlado tried not to show his surprise. He flashed on an image of Popovic's body in the boot, face down like Benny's, flesh pale and lifeless like Benny's, the dark bloodstain across his back.

'Now there's a man with some real army connections who, if we find him, can help us,' Harkness said. 'Not just with Andric, but with Matek, too. Same shady friends. And from what I've heard, certain parties have already been working on cutting an immunity deal in exchange for Popovic's testimony. I don't want to say it's us and I don't want to say it's your people, Guy. It might even be all of us, under the auspices of the Tribunal. Or so I've heard.'

This was news to Pine, apparently.

'A deal? He's been under indictment for more than a year, if that's what you mean. A sealed indictment, granted. But there's nothing beyond that.'

Janet, looking pained, spoke up. 'Actually, Calvin, there have been talks going on at levels well above us for quite some time. I can't speak with authority, but Spratt and Contreras have wanted to reel him in for reasons other than prosecution. Popovic apparently knows things about a lot of higher-ups, and not just Andric.'

'I won't disagree,' said the Frenchman, still looking down at the table.

'Excuse me,' Harkness said, 'but might this be a good

time to ask our Balkan friend Mr Petric to leave the room?'

Vlado tensed. He wondered what more Harkness had learned during the past few days about Popovic, and what that might mean for him. There was no way he was leaving the room voluntarily, but he needed someone to speak up for him. When help finally arrived, it came from an unlikely corner.

'Personally,' LeBlanc said, 'I don't see why anyone should have to leave.'

'*Personally*, I'd agree,' Harkness answered testily. 'Professionally, the smaller the loop the better.'

'But Paul,' LeBlanc continued, with a look that said the conversation had gone right where he'd wanted, 'as far as Vlado is concerned, all of this *is* personal. Or have you forgotten the connections that brought him to our attention. Don't you think he's earned inclusion?'

Vlado hoped the only connection they meant was his father. Judging from Harkness's sudden embarrassment, that seemed to be the case.

'Yes, of course,' Harkness said, reddening. 'I guess I'm just not used to including locals on matters like these. No disrespect intended, Vlado.'

'None taken, Paul,' Vlado said, lingering on the name. 'After all, it's only my country.'

LeBlanc bowed his head, suppressing a laugh.

'Now that we've settled that,' Pine said, 'what does any of this have to do with Popovic, other than his status as a material witness against Andric?'

Harkness looked across the table at LeBlanc. 'Guy, you want to take a shot at that?'

LeBlanc shrugged. 'He's done work for both of us. Apart from whatever he's offering the Tribunal.'

'He's given us some pretty good stuff,' Harkness said. 'Help with military targeting. The latest word on the thinking of the Yugoslav leadership. He's become quite the turncoat. For a price, of course.' He stared at Vlado. 'And it could certainly cost him his life if word ever got out. Assuming it hasn't already.'

'You think he might be dead?' Pine said. Vlado pressed his hands together beneath the table.

'It's a possibility,' Harkness said.

'Unless he has dropped out of sight in order to help Andric,' LeBlanc added. 'Another possibility. Maybe Andric outbid the Tribunal for his services.'

'Wouldn't make sense,' Pine said. 'Not if turning evidence against Andric was really his ticket to freedom.'

Harkness and LeBlanc exchanged glances, Harkness with what appeared to be a look of warning.

'There are other factors,' LeBlanc said. 'But I'm afraid I can't share them just now.'

Pine turned to Janet. 'Do you know what the hell they're talking about?'

She lowered her head. 'No.'

'Sure about that?' he said testily. 'Given your connections with "the community"?'

When she looked up, she was clearly angry.

'Positive. And don't question my word again, especially with regard to my so-called connections.'

Vlado was still trying to put the pieces together when he looked up to see Harkness chuckling at him.

'You're looking a bit flabbergasted, old boy. Welcome to the wilderness of mirrors.'

'Wilderness of mirrors,' Vlado repeated. It was an interesting phrase.

'A paranoid old spy said that once about the intelligence community,' Janet explained. 'Mostly because he never learned to tell the difference between the real images and the reflections. Pretty much sums up this situation, I'd say.'

'While we're on the subject of bewilderment,' LeBlanc said, 'in my opinion, all three of these disappearances may be connected. Matek's included.'

Harkness shot him a dark look. 'I believe we're talking out of school now, Guy.'

'We do all want the same thing, don't we, Paul?'

'You tell me. But as long as that cat's out of the bag, may I offer some more advice?'

'Why not,' Pine said, 'since you're going to tell us anyway.'

'Wherever you go, watch your step. You're fooling yourself if you think Matek doesn't have international reach. You've already whistled past the graveyard once, gentlemen, and look where that got you. Blunder into Italy and it might be worse. So why not leave it to the professionals?'

'I thought we were professionals,' Pine said.

'You know what I mean. Besides, it might be more productive looking for Popovic first. And from what I know of the man, there are already plenty of good leads in Vienna, in Zurich, and especially in Berlin. You're a Berliner, Vlado. You must have some contacts in the

Yugo community there. Surely someone would have spotted Popovic by now, no matter what name he's travelling under.'

Vlado wondered if he was the only one in the room who thought Harkness's smile suddenly seemed predatory. Who should he fear more, he wondered, Matek or Harkness? Yet he was about to further entangle himself with both, drawn deeper into their interests by the tether to his father's past. The challenge was to keep the tether from becoming a noose.

'I have a better idea, Paul,' Janet said. 'How about if you show us how the pieces fit, then we'll be able to help you even more. Seeing as how you think that's our job.'

'We've already offered more information than I'd wanted,' he said, glancing pointedly at LeBlanc. 'But if you can be specific about what you want to know, maybe I can help.'

It was the old bureaucrat's trick. I'll tell you what I've got as long as you already know. But Janet called his bluff.

'I'll be very specific. There is a piece of Matek's security file I can't get my hands on. His repatriation documentation from nineteen sixty-one. Apparently you've seen it, but every request I make comes back empty.'

'That's not ours to deliver, I'm afraid. You'll have to ask the Yugoslavs.'

'Well, maybe you should make a little more effort to free it up, especially if Belgrade still wants old Ustashe criminals like Matek taken care of.'

260

'I didn't say they hadn't delivered it. I said it wasn't ours to deliver to you. Some things are given to us conditionally. With certain restrictions.'

Her face was rigid. 'That's nonsense.'

'No. It's called diplomatic protocol. Happens all the time.'

'You know damn well there are ways around that kind of protocol. Especially from where you sit. And I'm not talking about your desk at the Department of State.'

Well, at least someone had finally stopped dancing around the subject, Vlado thought. Harkness was clearly displeased, although LeBlanc wore a prim smirk.

'No need to make this personal,' Harkness replied coolly. Then, with a leer at Pine, 'You, of all people, Janet, should know not to make things personal. Clouds your judgement.'

Janet went scarlet, Pine as well. LeBlanc shuffled through some papers, his expression as bland as if he'd just sat through the world's most uneventful meeting.

'Well, lady and gentlemen,' Harkness said with a note of triumph, rising suddenly from his seat. 'We seem to have covered the necessary ground. Best of luck in your misguided pursuit, however far afield you might stray. And cheers.' He raised his water glass, as if toasting the end of a cricket match with champagne.

No-one joined him in the gesture.

'Well, that was an experience I could have lived without,' Pine said a few moments later, still steaming.

He, Janet and Vlado were in the hotel coffee shop. 'Do either of you have any idea what they meant about connections between the suspects?'

Janet shook her head. 'But it's bound to be in the files somewhere. Or maybe Fordham knows. Why else would Harkness want to steer us away from Rome? I'm betting Popovic is nothing but a dead end.'

He was certainly that, Vlado thought, wanting only to change the subject.

'Tell me,' he said. 'Harkness and LeBlanc aren't just diplomats, are they?'

Pine smiled. 'They're spooks, you mean.'

'Spooks?'

'Spies. Intelligence. Or in the case of Harkness, CIA, with diplomatic cover.'

'Yes. Spooks, then.'

'Maybe. It's always been the assumption, even if nobody talks about it.'

'Why doesn't anyone just come out and say it?'

Janet laughed. 'You mean, "Hello, I'm Paul Harkness, CIA"?'

'No. But one of you might have told me.'

'I guess you get used to dealing with people like them when you work in places like this,' Pine said. 'Besides, you never know for sure.'

'So you just deal with them the same way you would with any outsider,' Janet added. 'Even if they're straight-up diplos they're going to have their own agenda, and believe me, some of them are every bit as devious as any spook. So we co-operate when we have to, but otherwise keep to ourselves.'

'But you're both Americans. So you must be on Harkness's side. At least a little.'

'Sometimes I wonder,' Pine said.

'Just think of it as us, the Tribunal, versus everybody else,' Janet said.

Vlado shook his head. Everyone on the same side, yet all of them working for someone else. Perhaps this was Bosnia's future, a conflict that would mature from a bludgeoning match to a sneaky and surgical meddling.

'You were right, Calvin,' Vlado said, 'our politics are nothing compared to all of this.'

'So, tell me more about Robert Fordham,' Pine said. 'Is he really a lying windbag?'

'If so, then he's the most reluctant windbag I've ever come across. It took me a good half-hour to convince him I was legit. He even called to verify I was on the level. I guess his reliability depends on how good his memory is. But he's about the only person left from Matek's Roman days. Strange bird. Bit of a hermit. He was a Foreign Service brat growing up – that's where he learned his Italian – but didn't move to Rome full-time until six years ago, after his wife died. In nineteen forty-six he made it to Rome the hard way. Landed at Anzio with the US Fifth Army, then slogged his way north. When the war ended, his State Department daddy wangled him a posting to an army counterintelligence outfit. The 428th. The rest is in here.' She handed them a cream-coloured folder stuffed with papers.

'What did Harkness mean when he said Fordham had washed out?' Vlado asked.

'In forty-six he seems to have run foul of his superiors.

The details are hazy. He also didn't get along too well with Angleton and some of the early CIA people.'

'Who's Angleton?' Vlado asked.

'Funny you should ask,' Janet said. 'He's the guy who came up with the "wilderness of mirrors" phrase, mostly because he ended up lost in it. He was fighting the Cold War before most people knew it existed. By the end of his career he was seeing double agents under every bush. Anyhow, I guess in Angleton's view Fordham didn't exactly graduate with honours. He went back home and became a banker. He wanted to join the Foreign Service but flunked his security clearance. Probably due to Angleton.'

'So he has an axe to grind,' Pine said.

'Possibly. But it's him or nobody.'

'There is one other thing,' Vlado said. 'Maybe it's a lead, maybe it's not.' He pulled the old photo from his pocket and told them about his Aunt Melania. 'If she's still around, she might be worth talking to. Her house is in Podborje.'

'Interesting,' Janet said, studying the photograph. 'Where's Podborje?'

'Two-hour drive at the most, even on bad roads.'

'You think she's still alive?'

'These farm women are pretty tough,' Vlado said. 'There's an old joke about Herzegovinian women. "Why do the husbands always die before their wives? Because they want to."'

Pine laughed loudly, Janet less so. But they agreed that the trip was worth a try. Vlado and Pine would make the drive in the morning.

'OK, then,' Janet said, bringing the meeting to a close. 'Then you'll be heading south before I'm up. Just make it back in time for your flight to Rome. Then we'll see how far you can burrow into Matek's past.'

Vlado smiled grimly. He'd never been to Rome, but the past was becoming familiar territory.

'Time travel,' he said. 'I seem to be doing a lot of that lately.'

16

They left before the sun was up, driving through the darkness into high mountain passes where dirty piles of snow lined the roadside. But by the time they reached the turn-off south of Jablanica, steam was rising from the pavement into the early light of what would be an unseasonably warm day.

'From what I remember, it's pushing it to even call it a village,' Vlado said. 'A few farms and houses, pretty scattered. But I do remember you can see my uncle's place from the top of a hill, just before the road goes into the valley.'

After they turned off the main highway, the roads were more like glorified goat paths, all dirt and gravel, even more rutted than the one to Matek's compound.

'Jesus,' Pine shouted as the Volvo scraped its undercarriage on yet another hump of stone. 'Hope the EU doesn't mind investing in another exhaust system.'

A few turns later, Vlado shouted 'Stop!' and Pine brought the car sliding to a halt at the edge of a hairpin turn. Vlado climbed quickly from his seat, stepping onto the grass verge of an overhang above a deep, narrow valley. Pine joined him, taking in the panorama. The morning breeze was soft in the rising heat.

'There. The second rooftop. See?' Vlado sounded as

enthusiastic as a small boy. The morning had the feel of a fresh start, the beginning of an adventure, especially with Rome awaiting them at the day's end. 'I can't believe it,' he said. 'I remember this exact view. My father made us all get out of the car. I think he even took a picture.'

'Let's just hope your aunt's still down there.'

'Oh, she's there,' Vlado said, smiling broadly. 'Look at the chimney.'

Wisps of white smoke swirled from one end of the red rooftop.

'Maybe it's somebody else.'

Vlado shook his head. 'Not in Podborje. When people die, there's nobody else to move in. No-one moves to places like this any more. Let's go.'

The descent took another fifteen minutes. They hadn't passed another car for at least an hour. They pulled up in front of a plastered brick house with a red tile roof. Just to the right was a weathered wooden barn. Beyond were brown fields, stubbled with weeds and the remnants of last summer's corn. The valley was quiet, no sound but the wind across the fields, and the air smelled of smoke.

Snow still covered some of the small lawn, melting fast. From the barn came the slapping sound of a wooden door, and they turned to see a short, stooped woman in a long skirt emerge with two steaming pails of milk, one in each hand. She eyed them sceptically, these visitors with their modern white car, but she never stopped walking towards the house.

It was her, Vlado realized, although he'd remembered

her face as smooth and brown. Now it was creased and collapsed, yellowed and spotted, like one of those handicraft dolls made of dried apples. But there was still strength in her movements.

'Aunt Melania?' Vlado ventured tentatively.

She stopped, carefully setting the pails in the mud, squinting into the morning light.

'Vlado?' she croaked in a high but strong voice. 'Is that you, boy?'

Vlado nodded, and she dropped to her knees as if shot, rapidly crossing herself and muttering words they couldn't hear. They rushed to her side, but she was smiling.

'Please,' she gasped. 'Careful of the milk.' Then she stood, wrapping Vlado in a wiry embrace before stepping back to look him in the eye as if he were the eighth wonder of the world. A rooster strutted forward, clucking nervously as it inspected the intruders.

'I never thought I would see you again,' she said. 'Especially when I heard your father was dead. He must have told you how much he never wanted to see us again.'

'No,' Vlado said. 'He never did. But I do remember coming here.'

She continued peering at him, as if searching for signs of falseness. Appearing satisfied at last, she said, 'Come inside. I have something for you, but first I'll make coffee. And I'm baking bread. You will eat.'

Once inside, Vlado introduced Pine as his 'friend from America. He won't understand anything you're saying, though, so don't worry.'

She laughed. 'It will be just like your father, then. He never understood what I was saying either, or pretended he didn't. Your mother, though, she always knew I was talking sense.'

The house smelled of warm bread. She seated them by a rough table, built much like the one Konjic had made, and pulled a brown loaf from the mouth of a huge oven, then put a pot of coffee on to boil, making it the Turkish way, from a grind finer than dust that left a muddy sediment in every cup.

'Me and the woman at the next farm, we bake for each other,' she said. 'She's a widow, too. We live a mile apart, so we take turns making the walk. She won't be here for another hour, so we have plenty of time to talk. But first, some eggs. Come.'

They followed her back outdoors, trooping past the barn with its smell of manure and damp coldness to a weathered hen house, where she stooped among the birds, their wings flapping as she pulled an egg from each of six nests. Returning to the kitchen she took a blackened iron skillet from a hook on the wall and began scrambling the entire batch. She put plates and forks before them, and seated herself at the end of the table.

'I suppose I shouldn't be so surprised to see you, coming across the mountains with the sun barely up. And with an American, too.' She smiled, eyes gleaming with mischief. 'You were always going to be an explorer, you know. A traveller on the seas. Or that's what all your books were about when you were a boy. Is that what you've become?'

'I'd forgotten all that,' Vlado said, laughing. 'Wasn't Magellan my favourite? Because he'd been the first to go round the world?'

'Yes. You wanted to be the Yugoslav Magellan. You said you wanted to sail for Tito. You should have seen your father's face when you said that. It was all he could do not to shout at you, but he held it inside. Your mother and I had a good laugh and just egged you on. We were terrible.'

'And Uncle Tomislav?'

'Oh, he didn't worry about those things any more.'

Vlado paused long enough to interpret for Pine, who had been silent up to then. That prompted a question from Aunt Melania.

'I saw the EU symbol on your car. Is that who you're working for?'

When Vlado told her they were working for the War Crimes Tribunal, her eyes widened. She reappraised Pine with greater scrutiny, then asked, 'Is that the reason you're here? War crimes?'

'Yes, but it's very complicated.'

'Those things usually are.' She was looking down now, cradling a coffee cup in her lap. 'How much did your father tell you about the war?'

'Nothing really. But I've learned a few things in the past week. About what he did. Where he was. That he went to Italy afterwards, things like that.'

'Then maybe you can understand why he and your Uncle Tomislav never really got along later.'

'Because of the war?'

'Mostly because of what happened afterwards. Your

270

father had been travelling with another boy from here. Pero Rudec.'

Pine heard the name, and strained to work out what was being said. Vlado hoped Pine would have the good sense to be patient and not interrupt.

'Yes. I've heard of this Rudec.'

She shook her head, sipping her coffee, then spoke very slowly, gravely. 'Then maybe you also know about a man named Josip Iskric.'

'Yes. He's my father.'

She nodded, saying nothing for a few moments. 'Iskric was my name too, of course. Until I married your Uncle Tomislav. Our family lived all over this valley. There are only a few of us now. A lot of them were killed in the war.'

'Tell me about the war.'

'Afterwards was the worst. That's when your father and Pero left the country. But your uncle stayed, and the new authorities, Tito's people, put him in gaol for a while. Him and some others from the local militia. He had never gone in for the politics. He fought in the Home Defence Army because all his friends were doing it. But he never sewed a big U for Ustashe on his shoulders like some of them. Like your father for one, at least for a while. And like that Rudec for another, as if he ever cared about any cause but his own.

'But your uncle wasn't interested in causes, and I think that's what saved him. Some of our friends in the village, the Seratlic family, were Serbs. They survived. Someone must have hidden them during the war, because by the end of the fighting the other Serbs in the

271

valley were all either dead or gone. Taken north. But Seratlic vouched for Tomislav. Why, I don't know, because Tomislav wouldn't have spoken up for them, and he certainly wouldn't have hidden them. He always did as he was told. But we'd once sold them milk at fair prices, when their father had a dairy. So your uncle got out of gaol. Some of the others stayed inside. A few were shot. Quick trials that no-one ever saw. You'd read a paragraph in the newspaper, and that was it. It was a bad time.

'We thought your father was dead. Rudec, too. And when we didn't hear from them for a few years, we were sure of it. My only brother, gone. Then in nineteen sixty-one we got a letter from him. He told us to burn it after we'd read it. It didn't even come by the regular mail. It was brought by some old man on a mule who'd got it from someone else on a train. It didn't have his real name in it, but we knew who it was from what he said.'

'Do you still have it?' Vlado asked, more as a son than an investigator.

'We burned it, like he asked. He told us that someday he would visit, but that for the moment it was too dangerous. He said he was near Sarajevo, that he'd learned a trade and met a woman. But he didn't tell us his new name, or his village. When you were a boy, I only knew you as Vlado. Maybe now you can tell me your last name. I have always wondered. Can you tell me?'

'Petric,' said Vlado, feeling fraudulent as he stated it, a creation of forgery and deception. 'Vlado Petric. It has always been my name.'

She nodded curtly, accepting it.

'Before you go on,' he said, 'I have to tell my friend a little of what we've been saying.' He brought Pine up to speed, leaving out the part about his name.

'Ask her if your father's letter mentioned Rudec,' Pine said.

It hadn't.

'But Rudec is alive, isn't he?' she asked. 'This visit is about him.'

'Yes. Only now he goes by the name Matek. We're looking for him. Partly because of the past. Partly because he killed one of our colleagues.'

She shook her head slowly, regretfully.

'Then I will help if I can. But I'm afraid I don't know much. He never returned. Never wrote or sent word to anyone. Only your father came back, and even he had to sneak into the valley. He said that if anyone ever found out his real name they would put him in prison, or shoot him. But of course Tomislav, being a man, had to talk about the war. So after dinner, and after the third glass of brandy, Tomislav began asking questions. About the war, and the year your father went north.'

Vlado knew where north led – straight to the Sava River, and Jasenovac.

'He wanted to know what had become of Rudec, and where they'd gone, what they'd done all those years. Maybe your father had been led astray by bad politics, Tomislav said. By all those men who went goose-stepping with the Germans, wearing their big Us. Bowing down to priests and politicians, as if it was

273

some kind of crusade. Because by then, of course, your uncle was only listening to what Tito had to say. So he and your father argued, then they fought. Fortunately by then they were so drunk they couldn't do much harm. They broke a few glasses, knocked over some chairs.'

'I saw them through the window. Like two bulls in a ring. Snorting and pawing.'

'Two *drunken* bulls.' She smiled, showing her missing teeth. 'But your mother and I got them to bed. We only had to lay them down and they passed out.' She stopped speaking, as if that was all she had to say on the matter.

Vlado drank the strong, bitter coffee, feeling the pleasing, familiar grittiness on his tongue. Somehow it tasted better here, in this quiet valley hidden in the hills.

'Tell me more about Pero Rudec,' he said. 'You knew him?'

'Oh, yes. A handsome boy, especially when he wore his uniform from the officer's academy. But he was always a little unsettling, too.'

'How?'

'Oh, you know. Always the first to do everything, especially when it came to girls. Always looking for the easiest way to do something. The short cuts. But he also knew how to make the parents like him. Being sweet to the mother while trying everything under the sun with the daughter. Some of the fathers saw through it and chased him off, but he was pretty sly.'

'You went out with him?'

'Oh no. He was forbidden fruit. And I was already

274

promised to Tomislav. A good thing, too. Soon everyone knew that a girl down the valley, Mirta, was pregnant. But it was just after the war had started, and that gave Pero a chance to get away. Tomislav and your father signed up for the local militia. But Pero volunteered for a special unit heading north. A sort of Ustashe SS, only they didn't call it that, but I think he liked the idea because it took him away from Mirta and her father. Of course he had to put a different face on it, talking about his valour and his duty. But no-one believed him. I think he also liked the idea that he might collect some booty. Like a pirate.'

'People knew there would be booty?'

'People had already heard what these units were doing. Burning villages and taking everything. Trying to wipe out the Chetniks. Some volunteers had already come back because they couldn't stand it.' She shook her head. 'I don't think Pero felt one way or the other about the Chetniks, but he never came back.'

'What was it like here?'

'There were raids by all sides, back and forth across the hills. In the last year of the war a group of Partisans or Chetniks, no-one was sure which, attacked and burned a village near here. Tomislav and your father were the first men to get there afterwards. Every family had been murdered in their beds. Everyone wanted revenge. And that was when your father went north.'

'In the last year of the war?'

'Yes.'

Vlado was puzzled. The file had clearly said his father went north two years earlier, at the same time as

275

Matek. He attributed the discrepancy to the haze of his old aunt's memory, knowing how these things could get jumbled over time.

'But Tomislav stayed?'

'His father wouldn't let him go. Our father felt the same way. But Josip went anyway. He was determined.'

Thus was a war criminal born, Vlado thought. Seeking vengeance and finding it, but a vengeance of the most terrible sort.

'And he ended up at Jasenovac.'

'Is that what you've heard?'

'Yes. Along with Rudec.'

She was silent a moment, playing with her napkin.

'I'd always heard that about Rudec,' she said. 'But I was never sure about your father.'

'Is that what he and Uncle Tomislav were arguing about that night?'

'Who can say? Your mother and I couldn't stand the noise, so we left them alone out there in the back. Then we heard things getting worse, but by the time I got downstairs they were on top of each other.'

'So you never really found out what set them off?'

She paused, as if reluctant to continue. 'Something about Rudec, if you really want to know.' She stared at the floor. Pine must have sensed the change in her tone, because he was suddenly more attentive, leaning forward in his chair.

'What was it?'

'Oh, Vlado, you really don't want to know all this. The past is the past. Let it stay in the ground.'

'Someone else has already dug it up, I'm afraid.'

She sighed, then placed her coffee cup on the table and straightened in her chair.

'Tomislav told me about it the next day, after you had all gone. Even then he couldn't quite remember why things had got so out of hand, once he started explaining it. But Rudec's name had come up. Tomislav had heard some things after the war. About that place you mentioned.'

'Jasenovac.'

'Yes. Rudec and a few others had apparently been some of the worst. All the wild stories about the killings, the torture. I'd always wondered if maybe it was just Tito's people making it up. But the Seratlic family, the ones who'd helped Tomislav, they'd heard it from cousins who'd survived the place. They said all of it was true.

'But your father told Tomislav to stop repeating those stories, especially the ones about Rudec. He said it was too dangerous. And Tomislav thought your father was being a coward. But your father insisted, and said Tomislav should never say those things to anyone. Tomislav lost his patience. And, well, you saw the rest out of your window.' She paused again. 'But the oddest part was what your father did the next morning.'

'Leaving early the way we did?'

'Before that. Before you were even up. Tomislav was still asleep, snoring. Your mother was packing. I was in the kitchen, still restless from seeing them the night before, my husband and my brother rolling on the ground like a couple of animals. I was making bread when your father came down. He told me he was sorry things had gone so badly but he was really worried about what would happen if we talked about Rudec, or whatever he was called now. Your father said it would hurt him more than Rudec, because of things that had happened after the war.'

'*After* the war?'

'Yes. In Italy.'

'But not during the war.'

'No. Your father wouldn't talk about those years. Not a word. Especially about the time after he went north.'

'To that place.'

'Yes. To that place.' She lowered her head.

'They were in Rome for fifteen years,' Vlado said. 'A lot could have happened. He could have been talking about anything. Work that they did against Tito, maybe.'

She shook her head. 'Not in Rome. Later. When they were on the coast. In some other town, where he and Rudec were for years, your father said.'

There had been nothing in either file about that.

'I didn't know they lived anywhere but Rome.'

'They only stayed in the city a year or two, he said. Then they went south. Looking for work, I think, or maybe because it was cheaper. He didn't say much beyond that. But he did say he hadn't wanted to leave. He said he was happy with his new life, with you and your mother. But – and I'm trying to remember exactly how he said it, because it was so strange. It was something like, "I love my new life, but I never really finished my old one." Then he gave me something, and I understood at least part of what he meant. But not for sure, because he never said anything more. He just gave it to me and told me never to throw it away, but never to let you or your mother see it. I think he couldn't bear to destroy it, but was afraid to keep it in case one of you might find it.'

'What is it? Do you still have it?'

'Yes. And maybe I should have kept his wish and not told you about it. But if it will help you find Rudec . . .' She shrugged. 'Because he is part of it, too.'

'Show me, please.'

She nodded, placing her palms on the table and slowly pushing herself to her feet. In passing she laid a hand lightly on Vlado's head, in the manner of a priest offering a blessing. 'It's in my dresser drawer, where it has been since that night. I never even showed it to Tomislav.'

She hobbled off, stiff after their hour at the table, seeming years older than when they'd arrived.

'What's happening?' Pine whispered. 'Where's she going?'

'She's getting something my father left here, years ago. When I was a boy.'

Pine said nothing. There was only the sound of chickens outside the window, clucking and scratching, heads bobbing in the sunlight. Aunt Melania returned with a small square of paper. When she turned it over, it was an old photograph. She handed it to Vlado. The tones had browned but the focus was sharp.

It was his father, smiling broadly, a young healthy man standing with his arm round the shoulders of a smiling woman whom Vlado had never seen. They stood by a ladder, which was propped against a lemon tree. Gauzy netting was stretched across the treetops, filtering the sunlight. Next to them was another couple, and it took only a few seconds for Vlado to recognize the features of Pero Rudec, or Matek, as they knew him now. His aunt was right. Matek had been handsome, with just enough of the rogue in his expression to seem mysterious. The foursome was in a small grassy clearing, surrounded by citrus trees. On one side of the grass was a ring of white stones, darkened in the middle, as if someone had made a campfire.

The woman with his father was thin and dark-haired. They seemed quite at ease with one another, whereas Rudec's companion seemed stiff, ill at ease, or perhaps that was Vlado's imagination.

'Do you know her name?' Vlado asked.

'No. He never said a word of explanation. He only asked me to keep it.'

'May I have it?'

'Yes,' she said. 'And take this one too. He sent it later.'

It was a picture of his father and himself up in the mountains, admiring the view. Vlado recognized the view, a few miles outside Sarajevo, with Mount Jahorina in the background. He looked about six, in shorts with knobbly knees and blocky shoes. His father stood behind him. Both were smiling broadly, the same look of ease that his father wore in the picture from Italy, only in this one his large, strong hands were placed protectively on his son's shoulders. Were they the hands of a killer? Vlado felt his eyes brimming, so he took a deep breath and looked again at the other photo, turning it over for an inscription. There was only a studio stamp: 'Martelli Fotografia. Castellammare di Stabia. 1958.' He'd never heard of the place. Perhaps it was the town on the coast his aunt had mentioned.

'Just pictures?' Pine asked. He sounded disappointed.

'Maybe we'll learn more in Rome,' Vlado said. 'And this other place.' He turned the photo over again, saying the name slowly. 'Castellammare di Stabia. Maybe we should go there, too.'

'Maybe,' Pine said, sounding sceptical.

Aunt Melania, who hadn't understood a word of their English, said, 'Would you like a piece of advice from an old woman, Vlado? Something that will last longer than just a cup of coffee and a warm slice of bread?'

'Why not?' he said, smiling at her. But he saw she was serious.

'Don't go there.' She pointed to the photo. 'Leave those things where they belong.'

'I'm afraid it's too late for that now.'

She nodded, as if resigned to his answer. 'Well, if you have to. Maybe it will even be for the best.'

The look on her face said she didn't believe it for a moment.

17

Robert Fordham gazed down at the streets of Rome from his balcony on the fourth floor, wondering what he'd got himself into. On a warm November Saturday like this it was easy to forget the weary dishevelment that had reigned half a century earlier. Today the view was of nothing but prosperity – stylish hordes out for fresh air in sleeveless majesty. Older women squeezed vegetables in the market, the younger ones window-shopped. Close your eyes and the exotic orchestra of the streets kicked in – buzzing Vespas and honking cabs, a tinny choir of cellphones.

Yet, within the hour, and by his own free will, he would be conjuring up the grim post-war mood of 1946 – and for a pair of strangers, an American and a Bosnian, the same sort of tandem that had once done him so much harm.

He sighed at his foolishness. Ever since giving his consent the previous morning his cautious nature had been in turmoil. Already wary of phone calls, of repairmen, of any visitor other than his housekeeper, Maria, he was now seeing threats in every strange face. Before taking his regular walk that morning he'd found himself reverting to the small tricks of a very old trade, leaving behind markers and telltales to determine if anyone had entered his apartment – or tried to – while he was out. He'd stopped at every corner to look over his shoulder, guarding his flanks. He'd scanned every parked or passing car, looking for an excessive number of antennae, and he'd been more relieved than he cared to admit to find his front door undisturbed on returning.

Stir up enough memories from a brief and intense time in your past, he supposed, and the old habits and fears returned with them. But part of him believed that it was only prudent to feel this way. There were still too many unforgiving people out there, with memories as long and clear as his, and Rome was his last refuge. He had long since given up the stern clapboard villages of New England for the eternal mess and glory of this ancient sprawl along the Tiber, having made it his solemn duty to live and eat well, while worrying as little as possible about the past.

Why, then, had he agreed to venture back to that era when the city had been exhausted, creaking along on pushcarts and horse-drawn cabs in a medieval gloom of hunger and want. The lure certainly hadn't been the woman who had telephoned to make the request. Janet something or other, supposedly with the War Crimes Tribunal. She'd been friendly enough, and her bona fides checked out. But something in her manner had carried the unmistakable whiff of the Agency, or some similar organization.

The Tribunal was only the latest outfit seeking to tap his memory. Earlier supplicants had been nameless men in grey, still trying to tidy up after so much sloppiness. They'd knocked at his door, said little, then left with curt nods when he politely declined. A later one had posed as a journalist, a clever effort, but no thank you. Another had approached him at a café, unannounced, with the bluster and bonhomie of a long-forgotten acquaintance. 'Just happened to be on vacation, old boy, so imagine bumping into you here. Let's talk about old times, shall we?' No sale for that one, either. Fordham had learned the value and safety of silence as well as anyone. After all these years, why give them a reason to move against you?

He would have said no this time, too, until he'd heard the name that finally flushed him: Petric.

Could there possibly be a connection? And in such an unlikely quarter as the War Crimes Tribunal? He hadn't spoken their language in years, and for all he knew there were thousands of Bosnians named Petric. But he doubted it, and for the briefest of moments as he scanned the pavements below he saw not the shoppers with their strollers and motorbikes, but wispy visions of that other time: thin grimy boys in dark shorts siphoning petrol from his motor-pool jeep, hunched old men peddling re-rolled cigarettes at the kerb, and raven-haired prostitutes in all their rumpled glory, offering a half-hour of tenderness for a pittance of lira or US Army scrip. For a little extra they would even accompany you afterwards on a stroll, arm in arm through the Borghese, where giggling boys by the duck pond climbed trees to toss pebbles at the GIs and their dates.

The shadow that inevitably fell on such memories was a hunched Balkan figure disappearing round a corner, a sharp, underfed face with dark eyes, a face that could read your deepest ambitions and play them to the greatest possible advantage.

'Signor,' a woman's voice said, returning Fordham to the here and now. It was his housekeeper, Maria. 'Your guests have arrived.'

He turned from the sunlight and stepped indoors, where the plaster walls always seemed to retain their midwinter chill. 'All right,' he said with resignation. 'Let them in.'

A maid met Vlado and Pine at the door when they reached the fourth floor. Signor Fordham had only recently woken from his nap, she informed them gravely, although the man who emerged to greet them looked far from groggy or ill prepared. He regarded them warily, his gaze lingering a shade too long on Vlado. Then he advanced with his hand outstretched but quivering slightly, as if he'd been shaken by what he'd just seen. China-blue eyes shimmered. A full head of white hair swept back neatly from a high fore-head. He was tall, about Pine's height, and in spite of a slight stoop there was something military in his bearing. Considering the occasion, he was dressed almost formally, in wool slacks and blue blazer with a starched white shirt.

'Welcome to Rome, gentlemen. I'd hoped the subject of Pero Matek would never come up again in my presence, but I'm hardly surprised it has. Too nice a day to stay indoors, so I thought we'd go out on the balcony. Coffee?'

'Please,' both men answered, and he nodded to Maria.

'One little matter first, if you don't mind. If you brought any identification from the Tribunal, I'd like to see it.'

Vlado glanced at Pine as they pulled out their wallets, fishing ID cards from the small stack of lira they'd picked up at the airport. Fordham gave the cards a long look, comparing their faces to the photos before handing everything back, offering no apology for his apparent mistrust.

They took seats on the balcony, a trifle uneasy after that display. From Vlado's quick inspection the apartment had seemed a spartan place, with few signs of the clutter that usually filled the homes of the old, especially the prosperous ones who had travelled widely. No collections of photos or relics or memorabilia. Only one or two paintings. The furniture might have been from an upscale hotel, it was so generic. The balcony offered the lushest display – a floor of painted tiles with an ironwork table and chairs, enclosed by tall hovering plants in giant terracotta pots. It was like some nook in a forest. Before sitting, Vlado briefly sampled the view – a torrent of pedestrians and mopeds streaming downhill from the Colosseum, which glowed in the near distance in the amber of late afternoon.

'One more thing before we start,' Fordham said. 'Were you followed on your way here?'

Pine seemed taken aback. 'We, uh, pretty much came straight from the hotel,' he said finally. 'And we went straight from the airport to the hotel. I guess I wasn't really looking out for it. It's not exactly part of our training.'

'I suppose not,' Fordham said, sounding disappointed. Pushing himself to his feet, he stepped gingerly towards the edge of the balcony, leaning out to allow a view without revealing himself to anyone below.

'There's a man down there,' he said, returning to his seat. 'Doorway across the street, reading a newspaper. Blue jacket, green tie. Showed up just before you arrived. He with you?' He looked first at Pine, then at Vlado.

Neither had any idea who he meant. Pine got up for a glance, but Fordham hastily motioned him back to his seat.

'No sense attracting further attention. Probably nothing. Just a feeling.'

'You know, it's *us* looking for *him*,' Pine said, trying to strike a note of levity. 'Not the other way around.'

'It's not Pero Matek I'm worried about. It's the other ones.'

'The other ones?' Vlado said.

'The problem is that neither of you has any idea what you're dealing with. Just like I didn't.'

'That's why we're here,' Pine coaxed. 'To find out.'

'I may be doing us all a disservice by telling you. These things happened a long time ago, but in some quarters they haven't lost their currency, or their potency. It has a long half-life, this kind of information. Some of it should have been buried in lead and locked away.' He turned towards Vlado. 'You should know that as well as anyone, I'd expect. Are you his son, or is the connection more distant? I'm referring to Enver Petric of course, born Josip Iskric.'

'My father,' Vlado said, feeling as if his one advantage in the interview had been stripped away. How had the man worked it out so easily? Surely not from the Tribunal. Maybe it was the sort of deductive leap made possible by an overly suspicious, even paranoid mind. Yet, for an irrational moment, Fordham seemed like some sort of spirit guide, an eccentric old mystic who could gaze through the foliage of his balcony into the mist of the past. His blue eyes glinted. Powerful emotions were at play, but Vlado couldn't read them.

'I suspected you might be his son the moment I heard your name. When you walked in the door I was certain. Those eyes. The way you listen. That earnest quality.'

That word again. Vlado winced.

'It's the only reason I agreed to see you at all. Even then, that woman who called nearly put me off enough to refuse.'

'Janet Ecker?' Pine said. 'What'd she say?'

'It's not what she said. It's the way she was. Like the man I just saw across the street. Again, nothing definite. Just a feeling. Schmoozed me just like they would. People from the Agency. The ones who've been coming round here for years, trying to get a rise out of me. I guess I was worried she might be from their world instead of yours.'

Vlado and Pine exchanged glances. The old man's

precautions suddenly didn't seem so fussy, and certainly not laughable.

'It's not easy,' Fordham said, 'breaking cover like this. Maybe I'm still seeking expiation. Forgiveness of sins. Though God knows I'm not Catholic.'

'Expiation?' Vlado asked.

'That part comes later,' he said, still unreadable. 'Patience.'

He stood, creeping again to the edge of the terrace, leaning the way he had before. Apparently satisfied, but revealing nothing, he returned to his seat.

'What do you know about those days, anyway?' he asked Vlado. 'Your father ever tell you much?'

'Nothing. I didn't even know he'd lived here until a few days ago.'

Fordham nodded, apparently unsurprised. 'Then I suppose the only way to tell you this story correctly is to take you to the scene of the crime,' he said. Vlado wondered uneasily what the crime might be. 'Besides, it's a fine Roman afternoon, and this weather won't last. Come on. I'll call us a cab.'

When they emerged downstairs there was no sign of the man with the newspaper and the green tie.

The ride was a strange one. They changed cabs twice, and Fordham spoke only to the drivers, waving off their questions. They rode north through the city, up past the ruins of the Forum, then along crowded streets past the shoppers and off-season tourists, squeezing past the top of the Spanish Steps before veering west towards the river. Not until they caught the third taxi, by the

Tiber, did Fordham stop turning incessantly to look out the back.

Settling at last into his seat, he said, 'What do you know about the way things worked here in nineteen forty-six?'

'Just what we've seen in the cables,' Pine said. 'And those weren't rich on context.'

Fordham nodded. 'The city itself wasn't so different. It was the people who were an unholy mess. Refugees from half of Europe, and nobody had a dime. But if you were on the run or had something to hide, it was a great place to be. The Italians were too busy purging each other to worry much about other nationalities. The politics would go left one week, right the next. Just like today, only now it's every month. The carabinieri pretty much left it up to us and the British to sort out the foreigners. Croatians and Ustashe were my department. I was one of eight officer investigators with the 428th CIC detachment. Army Counterintelligence. We had a little office at 69 Via Sicilia. British Intelligence was upstairs, thinking they still ruled the waves. Then there were the leftovers from OSS, James Angleton and his people, technically still working for the army even if officially without portfolio. The CIA wasn't born yet. Angleton was a strange one. Tall and skinny. Wore a big coat, big hat. One of our people went to see him once and found him crawling on the floor, checking for microphones. Which of course made us wonder if he'd bugged *us*. He was already more worried about Moscow than surviving Nazis. Hated Tito. Saw any Ustashe types as potential allies.'

'Were there a lot of Croatians here?' Vlado asked. 'And Bosnians?'

'Thousands. Coming out of the DP camps or down through Austria. A lot of them wanted to get to Argentina or America. Ante Pavelic himself ended up as Juan Peron's security adviser, you know. There should have been a song about him in *Evita*. We were supposed to be rounding them up, but somehow they kept slipping through the cracks, mostly with the help of an evacuation network run by some Croatian priests, over at the Cofraternity of San Girolamo. That's where we're headed. San Girolamo. Father Krunoslav Draganovic ran the show there. He was also head of the Pope's Relief Commission for Refugees, which tied him in to all the DP camps. Sometimes they sent people back across the border, with our help, to plant bombs or generally raise hell. But mostly they shipped all their bad eggs to safety overseas. Gave them new names and put them on freighters to Argentina, the States, Canada, you name it. Everybody called Draganovic's network the Ratline. It's how Klaus Barbie got away.'

'The Butcher of Lyon?'

'Yes. It was more than a little embarrassing when it came out later that we'd helped him get away, with Draganovic pulling the strings. The cover-up said Barbie was the exception, not the rule.'

'You don't agree?' Pine said.

'Nobody would who was here then. But the proof's gone by now, of course. Which is why I keep my mouth shut.'

He paused to give further instructions to the driver.

They were still headed up the Tiber, in traffic growing heavier by the minute. The dome of St Peter's loomed in the distance to their left.

'The day I met Matek I was looking for a Nazi. An old SS man we kept rounding up and the British kept letting go. Fiorello, our CO, was determined we were going to keep picking him up until the Brits kept him locked up. That's the way it was then. You were never sure who was on your side one day to the next. We had a list of his mistresses, and we'd visit them one by one until he turned up. I drew Inge, who I always thought of as Marlene Dietrich, mostly because of the way she talked. She lived in a run-down old pension on Via Abruzzi, a place full of exiles. Always smelled like boiled cabbage.

'Well, Inge was in, but our SS man wasn't. He'd dumped her for some new gal across town, so I phoned in the name from downstairs and decided to check the books. That's how we made the rounds then, checking registration records then visiting the newcomers, making sure their papers were in order. Just about everybody had some kind of information, and usually all it took to get it was a few cigarettes. And that day, Matek's name was the latest entry. So I paid him a call.'

'You spoke the language?' Vlado asked.

'Serbo-Croatian? Some. But Matek had learned some Italian at Fermo. He'd just arrived, and was pretty skinny after all that time in the camp. It was clear his papers were a rush job, but he had that look in his eye that dared you to do something about it. He said Father Draganovic himself had got him out of Fermo, so right

292

away he had my interest. The father had driven down to the camp in a US Army staff car, which somehow didn't surprise me. He'd held a Mass for a few hundred Croatians, then asked anybody with special requests to see him afterwards. Matek had got a job at San Girolamo working as a typist and driver, which piqued my interest further. I'd been trying to get a hold of some information there for months.'

'What kind of information?'

'They kept a master list of all the émigrés – names, aliases, military rank – everybody they'd ever housed or fed or were trying to ship out, including all the big Ustashe types in hiding. We'd turned another worker who was supposed to slip us a copy, but a week later they fished him out of the Tiber. So you had to be careful.'

'Did Matek tell you his military background?' Vlado asked.

'A few lies. But we didn't concern ourselves too much with that, because within a few days an order came down from Washington to go after Pavelic, the dictator himself, and suddenly Matek was our best bet for an insider.'

'This was when?' Pine asked.

'June nineteen forty-six. Tito's people had been screaming for months that we were hiding Pavelic in Italy. I think somebody in Washington finally got tired of hearing it.'

'Were we?' Pine asked. 'Hiding him?'

'We certainly hadn't been looking for him. Especially people like Angleton. But our guys were game for the chase, and the word around town was that Pavelic was holed up at Castelgandolfo, the Pope's summer residence, out with the peacocks and chicken coops. Supposedly some of his old security chiefs and cabinet members were there too. The only way to know for sure was to get that list out of San Girolamo. And damned if we didn't, with Matek's help.'

The taxi reached its destination, stopping by the bridge at Ponte Cavour, beneath the leafless sycamores lining the Tiber.

'Best to keep moving as we talk,' Fordham said, looking around quickly as they crossed a busy street. 'Makes it harder to eavesdrop.'

Pine rolled his eyes.

They walked into a modest but spacious piazza, one side of which faced the boulevard by the river. There was a high grassy mound at the centre of the square that seemed to glow in the evening light. Bordering the other three sides were long five-storey buildings of fairly recent vintage, by Roman standards, boxy and severe, with rows of narrow rectangular windows. The ones on the north and east sides were made of scrubbed white marble, but the one at the south end was ugly brown brick. It was joined to a faded dark chapel that looked centuries old.

'The mound is the mausoleum of Caesar Augustus,' Fordham said. 'Everything else in the square is a Mussolini creation, and that damned ugly hunk of bricks at the south end is San Girolamo. The Croatians couldn't afford the marble, I guess. But it worked well enough for Draganovic and his Ratline.'

Fordham pointed to the marble walls of the nearest building, just behind them. Beneath the windows were carvings of ancient Roman armies but also of the Fascist armies of the Second World War. Latin inscriptions ran overhead, with Mussolini's name prominent, along with a reference to his distant predecessor, Augustus.

'Hard to believe it's still here,' Vlado said, having grown used to Berlin, where every remnant of the Nazis had been bombed, buried or annotated to museum status.

San Girolamo also displayed the art of the era, with three huge, colourful mosaics looming above the fifth-floor windows. Jesus was in the centrepiece, a fawning crowd at his feet. The two flanking pieces featured priests ministering to crowds, presumably in Croatia. The inscriptions on this building were also in Latin, although the checkerboard symbol of Croatia was featured prominently. There was spray-painted graffiti on the bricks – a skull and crossbones topped by the words 'Gioventu Nazista'.

'What does Gioventu mean?' Vlado asked.

'Youth,' Fordham said. 'Nazi Youth. Guess they still feel comfortable here.'

The place made Vlado edgy, and for the first time in all his travels he could sense his father's lingering presence, a wan ghost in worn clothing drifting beneath these words and images, saluting an armed guard on his way through the door. Such petty players, his country-men, in these great struggles of the continent; instigators and assassins who lit the bonfire of Europe then went off to fight among themselves. Even the great

295

Pavelic, killer of millions, had been a sort of nothing here, hiding in cassocks and convents, then sailing in the belly of a freighter under an assumed name.

'Looks like the Croatians felt right at home here,' Pine said.

'Oh, they were great allies. Another Catholic nation getting cosy with Germany, and right across the Adriatic. It was a friendship for the ages, which is why the Vatican took it so hard when Tito gained power.'

'But if they couldn't afford the marble,' Vlado asked, 'how did they afford the Ratline?'

'Draganovic supposedly had a few crates of gold right there in his office. Looted from the State Bank of Croatia as the war was ending.'

Vlado remembered the reference to Matek leaving Zagreb in a convoy of trucks carrying 'assets of the State'. No wonder the good father had helped him get out of the DP camp.

'Probably had two hundred pounds of it. The British helped him bring it up from a monastery in Austria.'

They paused, facing the brown walls of San Girolamo. The mosaics were barely visible in the fading light.

'Can we go inside?' Vlado asked.

'You might be able to talk your way in. But everything will be locked up. Just like on that weekend in forty-six.'

'Matek had a key?'

'Several. To file drawers and offices. He'd stolen them, of course. Just for a day or two. Had us copy them, and kept a few of the copies for himself. That was part of his bargain.'

'What else did he ask for?'

'Oh, he wanted the moon. But no cash, we insisted. So he came up with a wish-list. Quite eclectic. A few tools. Some cigarettes. But mostly a lot of passes and travel documents, for freedom of movement. We weren't giving him those until he'd got us the goods, of course. He also wanted documents for a friend. A confederate. He'd concluded he couldn't pull it off without an extra set of hands.'

Vlado let that sink in a moment.

'My father.'

'Yes.'

'So that's when you met him.'

'Just before the break-in. I had to make sure we approved. And I did, with reservations.'

'Because of his war record?'

Fordham nodded grimly. 'But probably not in the way you think.' He looked around, as if worried again about eavesdroppers. No-one was in sight, but darkness was falling. The air was chilly.

'Gentlemen, if we're to continue, and if I'm to give you what you really came for, there are better places to talk about things like this. That blue van over there's been giving me the creeps since we got here.' Neither Vlado nor Pine had noticed it. 'And some of it I'm still not sure I should be telling you. For your own good, as well as mine.'

'Meaning what?' asked Pine, who was still looking around for the blue van.

Fordham pursed his lips, suddenly looking older than he had all afternoon.

'Meaning that just because it's fifty years old doesn't mean it's lost its ability to do harm. Even to kill. But after fifty years, I suppose it's finally time for me to come clean.' He turned towards Vlado. 'With you, in particular.'

18

Another three-taxi relay took them to a restaurant called Rimini's. It was one of Fordham's favourites, and he apologized personally to the proprietor for arriving so early. It was barely 6 p.m.

'No better than tourists. But we'll pretty much have the place to ourselves.'

Even so, Fordham was edgy whenever a waiter approached, eyeing the kitchen door at the sound of every coming or going. Rimini himself seated them near the back, then paced nearby for a while, as if unsure what to make of these sullen early arrivals. It was a good ten minutes before he brought them menus.

Vlado was hungrier for information than food, but not until Rimini took their orders did Fordham return to the subject.

'Meeting your father was Matek's idea. He'd told your father I might be able to help him return home. Of course, Matek didn't tell me any of this until five minutes before the meeting. Said it would be up to me to bring up our plans for San Girolamo. So I handled it very clumsily.'

'Was Matek there?'

'In the hallway. It was at your father's pension, which was worse than Matek's.' Fordham flinched as a waiter materialized with the first course – a bounty of antipasti in bright reds and greens.

Vlado tried to imagine Fordham as a young man, the face smooth and well fed, the swagger of a soldier whose war was won.

'So you told him about the plan,' he prompted.

'Not completely. Didn't want him running back to Draganovic with the details.'

'Did you think he might?'

'Not really. As a driver he'd ferried around enough of the father's guests to realize the sort of business they were in, the power they could wield. And everyone had heard about the poor fellow fished out of the Tiber. So the minute I raised the possibility of procuring a little information, he shut down. Asked me to leave.'

'Did you?'

'I was too defeated and embarrassed not to. But I came back.'

'He changed his mind?'

'No. Turns out Matek had been counting on your father to refuse, but he'd wanted me to see what we were up against. Matek believed your father's reluctance only made him more desirable. He didn't want to work with anyone who didn't have a healthy fear of Draganovic. He said the key was making your father fear us more.'

'How?'

'With his security file. By putting him in a position where he'd either have to help us or be revealed to the authorities. Your father had spent some time as a guard at Jasenovac.' Fordham hesitated, lowering his fork. 'You knew that, I hope.'

Vlado nodded. His stomach clenched, and he gently put down his fork.

'But of course that wasn't enough for Matek. He wanted to rig up the worst possible dossier – massacres, atrocities, eyewitness accounts – then show it to him and say, play ball or else.'

Vlado flushed and glanced at Pine, who had also put down his fork and was staring intently at Fordham. Pine's expression seemed both embarrassed and angry. Remembering the vivid account he'd read two days earlier, Vlado wondered now how much had been fiction. He felt a jealous anger brewing, this time on his father's behalf.

'So his father's file is all a lie?' Pine said, barely in a whisper.

'Pretty much. As far as anything detailed goes, anyway.'

'And you agreed to this plan?' Vlado said, leaning forward, his voice rising.

'Please.' Fordham looked around nervously. 'I didn't, in fact. I checked with Fiorello, just in case, and he agreed. Matek would have to find somebody else. Someone we could lure with a carrot, not a stick.'

'But that's not how it worked out, was it?'

Fordham shook his head, looking doleful. He dabbed his mouth with a napkin. 'We were pressured from upstairs. Someone at the embassy. Young hotshot from Washington on special assignment from State. He'd been making the rounds in Europe, and had taken a personal interest in the hunt for Pavelic, so he calls me over to his suite at the Grand Hotel. Big corner room with the windows open and the shutters thrown back. "You have a job to do, Robert," he says. "And I'd hate to see a fine career ruined because of some philosophical objection." It was get in line or get out of the way. So we got in line. And it turned out that Matek and your father weren't the only players in the deal.'

'Who else?' Vlado was terse now, an interrogator in tone and demeanour. All that was missing was the bright lamp. If he could have he would have tied Fordham to the chair and made him stew until it hurt.

'There was an agent Angleton wanted to run. Some low-level Ustashe hiding out at a convent. He was going to take a radio and explosives, cross the border and raise hell. After a year of good deeds, they'd give him safe passage to the United States. But he had a dirty file. Dirty as they come.'

'So you switched his file with my father's.'

'Not switched. We wouldn't have wanted any Jasenovac reference in his dossier. But his records made a convenient case history for your father. Real witnesses talking about real events.'

'I know. I've read them.'

Fordham swallowed heavily, then nodded. 'It let us kill two birds with one stone, as it were. Gave our operative a new identity and put your father in chains, figuratively speaking. Not that the operative ever amounted to much. Tito's people caught him inside a week. Shot him.' Fordham turned his eyes to his plate, sopping up a puddle of oil with a crust of bread.

Vlado reached across the table and grabbed Fordham's hand, squeezing the wrist, then leaned into his face.

'You're not eating anything until you've finished talking!'

Pine watched open-mouthed but did nothing to stop Vlado. Fordham glanced nervously at a couple that had just entered the restaurant, but this only drew further ire.

'Don't look at them,' Vlado hissed. 'Don't look anywhere but at me until you're done. I want to know exactly what happened next. Every detail. When did you tell my father?'

'The following week.' Fordham's voice was shaky, barely audible. He looked at the hand gripping his wrist with an expression of alarm. Vlado eased his grip, but not his gaze. 'I took the file over to his pension.'

'What did he say?'

'Told me it wasn't him. Said he'd heard stories, seen some things he hadn't liked, but nothing like this.'

'Did he say what he *had* done?'

Fordham shook his head. 'And I didn't ask. That would have been admitting we'd doctored his file. But at some level he must have known what had happened, because he said, "This is Pero's doing, isn't it?" I said I didn't know what he was talking about. That we'd pushed Matek the same way we'd pushed him. I knew he didn't believe me. He was angry. He . . . grabbed me for a minute. By the wrists.' Fordham looked away, and Vlado flushed in spite of himself. Slowly he let go of Fordham. 'Then he sat down on the bed.'

'And he agreed?'

'Not at first. Said he could embarrass us as much as we could embarrass him. I told him to go ahead and try.

303

I told him we'd throw him back across the border with a big U sewn to his britches and a rap sheet a mile long. They'd shoot him at sunrise. And with that he gave up. Besides, we were still offering what he wanted most: the opportunity to go home. Work for us, I told him, and we'd make the file go away. Give him a new identity, clean as a whistle: Enver Petric, the village farm boy who'd sat out the war, and an ethnic Muslim into the bargain.'

So this was where Vlado's name had come from: a lying spy and a murderous scoundrel. Vlado then asked the question that had been lurking behind his anger all along, although he wasn't yet sure he was ready for the answer.

'What was my father's actual record then?' His stomach fluttered as if he'd just leaped from a diving board.

'I never allowed myself to read it,' he said.

'Never *allowed* yourself?' Vlado's fist struck the table. Pine placed a hand lightly on his arm. The couple at the front table looked up with startled expressions, and a waiter approaching briskly with a tray full of steaming platters paused in mid-step. They waited in silence while he distributed the food, but Vlado didn't take his eyes off Fordham.

'I was afraid of how clean it might be,' Fordham said quietly, after the waiter departed. 'Although he *had* been at Jasenovac. That I knew for sure.'

'But only for a few months,' Vlado countered, some of the steam gone from his voice. 'And it was right at the end of the war.'

'Look,' Fordham said, and for once he didn't seem to care if he was overheard, 'I don't defend what I did. But do you have any idea how many people they could kill at Jasenovac in just a month? Let alone two. Or by what means? Are you at all familiar with how they concluded their business at the time your father would have been present?'

Vlado said nothing.

'Well, I'll tell you, since you're so eager for *every* detail.'

Now it was Vlado who was looking around the room.

'Look,' Pine interrupted, 'I really don't see any need to—'

'I do,' Vlado said. 'Let him finish.'

Fordham nodded soberly. 'I've been feeling guilty about this for more than fifty years. I should have owned up to it long ago. Should never have been a party to it. But even if your father did nothing but dig latrines he knew what he knew and held his tongue. He kept it all to himself while murderers like Matek walked free. OK, so we found a way to shut him up. But why hadn't he spoken up earlier? As an investigator, you know as well as anyone what it means to conceal the guilt of others.'

'Believe me,' Vlado said, feeling a queasy kinship, 'I know.'

'So did they even carry out the burglary?' Pine asked.

'Oh, with flying colours. First Saturday night in July. While I waited across the square in a jeep. After an hour they came lumbering out with a couple of boxes like they owned the place. None of the guards even raised an eyebrow. Amazing. Matek had a big bulge in one of his coat pockets, a fat envelope he'd stuffed in there for himself. We spent the rest of the night photographing everything so we could and put it all back on Sunday. It was a windfall – every name of every émigré, including their aliases. Enough to keep us busy for weeks. But of course there were gaps, too. Correspondence with the Vatican that we'd expected to see. Correspondence with Angleton, too, which personally I wanted as much as anything. I wanted to put him out of business.'

'You think that was the sort of thing Matek kept for himself? The envelope in his pocket?'

'That's my bet. At first I thought he'd turned it over to Angleton, that Matek had been working for him as well. Later I wasn't so sure. But it would have been some of the biggest sticks of dynamite in the whole barrel.'

'Then why didn't you withhold his passes?'

'I tried. I was overruled. The man upstairs again.'

'Who was he?' Pine asked.

Fordham smiled ruefully. 'It's the one question I haven't yet decided whether to answer. It's the one name they'd still want me to keep to myself. But I suppose if I wanted to play it safe I shouldn't have met with you at all. They'll assume the worst anyway.'

He paused for a moment, as if collecting himself. He dabbed his face with a napkin, then gestured towards the food.

'Do try some of this before it gets cold. It's quite the best there is in Rome. There's fish coming too, along with a little veal.' Then he took a bite.

Vlado was willing to indulge him for the moment.

Fordham raised his glass of wine, as if he was about to propose a toast. But all he spoke was a name.

'Samuel Colleton.'

'He was the man upstairs?'

'Well, well,' Pine said.

'Who is Samuel Colleton?' Vlado asked.

'Number two man at the State Department. But the job he really wants – has always wanted – is to be head man at the Agency. And that job comes open when the current director retires in May. Colleton's not the only contender, of course, and he's the oldest, a disadvantage. But apparently a certain momentum has been building, a feeling that maybe the old man deserves one last moment of glory – a sort of lifetime achievement award. Which is why any hint of scandal from his past would sink him. Reputations are at stake, gentlemen. And perhaps more.'

'Harkness,' Pine said.

'Pardon?' Fordham said.

'Paul Harkness. A State Department operative out of Sarajevo. He helped put together our botched operation. Technically, Harkness works for Colleton, and might still be working for him if Colleton gets the promotion.'

'Ah,' Fordham said. '*That* kind of diplomat.' He chuckled mirthlessly, relaxing for the first time in a while, shaking his head as he scooped another bundle of noodles onto his plate. 'These kinds of things always end the same, don't they? Just as you're ready to make your move, your operation goes to hell in a handbasket, and nobody on the ground ever knows why. Exactly what happened to us with Pavelic.'

307

'Someone botched it?' Vlado said.

'New orders from Washington, right after the break-in. Our hunt was postponed until further notice, leaving us dead in the water. Then Matek sank us.'

'Matek?'

'He skedaddled. And I got the sack. All after a big mess over at Draganovic's personal quarters, at 21 Borgo Santo Spirito, right next to St Peter's. Official Vatican property, so you couldn't touch him there. But the sidewalk out front was fair game, and Matek phoned me from over there a week after the break-in. Said if we came right away we'd find the ones we'd been looking for, arriving in a car with diplomatic tags. We presumed he meant Pavelic, riding around in Draganovic's car. But we'd have to grab him between the car and the front gate. Violating Vatican extraterritoriality was the great taboo. So a couple of us rushed over there knowing it would be a close shave.'

'I thought you'd been ordered off the case?'

'But no-one had said what to do if he fell into our lap. We drove over, parked around the corner and waited on the sidewalk. Ten minutes later a black car with diplomatic tags comes cruising in. We grabbed the first two guys out. Didn't recognize either one, but we had to do something, so we said we were taking them in for questioning. But by then there was a huge commotion. A bunch of nuns had come down the steps to see what all the fuss was about. They're shouting, lecturing us in Italian, Croatian, English. You'd have thought it was Christmas Eve in St Peter's, we had such a mob.

'Somewhere in the middle of all this I notice a truck pulling out from an alley just down the street. I got a glance at the driver, and I could have sworn it was Matek. Grinning. And all I could think was that we'd been had. But we took the two fellows back to Via Sicilia anyway. Checked their names against our list of suspects, and of course they weren't on it. So we apologized. And I think it might have blown over if not for the official complaint. The worst kind. An eyewitness claimed we'd violated extraterritoriality. Said we'd grabbed them inside the gates. And the complaint was filed directly to Angleton, who was going to make sure it stuck.'

'One of the nuns?'

'No. A clerk named Pero Matek. With a corroborating account from Josip Iskric.'

'But you were his meal ticket,' Pine said.

'His *expired* meal ticket. From then on I could only have been a hindrance. The next morning we were hauled in to see the ambassador. I was packing my bags by the end of the week. Transferred to Vienna, where I spent a year carrying messages between the British and the Americans, in an office where everybody knew about my great fuck-up. The following year, of course, Ante Pavelic caught a freighter to Argentina.'

'Great,' Pine said, shaking his head.

'Yes. Perfect. So at the end of my hitch I went back to Harvard. Got my degree and put in for the Foreign Service. Passed the exam but never got a posting. Failed the security clearance. Thanks to my good friends back in Rome.'

309

He paused, looking off into space, then resumed in a quieter tone.

'Years later I ran into Fiorello in Boston. Ancient by then. Cataracts and hypertension. Died the following spring, so I guess he was wanting to square accounts. He told me a story that had made the rounds after I'd shipped out. Around the time of the break-in, Draganovic had apparently got skittish about his crates of gold, the stuff they'd looted from Zagreb. Decided that the office wasn't safe enough, so he'd moved them to his place at Borgo Santo Spirito, where we'd made our famous "arrest". But both crates were stolen by two nameless conspirators who vanished into the mist, destination unknown.'

'Matek and Iskric.'

'That was my guess. Since then I've always wondered if all we were doing that day outside the gates was providing a noisy diversion for a heist. Fiorello said no-one came out of the affair very happy, including Angleton's people. They were kind of uneasy for a while, as if more than just gold had been lost.'

'Stolen information?' Vlado said.

'Maybe. The best way to hurt an Angleton is to steal his secrets. And talk about a long half-life. That stuff would still be radioactive.'

'So no-one ever saw them again? Matek or my father?'

'Not a trace. But I did hear something just before I left for Vienna. The Croatians had reported a stolen truck, and the morning before I caught my train they found it. Empty, of course, and out of gas. On the side of the road, just outside Naples.'

Vlado thought of the photo of his father and the unknown woman, standing in the citrus grove, with Matek, near the town he'd never heard of.

'Calvin, where's your map of Italy?' he said.

He pulled the photo from his satchel as Pine shuffled through a briefcase. They awkwardly unfolded the map, shoving plates aside with a clanking of china and silver. Vlado checked the name of the town stamped on the back of the photo.

'Near Naples, you said?'

Fordham nodded, smiling now, as if suddenly caught up in the spirit of their chase. 'Yes. Practically at the foot of Mount Vesuvius.'

'Castellammare di Stabia,' Vlado said, thumping a finger in triumph against a spot on the map. 'Right across the bay from Naples. Not far from Vesuvius.'

Pine broke into a smile. 'I'd guess we'll be staying at least another day in Italy,' he said to Vlado.

19

Vlado was woken the next morning by the sound of voices, a conversation drifting just beyond reach. The sensation was so vivid that he groggily got out of bed to open the door, half expecting to find a pair of young men outside dressed in the clothes of the 1940s. But the hotel landing was empty, every door closed.

It was barely light, not even seven, on his last morning in Rome – his first and only one as well, he reminded himself. Time to get moving if he was ever to catch up with the wandering spirit of his father. Lead me to Matek, he thought. Show me the way to your old enemy.

Coming more fully awake, he splashed his face at the bathroom sink, realizing that the voices he'd heard had been the last snatches of conversation from a waking dream – the young Fordham and the young Enver Petric, squared off in his father's shabby room somewhere across the city. For a fleeting moment, as he inspected his dripping face in the mirror, he was oddly certain that if he were to climb to the hotel rooftop he'd be able to pinpoint exactly where the conversation had taken place. It would stand out like a tiny beacon on the horizon, shining among the TV antennas in the blushing haze.

But Vlado had another destination in mind; a final

stop before he and Pine journeyed south. He threw on his clothes and went downstairs, heading into the street. He craved coffee but didn't want to waste time in the hotel. The strange weather was holding, so the morning chill was bearable, and within a few blocks his stride loosened. He unbuttoned his overcoat, taking in the smells of baking bread and brewing coffee. The Romans were throwing open their shutters to the morning, heeding the Sunday call of ringing church bells.

A few blocks later he crossed the Tiber and gazed down at the greenish-brown water, flecked with litter. The same current had scoured centuries of empire and conquest, outlasting all the barbarians and Fascists and occupying armies. His father had taken just such a walk, perhaps, on just such a morning, a devout young Catholic on his way to Mass. Yet he'd been willing to forsake name and religion to return home. Why, then, had he remained in Italy for fifteen years? And what had finally driven him back across the border?

It took ten minutes to reach the periphery of St Peter's Square, where the cathedral's huge dome filled the sky. Cutting left up an alley he reached a narrow cobbled lane, which he knew from his map would be Borgo Santo Spirito. Checking the house numbers, he made his way to number 21, at the end of the block, only a stone's throw from the colonnade round the massive empty square. The building was still a convent, five storeys of beige stucco and arched windows, just as Fordham had described it. This was where Draganovic had lived but, more important, where Matek and his father had last been seen, presumably while making their boldest move, escaping Rome with a truckload of someone else's war booty.

Out front, someone had just hosed down the brick pavement. An iron gate beneath a stone archway led up a long flight of marble steps to the entrance. There was a small plaque on the front wall: 'Zona Extraterritoriale Vaticano'. Even now, you couldn't make an arrest here, and Vlado smiled at the thought of the young Fordham standing at this very spot, cursing his luck. But the building itself was a disappointment. Somehow he'd hoped – irrationally, he knew – that it might offer some sign, or message. But the plaster walls were mute, the windows stared blankly. The same was true of the alley just down the lane, where Fordham must have spotted Matek's grinning face in the window of the departing truck. There were no portals into the past here. Nothing but the rainwater smell of the rinsed cobbles, the lonely whine of a Vespa from the next street. His excitement from earlier that morning drained away. What had he been thinking? The key to everything was not so much the past, he realized, as it was those who had survived it, then twisted history to their devices. Look forward not back, he told himself, unless you wish to be blindsided.

Vlado solemnly began retracing his steps back towards the hotel. By now, a dull ache in his forehead was fairly screaming for caffeine, so he stopped at a bakery that was just opening for the day. He ordered a roll and an espresso, and sat at a small pavement table. He stirred in a lump of sugar and sipped from the tiny cup, strangely deflated, watching an ageing priest in a black frock beetle his way towards St Peter's. Then a voice came at him from behind, strong and clear and very American.

'It's really a mistake, you know, going to all these old places. Your father's world is gone, and so is he. Let it rest.'

It was Harkness.

He pulled up a chair and leaned forward, the big pink face only a foot from Vlado's. He was decked out neatly in a sports jacket and pressed slacks, every bit the country gentleman, looking as if he'd shaved, showered and already read the Sunday papers. Harkness was still two steps ahead of them, Vlado realized, right where he must have been all along.

'I only say this for your own good, of course.' He was smiling now.

'Of course,' Vlado said, too shocked to say much else. 'So why are you following me?'

Harkness ignored the question. 'A word of advice, if you care to listen. Not that anyone has so far. None of this will help you find Matek. It might lead you in the right direction for a while. But in the end he'll outsmart you or kill you. Or just when you're ready to make your move, the Tribunal will jerk back your leash. Pine's bosses don't operate in a vacuum, you know, and soon enough they'll realize the two of you, as well as your little friend Janet Ecker, have wandered into places that have nothing to do with Tribunal business and everything to do with mine.'

The name Colleton formed on Vlado's lips, but he resisted the temptation to speak it.

'So you don't want Matek caught?'

Harkness shook his head. 'To the contrary. There's nothing I'd like better. You seem to forget that it was my idea to arrest him.'

'Then what does it matter if we pursue him?'

'Let's just say that things got complicated once he headed for the hills. And it hardly helped when Branko Popovic dropped out of the picture. For good, I'm now told. Meaning that you, in particular, owe me one. Meaning that it would be a very bad idea mentioning any of this conversation to Calvin Pine.' He leaned closer, lowering his voice. 'Besides, you should be home with that family of yours, making sure the police don't get too nosy. LeBlanc's there already, you know. Poking around in Berlin.'

Vlado had heard enough. He reached for the bill, but Harkness was quicker.

'Allow me,' he said, laughing when Vlado tried to snatch it back.

'I don't think Jasmina wants you blowing your pay cheque in overpriced tourist cafés.' Vlado flinched at the mention of his wife's name. 'Which reminds me. He's been calling her again, you know. Our friend Haris. Berlin can be so lonely this time of year. Who knows, maybe he'll make it back there before you do. Unless someone else beats you both to the punch. Branko Popovic didn't operate in a vacuum either, Vlado. He had plenty of friends. You really ought to call home more often, you know. And, please, let's not bump into each other again. The next time it won't be so pleasant. Ciao.'

Harkness got up, paid the bill and headed towards St Peter's, disappearing beneath the shadows of the colonnade without once looking back. Vlado was left standing by his table, where his roll lay uneaten on the plate. Stomach knotted, he walked slowly at first, then quickened his pace, and before he knew it he was running, sweat beading on his forehead, going full tilt for the hotel.

After a few blocks he stopped in confusion. What good would it do, hurrying back, when his phone line would be blocked, as it had been everywhere else? He pulled out his wallet, shuffling through the small stack of lira. There was just enough, only because Harkness had picked up the tab. He stopped in a small *tabacchi* where the proprietor was just rolling open the metal grille, and he bought a 10,000-lira phonecard, hoping it would give him enough minutes to Berlin.

Jasmina picked up on the first ring, sounding sleepy and warm, speaking from their bed.

'Hello. Sorry to wake you, but I've got to hurry. There are only a few minutes on the card.'

'Vlado? Finally.' She sounded relieved. 'It's so good to hear from you.'

'I'm sorry I haven't been able to call.'

'A secretary told me you weren't allowed. She said it might be a week or more, so this is a nice surprise. You're in Sarajevo?'

She didn't sound alarmed, which was something, he supposed. Perhaps Harkness had been bluffing. If so, it had worked.

'I'm in Rome. Since yesterday.'

'And you went without me? I'm insanely jealous.' She laughed, but he thought he detected a nervous edge. Was she alone? Of course she was. Don't be a fool for the man's bluster. 'Sonja will be jealous too. I'd put her on if she was up.'

Vlado checked the digital display on the phone. The card was draining alarmingly fast.

He was already down to 6,000 lira.

'No. Let her sleep.' Vlado already felt guilty for doubting Jasmina. It was Harkness who'd been lying. 'We're driving south today, leaving in an hour. I just wanted to make sure everything there was OK.'

She must have detected the tension in his voice because her tone changed as well.

'She really misses you, Vlado. And so do I. It's too much like during the war.'

'I'm sorry. And I'm glad. It's good to be missed.'

The meter had dropped to 4,000. He had to find some way of warning her, quickly, without either alarming her or having to explain too much. But she pre-empted him.

'Vlado, a strange thing happened yesterday. It upset me.'

'Yes?'

'You remember . . . Haris?'

'Yes. Go on.'

'He telephoned. From Sarajevo. When I first heard the static I thought it was you. He had a message for you. It was you he wanted to speak to, in fact. But he seemed to know you were out of the country.'

The coffee was burning a hole in Vlado's empty

stomach. The meter was down to 3,000. He thought of Harkness, smiling, somewhere out on the streets of Rome, leisurely awaiting his next move.

'What was the message?'

'He said they'd come looking for him, and he wanted to know if you were the reason. I asked what he meant, but he said you'd know, and that he had to go. He sounded scared. Then he hung up.'

So. It hadn't all been a bluff. Maybe none of it.

'What did he mean, they? Who's looking for him?'

'He didn't say. I thought you'd know. I couldn't sleep after he called. What haven't you told me, Vlado? What should Sonja and I do?'

2,000 lira.

'Stay at home, away from work, for a few days. Keep Sonja with you. There's more we need to talk about, but there isn't time now. I've kept too many secrets from you. I'm too much my father's son. I'm sorry, I know I'm not making sense. Go to the Vrancics down the hall if you need help. Go to the police if you have to. But try not to worry. Everything should be OK.'

'Vlado, are you in trouble?'

1,000 lira.

'I might be. I don't know. But I should be finished here in a few days. I'll be home as quickly as I can. I have to go, the phonecard's running out.'

'I love you. Goodbye.'

The connection went dead before he could answer.

'Goddamnit!'

His shout drew the disapproving stare of a passing nun as he slammed down the receiver. Here he was, in a city where cellphones bleated from every pocket, and he couldn't even arrange a decent call home. He cursed Pine, the Tribunal, the city of Rome. Then he cursed Harkness, but the thought of the man's face dimmed his anger with apprehension. His first impulse was to try and catch the next plane to Berlin. To hell with everyone else.

But that was exactly what Harkness wanted. And no matter how ruthless the man might be, Vlado doubted he was the sloppy type. His threats had hit home, but Vlado's gut feeling was that he'd exaggerated to make a point. Perhaps he'd even found Haris and put him up to making the call. How else would he have discovered by now that Popovic was dead? Did Popovic still have goons out there? Probably. But they'd be fighting over the leftovers, more dangerous to each other than to him or his family. Or so he hoped. What had Harkness called it during the meeting in Sarajevo? 'Whistling past the graveyard.' Another American idiom that seemed all too apt.

He felt a keen sense of urgency, as if the meter on the phone was still clicking downwards. He'd have to be more careful than ever, and faster, more efficient. If they didn't find Matek within the next day or so, they might never, and all remaining secrets would stay buried.

Back at the hotel room, he found that Pine had slid a note under his door.

'Vlado. I'm picking up the rental car. Back by 9. Calvin.'

Just as well. On the walk back he'd come up with an

idea, and this might give him time to carry it out. If his father and Matek had indeed robbed Draganovic, they wouldn't have relied on fake identities from San Girolamo to help them make their way south. And if their booty included some of Angleton's most embarrassing secrets, they wouldn't have wanted to use the identities furnished by the Americans either. The case file had told him of only one other reliable source for bogus identity in those days, and that was the Red Cross. For once, he had an inside source. He pulled Amira's card from his satchel. If only he had a phone.

He checked the line, just in case, but it was blocked. Ducking into the hall, he saw a maid emerging from a room along the corridor. The door was open. Gently shutting his own door he stepped towards the linen cart, where the maid was collecting a stack of fresh towels.

'*Scusi*,' he said, brushing past her as if he owned the place. You did these things with confidence or you didn't try them at all.

'*Signore?*' she said.

'I'll be right out,' he said briskly. 'Then you can finish.'

Shutting the door behind him and setting the security chain, he saw a man's clothes and a newspaper spread across an unmade bed. He picked up the receiver, punched 8 for an international line. The dial tone sprang to life.

He keyed in Amira's home number, grateful that she'd written it on her card, and as the number rang, it really did feel as if he'd gone back to his life during the siege – his wife had once again become an infrequent, distant voice in Germany, and he was alone and in need of a favour from this woman in Sarajevo who had paid so dearly for helping him the first time.

'Yes?' The voice was drowsy and languorous. He'd woken her, just as he'd woken Jasmina.

'It's Vlado. Vlado Petric.'

'Of course.' As if she wasn't the least surprised. She must have cupped a hand over the receiver, because he heard her speaking to someone else, the words indistinguishable. Probably her foreign boyfriend. And Vlado again felt the irrational stab of jealousy, followed by a flush of guilt.

'Go ahead,' she said, all business now.

'I'm in Rome. But I need some information the Red Cross may have. Old stuff, from fifty years ago.'

'And you thought maybe I could look it up for you.' Not happy about it, but not angry either.

'It's just that, well, I'm not sure that going through official channels would do much good. It's not something they'd be proud of.'

She laughed. Whatever reserve she'd maintained had dissolved. 'And what will it be next time, Vlado? Will you need me to break into a building for you? Go ahead. Tell me what you need. Then I'll decide if you deserve it. Is it for the Tribunal?'

'Yes. But it's personal too.'

'These kinds of things usually are in our country.'

He told her he was looking for records of two Red Cross passports issued in Rome during the last week of June or the first week of July 1946, around the time of the break-in at San Girolamo. Most likely they would have been issued the same day, to males ages 23 and 25. Then he gave her their dates of birth.

'Under what names?'

'That's what I'm trying to find out. They would have wanted new identities. Evidently it was fairly common then.'

'Common now, too. At least in some quarters of the IRC. But I never said that, of course. Let's just say that some employees don't always maintain their spirit of altruism when faced with the prospect of a windfall profit for a few mere documents. Especially during wartime. Especially in shitholes like this.'

'Whatever you say.'

'Do you have a nationality?'

'It was a pair of Yugoslavs, ethnic Croats. But if I had to guess I'd say they'd want to be listed as Italian, so they could stay awhile. Maybe with an address near Trieste, somewhere near the Slovenian border, so it wouldn't be implausible for them to have Slavic accents, or to know Serbo-Croatian.'

'A lot of the older stuff has been computerized. Leave it to the Swiss to digitize every possible record. In which case it's lucky you reached me on a Sunday. I can surf on the office computer with none of the administrators around to ask what I'm up to. Which is no guarantee I'll find it. If it's still only in paper form, I might not be able to track it down until Monday, if then. But you're right about going through official channels. Total waste of time. How'd you end up in Rome?'

'Long story. And we're heading south in half an hour.'

'Still with the American?'

'Yes. Still with the German?'

She laughed. 'I'll do what I can, Vlado. Try me tomorrow at the end of the working day. Here, not at the office.'

'OK. And thanks.'

'No need. The more of the bastards you can put away, the better. Talk to you tomorrow.'

Vlado stepped into the hallway. The maid had disappeared into some other room.

He met Pine in the lobby a few minutes later. It was just before nine, and the rental car was parked out front. Vlado wondered what he should say, if anything, about the morning's events. Nothing, he supposed, given all the warnings. Somehow it seemed safer keeping it all to himself, although it made him feel guilty.

'I called and got us a hotel in Castellammare di Stabia,' Pine said. 'But damned if I've decided what we'll do when we get there, other than spend some more of the Tribunal's money.' Then he smiled and picked up his bags. 'But I guess we've got three hours to come up with an answer. C'mon. Let's hit the road.'

20

As Vlado and Pine were climbing into a rental car in Rome, Pero Matek was gazing out of the window of a train.

It had been a long two days, he reflected, although much easier than the last time, when it had taken months, even years, and every turn had been fraught with either ambush or deception. One enemy after another, from armies to investigators to priests. But he'd had the energy to deal with it then, outwitting all comers even when operating without food or sleep. Now, just one day in a car and a second day aboard trains had exhausted him.

He hadn't helped himself by making the journey longer than necessary. The most direct route would have taken him west by northwest to the Croatian coastline, then up along the shore, cutting the corner at Slovenia towards Trieste — a circuit of the upper Adriatic, like some tourist with his Baedeker. But he'd headed for Austria instead, spending the first night just across the border, waking up in Villach to a warm morning with steam rising from the streets. He'd dumped the car, which had been stolen anyway, and since then it had been trains all the way, zigzagging down the boot of Italy until he found himself in a second-class compartment crawling round the Bay of Naples. The view towards the water was blocked by industry and crumbling apartments, so he turned in his seat to look inland, up towards the imposing brown cone of Vesuvius.

The top was bare, levelled by its last great blast in 1944, only two years before his own arrival. He remembered the way the mountain had been smoking then, a sulphurous steam that had made him uneasy, bringing to mind all those ancients fleeing for their lives at Pompeii and Herculaneum. Panic was the same no matter what its era, and the fear that drove mobs disgusted him.

He thought of the crowds along the northbound road out of Zagreb in the last month of the war, refugees clogging the highway with their carts and bundles, slowed by their belongings when they should have just cut and run.

Or, worse, the crowds during the fighting in the Kosarev Mountains – the churches full of people, all of them screaming while his men encircled the building. The mob had started breaking their own damned stained glass just to try and save themselves, until a few machine-gun bursts convinced them to remain inside. Then the fires had begun, his men pouring petrol by the gallon, wasting it, an inefficient way to do business when you could sell the surplus at a premium. The noise made by the trapped crowd had reminded him of cavitation in the bottom of a kettle as it comes to the boil, when the excited molecules make a clattering noise like fingernails tapping. The angry buzz of

326

hornets in a shaken nest. And you killed them the same way, with smoke and flame, to make sure none would ever sting you. Roasted alive, the propagandists had said later. Well, burned certainly. But by the time the roasting began they'd been dead enough.

He turned from the window. The man next to him was getting up, a bag of apples in his hand. Matek checked the station name. Still five more to go on this rattling local that seemed to stop every mile, dotting the arching coastline all the way to Sorrento, which even at this time of year attracted holidaymakers. He spotted a pair of young Germans with backpacks, a few middle-class Britons and their pale brood. No Americans though, thank God, so the only noise in the carriage came from the Italians, especially the two near the front, arguing loudly above the rattling, their arms moving as if they were conducting an opera, some energetic scene from Puccini. It had turned into an unseasonably warm weekend, so he supposed he had to expect some holiday crowds. The views from the bluffs of Sorrento and Positano would be no less spectacular because it was winter. The swimming pools would still be heated, the restaurants still overpriced, the shops still full of everything that was coveted and useless. But for him there would be only a few calls at a few old stops, a brief interlude to collect on an insurance policy of sorts, a retirement fund, something he'd set aside long ago for some major unforeseeable emergency, for which his current predicament surely qualified.

At last the train screeched and shuddered into his stop, a grimy and crowded port city that he had once called home. Hardly anyone else was getting off here, he noted with pleasure as he stood up with his small canvas bag – he still knew how to travel light. But the journey had drained him. As he made his way down the aisle he felt the fatigue in his calves and at the backs of his eyes. He could never have made the journey of 1945 now. He'd have become one of the thousands left for dead, strafed by the Russian planes and rounded up by the Partisans. Herded into long lines and shot. Then, the mass graves. Had there ever been an era when his countrymen hadn't been digging them?

He walked slowly into the town along narrow streets, and within a few blocks he found a small pension that seemed suitable. It was a bit down-at-heel on the outside, but the room was clean and the rate cheap. The proprietor was kind enough. She was roughly his own age, probably a widow from the way she hovered over him, seemingly with little to do but talk and ask questions. Not that he was answering. His Italian continued to bloom, his fluency returning faster than he would have guessed. Yes, he would do just fine here. And after the woman finally left – a trifle too nosy for his taste, he decided – he threw open the shutters to let in the air.

Beyond a church spire a sliver of the Bay of Naples was visible, glittering in the morning sunlight. And if he leaned just a bit to the left, there it was, the great cone of Vesuvius. He had forgotten the way the volcano dominated the entire basin, the way she made every village seem vulnerable to her brewing and steaming. But she was quiet today, as she had been for years. Like his own life, he reflected. And surely one measure of greatness, whether you were a man or a mountain, was how well you could emerge from dormancy, how deftly, and with how much residual power and skill.

He had some time to rest now. No sense in acting hastily, especially when there might soon be others to contend with. Perhaps by now the investigators had discovered his old identity, and if so they might have discovered other things as well. From the moment he'd heard from his informant Osman in Travnik he'd known he'd have to keep moving for a while. The boy, the son of Enver Petric, had been unnerving enough, turning up out of the blue like that. But then Matek had learned that he was travelling with an American, and the name Calvin Pine had sounded familiar. A short search on the internet had easily turned up the man's background: the War Crimes Tribunal in The Hague. He'd have been a fool to wait for their next visit. Handcuffs and a show trial, the end of everything.

Thinking of them now only made him irritable. His plan to booby trap his office with mines had seemed elegant at the time, but he realized now it had been too imprecise. Better to have simply sent a few thugs down the mountain to murder them in their beds, especially the son of Petric, with his father's eager eyes and earnest determination. The sort who wouldn't give up until you put a bullet through his brain. Instead he had killed neither of them. Just some third wheel. The other three mines hadn't even gone off. Or else Azudin had found some way to fuck it up. He'd cursed when he heard the victim's name on the radio. A fellow he'd never heard of, yet a killing that was just as likely to make them hunt for him. So much for elegance.

And what if they turned up here? Local talent could handle it, of course. It was as easy to find in Italy as it was at home. Easier even, once he'd had a day or so to get the lie of the land. Or he could take care of things himself. The gun was in his bag, and now that he was back on a war footing, it seemed only natural.

But he'd found the radio bulletin yesterday from eastern Bosnia even more disturbing. A botched raid by the French. The escaped general still at large. It was too much of a coincidence that they were both on the run at the same time, and Matek was convinced he would soon have at least one other visitor to keep him company.

He unpacked his bag and sprawled on the bed. Later he would have a nice dinner, some wine – a decent vintage – and a bowl of pasta, nothing too heavy. Then, early tomorrow, he would find the right place to begin doing business, a vantage point that would let him take stock before making his move. But for now, rest.

He laid his head on the pillow and closed his eyes. The surprising warmth of the coastal breeze in November reached him through the shutters which drifted and slapped lightly against the wall. By late tomorrow, there might well be quite a show to watch, and he wanted to be rested for his part in it. As he tumbled towards sleep, he felt like a man with all the time in the world.

21

Vlado, exhausted, fell asleep not long after Pine pulled onto the autostrada heading south, with the windows down and the breeze in his face. He woke later with a start, having no idea where they were, or how much time had passed. It was warmer, the traffic heavier. To the right, the ocean glittered in the distance. Glancing left he was startled to see a huge brown mountain, lopped flat at the top. Vesuvius. He wished Sonja was here to see it. They'd hike the trail to the top. Peer down into the crater.

Pine hadn't yet noticed he was awake, and Vlado watched him. He looked relaxed, steering with one hand, sunglasses shining, an elbow propped on the open window – the very picture of a relaxed American travelling without a care in the world, spiky blond hair tossing in the wind. He was easy to work with, a pleasant fellow. But more to the point, Vlado trusted him, and he had a feeling that was going to be more important than ever in the next few days.

Pine glanced over, saw that Vlado's eyes were open.

'Quite a sight, huh? Wouldn't want to be around when she blows.'

'How much further?'

'Twenty minutes. Maybe thirty with the traffic. You had a pretty good nap. I think you needed it.'

Vlado nodded, still groggy.

'I've been thinking,' Pine said.

'About what?'

'Matek. Him and your father driving down here in that truck. Assuming that was who Fordham saw, of course. I guess we have to assume that or we might as well not be here. Let's say they ran out of gas somewhere around here. They'd have to find some way to keep moving with two crates of gold. Assuming, of course, that they took the crates to begin with.'

'Sounds right for Matek.'

'If you had a bunch of gold bars at your disposal, you'd be able to afford any kind of help to keep you moving. Except you wouldn't exactly be able to melt into the landscape once you started spreading gold around. Matek strikes me as too careful to have done that. He'd have kept it hidden, at least for a while. I also doubt they'd have been able to take much of it with them when they slipped back into Yugoslavia. For that matter, why go back at all when you've taken fifteen years to build a life here and have a nice nest egg salted away. Unless you had to leave, and leave in a hurry. Which is all my way of saying that I think it might still be here. The gold. The documents they stole. All of it. Or whatever they didn't spend in fifteen years. Sound plausible?'

'Sounds like you want it to be plausible.'

'Not much point in us coming here otherwise. Matek would certainly have no reason to come back.'

'Except for the woman, maybe. The one in the picture.'

Pine cocked his head. 'You really think that's his style? To be pining away all these years for a woman?'

'No. Just trying to convince myself too, I suppose. I don't want this to be a dead end.'

'Maybe it isn't, even if he's not here. Spend fifteen years anywhere and there's a good chance that somebody left behind will have an idea of how to find you later.'

'Possibly.'

'Or possibly not. I dunno. The more I think about it, the more I wonder about all our assumptions. They're mostly based on the recollections and conjectures of a paranoid old man. And if all his secrets are so damned dangerous, how's he lived to the ripe old age of, what, seventy-eight?'

That thought silenced them both, and Vlado couldn't help but remember what Harkness had said about their short tether. If he was right, this would be their last stop, whatever happened.

'At least the weather's nice,' Pine said. 'At the worst we'll have a couple days' vacation.'

'With a few more nice meals.'

They drove on, watching the signs for Castellammare.

'So what do you think you'll do when this is all over?' Pine said. 'Now that we've turned your life upside down. Think you'll move back to Bosnia?'

'Hard to say.' He tried not to think of Popovic, or of all the people who might have worked for him, still in the country. Or of Haris, who'd gone back and may have got into a jam. He didn't think Jasmina wanted to go back anyway.

'Jasmina doesn't like Germany, but she likes what's happened to her there. You'd think the ones who lasted out the whole war would be all the tougher for it, but they're not, they're worn out. She's stronger. More forceful. You ought to see her with a German butcher. Fights him by the gram, and comes away gloating about it. She was happy to have me back but she's a different person. Sometimes I like it and sometimes I don't.'

'Sounds like what she said about you.'

'What do you mean?'

'We had a chance to talk in Berlin. While we were waiting for you to get home from work. She said the war had hardened you. And part of it was good. She said there would never be anything that could beat you or break you after you'd survived the siege. But she worried about you, too. All those emotions you'd stored up. She said you'd learned a little too well how to keep things from bubbling to the surface. It's what you'd expect a woman to say about a man, I guess. None of them think we can communicate. But still.'

Vlado nodded, feeling his heartbeat quicken. He desperately wished he was home. If he were there right now he'd finally be able to talk about everything, not just from the past few days but from all seven years. It would come out of him like an illness, a dark liquid purged from his system. Yet there would be sweetness as well. And then he would share a drink or two with Jasmina, and as the night grew still they would slink off to bed, and enjoy a welcome bliss where there was no past but their own.

'How'd you two meet?' Pine asked.

Vlado smiled. 'Like peasants. I was the city boy visiting her village, staying with some old friends of my mother's. There was a big celebration for the Feast of St Damien, the village's patron saint.'

'I thought Jasmina was a Muslim name?'

'It is. But no-one missed a feast like this. Lambs on a spit. A big dance. And it's where all the courtship took place. Especially if your parents were part of the old ways, and hers were. So there I was, the city boy in his blue jeans. I held myself above all that courtly business and the stupid traditional costumes. But they made a big circle and went round and round, dancing the *kolo*. Once that starts you can't help but join in. And I saw this girl on the other side of the circle looking at me, so I smiled back. I think she liked that, liked the fact that a city boy so disdainful of it all still found time to check out the local talent. She was fed up with all the farm boys with thick necks, especially the ones her parents kept picking out. So we spent the evening talking, way too much for her uncles' and aunts' liking, but her mother was OK about it. To hell with tradition for a change.

'After that I started driving out from Sarajevo at weekends, borrowing my father's car. All very formal for a while, and always with a chaperone, but she minded it more than I did. I thought it was rather charming. Romantic. And it was always such a victory when we managed to sneak away.'

Vlado remembered one such time in particular, slipping off to a farm pond during another feast day, darting barefoot through the pines, tiptoeing on his tender city-boy feet in a way that had made her laugh. They reached the water's edge and shed their clothes without a word or a prompt – the entire village was off somewhere else. They plunged into the cool water, laughing, playing like otters, lithe with their touches and feints. Then, drying off, they looked each other in the eye and understood what their future would be without even speaking, and they tumbled together onto the grassy bank, wet bodies moulding to each other, sliding and warm. He pressed his face to her hair, smelling the pond, and afterwards, as they held each other, they spoke of what their lives would become, adorning their futures with the sort of dreams they had never before admitted to anyone. Four months later they married – more dancing of the *kolo* – then a golden age with a child and success, and no hint of war or upheaval or separation.

If Jasmina had known of all the trials ahead, Vlado wondered whether she would have come along with him anyway, especially if she could have foreseen his latest and darkest secret. It was this painful question which at last burst the dam of his thoughts, and made him realize he had to tell Pine everything, no matter what – that if he didn't do it this instant, he might never, and somehow it would poison them all.

'Calvin, there's something I need to tell you. Something that may be related to the case. Or maybe not. Only Harkness and LeBlanc probably know for sure. But you need to be told.'

Pine furrowed his brow, obviously caught by surprise.

'OK,' he said. 'I'm listening.'

So Vlado told him all about Haris, Huso and Popovic, and the body in the boot. He held back only when it came to Harkness – the man's threats, and Vlado's worst suspicions. Those, at least, would have to wait until he knew his family was on safer ground.

When he was finished, Pine shook his head slowly in apparent sympathy. 'Jesus, what a spot to be in. No wonder you looked so wary when I showed up in Berlin. But don't worry. Nobody will hear it from me. The Tribunal needs to know Popovic is dead, but nobody needs to know my source. They probably suspect as much by now anyway, given how long he's been missing.'

'Thanks. But I can't ask you to protect me. Not once our work is finished. You'll have to tell them what you know. Or maybe I'll tell them first.'

Pine scowled. 'You think you're the only cop I've ever had to cover for? In Baltimore it must have happened once a month. Planted evidence? Look the other way, buddy. Botched warrant? Here, sign this one instead, the date's been changed. A little trigger happy in that shoot-out? Hey, that's the streets, the guy was dirty anyway. At least with you the victim was truly deserving, not some fifteen-year-old from a housing project with his mom strung out on heroin. It's why I left. Why I volunteered for the Tribunal. What could be a clearer and cleaner mission than hunting genocidal maniacs? Even an old one like Matek.' He paused, shaking his head again. 'But look at us now, wondering who's calling the shots, or how long we'll be able to stay on the case. Confess later if you want, but you might think first about your wife and daughter.'

He already was thinking about them, wondering with each passing mile if they were all right. Vlado nodded, relieved that he'd spoken but still unsure of his next move, half wishing Pine hadn't let him off the hook so easily.

Pine had already moved on to other matters, such as what bearing Vlado's revelations had on their pursuit of Matek.

'So how was Popovic supposed to fit into all this?' he asked. 'It still doesn't make sense. From what I gather, Popovic has been a sort of glorified errand boy for Harkness since the war ended. When he wasn't out killing Kosovars, anyway. And he almost definitely had ties to Andric. The whole sick crowd of Serb generals and paramilitaries. It's why he was so valuable to the Tribunal as a possible witness. But I'm damned if I know how he connects with Matek.'

They were silent a while, turning over in their heads what they knew, or thought they knew.

'Then there's LeBlanc,' Pine finally said. 'I wouldn't underestimate his ability for mischief any more than I would Harkness's. For all we know Castellammare could already be pretty crowded. And if they know more than we do . . .' He shrugged. 'Everything might be over before we even get started.'

'Just like what happened to Fordham.'

Pine nodded grimly. 'Where would you go first then, if you were Harkness or LeBlanc?'

Vlado shook his head. 'I don't travel in their world. I

can only tell you what a policeman would do.'

'Good enough for me. I'm just a prosecutor. What does the out-of-town cop do first?'

'Visits the local police. Partly as a courtesy, partly to get a few more eyes and ears working for you. You don't mention any crates of gold, of course, unless you want the whole town in an uproar.'

Pine frowned. 'I don't exactly want the local yokels to know what we're up to. Not yet. I've had enough dealings with the carabinieri before. Too military. They're breathing down your neck until you're boarding the flight home.'

'Then go to the Polizia di Stato. It's who I dealt with whenever we had to contact the Italians over smugglers or fugitives. You're more likely to get somebody in a suit. And they hate the carabinieri more than you do.'

'You're kidding.'

'Big rivalry. They monitor each other's scanners. Steal each other's sources. It's all very Italian.'

'I should travel with Europeans more often. Broaden my world view.'

The autostrada ended just as it reached Castellammare di Stabia, giving way to a winding two-lane road that crept up and over hills, hugging the rocky slopes that fell away to the Amalfi. The town – more like a city – was the gateway to a string of resorts, with the grey hump of Capri visible offshore in the distance. Castellammare had once been a resort itself, going back to ancient times when its mineral springs fed Roman baths. Those gave way later to green parks and princely villas. Locals still liked to think of their town in those terms, but the dominant sights today were gantry cranes and bustling wharves. It was the last oily smudge of industry before the shoreline gave way exclusively to leisure.

It was also home to terraced citrus groves, mostly lemons, harvested for every sort of product, including a strong local liqueur.

'Look,' Pine said, as they passed the first of the orchards. 'Like the one in your photograph.'

Vlado had been thinking the same thing, although at this time of year the trees held no fruit, so there were no workers up on ladders. Nonetheless, he felt strange seeing the orchard, as if he were moving ever closer to the heart of something he wasn't yet sure he wanted to reach.

22

They checked into a small hotel with decent views and an attentive staff, who seemed to have little to do in the off season. The bellman threw open a window to freshen the room, and Vlado took deep breaths of the briny air off the sea. His room faced the mountains, not the ocean. The manager had apologized – sea views were more popular, not to mention more expensive – but Vlado preferred it this way. Who wanted to be enticed by sparkling green water when it was still too cold for swimming? Give him the hills and the terraces, with the narrow roads disappearing into rocky folds.

He rummaged in his satchel and pulled out the old photograph, studying it again while the piping chatter of children drifted to him from the streets. For what must have been the twentieth time, he looked closely at the face of his father, then at the woman's. It was clear, as it had been every other time he'd looked, that their relationship had been no mere fling, even if it had endured for only a summer. They seemed completely at ease with one another. Or perhaps he was reading too much into it, a troubled son trying to make the best of things. Maybe their contentment was just weariness, resignation, a moment of repose at the end of a long and tiring day, climbing those ladders and shaking lemons from the trees.

There was a knock at his door, followed by Pine's voice.

'Ready to roll?'

'Be right there.'

The regional headquarters for the Polizia di Stato was only a kilometre away, so they walked, stretching their legs after the long drive. The building was an eyesore of sharp corners and dark glass, tucked at the edge of the port. A din of clanging metal and whining forklifts drowned out the street noises as they approached. Inside the entrance to the building was a reception counter, behind which were rows of desks piled with papers. The few officers on weekend duty strolled about in two-tone blue uniforms, coffee in hand, cigarettes burning in their lips. Pine sized it up right away.

'Typical cop shop,' he said. 'You sure about this?'

'Maybe we'll get an atypical cop.'

A woman up front asked them a question in Italian, but when Pine responded in English, she replied crisply in kind.

'What is your business, gentlemen?'

'We're from the War Crimes Tribunal in The Hague,' Vlado said, taking the lead if only because he'd dealt with the Italian police before. 'We're here as a courtesy, and to alert you to the possible presence of two suspects.'

'I have just the man for you,' she said, picking up a phone.

'Two?' Pine said under his breath.

'Think big. They'll be more impressed. And Harkness did say the cases were connected.'

'Just like he said Fordham was a lying windbag.'

'Detective Inspector Torello will see you,' she said. 'Follow me.'

She led them to a nearby door, then through a maze of desks to a glassed-in office in the back, where Torello was waiting expectantly in the doorway.

He was tall and slender, and wore a suit – just what they'd wanted, unless he turned out to be some sort of glorified public relations functionary – and seemed attentive and alert. The office eager beaver, Vlado thought, willing to do overtime and weekend work if that's what it took to get him out of this backwater.

'I'm assuming you'd rather speak English,' Torello said, 'and mine is quite good, if I say so myself. Welcome to Castellammare, gentlemen. When did you arrive?'

It was a social question with a point. He wanted to know how long they'd already been prowling around on his turf.

'Just got here,' Pine said. 'Drove down this morning from Rome.' He gave Torello his business card.

'Well, I am of course at your service, although our usual run of international cases is smugglers and refugees.'

'You could say these fellows are refugees,' Pine said. 'Suspects who've recently eluded us in Bosnia, and we have reason to believe one or both might be in your neighbourhood.'

Torello raised his eyebrows, then offered cigarettes

from a desk drawer. Vlado took one; Pine shook his head.

Torello was handsome, and wore no wedding ring. Yes, he was ambitious all right, Vlado thought, or he'd be out on some beach with a young woman on a warm Sunday like this. Vlado looked for family pictures and found none, but did notice a pressed dinner jacket, fresh from the cleaners, hanging from a hook in the corner.

Torello studied Pine's business card a moment.

'So tell me who it is you're looking for and why you think they may have come here.'

'We can give you two possible names for one of them,' Pine said. Vlado knew he had no intention of answering the second part of Torello's question. 'Pero Matek or Pero Rudec. The other fellow you may have heard of. Marko Andric, Serbian general. One of our ranking suspects. I've got particulars and a photo of each if you've got a copy machine handy.'

'Of course. And I'll check with some of the hotels and pensions this afternoon to see if any holders of Yugoslav passports have registered recently. I'll also provide you with official letters of introduction, if you like. They'll be helpful if you plan to make any inquiries locally. Will you be?'

He was good. Offering a service while poking his nose a little deeper into their business. Pine hesitated, so Vlado answered.

'We might be. What can you tell us about the local citrus growers? Their hiring practices, and any employment records they might keep.'

'Right now they're not very busy. They won't be

hiring seasonal help for a few months. As for records,' he shrugged, 'same as everyone else, at least in principle. But with the seasonal hires you can never be sure. We find some illegals now and then. Albanians. A few Bosnians too. You think your men might be looking for work?'

Vlado looked at Pine, unsure whether to take it further. Pine nodded.

'One of them might have worked in an orchard a while back.'

'How long ago?'

'Fifty years. Maybe nineteen fifty-two. Or as recent as sixty-one.'

Torello raised his eyebrows. 'Right after the war, then. Well. Those were interesting times here.'

'How so?'

'In the usual way of wars. There were no jobs, really, so anyone making money was probably doing something illegal. Lots of people on the move. And the soldiers, of course. Occupation forces. Mostly Americans, who seemed to like hanging around on the beach, or so I gather from some of the older people. I can give you the names of some of the larger growers. Their offices will be open tomorrow. I doubt their records will be much help, if they even have any from that far back. But it's worth a try, I suppose.' He paused, knocking the ash off his cigarette. 'In the meantime, answer me this, please. Why would not just one but two Balkan war criminals on the run, with all of Europe to choose from, want to come to this little blight on the pretty Amalfi coast?'

345

'I guess we'd like to know that too,' Pine said. 'To be frank, our coming here is sort of a shot in the dark.'

Torello smiled crookedly, as if to say he could live with that lame explanation for now. 'Leave me the number where you're staying. I'll send over the names of those citrus growers later this afternoon, along with the letter of introduction.'

Another deft move, Vlado thought, finding out right away where he and Pine were staying. But unless some local policeman turned up one of their suspects, and the chances of that happening seemed pretty remote, this was probably the last they'd see of Signor Torello.

They ate a big lunch on the way back to the hotel, deciding to enjoy the afternoon while they could. They'd been on the move almost constantly for three days now, and the meal gave them a much needed chance to unwind, even if Vlado kept expecting to see Harkness at any moment, grinning from the next table.

As the waiter cleared away their dishes before bringing coffee, Pine leaned back in his chair, patting his stomach.

'It is true what they say. The Italians know how to live. Have your big meal in the middle of the day, then sleep it off. Is that how Bosnia was before the war?'

'Except for the food and the naps.'

They laughed, enjoying the warmth and the smell of the sea.

When they returned to the hotel, the information from Torello was waiting for them as promised, copies for each tucked into their key slots.

346

'Efficient as a German,' Pine said. 'And on a Sunday.'

'He'd very much like to know what we're really up to.'

'I got that impression. Shit. What's this?'

There was a pink phone message at the bottom of Pine's pile.

'Call ASAP. Urgent. Janet,' he read aloud. 'So much for a restful afternoon. You better come up. You can listen in. It's one of those places with an extension in the bathroom.'

Janet Ecker answered in the middle of the first ring. She was at her desk on a Sunday, which was unusual enough. But her news was even more extraordinary.

'I've found the connection we were looking for.'

'You mean the one between—'

'No need to say the names. Between the old one and the new one.'

'You really think this kind of security is still necessary?'

'Probably pointless, especially considering what I've been up to all weekend.'

'Which is?'

'Shaking every tree in the forest to see what might drop out. I've been in touch with all my old contacts in the community, as you like to put it, so who knows how many alarms I've tripped along the way.'

'But productive?'

'Not until an hour ago. I was beginning to feel like a teacher who'd walked into a classroom to find students cheating in the middle of an exam. Everybody was silent. Even scared. And I'm talking about people who are gossips by nature. They wouldn't even return

347

my calls, and the few who did were no help. Then I got a telegram, of all things. In cipher. A code I still understand, fortunately. Directing me to an overnight delivery service, where a package was waiting.'

'Sent to a fake name, of course.'

'Of course. Very cloak-and-dagger. Always part of the game with this one. But apparently the word had gone out: say nothing to me or anyone at the Tribunal.'

'So what was it?'

'A copy of an old intercept from nineteen sixty-one, out of an NSA listening post in Zurich. Transmission from the Yugoslav interior ministry to Swiss banking authorities. Part of a Yugo search for looted federal assets via the State Bank of Croatia in April of nineteen forty-five. The meat of it was notes from a debriefing conducted by a military security officer at a coastal border post. He'd interrogated two repatriating Yugoslavs who'd come across the Adriatic. Pero Matek and Enver Petric. The officer questioned them for four hours and detained them overnight. Then he let them go. No charges. Curious, given the information they passed along.'

'Which was?'

'Tales of gold they'd seen in Rome. Cratefuls. Plus all the dirt you'd care to dish on Father Draganovic. Names of fugitive war criminals who'd been spirited away, and so on.'

'So why let them go?'

'Bribed, I'd guess. Either with money or privileged information.'

'What makes you say that?'

'Common sense, for one thing. The name of the security officer, for another. An up and coming army lieutenant.'

'Marko Andric,' Vlado said.

'Exactly. He was twenty-two then. Spent the next thirty years working his way up the chain of command, which by the time Srebrenica fell left him in charge of a brigade in the Drina Corps. During that time he requested permission to travel out of the country at least six times. To follow up on whatever tips Matek and Petric might have given him is my guess.'

'Destination Italy?'

'We'll never know. Every request was denied. Not unusual, given his rank. They were always edgy about defectors. But he'd at least have had the clout to make sure Matek never left the country either. Or Petric. Their names were probably on some sort of border watch list. And when things might have started opening up in the years after Tito died, the war began, so Andric was still too busy to travel.'

'Until now, when he drops out of sight the same day as Matek,' Pine said. 'After our friends Harkness and LeBlanc have arranged a joint operation to round them up.'

'So maybe we really are looking for both of them,' Vlado said.

'Then what would the Popovic connection be?' Pine asked. Vlado found that he still flinched at the mention of the name. He waited for Pine to pass along news of Popovic's death, wondering how he'd explain it. But Ecker spoke first.

'Who knows?' she said. 'Courier? Middleman? Or maybe just something out of Harkness's imagination to throw us off the trail. It seems to have worked with LeBlanc, anyway. Last I heard he was in Berlin, looking for him.'

This was bad news, Vlado thought. And yet another point on which Harkness had apparently been telling the truth. Perhaps none of his warnings was a bluff, a sobering thought to say the least.

'If only we had better leads,' Pine said.

'What *are* your leads?' Ecker asked.

'Lemon groves. That's about it. Matek and Petric may have worked in some, assuming they even lived here. All we've really got for proof is a label on the back of Vlado's photograph.'

'Well, whatever you do, move fast. The way I've stirred things up, I have a feeling it's not going to be a very pleasant Monday around here.'

23

Vlado and Pine were silent after hanging up. Pine came into the bathroom to find Vlado still seated on the edge of the tub.

'I figured there was no sense mentioning Popovic was dead,' Pine said delicately. 'Not yet, anyway. There'd be too much explaining to do.'

Vlado nodded, supposing he should feel grateful. He pondered what they'd just learned. Matek would probably find it easy to blend in here, having lived in Italy before. Andric would be a fish out of water. Everything about him, the way he dressed, the way he talked, perhaps even the food he ordered, should make him stand out, and easier to find. If both were truly here to retrieve two crates of gold, they'd need help, even if they knew where to look. Help from the docks, perhaps. Or a labour pool. Torello might know where to ask around, but that would involve telling him more than Pine wanted.

'Truck rentals,' Vlado finally said. 'That might be one place to start, if we really think one or both of them are here to dig up buried treasure. Trucks and cheap labour because it won't be a one-man job. Beyond that and the citrus groves, who knows?'

'Either way, you've got to figure it's a race. The news

has been all over the papers about both of them, for anyone paying attention. Unless they've stayed in touch with each other.' He looked at Vlado with raised eyebrows. 'Partners in crime maybe?'

'You really think Matek's the sharing type?'

'No.'

'Me neither.'

Nor did Vlado believe that either Matek or Andric would necessarily pose the biggest threat. Harkness could be a third seeker of fortune in the formula, though perhaps more interested in information than gold. A three-way race, then, between cut-throat competitors, each with his own brand of malice. If Vlado had his way they'd bring Torello more fully into the picture, plus as many men as he could spare. Safety in numbers sounded like a good idea just now.

'It's almost five,' Pine said. 'Might as well take a rest while I can. Maybe we can grab a light dinner later.'

After their heavy lunch, Vlado didn't even want to think about food. What he needed more was a walk. Something to calm his worries. He wished he had another phonecard, if only to check in briefly with Jasmina. He made a note to casually ask for a few more lira when Pine and he were out later.

'See you later, then,' he said. 'I'm going to have a look around the town.'

'Tell Andric hello for me if you bump into him. Maybe he's at the hardware store, buying a shovel.'

Andric and both of the others, Vlado thought. Strange how such a big place could seem so claustrophobic.

He left the hotel anticipating a long leisurely stroll,

far into the hills and orchards above the town. But the first mile and the first few hundred feet of elevation reminded him of how weary he was. Too much strain, too much moving around. He'd slept in one strange bed after another, and faced too many strong and vivid revelations, their after-images burned into his brain like a series of lurid photos. He, too, needed to lie down, despite his earlier nap in the car.

He returned to find a message from Pine right on the pillow, like a bedtime mint. Maybe later Pine would turn back his sheets for him, he thought, mildly irritated at the intrusion.

The message was simple and direct: Vlado, call Robert Fordham. There was a number with a Rome area code. But Pine had ensured that his phone line was again blocked from making any long-distance calls, irritating him further. No matter how much trust Vlado had earned, Pine was still being the loyal foot soldier about sticking to these silly security rules. Why bother leaving the message, then? Perhaps Fordham had called to offer another *mea culpa*. Or maybe he'd thought better of his confession, and wanted to recant. The whole business seemed wrong, so he walked to Pine's door and knocked hard.

'Just a minute,' a faint voice answered. In a moment Pine poked his head out, hair in all directions, eyes bloodshot. 'What time is it?'

'A little after six. I just got your message, but my phone's blocked, as you know, so I need to use yours.'

'What message?'

'This one.'

Pine frowned at the white slip of paper, examining the slanted handwriting in blue ink. It was written on hotel stationery.

'I didn't write that. Probably the front desk. Either way I guess you need my phone. Mind if I listen in from the bathroom?'

'As long as it doesn't get too personal.'

Vlado keyed in the number, envying Pine the freedom of an open line. Perhaps he could coax a call home out of him later. A woman answered, saying something Vlado couldn't understand. Presumably it was Fordham's housekeeper, but when Vlado asked for him she rattled off something unintelligible. He tried the name he remembered.

'Maria?' he said, but that only produced another burst of babble, and when Vlado continued to flounder the woman hung up.

'That was weird,' Pine called from the bathroom. 'Almost sounded like an office. Maybe we can get someone at the desk to do it for us. They can at least translate long enough to find out what's going on.'

They took the lift down.

'I need some help responding to the message you left,' Vlado said to the desk clerk.

'And your room number, sir?'

'Three one one.'

The man turned, inspecting the key boxes. 'I'm sorry, sir. You have no messages. Were you expecting a call?'

'No. This message.' He held out the slip of paper from his pillow. The clerk eyed it curiously, knitting his brow. Vlado began to get an odd feeling about it. 'It was delivered to my room.'

'Not by anyone here, sir. There would have been a light flashing on your phone, and the message would be in your key box, or on the in-house voicemail. Perhaps a friend dropped by while you were out.'

Vlado and Pine exchanged worried glances.

'But it was on my pillow.'

'Most unusual, sir. Just a moment.'

The clerk picked up a phone and made two quick calls, speaking only a few words each time, nodding briskly before hanging up.

'I'm sorry, sir, but neither the housekeeping staff nor the concierge has been in your room since you checked in. They'd be the only ones who could have delivered it. Unless you've entrusted someone with your key.'

Pine looked at Vlado. 'What do you think?' he said.

What Vlado thought was that Harkness must be in town. But if he said so he might have to explain more than he wanted about his earlier run-ins with the man. But Pine had reached the same conclusion from another direction.

'Sounds like spook behaviour to me. Harkness or LeBlanc, trying to shake you up. Unless LeBlanc really is in Berlin.'

'Then what does the message mean?'

'Only one way to find out.'

Pine turned back to the clerk, who was watching with interest.

'Could you call this number for us? We tried from my

room but couldn't get past the woman who answered. Neither of us speaks Italian. But it's this fellow, Fordham, who we're trying to reach.'

'Certainly, sir.'

He dialled while they waited.

'*Un momento*,' he said quickly, placing a hand over the receiver and turning towards Vlado. 'This Mr Fordham. She wants to know if he is a patient.'

'A patient?'

'Yes. This is a hospital you've called.'

'I don't know. But he's not a doctor.'

The clerk spoke some more, then picked up a pencil and made a few notes. After a few moments he gently replaced the receiver and turned to them with an expression of grave concern.

'I'm sorry,' he said softly, 'but your friend Mr Fordham isn't taking any calls. He is in the intensive care unit.' He paused, as if considering whether to continue. 'I'm afraid they don't expect him to survive the night.'

Vlado felt as if his stomach had dropped to his knees.

'Jesus!' Pine hissed behind him.

'Did she say why he was admitted?' Vlado said. 'Was it his heart?'

'Some sort of seizure, apparently,' the clerk said. 'Of unknown origin. She said his illness was not yet diagnosed.'

'That sounds like spook behaviour too,' Pine said. 'Of the worst possible kind.'

24

A wave of cold grey weather rolled in overnight from the Bay of Naples. The false spring fled, and with it the sharp golden light that had scrubbed the town of its age and heaviness. The sea had turned dark and choppy. The hills above the town had seemingly vanished, cloaked now by the drooping clouds. It was the sort of dreary winter morning, in other words, that made it difficult to get out of bed.

But as Vlado and Pine were meeting for an early breakfast, Pero Matek, undaunted by the misty chill, was arriving refreshed and renewed at the entrance of the lookout post he'd chosen that morning.

It was perfectly located, just across the street from a huge stone arch that would be the focus of his vigil. And because the chosen vantage point was a small and pleasant café, he wouldn't have to pass the time without warmth or sustenance. He sipped his first cup of coffee while scanning the surroundings. Besides the commanding view, the café also met his other needs: a rear exit, should he need one; suitably dim lighting, accentuated this morning by the prevailing gloom; and a calm and agreeable waitress, the sort who probably wouldn't mind letting an old man monopolize a single table as long as he tipped regularly and well, and perhaps even flirted a bit.

The day before, Matek had done a little shopping, buying some decent clothes, something more like what the locals wore. No more peasant garb; that look was gone for ever. He felt a little embarrassed by the silly hat and these bulky sunglasses, especially on such a cloudy day. But cover was cover, and who knew whether the local police had been alerted, or perhaps even been offered a photo.

As he opened his newspaper, he wondered fleetingly what poor Azudin was doing now. The boy was probably still in a panic over the exploding mines. At least he'd dutifully carried out his last orders. Although that would be the end of Azudin's career, of course. Just as well. The boy never could have stood up to all those country roughnecks. The timid authorities of the Travnik municipality would probably feel emboldened to begin dismantling his sprawling operation now – after parcelling out a percentage to their superiors, naturally. Matek sighed. It had all been built with such patience and skill. Ah, well. Never too late to build something new, although this time his fortune would arrive ready-made.

He checked the time with the waitress, but only for the sake of accuracy, of keeping his bearings. It was far too soon to make any further moves. He was here merely to keep watch and pass the time. Further action now might attract the attention of the competition. Best to let someone else move first. Then he would tend to the business of clearing the field for his final play.

His only other duty this morning was to recruit a young confederate, some lad with little to do and no schooling on his mind, and it wasn't long before he spotted a likely candidate lingering outside.

'Boy,' he hissed, feeling proud that he could speak Italian with virtually no accent. 'I've got something for a lad like you who might be willing to show a little initiative.'

The child was probably around twelve. Old enough for the necessary stamina, but probably still young enough to fear a tone of authority. He was wide-eyed, skinny, a little wary too. Just the sort who'd appreciate an easy way to make a few thousand lira with a minimum of effort.

'How would you like to do me a favour and make some money?' The boy backed away from the table just a shade. 'Nothing to do with me, mind you.' No sense having the boy think he was some sort of old fairy. 'I just need someone to help me watch that old stone gate over there. The arch across the street. *Sí?*' He held out two ten thousand lira notes. More money than the boy would probably see in a month. The eyes lit up. Perfect.

'*Sí,*' the boy said eagerly.

'There's a man I'm waiting for,' Matek said, lowering his voice so the boy would lean closer. 'A man who will be going through that entrance, then leaving through it, once he's done his business. You won't need to recognize him, because I'll be watching for him. But it might be hours before he comes. He might not come at all. But if he does, and when he exits, I'd like you to follow him. I'm old, and can't do it myself, so I need a set of fresh legs like your own. He'll be from out of town, so he'll be going back to some pension or hotel. I just need to know which one, and which room. It would mean a lot to me.' Matek unfolded five more ten thousand lira notes, holding on to them this time. 'And these will be yours if you can find that out. Can you do that? Do you have the day free to earn a nice wage like this?'

The boy nodded solemnly, as if too stunned by his good turn of fortune to speak.

'Good,' Matek said, smiling warmly. 'That's very good. So when any man passes through that arch, you look my way. And when it's the right one, I'll nod and raise this newspaper in the air. Like this. You see?'

The boy nodded gravely once again.

'Very good then. And remember, this could take hours, even all day. That's OK with you, right?'

'*Si*,' the boy said, regaining his voice. And without further prompting he took up station just across the street in a Plexiglas bus shelter that would protect him from the rain and mist, yet allow a full view in both directions. He took out his new money from time to time, scrutinizing it as if fearful it might have vanished, or transmuted to mere paper. But after a while he seemed satisfied that there was nothing illusory about the day's windfall, and he settled down stoically to await the call to action.

Satisfied that he had chosen well, Matek settled back into his chair and resumed the guise of studying his newspaper, even reading a line or two. He might as well find some way to pass the time. But if there was one thing that an old man knew, it was patience. And after fifty-two years of waiting, what did a day more matter?

By early afternoon, Matek had removed his sunglasses, deciding that on a cloudy day they attracted more attention than they deflected. The ridiculous hat remained in place, if only because it seemed perfectly in keeping with what the locals wore. He had read six different newspapers cover to cover, and his young confederate across the way had seemed in danger of nodding off several times. Matek was bored with his table, bored with the view, bored with the tired old arch that stared back at him with nothing but greyness. He was bored as well with the seemingly endless clatter issuing from the café's kitchen. But his waitress had been tolerant and polite, even if not as attractive as he would have liked. Only an older man would have been allowed to get away with this sort of camping out, he reflected, while ordering only a few coffees, a light lunch and a bottle of mineral water. Or maybe it was his generous tips that had done the trick.

From time to time, he had experienced fleeting bouts of panic. Perhaps he'd arrived too late. Maybe his quarry had come and gone. Or worse, perhaps the items he'd come for were gone altogether. Discovered by chance and looted years ago. He'd certainly heard of worse luck. But such moments passed quickly. He'd planned too well and for too long to be upstaged even by ill fortune.

Then, looking up once again from his paper, as he

weighed whether he could stomach yet another cup of coffee, he saw a face that banished all thoughts of failure. The man was across the street, walking slowly, headed straight for the arch. He, too, wore a hat, although his had not been as wisely chosen – no-one in this town would be caught dead in it. In fact, to Matek's eye the man's entire appearance, from his clothes to his movements, screamed Balkan with a capital B, even if he doubted anyone from around here had a similarly discerning eye.

Fortunately, the boy was paying attention, and sprang to his feet the moment Matek gave the sign, nodding and raising the rolled-up paper as if preparing to scold a dog.

The man paused for a moment, then passed beneath the arch. His hair had gone grey, and he seemed rounder towards the middle. Matek had seen enough newspaper photos to know what changes to expect. The eyes, he knew, would be the same, that blue-grey coolness which, so many years ago, had alerted him to the likelihood that the fellow was a hard bargainer, but a bargainer nonetheless.

Matek suddenly leaned forward across the table. Who was that lagging in the man's wake, floating to the rear as if on a long leash, if only the first man had the gumption to realize it? That was one of the pitfalls of being a general, Matek supposed. You grew accustomed to having others watch your back. Because it was clear this second fellow was using too many of the old tricks to be anything other than a shadow, a man on the make, now pausing to light a cigarette, then simply waiting, just like the boy, his eyes on the arch.

Then the man turned away from the arch, well before his quarry had emerged. In fact he was heading in this direction, glancing towards the café. He stopped at the rack of newspapers, and for the briefest moment he seemed to glance at Matek, who retreated behind his paper. When he peeped over the top, the man was still at the news-stand, scanning the headlines. Was he local? Perhaps. Or British? That would be the better guess. Then the figure turned and headed back the way he had come, stopping occasionally to glance in a shop window, but inexorably heading out of sight.

A false alarm, it seemed, but one Matek could have done without.

It was another fifteen minutes before the first man emerged back through the arch, and the boy was off in pursuit like a cat, as if he'd been born to the job. Matek smiled, briefly considering a tip when the boy returned with the information.

But no, he concluded. A bargain was a bargain. Besides, he'd soon have more pressing business to attend to.

25

Vlado and Pine worked fast on Monday, but their labours produced little more than sore feet and empty stomachs. They roamed the suddenly chilly town from its docks to its foggy hillsides, checking pensions and truck rental agencies, citrus growers and labour pools. But none of it turned up any sign of Matek or Andric, or anyone with a Balkan name or connection.

Their visit to one of the lemon growers was typical – half an hour of waiting to see the boss, even though this was the slow season, a time for pruning and book-keeping. At the first mention of employment records the man gave them a wary sidelong glance, as if sniffing a sting operation by labour regulators. He went so far as to hint at a possible bribe before being convinced they were truly who they said they were. At which point he lost interest altogether, assuring them that in the years following the war, workers had come and gone like fruit flies, too numerous and insignificant to count, much less keep any record of their names and wages. As for payroll taxes, that was for chumps, for men of little influence and less intelligence.

'He reminded me of some of my father's clients back home. That's probably how they still think of their employees, as fruit flies,' Pine remarked.

But it was the perfect sort of supervisory attitude, Vlado thought, if you were a worker trying not to be noticed or traced. With employers like that, this would have been an easy place to lie low in the chaotic years following the war.

They returned to the hotel at dusk. Vlado was heading towards the lift with his key when he heard Pine groan behind him. Vlado turned to see him at the front desk holding another phone message.

'Janet again?'

'Worse. Here.'

It was a fax on Tribunal letterhead, and the message was as terse as a telegram. 'Contact Chief Prosecutor Contreras at once at the following number. Make no further contacts, repeat NONE, by phone, interview or otherwise with regard to this case. Return passage booked. Details to follow. Spratt.'

Vlado checked the timeline across the top. The fax had arrived two hours ago.

'And there's this one,' Pine said, holding aloft a second sheet. 'Came in a few minutes ago. Our itinerary. Ten a.m. flight out of Rome, which means we'll have to leave around five in the morning if we're going to make it.'

'They're recalling us?'

'Looks that way. Let's hope it's either the result of a hot tip or a change in strategy. Care to listen in?'

Vlado felt suddenly panic-stricken. To come all this way and feel they were so close to a breakthrough, only to be recalled, or perhaps redeployed, although his better judgement told him the former was likelier. For the moment his only solace was imagining Spratt's reaction, his ears spouting steam like those of a cartoon character.

'C'mon,' Pine said. 'Let's get it over with.'

Vlado took up his appointed listening post on the edge of the tub. The only sound was the slow drip of the bathroom tap. A secretary answered and quickly patched them through, then Contreras came on the line with the brusque tone of a news bulletin, without the slightest pleasantry or preamble. He was no longer playing the gracious and charming grandee, the welcoming cheerleader for justice in all nations. He was instead the imperious judge issuing a fiery proclamation from the bench.

'Are you aware, Mr Pine, that between you and your partner's actions, as well as those of Janet Ecker, the American State Department has now lodged an official complaint with my office?' His voice rose on the word 'official', as if that put their transgressions on a par with mass murder. 'They say, and not without some justification from what I've heard at my end, that you've been inquiring into matters and places that are completely out of bounds. And frankly I can't help but wonder what sort of freelance operation the three of you are running. Can you tell me that?'

'None, sir. We're just pursuing leads on the possible whereabouts of—'

'Pursuing leads? Do you call harassing an elderly former intelligence agent merely pursuing leads? To the point where he has apparently suffered some sort of stroke? Or poking around old intelligence files, not even

366

officially declassified, as merely pursuing leads?'

'We were harassing no-one, sir. The man spoke to us of his own free will.'

'The same man, I presume, as the one who for years has been discredited as hopelessly unreliable. To the point that he became an embarrassment to his own government and was relieved of his duties. But nonetheless he, too, filed an official complaint about your behaviour, before his misfortune.'

'Fordham? But he's . . . He spoke to us willingly.'

'We received it straight from the American Embassy in Rome this morning.'

Pine said nothing in response. Janet Ecker had been right. Someone was pulling out all the stops, and it could only be Harkness and those above him.

'Exactly what you're trying to accomplish, none of us are sure,' Contreras continued. 'But given the level of betrayal we seem to have experienced on this case to date, not just involving the escape of Andric but that of Matek as well, several of us have begun to question the motives of all of you. And bringing in the Bosnian on this, which I'm told was your idea, was our first mistake.'

'My idea?'

'We were wrong to expect objectivity from a native. His personal connection to all this only made matters sloppier once things began to fall apart.'

Vlado bit his tongue. Contreras obviously wasn't aware he was on the line, and he would have hung up then and there if he could have done it without drawing attention to his presence.

'As for you and Miss Ecker,' Contreras continued, 'whatever grudges you may have against your old employers have no place in your current work.'

'But we—'

'Enough. This is not the proper forum for defending or explaining yourself. There will be ample time for that on your return. You're to leave Italy tomorrow, and in the meantime you're to make no further calls, conduct no further interviews and pursue no further leads, as you choose to call them. And you're expressly forbidden from any further contact with local law enforcement. There's nothing to be gained from disseminating our embarrassment any further. Clear on all counts?'

'Very clear.'

'Report to me as soon as you arrive. Bring Spratt with you, as well as the Bosnian. He'll be discharged from employment and returned to Berlin. The sooner the better. Until tomorrow, then.'

'Yes, sir.'

So this was how it would end, Vlado mused as the line went dead. He raised the mute receiver like a hammer, then brought it down across the edge of the tub, cracking the porcelain as well as the receiver. Let the Tribunal pay the damages, he thought savagely, his elbow aching with the shock of the blow. He gazed at the dripping tap, still marking out the seconds, then rose stiffly from his uncomfortable perch. The jolts and agonies of the past several days had been difficult, but they had at least led to the doorstep of discovery, or so it had seemed. Now he would be turned away before even knocking, and all he'd get for his trouble would be the humiliation of a peremptory dismissal. He wondered vaguely what had become of all the grand promises of resettlement, of finding him a new job as an investigator, but none of that seemed relevant now. At least his family would be safe, although maybe even that wouldn't hold true if LeBlanc or Harkness leaked word on the fate of Popovic.

'Sorry you had to hear that,' Pine said, appearing at the bathroom door. 'Pretty brutal.'

Vlado nodded, too angry to speak.

'I'm sorry, Vlado. You've been treated terribly. And for what it's worth, using you *wasn't* my idea. Well, you know where it came from. But I guess somebody has already started re-writing the history.'

'Yes. Funny how that keeps happening.'

'If I—'

'Never mind,' Vlado said. He was quivering with both anger and anguish. 'Just . . . never mind.'

'Well, I guess there's nothing left but to sit tight. We'll get some sleep and clear out as early as possible in the morning. Maybe later we can grab some dinner, if you feel up to it.'

Vlado could think of no suitable reply, so he left, walking numbly to his room. After shutting the door he sat on the bed for a few minutes. Then he rose to unlock the small refrigerator of the minibar, peering inside at the neat row of soft drinks and spirits and beer. He selected a small bottle – Scotch whisky, not at all his favourite, but it would do, and so would the rest of the little bottles, regardless of their contents. Once again, the Tribunal could pay the damn tab. He would drink the place dry. Call for room service.

But halfway through the first swallow he found he had no taste for it, and he poured the rest down the sink. He opened the window, then the shutters, gazing up into the dim haze of the hills, the contours of the land barely visible in the evening gloom. It was too cold to look for long, so he shut the window. The room was now raw with sea air. Then he lay back on the bed, his shoes still on. The red digital display of the clock on the bedside table said 5:37. The people in the streets were headed home to meals and quiet evenings. The end of the workday. Then he remembered Amira, and her invitation to call. Perhaps she had found the names, the ones from the Red Cross passports, if they'd ever existed. Officially, it was now useless information, he supposed. But only if you were working for the Tribunal. He'd just been as good as fired. So why obey orders when all promises had been broken? He sat up, reaching for the phone. He was still a policeman, still a curious son, eager to learn what he could. Without thinking he punched the number for an outside line, only to be connected to the night manager, who politely reminded him that his line was blocked.

Of course, he thought. Never trusted and never really considered anything but a utility, a lubricant for a rough and hasty coupling that had gone awry from the beginning. That angry thought was enough to get him out of the door, his coat and satchel in his hand, his heart beating in the way that fingers drum a desktop in impatience and irritation. He ran down the stairs, too impatient to wait for the lift, then burst through the lobby and barrelled into the evening air. Briefly he paused to pull on his coat. It took only five minutes to hunt down a *tabacchi*, where he used the lira he'd cadged from Pine the night before to buy a phonecard. Then he found a payphone and dialled Amira's home number, pen and notebook at the ready.

She answered immediately, sounding as eager as Janet Ecker had yesterday. Happy, even.

'I think I've found what you were looking for,' she said. 'Two names. Both Italian, with birth dates matching the ones you gave me. Do you have something to write with?'

When she was finished he thanked her, told her he'd be in touch, then hung up, sorry to be so abrupt but wanting to preserve every possible second on the card. A block later he ducked into a café. When a waiter approached he reached for his wallet, calculating what he might be able to afford. But all he really wanted now, he realized, was time, so he waved the man away, then rummaged in his satchel until he found the photo.

He scanned his father's face, then the woman's. 'So who is this woman you're with, Signor Giuseppe DiFlorio?' he said to himself in a low voice. 'Your lover? Your wife? And is she still alive?'

He carried his satchel to the bar, marshalling the fragments of his meagre Italian.

'*Telefono libro?*' he asked uncertainly.

'*Sí,*' the barman answered, stepping a few feet away and reaching low for a thin, dog-eared volume, which he plopped onto the polished counter.

'*Grazie.*'

'*Prego.*'

There were eleven DiFlorios listed. If she'd remarried – presuming she'd been his wife to begin with – then none of these would do the trick. But assuming she hadn't, and that she'd stayed in the town, and that she was still alive – a weight of assumptions that suddenly seemed crushing – then she might be one of these eleven. He was that close, perhaps. He scribbled down every number, returned the book to the bar, and walked past the baffled waiter back to the phone box outside. He inserted his card and began punching in the first number.

But with his limited Italian, what would he say? Even if he were fluent, he wasn't sure he'd know how to proceed. 'Hello. My father had the same last name as you and may have been your husband, can we talk?' Slow down, he told himself. Hang up and think this through.

Torello, he thought. His only hope. So he cradled the receiver and began walking towards the station, an investigator once again on the prowl.

26

In a small, gloomy pension a few miles across town, General Marko Andric decided that it was no use pretending he was a man of the world. He had been travelling for three days, yet still couldn't shake his uneasiness over being in a foreign land. In a word, he was homesick. And to think of all the times in years past when he had tried so hard to come to this very place, only to fail to secure permission. It had taken help from one of the enemy to finally make it possible, but now that he was here he was spending most of his waking hours feeling awkward and uncomfortable.

To his mind, the only way to cover new ground was with an army, tramping along in common cause. And his landscape of choice was rolling green hills, not these bare crags that tumbled straight into the sea.

The most jarring problem had been the language, an endless stream of bafflement that gave him headaches and made him feel like a child. The words here were like rubber balls, slippery and bouncing, moving so fast you could only grasp one or two at a time. By the time you had your pocket dictionary out, another twenty had bounded past.

The food, at least, was worthwhile, but even that was growing tiresome. What he'd really like now was a slab of meat, grilled to the bone, a substantial piece, not a mere slice or a few medallions like they served here. He pulled out a cigarette. Those, at least, were the same everywhere now. The American cowboy who ruled the world. After a few puffs he felt better, but he was worn out, sleepy. The strangeness of his journey had been giving him nightmares. Or that's what he chose to blame for the visions that had been visiting him lately.

The previous evening he had awakened in the dark believing that the dead were reaching out for him from the walls and floor, where they writhed like worms, their rotting fingertips outstretched, brushing against his bare arms and legs. Twisted faces had loomed above him, cursing incomprehensibly. Speaking Italian, no doubt. He had jolted to his senses, sitting upright and turning on the bedside lamp, comforted to find the walls bare and quiet. The ceiling was a blank. Children were setting off fireworks outside in the street below. That must have caused it all, he had told himself. But the taste in his mouth said otherwise. It was all too familiar. Lands, languages and cuisine might change, but the chalky dust of Srebrenica still coated his tongue, as if his system were unable to expel it. Even now, in the wake of a late afternoon rest, he could taste just a hint. So he set aside his cigarette and rose to rinse his mouth in the bathroom sink.

It was lonely, this way of living, and as he turned on the tap, swallowing, spitting, he wondered how long he'd have to endure it. His bare feet were chilly against the floor. Still cold and damp outside, he supposed, flipping back the shutter to see the clouds that had been settled on the town throughout the day. The daylight was nearly gone. Good. In a few hours, then, if all went as scheduled, everything would be over. Any moment he should have a visitor, someone who spoke his language, no less.

The thought was enough to get him moving. He threw on his clothes and allowed himself to feel some excitement. Taught by experience and rigid training never to expect anything to go smoothly, it had taken a while to finally begin believing this might happen, that everything might really come off without a hitch. He'd been feeling this way for a few hours now. Ever since he'd made his furtive reconnaissance, strolling past the place where the items were said to be stored. Thinking of the walk, he reached into his pocket. Finding nothing, he experienced a momentary panic. But then he felt it, rolled into a crease of the fabric. The old key. How amazing, he thought, that it still fitted the lock. He had tried it, ever so briefly, turning it just enough to slide back the bolt without opening the door. Then he'd quickly re-locked it. Too many visitors around at that hour to feel comfortable enough to do more. It would be more amazing still if everything remained. But such things were possible, he knew, having seen it happen in his own land – secrets going to ground in one conflict, only to be resurrected in another.

For a while during his walk he'd thought that he'd seen his contact, his benefactor, so to speak, although it wasn't as if the man's services came free of charge. It had been the briefest of glances, an eerie sense of footfalls that seemed to match his own. But when he'd turned for a look he'd seen nothing but a small boy and a man gazing at a rack of newspapers.

The moment had unnerved him enough to give him second thoughts about continuing his walk. And what if someone recognized him, or started to ask questions? He'd been jittery since crossing the border, too nervous even to read a paper or turn on the news, for fear of seeing his own face. Better to lie low, now that the hour was approaching. So much planning, and it had all come down to a single evening.

But now, as if answering his thoughts, there was a knock at the door. The maid, perhaps? Or was it someone he was expecting?

'Yes?' he said, easing towards the door, reaching for the gun that bulged from a pocket, in a jacket hanging on a brass hook.

'Marko? It's me.'

So it really was him, then, speaking his own tongue, although with the slightest difference in tone and timbre from how he sounded on the phone. He'd swear that much of the man's accent was gone too. Maybe it was just nerves. But it was such a relief to hear words he could understand that he neglected to take the gun from his pocket. His guest was early, but any good general knew that even the most careful plans changed and shifted.

So he opened the door unarmed, his first and last mistake. Staring back at him was an entirely different face from the one he'd expected, although it, too, seemed oddly familiar. Who is this old man? he wondered, but before he could ask he found himself staring at the barrel of a gun, a thick ugly thing with something heavy jammed on the end. A silencer. Not a good sign, even to someone so open to changes in plans.

'I know you, don't I?' he said, realizing as he spoke the words exactly who it was. 'Oh my God. Yes. From the border.'

The old man nodded. He seemed to be wheezing, slightly out of breath.

'Yes, now you remember,' the old man said. 'And you've come here to rob me blind. So I thought I would drop by for my key. I'll have it now, if you don't mind. Just tell me where it is. And no reaching into drawers or pockets, please, unless you want our little chat to end prematurely.'

The general was still trying to remember the man's name. Matek? Or was it Petric? He couldn't remember which of them had been the talker, the schemer, the one who'd ultimately come up with the plan that won his approval. But the man was now waving the gun in a very disagreeable manner, and General Andric felt his stomach going queasy, rolling on its side like a floundering ship. He wanted to burp, or worse; he could already taste the bile rising in his throat, flavoured by the infernal chalky dust. He licked his lips, a sticky sound.

'It's in my trouser pocket,' he answered, shamed by the quavering of his voice. His performance was dishonourable, and the general imagined his staff watching from the doorway, eyes downcast as they witnessed his humiliation, the old warrior melting into a pile of jelly. It was this thought, finally, that rallied him, and with a sudden twisting lunge he reached for the hateful barrel, once again a soldier on the attack.

He died a soldier's death, shot full in the front, the thumping, whooshing impact of two bullets throwing him clear to the window, where the rear of his head struck the sill with a loud bang. Slumping to the floor, back pressed to the wall, he looked down to see his entrails wriggling free like a nest of wet snakes. It made an awful slurping noise, all the more surreal for its painlessness. He felt only a vast and empty cold down there. Then, pouring into his head, a great rush of heat and blackness, as if someone had torn open a door at the top of his spine. A nimble claw of a hand darted into his trouser pocket, probing frantically, and the last thing the general heard was the voice of a gleeful old man, like some old troll in the woods.

'There you are,' the voice croaked. 'Just as I left you.'

27

Vlado was relieved to find Torello still at his desk. But his first question was the very one Vlado hadn't wanted to answer.

'Where is your American colleague?'

'Mr Pine is at the hotel.'

Torello seemed to consider this response carefully. Normally that would be a bad sign, an indication that maybe Vlado was about to be shown the door, exposed as the rogue operative he'd become.

But Torello wasn't frowning, wasn't nervous or reaching for his phone. If anything he seemed a trifle pleased.

'Tell me,' he said at last, 'you're not authorized to be here, are you? On your own like this.'

Vlado decided to level with him. 'We've been taken off the case. It seems we've become an irritant to US authorities. So I'm not here as a representative of the Tribunal. I'm now working for myself, mostly because my father was a colleague of the older suspect. Which I wasn't aware of until a few days ago, when the Tribunal roped me into this job. So for me it's strictly personal.'

Torello eyed him a moment. 'A missing persons case, then, is that how you'd characterize it? No longer a war crimes manhunt. In case my superiors ask later.' He said it with the beginnings of a smile. Vlado sensed a compatriot, even if he wasn't sure why.

'Exactly.'

'It's nice that we agree. Coffee? You look as if you could use some.'

'Yes.'

'And please,' Torello said, pulling a cigarette pack from his jacket, 'feel free to smoke. This isn't America, you know.'

'So you don't like Americans?'

'Far from it. I think Americans are wonderful. Especially their women, who seem to think Italian men are wonderful as long as we're taken in limited doses.' Torello's smile widened.

Yes, Vlado could just imagine him during the tourist season. The dark good looks that the rest of the world had come to expect of young Italian men. Slim and at ease, hair falling perfectly across the forehead, the impeccable English, and just enough sun in his face to suggest a man of action.

'But let's face it,' Torello continued, 'how often do people like you and me, from countries that generally remain on the sidelines, get the chance to do what we damn well please, especially when people from rather powerful embassies are demanding that we do otherwise? This fax, for instance, landed on my desk just this afternoon.' He handed it to Vlado.

It was a message from the US State Department urging police authorities to please check with embassy contacts in Rome before co-operating with any investigators claiming to be searching for suspects Marko

Andric or Pero Matek, due to unspecified 'diplomatic irregularities'.

'They shout. We jump. And look at the two of us, speaking their language. But I will uphold the letter of this memo, of course.' He held aloft the fax. 'So if, for example, an official representative of the Tribunal were to happen to telephone, looking for a missing colleague, I would of course have to refer him to these instructions, and say nothing. But a missing persons case for a visiting policeman from Bosnia? That's another matter altogether.'

Vlado let a moment pass, assessing the gravity of the leap he was about to make with Torello's help. He worried mostly about his family. He'd probably have a day, perhaps less, before being run to ground, either by Pine or Harkness. He also worried on Pine's behalf: he didn't want to ruin the man's career, although on one level he felt that Pine might actually approve. And if not? Likeable or not, Pine and the Tribunal had used him, and Vlado had earned his shot at rebellion.

'So, then,' Torello said. 'What brought you back here, looking for help?'

'These names.' He handed Torello the sheet of paper on which he'd written Giuseppe DiFlorio and Piro Barzini, followed by the eleven phone numbers for DiFlorios.

'DiFlorio was my father's name while he was here. Barzini was Matek. They probably arrived in the summer of nineteen forty-six and stayed until sixty-one. Then they went back to Yugoslavia. Why, I'm not sure, but my guess is that they had to leave in a hurry. Maybe some of the Ustashe people had finally found them. And they may have left something behind. Something Matek might have come back for.' Vlado paused. This was the one piece of information he still felt uncomfortable about disclosing, but there seemed to be no other choice. 'They may have left behind two crates of gold bars, plus some documents which the United States, even today, might find embarrassing, even damaging.'

Torello leaned back in his chair, exuding an almost boyish pleasure as he steepled his fingers. '*Fantastico*,' he said in a low voice. 'No wonder everyone is in such a, how would they say it, tizzy. A lather. Perfect.' Then his smile faded. 'But those names. I'm afraid those alone won't do us much good.'

'There was also this,' Vlado said, and he placed the old photograph on Torello's desk, then explained why he'd copied the eleven phone numbers.

'I was going to try simply calling them – a wild shot, I know.'

'A crap shoot, yes.' Torello seemed to enjoy collecting scraps of American slang as much as Vlado.

'But, well, I don't speak Italian. Only a few words.'

'I could make the calls for you, of course, but do we really want to start asking families all over town questions about this, getting them gossiping about who knows what? I don't think so. Checking records, that would be better.' He looked at his watch. 'I have a friend in the municipal authority who might be able to let us in after hours to look at marriage licences, death certificates, that kind of thing. But we can try here first. Police records. If your man Matek is as devious as it would

382

seem, I can't imagine him being able to stay anywhere fifteen years without getting into some kind of scrape. Come on. Into the basement.'

It took only twenty minutes. Torello thumbed open a few dusty ledgers of arrests and incident reports from decades prior to 1970. The rest had been computerized. The first line to catch their attention was a smuggling case from 1953. The suspect was Piro Barzini. His date of birth matched the one on the Red Cross passport. The charges were dropped.

'But look,' Torello said, thumbing to another page. 'This one is better.'

It was a 1961 citation, the report of accidental deaths by drowning. There were two victims: Giuseppe DiFlorio and Piro Barzini.

'It seems they decided on the ultimate exit for their return home, one that would leave no expectation of return. Some sort of boating accident. With no bodies recovered, of course. And look. They both had wives.'

So his father had married here. Even though Vlado had expected as much, the news went down like a ball of lead. Torello was still staring at the book, oblivious to the effect of his words. But when Vlado remained silent he turned and saw the Bosnian's expression.

'I'm sorry,' he said. 'This must be hard for you.'

Vlado shook his head and cleared his throat. 'What were their names?' he asked in a quiet voice.

Torello turned back to the ledger. 'Lia. And Gianna. Lia DiFlorio and Gianna Barzini. And if Lia is that woman in your picture, she probably still thinks of herself as your father's widow.'

'If she's still alive.'

'Let's see those phone numbers.'

Lia DiFlorio was the seventh name on the list.

'Her address is the same as in the police report. Still no guarantee she's alive. Her children might have kept the listing in her name.'

'Children. I hadn't even considered that.'

'Would you like me to call?'

Vlado swallowed hard. He nodded.

'Come on, then. Back up to my office.'

Torello keyed the numbers, then they waited. Just about everyone had cleared out of the station. There was no sound but the hum of the fax machine. The light of the desk lamp pooled around them as if they were characters on a small stage.

Vlado heard the line click, followed by a faint, '*Si?*'

'*Buona sera*,' Torello said. The rest was gibberish to Vlado, a rapid exchange that for all he knew was with a son or daughter, or someone else altogether. It was probably better not knowing what was being said. Just learn everything at once.

'*Sí, sí*,' Torello finally said, emphatically, waving his free hand in the air. '*Prego. Ciao.*' He hung up. 'It's her. And she will see us. Tonight.'

Vlado nodded, not quite convinced it was happening.

'I think she's as curious as you, actually.'

'What did you tell her? What did she say?'

'I told her I was a policeman, of course, and asked if her husband had been Giuseppe DiFlorio, the man reported drowned in 1961. She said yes. After that the

384

rest wasn't so hard. I told her we had some new information about the events of those years, but mostly I wanted to ask her about one of her husband's friends from those times. Piro Barzini. She sort of scoffed, and said something about Barzini not being much of a friend. And I told her I was with a colleague of mine from Yugoslavia who might be able to offer her more information. She seemed to find that a little strange, as you might expect. She even sounded a little fearful. But I wouldn't say she was alarmed. Then she invited us over, but asked us to give her a while to prepare. That means, I'm sure, that she needs time to cook for us. She's that type, I'm positive. It could be three a.m. and she would still feel like she had to feed us.'

'Just as well. I never ate lunch.'

'Then she will love you like a son.' Torello reddened, having let the words go before realizing their import.

But Vlado didn't mind. The moment had become so dreamlike that nothing would have jarred him. Well, almost nothing. He hesitated before asking the next question.

'Does she have children?'

'I didn't ask. She lives alone, for what that's worth. But I'd rather you were the one who asked that question.'

'Did you tell her . . . anything else about me?'

'I'll leave that to you as well. As hard as this is for you, it's probably going to be worse for her, finding out that her husband lived, what, another twenty-two years? You'd better bring that photo. She may need some convincing. And we should leave now. It's a good half-hour's drive. She lives way up in the hills.'

The pavements of the town were crowded with people heading for dinner, or straggling home. As the car began to climb, the road narrowed, and after about ten minutes they eased into a forest, then an open field, the road twisting as it rose. Halfway up the hillside they pulled free of the dense bank of clouds that had squatted on the town all day. The stars were out, and as Vlado gazed through the windshield he thought: I am going to my father's old house. He wondered if this road had once been a daily route home from work. He turned to look back down the hill, but the town had disappeared, its lights a pale yellow smudge against the clouds.

He felt awkward from the moment they entered the house. The old woman was nervous and fussing, flour on her hands, her apron still tied at the waist. The place smelled of spices and steam, a pot of pasta was on the boil. But Vlado's senses were on full alert for other reasons. He felt shamefully like a bloodhound, an intruder. He was a spy scenting and searching for any sign of a past life, any remnant of a presence that had vanished thirty-seven years ago. That meant scanning the walls for pictures, and looking for any sign of recognition in the woman's eyes. Fordham had immediately noted Vlado's resemblance to his father. Perhaps she would see it too, although Fordham had had the advantage of knowing the name Petric, and what that might signify. She'd probably never heard the name in her life.

The woman watched him and Torello closely as they walked into her living room, but the scrutiny was more in the manner of someone unaccustomed to visitors, of a wary soul assessing strangers who'd arrived after dark – and both of them policemen.

She didn't speak English, so they agreed that Torello would handle the questions and translate for Vlado. 'I'll identify you as a Bosnian policeman who has an interest in some of the events from her past,' Torello had said on their way up the hill. 'You can get more specific if you like.'

It had been too dark to get a good look at the outside of the house. It was set back from the road in the crease of the hill. But in front of a stone outcrop to the left was a grove of what looked like citrus trees. A welter of bushes and briar was on the right. Inside, the plaster walls were old and cracked, but whitewashed clean. The glimpse of her kitchen as they walked past revealed an ancient stove – reminiscent of the one at Aunt Melania's – with every burner in use.

As they settled on the couch, Vlado saw a small framed photo in the corner. Without thinking he crossed the room for a better look. Yes, he saw with a leap in his heart, it was Lia with his father. The photo had probably been taken within a year or so of the one in his satchel, but in this one they were on the beach. Round stones at their feet, clear waters behind them, with a steaming ferry visible in the distance. They wore the same look of deep contentment. It was the only photo in the room. There were no snaps of children, or babies, or anyone else.

'*Scusi,*' Vlado said, employing his limited Italian, realizing that both Lia and Torello were staring at him, Torello somewhat uneasily. He returned to the couch, then Torello began speaking. Vlado quickly lost track of the conversation, but did hear the name Piro Barzini and saw the woman frown. She said a few words in a low voice, then Torello turned to translate.

'I'm afraid this isn't going to be easy, and maybe not even productive. She seems very reluctant. She says her memory of those times is hazy. But I think it might be more the case that the memories aren't very pleasant. At least as far as Barzini is concerned. The moment I mentioned he was really our focus, she seemed to clam up. But if you have any ideas . . .'

'Yes,' Vlado said. 'Perhaps if we showed her my photo.'

'I'm not sure. Maybe it's too soon.'

'It will give us some credibility.'

'Or maybe it will just shock her. She's an old woman. Perhaps we should leave her in peace.'

'I'm afraid it's too late for that. If she finds out somehow that Barzini is still alive – and let's face it, he'll end up in the papers, one way or another – do you think she will be at peace then, wondering if her husband might have lived as well?'

Torello frowned. 'OK, then. Go ahead.'

Vlado pulled the photo from his bag, knowing he was about to rob this woman of part of her history, a loss he knew acutely. He handed it face down to Torello, who presented it to Lia DiFlorio. Her expression changed immediately, from stubborn scepticism to alarm.

She and Torello exchanged words in Italian, then she looked quickly at Vlado with wide eyes, a look of wonderment.

'She wants to know where you got it,' Torello translated.

Then the woman spoke again, and this time Vlado understood every word.

'Where did that come from?' she asked in fluent Serbo-Croatian, and somehow Vlado wasn't a bit surprised. 'I'm Slovenian,' she said, speaking to Vlado. Slovenia, yet another ethnic fragment of Yugoslavia that had come loose in the recent upheaval, forming its own state to the north of Croatia, and escaping virtually all of the fighting. But that hadn't been the case in the previous war. 'From near the border,' she continued. 'Not far from Trieste.'

'So that is how you met . . .' Vlado stopped short, having nearly said 'my father'. 'That is how you met Giuseppe DiFlorio. Because you spoke his language?'

She shook her head, her lips set in a tight line. 'No. When I met him he was known as Josip Iskric. He was a guard, and I was a prisoner. At the Jasenovac camp, during the war. You know of it?'

'Yes.' Vlado swallowed hard, his throat dry. 'I know of it. But you should tell me your story. Then I'll tell you mine. I think we have a few things in common.'

'What's going on?' Torello asked.

'It's complicated,' Vlado replied tersely in English. 'I hope you don't have any urgent appointments. We may be here a while.'

28

'We weren't at the camp long,' she said. 'Only about a month in all. We must have been some of the last arrivals. Just one busload from the fighting in the east. My family had been moving to another village with about twenty other people when the Home Defence Army picked us up. They didn't have the stomach to shoot us, and I don't think they knew what else to do with us. Things were falling apart by then anyway. And by the time we got to Jasenovac the place was in upheaval.'

They were seated in Lia DiFlorio's dining room. As soon as Vlado had filled Torello in on the rough details of her disclosure, they'd agreed to take a short break, partly because she insisted that they have something to eat before another word was spoken. She needed fuel if she was going to talk about those days, she told them, and said they would need it, too.

Vlado doubted he'd have an appetite, but once they sat down before the plates piled with pasta and sauces, his stomach reminded him that he'd missed lunch. By the time Lia returned to her story he'd finished the better part of the meal.

'They'd sent most of the women off to labour camps, in Germany and Austria,' she said. 'Slave labour in munitions factories. The ones who were still around knew all about it. But now the Partisans were coming. The Russians, too. The trains had stopped running north and no-one was going anywhere. So only the killing was left. They were going as fast as they could, especially with the men. They would take them out in the morning and shoot them, beat them, stab them, butcher them like pigs. Toss them in a hole or just throw them into the river. At night they burned the bodies in big piles. I'm sorry, I know you are eating, but if you want to hear the story I will have to tell it my way.'

Vlado nodded, transfixed. He put down his fork, and didn't touch his food for several minutes. Torello, not understanding the language, watched blandly and swallowed another bite of pasta.

'I could see some of it from the corner of the compound. Before, in our village, we'd always heard these things were happening, but I don't think any of us had really believed it. They'd taken some Slovenians earlier to Rab Island, a camp the Germans ran offshore. Nobody was sure what had happened to them, so this was all new to me, and I will never forget what it looked like. If I'd stayed there much longer, I'm not sure I ever would have recovered.'

She seemed to retreat for a moment into her thoughts, and Vlado wondered what images were playing out in her head.

'She's telling me about life in the camp,' he told Torello in English. 'Her family was there the last month of the war.' Torello nodded, still chewing.

'Some of the guards were pretty new too,' Lia

continued. 'They seemed almost as scared as us. Josip was one of them.'

So here we go, Vlado thought, steeling himself for the worst while hoping for the best.

'He was in charge of the women in my group. About a hundred of us. He would march us out to the fields where we were helping with the planting. It was April and some of the farmers had asked for hands. But every day we watched the horizon, the roads to the west, to see if the armies were coming. There were all sorts of rumours, so of course we were hoping we'd be rescued.'

'What were his duties?'

'Josip's?'

'Yes.'

'Giving us orders, mostly. Keeping track of us. Most of the time it was nothing complicated. Just telling us to march. Halt. Keep moving. Counting us off. That kind of thing. But on the very first morning I saw him looking at me, and I could tell he thought I was pretty. And so I encouraged him, returning his looks, smiling at him. Not because I thought he was any different from the rest of them – I would have killed him if I could have – but because I needed to feel I was doing something to survive. Anything, even if it was just flirting with a guard. Because every morning they made him pick out three or four of us to be sent with a detachment to the river, and all of us knew what happened there. The ones who left never came back, and once the planting was finished we knew they wouldn't need any of us. So we tried to work as slowly as we could.'

'He had to choose?' Vlado asked, gripping the edge of the table.

'Yes,' she said. 'He would do it quickly, without thinking too much. He'd pick some of the older ones, or the ones who were coughing, or sick. We all hated him for it, of course. He was the most powerful man in our lives. The moment he pointed his finger at you, you were dead. Our executioner. So I kept smiling at him, little smiles, so the other women wouldn't notice. For all I knew there were others doing the same. But so many of them were just skin and bones by then. I was nineteen and healthy, and wanted to be the last one on his list. He would always pretend he hadn't noticed, but I knew he had. And then, later, I forgave him everything. After what happened on the last day. When he helped us escape.'

Vlado's heart leaped. He tightened his grip on the table.

'He . . . he helped you escape?'

Even Torello seemed to sense something momentous in the air; he gently placed his fork on his plate and watched them both intently.

'Yes. He and some of the other guards, the newer ones. It was a few weeks later, and we knew the Partisans were closer because you could hear the shooting, all day long now. The guns and the Russian artillery. Sometimes we'd see a plane, flying low, Russian markings on the wings. But the killing went on. They were almost in a frenzy about it by then. Finally one morning there was a riot. In the men's section. Everyone knew that freedom was close but that the killing might come quicker, so some of the men rushed the guards. Then the shooting started. The reaction on our side was immediate. Suddenly everyone was running, and all the guards were shooting. Except ours. It was strange. I think we had the only group that didn't fire. They shouted at us instead. "Run!" they said. "Towards the back. Run! We'll cut the wires." For all we knew it was a trick, a way to shoot us in the back, but we ran, and they came with us. They cut the wires, and when we were through the opening they were still with us. There must have been six guards in all, and they seemed as desperate to get away as we were.

'Not everybody made it. The other guards saw us and fired. I think only twenty of us got clear, maybe a few more. And only two of the guards. Josip and another. A boy named Dario who looked about fifteen. We'd all hated him, too. But now he was running like everybody else.'

'What about the rest of your family?'

'They were killed.' She said it without changing her tone, but her eyes were looking straight at Vlado. 'My mother made it through the fence but she was shot. I saw her on the ground behind me. I didn't look back again. My father must not have made it out. Later I heard that the Partisans arrived after another two days, but he must have been dead by then. I don't know if he died that morning or not, but I never saw him again. It was a miracle, really, that any of us lived.'

'Where did you go?'

'We walked for three days, going north and, later, east. We wanted to get away from the fighting. Josip got

394

rid of his uniform and his papers, but he kept his gun. By then we knew he wasn't going to hurt us, but I think he wondered if we might do something to him. After a few days there were just six of us left. The others had gone in other directions, trying to get back to their villages. Some were Slovenians but most were Bosnians. Two weeks later we crossed the border into Italy. Half starved, but we made it. Some British soldiers picked us up and put us on trucks. A week later we were in a DP camp, in Fermo.'

'Why didn't you go home?'

'There was nothing left to go back to. Our village had been burned and my parents were dead. My brothers were off in the war – I didn't know where, we hadn't heard from them for more than a year. I thought about going to Lubljiana, to look for an aunt, but I didn't know what the situation was there, and I was too afraid to travel alone. And by then I was with Josip. I know it sounds insane. Being with your guard. But he had freed us, and he'd looked out for me on the road. By the time we got to the DP camp we were travelling as husband and wife, not because I was in love with him, but because things went easier for you if you were married, part of a couple. If you were unattached they might leave you in the camp for ever. With a husband you were resettled sooner. And Josip was worried they'd find out he'd been working at the camp. As long as I was with him, no-one would be suspicious. But it was because of Josip that I met Rudec, or Matek, as he was already calling himself. The one who later called himself Barzini.'

'At Fermo?'

'Yes. He was from Josip's village, a little place in Herzegovina, and they saw each other in the dining hall. Josip told me Matek had been at Jasenovac earlier – he didn't want to tell me much about what he'd done – but that he had been transferred to Zagreb, not long before my family arrived.'

Of course, Vlado thought. How else would Matek have ended up in the convoy going north with all that gold? The clever opportunist had found the easiest way out once again. And it was Matek who engineered their way out of Fermo, Lia told him, a clever way of keeping Josip indebted to him, she believed. The first thing he did was get travel documents for all three of them, shedding his old name of Rudec in the process.

'He never said how he'd done it. He just showed up one morning at our barracks with all the papers, and told us to make sure we attended a Mass that Sunday to meet a Father Draganovic, who would take care of us.'

After that, she said, things moved quickly.

'We went to Rome next. Josip wanted to go back to Yugoslavia, but Matek always had some plan, some scheme, and he knew how to make Josip do as he said. And one morning Matek showed up with more papers for us. Passports from the Red Cross. He said we were moving here, to Castellammare. So now I was Lia DiFlorio. Before, I had been Lea Breza. Josip was now Giuseppe, and Matek was Piro Barzini. I knew by then that I was in love with Josip, and wanted to be where he was. So we came here, and for fifteen years we were happy, though we were never able to have children. Or as happy as we could be, knowing that we couldn't go home, or that at any time someone might find out who we really were. And there was always Matek, with his plans and his schemes. Right up until the night when they left in a boat. Matek said they would be gone only a few hours. But they never came back.'

'In nineteen sixty-one?' Vlado asked. Very soon he'd have to tell her his own story, and he wondered how best to do it. He was certain now that she'd never have heard the name Enver Petric, that Matek and his father must have kept that identity a secret all along.

'Yes, nineteen sixty-one,' she said. 'On a clear night with a calm sea. The authorities concluded they'd drowned, but no-one ever found their bodies. There was only the boat, which washed up later. But by then . . .' She shrugged. 'I had nowhere else to go, so I stayed. But I've always wondered if they really died. If they ever really got into the boat at all. And now I have a feeling I'm going to find out. And that the news isn't going to be very happy. Is that right?' She gazed imploringly at him.

Vlado wanted to spare her feelings yet knew he couldn't. She had given him a tale of redemption that he hadn't thought was possible, but all he could offer in return was the knowledge of a betrayal. He took a deep breath, her eyes still on him, and he began – slowly, deliberately.

'There are three things you should know first. One is that Pero Matek is still alive, and may well be here, in Castellammare di Stabia.'

She took it without flinching, as if she'd expected no less.

'The second thing is that Josip Iskric lived until nineteen eighty-three. He reached Yugoslavia in nineteen sixty-one, probably after Matek gave him no choice but to return, and also to keep quiet about it. They crossed the Adriatic, and he became Enver Petric, and settled near Sarajevo.

'The third thing . . .' Vlado paused, feeling short of breath, as if there was hardly enough air left in the room for the three of them. 'The third thing is that I am Enver Petric's son, his only child.'

Lia placed a hand on her heart, seeming to falter. But her eyes were dry. She rose unsteadily from her chair and stepped towards Vlado, who had already stood to receive her. Placing her hands on his shoulders, she looked into his eyes, then slowly embraced him, tentatively at first, then tightly. Vlado hugged her back, feeling an odd mix of emotions. She wasn't his mother, but she was something almost like it, the only person close to a relative he had left from his father's side, except Aunt Melania. He felt her sob against him, a quiver that shook his breastbone, and he reacted as if it was some sort of signal, finally releasing his own emotions. A tight ball of heat seemed to melt in his chest, and his tears fell.

Torello, still seated, wiped his mouth with a napkin and coughed, looking off towards the other end of the room. There was no sound now but Lia's light gasping, like a weary swimmer who had just come up for air.

After a few moments she released him, backing away unsteadily. Vlado slowly dropped his arms to his sides, his shirt-front damp. She dipped a napkin into a glass of water and dabbed at her splotchy face, then at his, the wrinkled hands moving tenderly, almost in a caress.

'How much longer did you say he lived?' she asked, her voice steady now.

'Until nineteen eighty-three. I was nineteen when he died, the same age as when you went to the camp.'

She nodded.

'I only found the picture a few days ago,' he said, gesturing towards the black and white photo on the table. 'My father gave it to his sister a long time ago, when I was a boy. My mother, as far as I know, never saw it. She died a few years ago. But I didn't really know who you were until now. This evening.'

She nodded again, either too upset or too stupefied to say a word.

Torello cleared his throat. 'I would assume,' he said in a low voice in English, 'that the truth has come out about your father.'

'Yes. And now I suppose we need to somehow start asking the meat of the questions. Not that I'm inclined to do it.'

'Then we'll use that method they have in the American cop movies,' he said softly. 'Good cop, bad cop. I'll ask the intrusive stuff, the prying questions. She'll expect me to be that way anyway. You can fill me in on what she's told you, then rest a while. You look as if you need it as much as she does.'

'OK,' Vlado said, sitting down, drained, yet also transported by a new lightness. He looked at Lia, who smiled, and he smiled back.

Bad cop or not, Torello handled it well, Vlado

thought, if one could judge such things merely by tone or pacing. But it was also clear that Lia DiFlorio said few words in response to most of his questions, and ten minutes later Torello told him they knew little more than when they'd arrived, especially with regard to any crates that Matek or Vlado's father might have brought with them to the town. They had travelled to Castellammare separately, she said, with Matek and Josip going a few days ahead of her, by truck. She had gone by train, a slow and halting journey that had taken days.

Neither Josip nor Pero – Vlado couldn't think of them as DiFlorio and Barzini – had ever mentioned anything they'd brought from Rome, or any hiding place where they might have stashed valuables, and she knew of no place Matek might go if he were to return.

Did Vlado believe her? He wasn't sure. But he still felt, somehow, that she would help them, in her way, if she could.

After Torello had brought Vlado up to speed on his last round of questions, everyone lapsed into an exhausted silence. The two men lit cigarettes, and Lia leaned over to pull one from Vlado's pack.

'I gave up years ago, but tonight I can't help it,' she said.

'Where is my father's grave?' Vlado asked, thinking it might be worth a visit. Even knowing it was empty, it seemed a fitting memorial to the part of his father's life he'd never known.

'Not far down the hillside. I still go there to think about things. To talk to him about what I've been doing.

It's very peaceful there. But now . . .' She shrugged weakly, her voice trailing off. 'If I'd had the money I would have bought him a *cappella*, a big place I could really visit. But there just wasn't enough money.'

'Excuse me,' Torello said, perking up. 'Did she say something about a *cappella*?'

'Yes,' Vlado said. 'Is it some kind of grave?'

'It's a chapel, but when it is in a cemetery it is a vault, sort of a miniature chapel. Which would make it a perfect hiding place. Did she say that Matek, or Barzini, bought one?'

'No. She'd wanted to buy one for my father, but couldn't afford it. She managed just a plot and a head-stone. And she didn't buy it until after Matek and my father went missing, so the timing is all wrong.'

'Yes, you're right. I'm getting tired.' Torello frowned, the light gone from his eyes.

'What was he asking about a *cappella*?' Lia said to Vlado, who was beginning to feel like an international mediator, all of this back and forth in two languages while the others spoke a third one between themselves.

'He thought if Matek had bought one for his family, then he could have stored the crates he'd asked you about in it.'

'But he did buy one,' she said, with a sudden light in her eyes. 'For his son.'

Vlado slowly put down his cigarette on the edge of his dinner plate. 'Matek had a son?'

'Yes. He died very young, of influenza. So Matek went out and bought him a big *cappella*. Way too big for an infant, but that was Matek. He liked to make big gestures, to show off. It's in the same cemetery as Josip's headstone.'

'Surely even Matek wouldn't actually use his own boy's tomb as some kind of hiding place,' Vlado said doubtfully.

'The Pero Matek I knew would do it,' Lia said firmly.

Vlado turned towards Torello to translate, but Lia stopped him.

'No,' she said, holding up a hand, which only served to pique Torello's interest. 'I don't want them knowing. Not the local authorities. Please.'

'What's she upset about?' Torello asked. 'What's she saying?'

Vlado looked at her imploring eyes and nodded slightly. Who knew why she was acting this way, but he'd go along with it for now. He owed her that much at least.

'She's worried about Matek,' Vlado told Torello, trying to think fast. 'She's worried he'll come up here. Try to hide here, or make her help him.'

'Not likely,' Torello said dismissively, 'but I can have someone keep an eye on the place if it will make her feel better.'

'Tell her, then.'

Torello spoke, and Lia seemed to calm down, glancing at Vlado with a return nod in thanks. Then, switching back to her native tongue, she hurriedly gave him directions to the cemetery. It was on the way back into town, she said, only a ten-minute drive, marked by a large stone arch at the entrance. But the better route –

quicker and more direct – was on foot, directly downhill through the trees on a narrow path that began just across the road. Five minutes at the most.

She imparted the information without once using the word '*cappella*' or any other obvious phrasing that might have alerted Torello. Then she told Vlado that Matek's spot was in the northeast corner, only a few rows from the headstone marking the empty grave for Vlado's father.

Just then Torello's pager went off, and he excused himself to phone his office from the car.

'I'll be right out,' Vlado told him. 'I think we're pretty much finished here.'

When Torello had gone, Vlado placed both his hands on Lia's, grasping them as he rose to his feet.

'I have to go,' he said. 'But I hope to be back.'

She nodded. 'Matek's *cappella* will be the only one without flowers,' she said. 'The boy's mother stopped going there years ago. I don't even know if she's still alive. She wanted nothing to do with me after the men disappeared. I don't think her time with Pero was very happy. And remember, the name on it is Barzini.'

They were at the doorstep now. He could see Torello at the wheel, talking on the phone with the inside light on. As Vlado turned to say goodbye, Lia placed a hand on his face, pressing it lightly, almost as if she were a medium, trying to detect some remnant of his father's soul.

'I am tired,' she said. 'Talking about those times always wears me out. But this time, more than ever.'

403

Then, almost timidly, she asked, 'Did you say that his name was Enver after he went back to Yugoslavia?'

'Yes. Enver Petric.'

She smiled, lowering her gaze, dropping her hand to her side. 'He was definitely not an Enver. Only a Josip. A Giuseppe even. But Enver? He must have felt ashamed every time he said it.'

'I wouldn't know,' Vlado said, at a loss for words.

She looked up, reddening. 'But maybe that changed when you were born. Having a son would have made being an Enver worth it, don't you think?'

'I hope so,' he said with a hesitant smile, feeling embarrassed.

'Are you a father?'

'Yes. My daughter is nine.' And his smile broadened as he thought of Sonja, wondering what she'd make of all this.

'You wouldn't care what she called you. Any name she chose would seem right, wouldn't it?'

'Yes. It would.'

'Good, then.'

That seemed to give her a measure of peace, and she again placed a hand on his cheek, leaving it there for a few seconds. Vlado felt the roughness of the wrinkled skin, but also the warmth. Out of the corner of his eye he saw Torello, now standing beside the open door of the car, waiting.

'I should go,' Vlado said.

'Let me know what you find,' she said. 'Promise me that. And when you do, I may have something more to tell you.'

It seemed to be all she wanted to say on the subject right now, so Vlado resisted the urge to ask for more. They said goodbye, and he and Torello climbed back into the car for the long drive back down the hill on the narrow road that disappeared into the clouds.

29

'That was my dispatcher,' Torello said as Vlado got into the car. 'There's been a murder at a pension in town. They think the victim is Andric. Healthy male in his fifties carrying three different passports. Face matches the photo from Interpol. Not much to see down below, though. Two shots at close range, large calibre, probably with a silencer.'

So it was true then, their theory about why Matek and Andric might both be drawn to the town. And now the younger and stronger contender had fallen, leaving the way clear for Matek. Vlado realized he had better get moving, even if he knew of only one place to look. He'd feel better having Torello with him, even if Lia had been insistent about not telling the local police. He doubted she wanted him risking his neck.

But Torello apparently wasn't available.

'I'm heading to the pension now,' he said. 'It's down near the port, not far from the office.'

'It's probably best if I don't arrive at the scene with you,' Vlado said, making it up as he went along, 'considering I'm not even supposed to be here. But you should alert Pine. Have your dispatcher call him at the hotel. Then I can hear about it from him and meet you at the scene.'

'Suit yourself. But I can't waste time dropping you at the hotel. I'll have to let you out on the way.'

'Good enough.'

A few minutes later they reached the outskirts of the town. In the bright blur of a street lamp, Vlado saw a stone arch on the left, just as Lia had described it. 'Drop me here. Just remember to tell Pine.'

'Further along would be better, a lot closer.'

'Here is fine. I'll get a cab.'

'Whatever you say.' Torello sounded puzzled, perhaps a little miffed. The streets here were empty, and it was obvious that finding a cab would take a while. But he was in too much of a hurry to ask anything more, so he let Vlado out with a nod and a quick, 'See you there,' before accelerating away.

As the car's red tail lights disappeared round a curve with a squeal of tyres, Vlado walked quickly towards the arch, hoping he wasn't too late. The nearby shops were closed. The only sign of life was a small café, but even that was dimly lit, and the few customers had been chased indoors by the chilly weather.

No-one was in sight as he entered, which Vlado took as a good sign. Scanning the ground quickly, he saw no tyre marks. He doubted you'd be able to haul much out of here without a truck. Or maybe he was at the wrong place altogether. There were hundreds of likely hiding places, from ancient Roman catacombs to caves higher in the hills. And there was always the possibility that Matek had simply dug his own hole, a place where no-one but him would know to look. Although the rocky soil made that seem unlikely. Matek struck him as the type who'd cut a corner whenever possible. And what easier way to do so than stealing your son's tomb.

Just inside the cemetery walls was a small stone house, probably the caretaker's. As Vlado approached the door he worried again about the language barrier. If the caretaker didn't speak English, Vlado would only arouse suspicion, arriving with frantic gestures and no escort. But no-one seemed to be home. The windows were dark, and the place was silent. Vlado checked his watch. It was just after nine. Too early to be home for the night if you lived in a cemetery. Vlado crept along quietly nonetheless, heading for what seemed to be a wooden maintenance shed just to the rear. It was surrounded by a high chain link fence, padlocked at the front, but the fencing was old and loose. Vlado was able to pull back the gate just enough to squeeze inside. He opened the shed door and flicked his cigarette lighter. Two manual lawnmowers were parked cheek by jowl with a jumble of shovels, rakes and hoes. On a rough wooden shelf were more tools. One was a long, heavy crowbar. Vlado took it. There were also two battered flashlights. He tried the first, finding the batteries were dead, but the second one worked. He slipped back outside, pausing to make sure the house was still quiet before continuing. No sound but a few passing cars out on the street. The northeast corner, Lia had said. Vlado oriented himself by facing downhill, towards the Bay of Naples, which was to the north. He angled off to the front and right, and after about thirty yards he turned on the flashlight. His trousers were already wet from the dewy grass.

He would have felt better with some back-up, and for a moment he thought of returning to the street, trying to reach Pine before Torello did. But it was probably already too late for that, and his curiosity was stronger. Besides, all was quiet. Anyone loading up crates of gold bars would be making one hell of a racket.

He made his way downhill past a long white aisle of tombstones towards the far side of the lot. There, off to his right, and about a hundred yards from the entrance, was a wall of the *cappella*, like a miniature block of apartments, abutting a crease in the hill. Each was like a tiny chapel of granite or marble, with names and dates chiselled into slabs next to the door; little temples of the dead, where the bereaved could step inside, sheltered from the noise of traffic and the elements. The newer ones had smoked-glass doors, and as the flashlight winked past, he glimpsed bouquets of flowers and the greenery of plants. There were also flowers in brass vases.

Lia was right. There were flowers outside every *cappella* but one, which was about twenty yards down the row. Vlado swung the flashlight. The name 'Barzini' was engraved in stone. This one had a steel door, heavy looking and rusty at the edges. The boy's name had been Carlo: 1951–1952. A year old at the most.

The lock looked substantial, which was hardly a surprise. But there was just enough room to poke the teeth of the crowbar between the door and the jamb. Five minutes of prising and grunting finally brought the door free with a metallic shriek, followed by a loud snap, like a small gunshot.

Vlado checked behind him before entering, swinging the beam of the flashlight across the tombstones, but he saw nothing. There was still only the sound of a few cars and trucks grinding their way up the streets.

He pulled back the door and shone the light through the opening, then stepped inside, amazed at the spaciousness. His footsteps resonated as if he'd entered a cave. No flowers in here, either. Nothing, in fact, but a damp smell like wet concrete. Somehow it all felt familiar, and Vlado remembered the *Fahrerbunker* from his last day on the job in Berlin. The thought made him a little weak in the knees, then a breeze outside began to shut the door behind him, and for a few panicky seconds he envisioned being locked inside. But with the lock sprung that was impossible, and he chided himself, trying to relax. The door was so fouled by his jemmying that it merely tapped and bounced in the frame before finally coming to rest, a few inches ajar.

Resuming his inspection by flashlight, he saw granite ledges running lengthwise on both sides, presumably to be used as benches. The main attraction sat in the middle of the floor, a large stone tomb, about four feet high, three feet wide and more than six feet long. Much too big for an infant. Big enough, in fact, for a large man. Or other things.

The lid was a slab of marble, with the name engraved on top. Vlado ran his fingers beneath the overhanging edges. It looked heavy enough but didn't seem sealed in any way. He gave a test lift with one hand, but it didn't budge. He placed the flashlight on a ledge and pulled up with both hands, managing to lift the slab a few

410

inches and slide it over, just a fraction. It would be difficult, but not impossible. Before getting started he took
a final inventory, listening carefully for noises outside.
Still quiet.

Lifting with all his might, he began swivelling one
end of the slab slowly towards the ledge behind him. As
it began to ease free with a gritty, grinding sound,
warmer air from inside the tomb curled up around his
fingers, an eerie tickling sensation. He hoped there
wasn't a child's body inside, no matter what else he
found.

He shuffled sideways a few feet, still holding one end,
his shoes scuffing on the grit. Then he lowered the lid
as gently as possible onto the ledge before stepping to
the other end to repeat the trick, until the lid balanced
lengthwise along the ledge, nearly half its width overhanging precariously. With the flashlight resting low on
the other side of the room, the inside of the tomb
remained deep in shadow. Vlado was sweating, and
could feel the strain in his arms and shoulders. But now
came the moment of truth.

He retrieved the flashlight and pointed the beam
inside. The sight was electrifying: two wooden boxes,
nailed shut, with recessed metal handles folded down
on two sides. The black stencilled lettering on top was
in Vlado's language. 'State Bank of Croatia.' There was
no coffin. No body.

He felt for a moment like an exultant pirate. He wanted
to shout, to pound someone on the back and roar with
laughter. He hadn't felt this giddy in a long while, but it
was more important than ever to remain quiet. The

411

crates were nailed shut. He'd need the crowbar again, and he'd left it in the grass outside the door.

As he pushed open the door he felt the fresh wet air on his face. It was still quiet out here. Then the brightness of a flashlight beam exploded into his face, blinding him for a second, and before he could move another step he saw two dark silhouettes loom up suddenly on either side. A hand was clamped across his mouth and another across his right arm. He heard a metallic click, letting him know his visitors were armed, followed by a voice, speaking in English.

'Nice of you to get things started for us.' Harkness. 'And how convenient to find you literally at death's door, which is where you've been heading all along. Step back inside, please, so I can conclude my business and get the hell out of here.'

Vlado turned, and the other man swivelled the light. Vlado could now see that it was Matek. He said nothing. Even in the darkness something about him seemed different. Harkness held the gun. Before stepping through the door, Vlado considered bolting – anything instead of going back in there at gunpoint. But the nudge of a barrel in his back convinced him otherwise. A strong smell emanated from Matek. Sweat and effort and worry. Blood, too. He was breathing hard, a rasping that said he'd had a rough time.

'C'mon, now. Inside.' Another shove with the barrel. 'Keep your hands behind your back, where I can see them.'

Back through the door, their voices sounded hollow, stony.

412

'If you would empty your pockets, slowly please, and carefully place the contents on the floor. Particularly any firearms you might have.'

Vlado had nothing with him but a pencil, a few scraps of paper and some coins. When this was all he produced, Harkness poked his own hand in to make sure.

'Good of the Tribunal to send you into the world so well prepared,' he said. 'I can't tell you how much it pains me to see you here, Vlado. Headstrong and meddlesome as ever. But you've at least earned yourself a look inside the crates, I suppose. Besides, I need your help.'

'Sorry. It's not what I'm paid to do.'

'Fine. Then I'll shoot you. Your choice, family man. Just let me know when you've made up your mind.'

Vlado's chest went hollow. He'd been telling himself for the past few seconds that Harkness wouldn't do him actual harm; that the man might be ruthless and manipulative but wasn't a killer. Now he knew otherwise, and should have all along. He looked again for an opening, any chance to kick or lunge, but Harkness was keeping himself beyond range, and seemed as alert as ever. Gun raised. Pointed right at him.

Matek, on the other hand, still hadn't opened his mouth, and Vlado now got a good look at him. His expression was glum, defeated, a countenance suggesting that this was anything but a willing partnership.

'Pero, why don't you lean in and pry the top loose on that first crate. Vlado, back away, and put your hands on your head. Move an inch and you'll have a very ugly hole in your chest. Faster, Pero, and no tricks. You've already seen where that leads.'

As Matek bent over with a wheezing grunt, Vlado saw a dark, wet stain under his left armpit. Harkness saw Vlado looking.

'Don't worry about him. Tried to pull a knife on me, so I had to set him straight. Nothing fatal. He's still pouting about having to share.'

As if Harkness would really go through with such an arrangement, Vlado thought. Matek would be killed the moment they got clear of here. He wondered if Matek realized that. Perhaps the old man was also hoping for an opening, a final chance. If so, it would be two against one, if only for a moment.

Matek merely grunted in reply, but seemed to recover some of his energy. He glared at Harkness, looking covetously at the gun, then began working at the lid of the first box, using the crowbar Vlado had appropriated.

'Just pry it open on one side. We're nailing it shut as soon as we've seen what's in there.'

The wood snapped free, and even Matek couldn't keep from gasping, though he'd doubtless known what was inside. The flashlight beam glinted off neatly stacked gold bars that rose nearly to the brim, a dazzling sight in the darkness.

'Just as advertised,' Harkness said. Then he poked a hand inside, as if feeling for something that might be wedged at the sides. He came up empty. 'All right. Shove that lid back on. We'll nail it in a minute. Next one, please.'

Matek, still without a word, worked painstakingly at the second lid. Harkness was transfixed, and Vlado slowly began to lower his hands from behind his head. One inch. Then another. Then another. Harkness looked up quickly, swivelling the gun, the barrel coming to rest a few feet from his chest. The pitch of his voice rose by an octave.

'Next time you do that, you're dead. No more testing.'

The nails of the second crate screeched and groaned, and the lid hinged open. But the sight this time was a shock, though Matek didn't act a bit surprised. The box was nearly empty. No more than a few rows of gold bars were stacked at the bottom.

'Jesus Christ, Pero, you profligate old bastard. What'd you do, spend fifteen years trying to corner the local market in Limoncello?' But Harkness sounded more amused than upset. He was more interested in a fat, dog-eared brown envelope wedged upright to one side.

He pulled out the envelope, the papers practically spilling from one end. It looked like a hundred or more pages. Vlado stared at them, more fascinated than he had been by the gold. Somewhere in that pile, most likely, were the documents that had changed his father's life. That had, in their way, helped bring him into this world, he supposed. And now they might well usher him out.

'It's what you should have given us from the beginning, you welshing old thief.' Harkness put down the flashlight a moment, still aiming the gun with his other hand. Then he pushed the envelope against his overcoat, folding it lengthwise in a one-handed motion before stuffing it into a wide pocket. 'Now, gentlemen. Time for the real work. Pero, go and get the truck.'

Unbelievably, Matek did just that, disappearing for several minutes before Vlado heard the engine as the truck poked in through the cemetery gates and began crawling across the lot. Only his greed could be keeping him going like this, Vlado thought. Any other man would have driven down the mountain and got out of here. Matek either actually believed Harkness would split the take, or else he still held out hope of outsmarting the man, as if he held one last trick in reserve. Or perhaps it was simply the fatal hubris of a man who'd never yet been outfoxed.

Vlado, who'd waited in silence up to now, decided to get straight to the heart of the matter.

'Tell me, are you going to kill me when you've finished here?'

'Just keep making yourself useful and stay quiet, Vlado. You know I'm not the sloppy type. But you want to know the real shame in this? I wouldn't even be here now if it weren't for you. Popovic was supposed to be here, doing the dirty work. But you went and spoiled that, didn't you? Then Matek slipped the leash and everything went to hell. Though it's funny how things have a way of working out. Here you are, handy for the heavy lifting, while Matek has already accommodated me by taking care of the worst of the chores.'

'By killing Andric, you mean.'

Harkness seemed momentarily taken aback. Then he recovered, forcing a smile. 'So they've found the body, then, and already made an ID. Impressive.' His voice wasn't so smug now, and he glanced at his watch. 'Which branch of police?'

Nice to know there were a few things he hadn't found out about, such as Torello, for example. No sense telling him now.

Vlado merely shrugged.

'Not the carabinieri, I hope, or they'll be here with armour. All the more reason to work quickly.'

Matek had completed the drive up the grassy service road and stopped just short of the entrance. The cemetery entrance was visible through the open door, but the caretaker's hut was still dark and quiet.

'Get in here, Pero. There isn't much time.' Harkness was all business now. No more joking. 'Get a grip on that first crate, both of you. Use both hands. Drop it and you're dead. Take a hand off before I say so and you're dead.'

They bent into the tomb, gripping the metal handles on either side of the box, and heaved upwards. Matek in particular struggled with the weight, and for a moment they looked across the top of the crate at each other, and something seemed to pass between them, if only a shared recognition of their misery. The moment passed. As soon as the crate had cleared the top of the tomb they began shuffling towards the door with it. The handle was digging painfully into Vlado's hands, but he didn't dare rest them now.

'Good. Keep it moving. Steady. Just push slowly through the door and watch your step.'

They were back into the night air, a relief from the claustrophobia of the *cappella*. Still no sound but the

417

hiss and grind of light traffic. Vlado darted a glance to either side, and nearly lost his footing.

'Keep your mind on your work. You're not going anywhere without a bullet in the back. And don't think you can rouse the caretaker. He's having a fine time drinking down in the town, courtesy of the US Treasury.'

With another heave, they shoved the crate into the back of a small truck with a canvas cover on the back. It was unmarked. They slid the crate back a few feet, then turned towards the *cappella* again. Harkness was a good ten feet away. If Vlado was going to make a move, now was the time.

'All right, back inside. And to answer your earlier question, Vlado, no, I'm not going to shoot you. So breathe easy.'

A ruse? Probably, but it had the desired effect, giving Vlado just enough hope to keep him from trying anything stupid, like running, or rushing Harkness. He and Matek between them could possibly overpower the man, but the one who made the first move would pay the price, and neither wanted to give his life for the other.

They loaded the second crate, then Matek shut the gate of the truck.

'Back inside again,' Harkness said, and followed them into the *cappella*. 'Vlado, turn round and face the back wall, then slowly bring your hands down behind your back. Good. Pero, take this.' Vlado heard Harkness pulling something from his coat, wishing all the while that he'd taken his chance outside. His moment of

418

uncertainty had cost him. 'Wire his hands together.'

Matek worked slowly, the wire pinching into Vlado's wrists. He was making sure of a tight fit. So much for expecting help from the old man, or any sort of teamwork. Now it was too late for any move. His stomach sank towards his bowels, and he had an image of Jasmina and Sonja, silhouetted in a brightly lit doorway, slowly waving goodbye.

'Now turn round slowly and step into the tomb.'

It was awkward doing it with his hands behind his back, but he managed.

'Pero, step away, and don't move. Vlado, get down on your knees.'

'You said you weren't going to kill me.' His voice was shaking. He hated himself for it, for doing as he was told, for making these stupid and frightened comments. All those people trooping like lambs into the death camps. He'd have done exactly the same, fooled to the end, thinking he was helping his family.

'I say a lot of things I don't mean, Vlado. It's all part of diplomacy.'

Here he was, he thought, the wire cutting into his wrists and the chill of the tomb's stone floor drilling into his knees. He'd helped Harkness keep things neat by lowering himself into a place where his blood would pool in the blackness and he would be sealed for eternity, a hermetic disposal with the witting assistance of the victim. As Harkness eased the gun forward, Vlado decided on a final move, no matter how futile.

'Pero, please step back,' Harkness ordered.

His words were nearly drowned out by the roar of an

419

engine. A flicker of headlights darted through the opening in the door.

'Pero, see what the hell it is,' he said tersely. 'If it's the goddamned caretaker, he's going in there with Vlado.'

Matek pulled the door wide while Harkness glanced over his shoulder. Vlado inched forward on his knees, but Harkness swung the barrel back in his face, no more than a foot away.

'Hold still!' he hissed. 'Pero, who is it?'

'Two cars. Coming this way.'

'Fuck!'

Harkness again glanced away, and this time Vlado was close enough to lunge, trying awkwardly to strike like a snake, rising from his knees and bending at the waist while pressing his soles against the rear of the tomb for leverage. His head butted Harkness in the thighs, teeth against the wool of his overcoat, but the impact wasn't enough to knock him down. Harkness stumbled a step then turned, face enraged, the black barrel again in place as he tilted his head slightly to aim. He squeezed the trigger and there was a blinding flash just as an arm fell on the gun from the side – Matek, seizing his moment. A dart of flame creased Vlado's left cheek, and he felt the sting of splintering marble against his forehead as the slug crackled and bounced through the echoing roar, as if someone had tossed a lightning bolt into the *cappella*. Harkness twisted the gun free from Matek's grip and ran through the door, bursting into the cemetery like a horse from its stable, coat-tails flying.

'*Fermi! Polizia!*' a voice shouted on a loudspeaker.

Vlado's ears were still ringing from the gunshot. Headlight beams were swinging wildly in their direction now, and he threw himself across the low wall of the tomb then clambered awkwardly to his feet, his adrenaline on full throttle, though his hands were still bound painfully at his back. Through the door he noticed Matek off to one side in the shadows. Twenty yards to the left a dark shape bobbed among the tombstones, on the outer edges of the headlight beams.

'Fermi! Fermi!' the loudspeaker cried again, but Vlado had already ducked out of the blinding glare and was running after Harkness, head forward for balance with his arms behind him. He sensed dark figures somewhere to his left and rear, coming after them. The grass was slippery, and he nearly lost his balance, clipping a foot on the edge of a low-lying marker. Harkness was barely visible now, but Vlado could still see the gun in one hand. The man was in good shape, but being younger helped, and Harkness stumbled slightly as he, too, caught his foot on some low-lying stone. He must have heard Vlado huffing closer, because he glanced over his shoulder, his face pale in the dimness. The voices of the police seemed to be receding. They must have been closing in on the truck, perhaps chasing down Matek, or preoccupied by the *cappella*.

They were now on a rising slope, Vlado surging at an odd angle, barely keeping his balance but within ten yards of Harkness, driven forward by his anger. He saw Harkness pause, then turn, the gun outstretched, so he swerved wildly, stumbling to the right as he saw the muzzle flash, accompanied by a boom echoing into the hills. He dived towards Harkness's ankles as he lost balance, knowing that the next shot would probably be from too close to miss. He felt Harkness's legs buckling beneath his chest as he collapsed, still lunging forward. They hit the wet ground hard, taking his breath away, and he scrambled up the body in an awkward crawl, hands still wired behind him, Harkness was groping for something, perhaps the gun. Vlado flinched as there was a second flash, but this one was far smaller, and he saw that Harkness had pulled out a cigarette lighter and was stretching it towards the edge of the old brown envelope, which lay just beyond him in the grass. The flame lit the scene with an amber glow, showing the whites of Harkness's eyes. The corner of the envelope was just catching fire as Vlado moved towards it on his knees. Harkness squirmed beneath him, reaching far enough to grasp the envelope and flick it forward a foot. But the motion extinguished the flame, and as the spinning envelope came to rest, Vlado fell in a heap, his chest collapsing on top of Harkness's head. The smoke from the envelope was musty in his nostrils.

'You goddamned fool!'

Harkness's voice was a muffled shout from beneath Vlado's stomach. The man was thrashing like a buried animal trying to dig its way back to the surface. Vlado rolled off, looking around quickly for the gun but not finding it.

'Vlado!' another voice shouted from behind. It was Pine, moving towards them from twenty yards away.

'Over here. I've got Harkness.'

'I have a gun,' Pine said. 'So no sudden movements.'

Vlado sat up slowly, while Harkness remained prone, panting heavily and cursing beneath his breath. Pine knelt on the ground and picked something up.

'There,' he said. 'Now I really do have a gun. Must be his. Get up slowly, both of you. And if you think I won't shoot you, Harkness, think again.'

'You're damned fools, both of you, if you think this is the right thing to do. You especially, Pine.'

Pine ignored him. 'You all right, Vlado? Is that blood on your face?'

'Just a graze. I'll be fine if you can get this wire off my wrists. Where's Matek?'

'He's here?'

'You didn't see him?'

'No. The cops are all in a lather back there over the crates. Your buddy Torello found them in the truck.'

'Matek's wounded. He may not have gone far.'

'You better go tell the others. I'll take care of this one. Here, turn round and let me get that wire. Harkness, don't move.'

Harkness was still on the ground, spent. A policeman was running towards them through the tombstones, and Pine was happy to let him clip the wire off Vlado, who rubbed his wrists, his arms aching. Vlado picked up the singed envelope of documents and walked quickly towards the *cappella*. He found two more policemen by the truck, and one was Torello.

'We found a deed to the *cappella* in Andric's room,' he said. 'I thought we'd better hurry over. But I didn't think we'd find you here.' There was a slight note of

423

disapproval in his voice, but Vlado had bigger worries just now.

'Where is the other man?' he asked hurriedly.

'Your colleague, Mr Pine?'

'The other suspect. Matek.'

'I haven't seen anyone. Just you and that other American.' He gestured towards Harkness, making his way across the cemetery with Pine and the policeman behind him. They walked in single file, striding as slowly and carefully as pall-bearers.

Vlado checked inside the *cappella*, but found only another policeman poking around the tomb. Just outside the door he picked up Harkness's flashlight. It was still on, and he swung the beam in a wide arc into the distance. Nothing. All this, and Matek had again slipped away, a survivor for the ages. Vlado was sick with disappointment. At least he'd been able to save the documents. But where was Matek? He couldn't have gone far in the shape he was in, but if he'd reached the road he could have hailed a cab.

Vlado moved past a row of graves, peering into the darkness but seeing only stone angels, vaults and slabs of marble. Nothing living, and nothing stirring. Then the afterburn of his adrenaline made him sag on top of one of the headstones. He turned off the flashlight, pondering his next move, wondering how late the trains ran.

One of the police cars restarted its engine. They were probably eager to spread the word about the gold. By dawn the whole place would be crazed, and it would be harder than ever to get anyone to look for Matek. But for now they could at least alert the train station and the taxi dispatchers. Vlado got wearily to his feet in the dark. It would again become a slow, painstaking manhunt, one he probably wouldn't be allowed to join.

The police car began moving, and as it swerved, the beam of its headlights swept past Vlado, illuminating the ground before him. In that brief moment a single name leaped at him from the facing row of tombstones: 'DiFlorio.'

30

Vlado turned his flashlight back on to make sure it hadn't been his imagination, and there it was. Blood rushed to his fingertips as he stepped towards the stone. 'Giuseppe,' the inscription began, and he roughly deciphered the rest as saying, 'beloved husband of Lia'. Even though he knew that the grave beneath him was empty, Vlado was moved by the sight of the name. He crouched to place his fingers against the carved letters. Something of his father remained here – in this town, in these hills – no matter where his body reposed.

'So, tell me,' Vlado whispered, this time half believing he'd get an answer, 'where has your old enemy gone?'

But the only response was the chatter of a scanner from the second Italian police car. Vlado looked over and saw two of the officers lighting cigarettes. One was already writing up his report, seated on the bonnet of the car. Vlado reached into a pocket for his own cigarettes, feeling his nerves begin to calm. But as he shifted his flashlight he saw something else – two red droplets on the grass, shining up at him from a few feet past the headstone. The hair stood up on his forearms, and he bent down to touch. The drops were warm. With his flashlight he saw that the grass had been disturbed.

There was a rough path of smudged footprints through the dew, leading towards the low stone wall on the opposite side.

He stepped in that direction, soon finding another scatter of red droplets, then another, until the smudged footprints reached a small opening in the wall, where a narrow path rose steeply uphill through the trees.

Only a five-minute walk, he remembered Lia saying, and as he began to climb, a patchwork of images and observations began to take shape with a sudden coherence: the old photo of Lia and his father, showing a ladder propped against a tree near a small ring of stones; Matek's brooding silence at the *cappella*; the emptiness of the second crate. Lastly there was Lia DiFlorio, and the way she'd first reacted to the photo, then her adamant insistence that Torello not be told of the *cappella*. But come and see me afterwards, she'd said, and she would tell Vlado something more. With every step he took, the meaning seemed clearer, and he quickened his pace even as he heard Pine's voice from behind him, well down the hill, plaintively calling, 'Vlado, Vlado,' like a parent who has lost track of a wayward child. The sound soon faded, and within minutes there was only the night chirp of a few bugs, the snapping of twigs beneath his feet, a swish of branches overhead as he pushed his way upwards. The air was cooler here, moisture clinging to the trees. Above the canopy, only starlight. The clouds were gone.

The path reached the road, and on the other side was Lia's house, set against the hill. The lights were off.

Vlado worked his way round to the left, where he'd earlier seen the citrus trees. He spotted another droplet of Matek's blood. Harkness had insisted he'd done the man no real damage, but Vlado wondered.

He moved slowly now, looking carefully for places where the dew and the grass were smudged or trampled. He passed the house well to the left of the chimney, then eased back into trees, picking up another path, this one fainter, but stained here and there by the telltale droplets. A minute or so later Vlado found himself in a grove of lemon trees, and he thought again of the photograph as the path emerged into a small clearing. With the view before him now, everything fell into place, even in the dim starlight. There was the same bluff as in the photo, the same ring of white stones. He had assumed the stones were for a campfire, but now he saw that they formed the rim of an old well. Poking just above it were the top few feet of a long wooden ladder – the same style as the one in the photo. Vlado paused, listening carefully, and heard a tiny scraping sound, like that of a mouse gnawing at a skirting board. It came from inside the well, which surely was dry, and had been for at least fifty years.

Vlado stepped carefully to the rim and peered down. Some twenty-five feet below, illuminated by a flashlight, was the grey head of Pero Matek. He was stooped like an old troll, hunched over his coveted possessions.

'Looking for the last of your nest egg?' Vlado shouted.

Matek lurched in surprise, then picked up the flashlight and shone it upwards, momentarily blinding Vlado, who squinted but held his ground. For a moment

428

the old man said nothing, then he began to chuckle, a tired wheezing laugh.

'I was right,' Matek said. 'Just like your goddamned father. You never know when to let go.'

'Was part of his share down there? Or were you the only one who knew about this place?'

'*His* share?' The wheezing laugh again. 'His share was my agreement not to turn him in, plus the occasional handout. I got nervous about leaving everything down in the *cappella*. Always having to visit it whenever I needed to make a withdrawal. Those old women with their flowers do a lot of gossiping. So I gradually moved half of it up here. And now there's enough for both of us. Here, I'll show you.'

Matek bent over, but he straightened holding a gun, not gold. Vlado jerked his head back just as the shot echoed up the stone shaft like a blast of artillery. Now where the hell had that come from? One of the police cars, probably. Stolen in all the confusion as the old man had slinked away in the shadows, one last trick in his bag. But the shot had missed, and Vlado now held a momentary advantage. Taking care to keep himself beyond the narrow cylinder of Matek's line of fire, Vlado grabbed the top rung of the ladder, which was angled just out of harm's way. He gave a great tug, and by the time Matek realized what was happening Vlado had raised the ladder several feet. He heard the gun and flashlight clatter against the stones before he felt the ladder tug back. It was as if he'd just hooked a huge fish on a large, unwieldy pole, and for a moment his grip wavered as Matek pulled, gravity and leverage on the

429

side of the old man. Then Vlado stepped forward to brace his foot on the stone ledge, no longer worried about the gun, and pulled with all his might. There was a grunt, then a sharp cry of pain echoed from below, and Vlado nearly lost his balance as the ladder came free. He raised it, one rung at a time, until the whole thing teetered awkwardly above him and he let it tumble harmlessly into the grass.

He sagged back onto the wet ground, exhausted. Then he was startled by the sound of a woman's voice coming from the darkness of the trees.

'It's him, isn't it?' she said. 'It's Pero, down in the well.'

Vlado turned to see Lia DiFlorio standing in a long dressing gown at the edge of the path, her breath vaporizing into the night.

'Yes, it's him. But don't look down there. He has a gun.'

'I know. I heard it. That's what brought me outside.'

'Sorry to wake you.'

'Oh, I was awake already. Far too stirred up to sleep tonight.' She smiled just a bit, then the smile widened, and she broke into a satisfied laugh.

'How nice to see him playing the fool for a change,' she said. 'Especially when there's been nothing down there to claim for years.'

'You took it, didn't you?' Vlado said, with just the slightest hint of a scolding tone, to let her know she should have told him earlier. 'I wouldn't have told Torello, you know. You're probably entitled, after all you went through.'

'I was afraid. That gold paid for this house. Your father and I were barely able to pay the rent before.'

'Do you still have any?'

'Not much. But more than enough for me to live on. I don't spend it quickly. And Pero had already gone through a lot of it by the time they left. Which is one reason I never realized he'd hidden it in more than one place. I thought he'd put everything up here, until tonight.'

'So where is it now, the gold from the well?'

'In the house. Somewhere safe. I moved it about ten years ago. I was getting too old to keep climbing that ladder. Then, when you came and showed me that picture, I didn't know what to think. I was scared that you knew everything. But once you told me you were Josip's son, I wasn't so worried.'

They were silent a moment, as if sorting out their thoughts. The sound of digging came from inside the well, and a band of light wavered through the opening as the old man again bent to the false promise of treasure. Matek obviously hadn't been able to hear their conversation.

'There's nothing there any more,' Vlado shouted, easing towards the rim. 'Lia took it all.'

'Lia never knew it was down here,' Matek grunted stubbornly, still digging.

'Josip told me,' she said. 'In a note he left me, the day the two of you disappeared.'

With that, the digging stopped. No-one said a word. Matek hadn't heard that voice in nearly forty years, and it had silenced him as surely as a ghost would have.

Vlado sagged back on his haunches, trousers soaked by the dew. He took a cool, deep breath of the night air and looked at Lia, trying to read her face, but there wasn't enough light.

Their silence was broken by voices and footsteps approaching along the path.

'Probably the police,' Vlado said. 'They must have heard the gunshot.' Then he turned towards Lia, straining again to see her face. 'Don't worry. I'll never tell. And they won't believe him. It's the only secret still worth keeping in this whole mess.'

31

By late the next day, three nations and two local juris-
dictions were already fighting over custody of the gold
bars found inside the Barzini *cappella*. Italy was first to
lay claim, followed in quick succession by Croatia and
the Federal Republic of Yugoslavia. Envoys from Rome,
Zagreb and Belgrade were already en route, but they
would have to contend first with the municipal officials
of Castellammare di Stabia, who'd moved the crates
into the vault of a local bank. They'd done so over
the strenuous protests of late-arriving officials from the
Naples regional authority. By evening even the Polizia
di Stato were mulling over a counter-claim, seeing as
how nothing of value would ever have been discovered
if not for the independent actions of one of their officers
who, as they were already emphatic in pointing out, had
risked his life in the line of duty.

Italy's afternoon tabloids had already laid odds that
the fight would go on for years, and with each hour the
van of another TV crew arrived down the autostrada.
Swiss officials, meanwhile, had begun quietly inquiring
whether there was any reason they should be either
embarrassed or indignant.

Lost somewhat in this hurly-burly was the fact that a
major war crimes suspect had been killed in the town,

and that another more obscure figure, wanted on charges relating to actions half a century earlier, had been apprehended. And that an indignant American diplomat appeared to be in hot water.

And so it was, in the spate of interviews, interrogations and official paperwork that followed, that Vlado didn't see Pine until nearly noon of the next day, when he ran into him in the hotel lobby. They agreed to share a meal. Their flights back to The Hague had already been rescheduled. But the verdict on whether they were to be applauded or excoriated on their return apparently remained a work in progress, with Spratt and Contreras still monitoring prevailing winds from Washington, Paris and Berlin. Janet Ecker remained on administrative leave.

'Well,' Pine said, as they seated themselves, 'the early word is that Matek won't fight extradition.'

'To Croatia?'

'Yes. He's convinced he can beat the rap. He's apparently already been on the phone to his attorneys and his Swiss bankers. Seems to think that if he can get a running start, there just might be enough sentiment in his favour to keep him free, especially with a trial in Zagreb. Who knows, maybe he's right.'

'Maybe,' Vlado said. 'But he might be surprised. The Croatians may decide to make him an example. He offers the perfect chance for national atonement. And in the end, he wasn't even a good fascist, just a thief who stole from everyone, the Ustashe included.'

'Which reminds me. The Croatians may want you to

434

testify. If only to help establish provenance on some of the documents.'

'The documents,' Vlado said, shaking his head with a frown. 'If only I still had them.'

It was the one aspect of the previous night Vlado was glum about. He'd handed them over to Torello around midnight. Within an hour, outside forces had intervened and Torello had regretfully informed him that the envelope and all its contents were being moved 'upstairs', having somehow become part of the equation in the fight over the gold. Torello surmised that a swap was in the works: US backing of an Italian claim in exchange for the return of printed material which, by rights, was legally the property of the US Army, never mind what the priests at San Girolamo would have said about that argument.

'I never should have handed them over,' Vlado said. 'It's the same old story.'

'I wouldn't be so sure,' Pine said, and he slid a fresh manila envelope across the table. 'That's your set of copies. I've got one for myself. Torello slipped them to me around three in the morning, right after you'd gone back to the hotel. He was able to steal a few minutes at the Xerox machine just before sending the originals upstairs. I haven't had much time to look, but the little I've seen was interesting reading. Letterheads from Angleton, Colleton, the Vatican. Plenty of people to be embarrassed. And I did see your father's name once or twice about halfway through the pile, so I think you'll be pleased.'

'What will you do with yours?'

'I've already done it. Faxed the entire load to Janet's apartment. She's got some time on her hands now, as well as a few axes to grind. She assures me that by the end of the week she'll have sent copies to three congressmen on the intelligence committee, the Attorney General's resident Nazi hunters, plus a fully annotated set to a friend of hers at the *New York Times*. So much for enduring secrecy, huh?'

Vlado felt like laughing out loud, like dancing on the tabletop. It had been a wrenching and emotional week, but this was the perfect finish.

'So what does this mean for Harkness? Criminal charges?'

'Doubtful,' Pine said, smiling ruefully. 'He's already gone back to the US Embassy in Rome. For all I know he's left the country altogether. Taking a few shots at you probably made it a little tricky. But he missed, fortunately for both of you. The only person he actually hurt was Matek. That was apparently the argument from the US side, and given his connections, plus the fact he didn't make off with a penny, it was enough. The police are keeping his name out of it, and the press only seems interested in the gold. If anybody's going to be able to make a stink, it's LeBlanc.'

'Where's he?'

'Chasing false leads in Berlin, last I heard. Apparently he knew Harkness was up to something but couldn't figure out what. Who knows whether he knew about all the stuff buried here? But you can bet he'd like to have a look at these papers.'

'So Harkness gets off free, then?'

Pine shrugged. 'His career will suffer. That's something, I guess. He'd hitched his wagon to Colleton's, and they'll both be watching the wheels come off during the next few weeks. But chances are he'll get a nice settlement. Probably a new life somewhere warm.'

'A better deal than Robert Fordham ever got.'

Pine nodded grimly. 'I called the hospital again this morning. They said he passed away a little after midnight. I'm trying to get Torello to ask for an autopsy. But even then they probably wouldn't find an injection mark. Too easy to hide if you know what you're doing.' Pine lowered his voice. 'One other thing you should know, for what it's worth. Torello told me Harkness was making some noise last night about you and Popovic in Berlin. Don't ask me how he knew, but I'd assume this won't be the last you'll hear of it. Sorry.'

'It's OK,' Vlado said. 'I've decided to make a full report on all that.'

'What do you mean?'

'A sworn statement to the police in Berlin about what happened with Haris and his friend. What I did. Where the body is. They need to know.'

'Why? Why are you doing this?'

'Because I need to.'

'What, to confess? Then tell a priest.'

'No. Someone from my family needs to come clean.'

Pine grimaced, shaking his head. 'So it's for your father then. "Bless me, for he has sinned, and so have I." I guess some of the Catholicism really did rub off.'

'No. It's for my own peace of mind. And because it's

right. My father got his chance at redemption on the last day at Jasenovac, and he seized it. Lia DiFlorio is proof of that. For me there's no life to save, just a story to tell. Yesterday Harkness tried to use it against me, and I knew I'd be under that kind of pressure for the rest of my life.'

'Well, still not too late to change your mind, you know.'

'It is, actually. I spoke to a police lieutenant in Berlin this morning.'

For a moment Pine was speechless.

'I'll do what I can for you, of course.' He spoke slowly. 'I've got some contacts in German law enforcement. A few, anyway. And the Tribunal certainly owes you and your family. Everything may yet work out.'

'It already has,' Vlado said, surer than ever that he was right.

Epilogue

Berlin wore grey for Vlado's homecoming. But for once he didn't mind as his plane descended through successive veils of cloud. Even the maddening flatness didn't seem to register as the jet circled low, searching the dimness of a winter afternoon for the landing strip at Tegel.

The authorities, by previous agreement, weren't waiting for him. So far the Berlin police had bent over backwards not to seem jackbooted or Prussian. The lieutenant who'd spoken to Vlado in Italy had chatted with the bland, reasonable manner of a TV host arranging a panel on the euro as they'd discussed the likelihood of whether Vlado would remain a free man.

'It helps immensely that you came forward,' the officer said in crisp English. 'Given that you didn't actually participate in the killing, and given as well the circumstances of the victim's past, most factors weigh in your favour. Though of course we'll have to verify your account with the two primary suspects.'

No problems there. Haris and Huso had been only too happy to turn themselves over to international authorities in Sarajevo once the word went out, having spent the preceding days dodging undesirables from the Belgrade underworld.

Pine had done his part. He knew a German on the Tribunal who was a friend of a friend of the chief inspector. Two phone calls later, everyone felt better, re-balancing a scale that might otherwise have tipped unfairly against an uprooted Bosnian.

So it was that Vlado received the welcome that he had missed five years earlier. Properly alerted this time, Jasmina unearthed a dress she hadn't worn since before the war, to a wedding in 1991. Sonja wore her one and only party dress, already a size too small, but that only made it more affecting for Vlado, who took it as a sign his little girl was growing up too fast.

They were waiting just outside the security entrance at his gate, and he emerged into a joyous implosion of Balkan shouts and grasping arms. They exchanged the usual phrases that can never stretch large enough to enfold such moments.

'It's so good to have you back.'

'Good to be back.'

'Did you catch them all, Daddy?'

'Yes, Sonja. I'm finished with all that now.'

Then they drove home in a borrowed car – an Opel, not a Yugo – and Sonja chattered as if someone had been winding her spring all morning. Were there really windmills in Holland? Had he eaten much spaghetti? Was there still an emperor with rows of centurions? She squealed with delight when Vlado gave her a small box of Vesuvian stones, which he'd discovered at an airport gift shop in the nick of time.

They burst into their apartment on a wave of cooking smells and the fragrance of cut flowers. The memory of his dreary arrival five years earlier vanished in the steam of roast lamb and warm dumplings, and as they ate their way through the celebratory feast the wine blossomed like a benediction in Vlado's weary head.

Yet, when it came time to tell the stories – the ones he knew he must tell of his father, of Lia, of old wars and old sorrows that inevitably gave way to new ones – he felt strangely claustrophobic. It all seemed lodged in his throat like some bite too immense to swallow. And for a moment he felt the crush of those earlier years – alone in a siege with too much to think about and no-one to tell it to, his trapped words going stagnant.

Jasmina, seeming to read his thoughts, rose quickly from her chair. For a bizarre moment he thought she was going to slap him sharply on the back, as if he were choking. Instead she darted to a side table, an eagerness in her eyes.

'I meant to tell you,' she said brightly, reaching for something, 'this came for you this morning.'

It was a small white envelope, stuffed plump like a great ravioli, the right side plastered with Italian stamps postmarked Castellammare di Stabia. The handwriting was small and careful. He gently tore it open to find a short note:

'Dear Vlado. There is much more for us to know about

each other, and many memories to share about the man we both loved. Bring your wife and your daughter. My home was his, and now it is yours. Love, Lea.'

She'd spelled her name the Slovenian way, he noticed, and she'd enclosed seven black and white snapshots. New prints from old negatives, it seemed, made just for them. They were shots of his father, young and smiling, some with Lea, some with others; but none, he saw with relief, with Matek.

Proudly, as if he'd just drawn a winning hand at poker, Vlado fanned the photos before him on the table-cloth. Eyes shining, he looked at Jasmina, then Sonja, both cocking their heads as if they had a thousand new questions.

'Sonja,' he said, 'did you know that you had a . . .' What should he call her? '. . . step-grandmother in Italy. On the seashore. She's been a secret, all these years, but someday we might visit her, all of us.'

His audience was hooked, and Vlado was certain now that it would all come easily, even the darker chapters to be told later, on this thrilling night when he had at last come home.

Afterword

I owe a great deal to a great many for helping me complete this book.

Thanks to Tom Hundley, valued colleague and friend, for the germ of an idea that evolved into an important subplot, as well as for his hospitality to my family during our stay in Rome. Thanks as well to William Gowen, for sharing hours of vivid memories of his days as a US Army counterintelligence officer in post-war Italy.

Greatly assisting my historical research were Ron Neitzke, former Historian for the US Department of State, and distinguished Croatian historian Jere Jareb, who directed me to a wealth of old memos, reports and diplomatic cables on the subjects of looted Croatian gold and the escape of dictator Ante Pavelic, not to mention Dr Jareb's harrowing personal memories of Croatia during the final days of the Second World War.

Thanks also to authors John Loftus and Mark Aarons, whose book, *Unholy Trinity*, offered valuable perspective on the post-war 'Ratline' of Father Draganovic.

In preparing to write, and also during my work in Europe as a journalist, I had the pleasure and privilege of meeting in The Hague at various times more than a dozen prosecutors and investigators for the International Criminal Tribunal for the former Yugoslavia. Perhaps nowhere on earth will you find a more tireless, selfless and idealistic bunch. All accurate characterization of Tribunal operations should be credited to their contributions, and the brief paragraph from a Tribunal indictment, glimpsed by Vlado Petric in the fourth chapter, is an excerpt from the 'Jelisic and Cesic' indictment of July 1995. Any discrepancies or false notes concerning the Tribunal – this is a work of fiction, after all – are my responsibility alone.

In Berlin, thanks to friend and journalist Anja Kolaschnik, for help in meeting Bosnian refugees in the city, and to Amir Kahvedzic and Boslijka Schedlich for sharing their experiences and observations on the refugee life. In Sarajevo, Lejla Gotovusa, Emir Salihovic and others offered valuable insights on the city's post-war state of mind.

For guiding me beyond the choppy seas of the first draft, profuse thanks to my agent and first line of defence, Jane Chelius; to brilliant colleague and friend Scott Shane; and to Soho Press editor Juris Jurjevics, who owed me nothing but helped anyway. Many thanks also to editors Jenny Minton in New York and Selina

Walker in London, for deftly lighting the way to completion.

As always, I reserve my greatest thanks for my wife, Liz Bowie, for love, encouragement and support.

DAN FESPERMAN'S
SUPERB NEW NOVEL IS

THE WARLORD'S SON

HERE'S THE FIRST CHAPTER
TO WHET YOUR APPETITE

CHAPTER ONE

The sun does not rise in Peshawar.

It seeps — an egg-white smear that brightens the eastern horizon behind a veil of smoke, exhaust and dust. The smoke rises from burning wood, cow patties and old tyres, meager flames of commerce for kebab shops and bakers, metalsmiths and brick kilns. The worst of the exhaust sputters from buzzing blue swarms of motor rickshaws, three-wheeled terrors that careen between horse carts and overloaded buses.

But it was the dust that Najeeb Azam knew best. Like him, it had swirled down from the arid lands of the Khyber and never settled, prowling restlessly in the streets and bazaars as if awaiting a fresh breeze to carry it to some further, better destination.

In the morning it coated his pillow, a faint powder flecked with soot. In the evening he wiped it from his face and coughed cinders into a handkerchief, never quite able to flush it from either pores or lungs. Wherever he travelled it went along for the ride, a parasite, a little gift from his adopted home. He was respectful of its mysterious cloaking powers, because things had a way of disappearing in Peshawar — people, ideas, entire political movements. They would be loud and noticeable one day, only to vanish without a trace in the next, and with each new day someone or something else always seemed to have gone missing.

A Peshawar dawn nonetheless had its charms, and Najeeb liked to rise early to savour them. So, on a warm morning in mid October he stood in the darkness of his small kitchen a half-hour before sunrise, brewing tea while listening to Mansour's horse cart leaving for the bazaar. He knew without looking that the old man stood like a charioteer on a narrow wooden flatbed, reins in hand, pomegranates and tomatoes piled behind him, the baggy folds of his *shalwar kameez* flowing ghostlike in the pale light. The lonely clip- clip was soothing, yet also a sort of warning, like the ticking of a bomb. It was part of Peshawar's daily countdown to chaos. Soon enough the narrow streets would explode with vehicles, animals and people, beggars and merchants elbow to elbow along the margins as both cried out for rupees.

The loudspeaker of a nearby mosque crackled to life. Najeeb strolled to the living room, setting his teacup on a shelf and kneeling, lowering his forehead to the rug in prayer. This, too, was a ritual of tranquillity, yet it never seemed quite peaceful enough here.

In the tribal lands of his boyhood the *muezzin*'s cry had been a solitary call, haunting and lovely. He used to pretend the message was for him alone, and to Najeeb there was still no grander expression of power than the words *Allahu Akbar*, God is Great, when carried on a morning breeze across empty country-side. But in Peshawar there were more *muezzins* than he could count, and their calls became an unruly conversation – one voice trumping another in a war above the rooftops. Cats yowling over turf. Or perhaps Najeeb was turning into an infidel, a worldly backslider. A *Kafir*, as his father's Pashtun tribesmen would have said. Life never seemed half so holy now as it once had, and in a country where not only a man's calling but also his marriage were generally set in stone by age eighteen, Najeeb was still a work in progress at twenty-seven.

As a boy he'd roamed a wonderland of extremes, a rural princeling at play among bearded turbaned men with rifles slung on their backs, all of whom owed their allegiance to his father. After breakfast he might sprint barefoot through the dew of waist-high poppies, dodging marauding boys from the village with slingshots round their necks. As the sun climbed higher he sought the refuge of high defiles to watch smuggler parades of camels and horses, teatime caravans swaying and clanking through the passes. Then, off to bed on the verandah of his father's *hujera*, the men's guest house, where he gazed up at stars so icy bright that it seemed they might pierce his skull. Pleasantly weary, he stretched on a rope bed, eavesdropping on his father's guests and supplicants – smoky piratical gatherings in the *hujera*'s great room, with hubble-bubble hookahs and high-calibre bandoleers, lulling him to sleep with the streamside murmur of their mutter and growl, and the whine and hum of their radio, beaming news from the great beyond. Occasionally a burst of laughter or angry shout shouldered, but by morning there was only him and the *muezzin* beneath another clear sky.

Yet, that world also had its special cloaking magic. It was a place where one learned quickly to conceal his thoughts and dreams, and from his earliest years Najeeb's elders taught him to hold in his emotions, sheathing them like a weapon.

At the age of eighteen he abruptly left behind that world, dispatched across the seas to university in the United States. It was his father's idea, a vain stab at worldliness to impress a few haughty ministers in the government corridors of Islamabad. Najeeb went reluctantly, and for months he held himself sternly under wraps, bookish and brooding through a North Carolina winter amid airless dreams of home.

Then came the spring, and Najeeb emerged timidly from underground, sampling the bounty of bright new places that began to make home seem small, plain and crude. There were supermarkets as big as his village, libraries the size of canyons, lush trees alive with blossoms and songbirds. Then there were the women, practically naked compared to the ones he'd grown up with. They were a temptation, he knew, yet there was a holiness about them, too – as if heaven and hell had been rolled into one amazing creation of bare arms, exposed legs and lustrous heads of hair, their animated faces open to the world and all its possibilities. They soon became responsible for an altogether new kind of training in Najeeb's life. Tell us your feelings, they demanded. Share your thoughts. Having been exposed to Shakespeare in the same heady spring, Najeeb found himself torn in ways he had never anticipated. To feel or not to feel, that was the question.

And now, years after his homecoming, he was not only restless but trapped – banished from tribal lands by his father, barred from America by consular officials.

His father's action had followed a betrayal which Najeeb no longer cared to revisit. The consular ban was of a more recent vintage. The United States had decided the previous month that it no longer wanted his company, after his two worlds had collided in ways previously unimaginable in the burning skies of lower Manhattan.

So, he soldiered on in Peshawar, feeling as if he'd snagged a little of himself in each place he'd departed. And as each morning's peace dissolved he often found himself brooding over what was missing, sometimes believing that he, too, was disappearing into the Peshawar haze, as indistinct as the horizon. In a country where most people defined themselves by family or faith, Najeeb found himself resorting to a more American approach, seeking identity from his various occupations. For the moment, then, he was a translator and guide, a painter of birds, an un-employed computer engineer, and, most recently, a journalist of sorts, reporting for a rambling English daily called the *Frontier Report*.

The few people in Peshawar who knew Najeeb well could have added further labels – disowned son, enthusiastic fornicator, occasional imbiber of forbidden beverage, habitual consorter with foreigners – tireless seeker of any path, in other words, that might lead beyond Pakistan. And at this precarious moment in the city's history, when choosing sides was the order of the day, Najeeb remained dangerously neutral.

One thing no one ever called him was lazy, and today's schedule was particularly industrious. First on the agenda: a ride on his motor scooter to the humble offices of the *Frontier Report*, where as always there would be plenty to write about. His daily task was to fashion a digest of news briefs from the tribal hinterlands of the Northwest Frontier Province. It always made for strange reading – rustic feuds and oddball robberies, villages convulsed over the tiniest of matters. Perhaps someday he would collect them in a volume of curios for his friends in the United States, a Pakistani gothic that would finally make them understand what made this place tick.

The most important business of the day was scheduled for late afternoon, when Najeeb would meet yet another foreign journalist who wanted to hire him for guiding and interpreting. A fixer, the job was called, and today's client was American.

With most of the journalists so far the routine had been pretty standard. They spent their first few days doing interviews in the streets, liking the lilt of the word 'bazaar' in their copy and enjoying the way every merchant invited them inside for tea. Najeeb translated while fending off hordes of curious barefoot boys and legless beggars.

If there happened to be a demonstration that day, they covered it, taking care to stay upwind from the tear gas. Then came the obligatory visit to a *modrassah*, one of the religious schools that supplied the Taliban with so many foot soldiers. Black-haired boys kneeling in straight lines on scrubbed marble floors, heads bobbing as they recited the Koran. Then perhaps a chant or two of 'Death to America', before collecting quotes from the resident Holy Scholar.

Najeeb and his clients always shared an awkward laugh in the taxi afterwards, the reporter never quite sure where Najeeb stood on these matters, and Najeeb never eager to say, not when every cabby was a potential informant.

Then, unless there was some new wave of refugees to badger, Najeeb would escort his client east, three hours down the bouncing highway to the calm green sterility of Islamabad, to seek out bureaucrats and diplomats who might grant travel papers for the Afghan border. Because Afghanistan was the ultimate goal of every client, even if the border had been closed for weeks and would likely stay that way a while longer.

If it ever opened, Najeeb would probably cross it as well. Not that he enjoyed gunfire. But at a pay rate of $150 a day he couldn't afford to say no, because the one thing that might yet get him out of this place was cash.

Yet, even as his supply of cash reached $3,000 and counting, the American embassy grew ever more remote. A hasty security cordon that had gone into place after September 11 had crept ever further down the surrounding boulevards. Now, a mere five weeks later, you couldn't get within blocks of the place, and for the moment a visa was out of the question. Not only had most of the embassy staff left the country, but there was now a waiting list, a clerk told him by telephone. It might take weeks, even months. Meanwhile, reports filtered back from the United States of young Pakistani men disappearing into gaols by the hundreds, gone without a word of explanation. So Najeeb bided his time and stacked his crisp fifties and hundreds, stockpiling ammunition for a battle that might never come.

Such was the drift of Najeeb's thinking that morning when, still on his knees, he was startled by a whisking sound from over by the door. Had he completed his prayers? He wasn't sure. The loud-speakers of the mosques were silent. A rickshaw whined past outside, scouting for the day's first fare. He checked his watch – still time for another cup of tea – but his eyes were drawn to a spinning white object on the floor tiles. It was an envelope, just coming to rest. Someone had shoved it beneath the door. He listened for departing footsteps, but there was only the clopping of another horse, so he rose stiffly and crossed the room, throwing open the door in expectation of discovering the crouching messenger, caught in the act.

But there was no one. Nothing. And the stairwell was silent. It was as if the envelope had fallen from the sky with the first shaft of sunlight. Shutting the door, he picked it up – cream coloured and sealed, but not a single smudge. Whoever had sealed the cream coloured envelope had done so without a single smudge, meaning he was either clean or careful.

Najeeb tore open the top and pulled out a folded sheet of paper of the same creamy complexion. There was no letterhead or official markings, only a hand-written message in black ink, neat and cramped, giving the impression of someone not accustomed to writing. At the top were the numbers '24:30', and the writing below was in Arabic. It was a passage from the Koran. With no one there to watch, Najeeb allowed himself an irreverent smile. No doubt he was about to receive a scolding from a neighbour, some lesson in morals from a well-meaning meddler.

'Enjoin believing men to turn their eyes away from temptation and to restrain their carnal desires,' the first line said. 'This will make their lives purer.'

His smile widened. Someone must have seen Daliya exiting a few nights ago, and it probably wasn't the first time. The memory brightened his mood. Whereas he thought of himself as wispy and insubstantial, she was full and complicated, a soul worth clinging to. He continued reading.

'Enjoin believing women to turn their eyes away from temptation and to preserve their chastity; not to display their adornments.'

Oh, but such adornments. If this writer only knew. Another set of numbers followed, '24:39,' meaning the writer had skipped ahead. The next passage took his smile away.

'As for the unbelievers, their works are like a mirage in a desert. The thirsty traveller thinks it is water, but when he comes near he finds that it is nothing. He finds God there, who pays him back in full. Swift is God's reckoning.'

Najeeb wondered angrily what sort of 'reckoning' the writer had in mind. Did God's self-appointed scold also intend to be His avenger? He crumpled the page, then reconsidered, smoothing it out and reaching for a pen. This demanded a reply. He pulled his own copy of the Koran from between English editions of Philip Roth and Paul Auster, thumbing the pages. Where was that verse that had recently caught his eye? There. Just as he remembered. He'd be quoting it out of context, of course. In fact, he was likely misinterpreting it altogether, a thought that returned his smile with a gleam of mischief.

'2:79,' he wrote. Then he scribbled in rusty Arabic: 'Woe betide those that write the scriptures with their own hands and then declare: "This is from God," in order to gain some paltry end.'

He stuffed the page into the messenger's own envelope and resealed it with tape, then wrote on the outside in Urdu, 'A reply to this morning's visitor to apartment 12.' After a second mug of tea he grabbed his satchel and the keys to his scooter, taking care to lock the door before rushing down the stairwell. He posted the envelope by the mailboxes at the entrance, wondering how long it would be before someone took the bait. For a moment he had misgivings – why stir the pot? – and his stomach rumbled, as queasy as if he'd just eaten too much *chapal kebab*. He'd have to remind Daliya to take more care in her comings and goings. The city grew more dangerous and irrational by the day.

'Meddlesome fanatics,' Najeeb muttered on his way into the streets. 'They'll be the death of us all.'

**Read the complete book –
coming soon from Bantam Press**

THE WARLORD'S SON

Dan Fesperman

'The sun did not rise in Peshawar. It seeped – an egg-white smear that brightened the eastern horizon behind a veil of smoke, exhaust and dust. The smoke rose from burning wood, cow dung and old tires, meager flames of commerce for kebab shops and bakers, metal-smiths and brick kilns. The exhaust sputtered from buzzing blue swarms of motor rickshaws, three-wheeled terrors that jolted across potholes, darting between buses like juiced-up golf carts.'

Into this smoky chaos of sprawling humanity comes Skelly, a burned-out American war correspondent, now in harness again thanks to a messy divorce and too many children. Post nine-eleven, he's back in the game, in yet another new and extremely hazardous location, dropped from the skies after scarcely as much preparation as one might make for a weekend at the beach.

But first he must find a 'fixer'; someone local yet who speaks English, who's good on the ground, yet can arrange transport; a man who is essential to keeping one alive and safe, yet knows where the action is. And, for every war correspondent in Peshawar, the action is across the border in the mountain strongholds of Afghanistan . . .

Soon Skelly and his fixer, Najeeb, are driving dusty roads north, in the wake of Mahmood Abdul Khan – ex-Mujahadeen, ex-Taliban, currently good friend of the Allied forces. For Skelly has been promised the scoop of a lifetime, the sort that will allow him to write his own ticket back to the States. He and Najeeb are on the trail of the tribal leader whom every American is after, the biggest fish of them all . . .

0 593 05041 X

COMING SOON FROM BANTAM PRESS

LIE IN THE DARK

Dan Fesperman

'A DÉBUT NOVEL OF IMMENSE POWER'
The Times

Investigator Petric makes his living from the dead. Lately
business has been slow, what with the siege around Sarajevo.
Condoned killing has displaced the crime of passion; his
services with the civil police as a homicide investigator have
been less in demand. Unluckily one premeditated death does
land on the detective's desk. It is no abused lover or a distant
sniper's victim but a government official the chief of the
interior ministry's police – shot dead at close range.

In a thriller that recalls the first excitement of Martin Cruz
Smith's Moscow and the Vienna of Graham Greene's *The Third
Man,* author Dan Fesperman brilliantly renders the fragmented
society and underworld of Sarajevo at war – the freelancing
gangsters, guilty bystanders, drop-in correspondents, the
bureaucrats frightened for their jobs and very lives – and he
weaves through this torn cityscape one man's desperate, deadly
pursuit of the wrong people in the worst places.

'ONE OF THE BEST BOOKS I HAVE READ FOR A
LONG TIME'
Sunday Telegraph

'A haunting ice-cool novel – *The Third Man*
meets *Gorky Park*. Stunning'
Daily Mirror

'A QUITE ASTONISHING FIRST NOVEL WHICH INJECTS
THE READER INTO THE HEART OF THE DARKNESS WHICH
WAS SARAJEVO AT THE HEIGHT OF THE YUGOSLAV
CONFLICT. READING THIS BOOK IS LIKE BEING THERE. IF
FESPERMAN HAD TAKEN ME ANY CLOSER TO THE
ACTION I'D BE DEMANDING A FLAK JACKET . . . THIS IS A
HUMANE AND MOVING BOOK, A GREAT CRIME NOVEL. A
GREAT NOVEL, PERIOD'
Ian Rankin

0 552 77268 2

BLACK SWAN

MISSION FLATS

William Landay

Nothing much happens in Versailles, Maine. Until a body is found in a cabin up by the lake. The dead man turns out to be from the Boston DA's office, a prosecutor who had been investigating a series of gang-related murders in that city. Ben Truman, Chief of Police, heads down to Boston to follow the few fragile leads he has in the case. Not welcomed by the police there, he knows he really should get the message and disappear back to the sticks. Big city crime is way beyond anything he's ever dealt with before.

But still Truman refuses to let it go. With the help of a retired cop who knows all the angles, he becomes embroiled in an investigation which has its roots in a sequence of deaths which began twenty years previously.

From its violent and shocking opening, through vivid depictions of battle-scarred inner city Boston, to its intensely suspenseful conclusion, *Mission Flats* is the most thrilling literary crime novel in some years – combining intelligence and thoughtful, precise prose with page-turning action.

'The most promising début since Scott Turow's
Presumed Innocent'
Sunday Times

'Lyrical, keenly observed, and occasionally as dark as a wrong turn at midnight, *Mission Flats* is a harrowing, memorable début by a writer to watch'
Stephen White

'*Mission Flats* has action, excellent surprises and a powerful ending, but it also has strong, well-written characters. Landay's début novel is a cut above and I'm looking forward to his next book'
Phillip Margolin

0 552 14944 6

CORGI BOOKS

BANGKOK 8

John Burdett

In surreal Bangkok, city of temples and brothels, where
Buddhist monks in saffron robes walk the same streets as
world-class gangsters, a US marine sergeant is killed inside *a*
locked Mercedes by a maddened python and a swarm of
cobras. Two policemen the only two in the city not on the take
– arrive too late. Minutes later, only one is alive.

The cop left standing, Sonchai Jitpleecheep, is a devout
Buddhist and swears to avenge the death of his partner and
soul brother. To do so he must use the forensic techniques of
modern policing and his own profound understanding of the
mystical workings of the spirit world. Both will be vital as he
immerses himself in the moneyed underbelly of Bangkok –
where desire rules and where he will eventually find the
killer, a predator of an even more sinister variety. . .

'Cracking East meets West thriller introducing a half-Thai,
half-American cop whose Buddhist beliefs are as important as
his forensic skills. Terrific'
Observer

'A fantastic new thriller with an avenging Buddhist cop as its
central character'
Mail on Sunday

'Like a modern-day Indiana Jones adventure written by Evelyn
Waugh . . . One of this season's cleverest and most stylish
entertainments'
Wall Street Journal

'Quirky and highly entertaining . . . something to enjoy for its
sheer bravado'
New York Times

'A thriller as exotic as it is enthralling, and as provocative as it
is obscene'
Harpers

'Impeccably researched, this is sometimes poetic, often exotic,
and totally hardcore'
Daily Mirror

0 552 77140 6

CORGI BOOKS

A SELECTED LIST OF FINE WRITING AVAILABLE FROM CORGI AND BLACK SWAN

14900 4	THE WHITE RUSSIAN	*Tom Bradby*	£6.99
14951 9	THE DA VINCI CODE	*Dan Brown*	£6.99
77140 6	BANGKOK 8	*John Burdett*	£6.99
99979 2	GATES OF EDEN	*Ethan Coen*	£7.99
99686 6	BEACH MUSIC	*Pat Conroy*	£8.99
14578 5	THE MIRACLE STRAIN	*Michael Cordy*	£5.99
99985 7	DANCING WITH MINNIE THE TWIG	*Mogue Doyle*	£6.99
77206 2	PEACETIME	*Robert Edric*	£6.99
77268 2	LIE IN THE DARK	*Dan Fesperman*	£6.99
14923 3	THE VETERAN	*Frederick Forsyth*	£6.99
13678 6	THE EVENING NEWS	*Arthur Hailey*	£5.99
77082 5	THE WISDOM OF CROCODILES	*Paul Hoffman*	£7.99
77109 0	THE FOURTH HAND	*John Irving*	£6.99
14901 2	WALLS OF SILENCE	*Philip Jolowicz*	£6.99
15021 5	THE ANALYST	*John Katzenbach*	£6.99
14970 5	THE BUSINESS OF DYING	*Simon Kernick*	£6.99
14584 X	THE COLD CALLING	*Will Kingdom*	£5.99
99859 1	EDDIE'S BASTARD	*William Kowalski*	£6.99
14944 6	MISSION FLATS	*William Landay*	£6.99
99807 9	MONTENEGRO	*Starling Lawrence*	£6.99
77133 3	MY WAR GONE BY, I MISS IT SO	*Anthony Loyd*	£7.99
14870 9	DANGEROUS DATA	*Adam Lury & Simon Gibson*	£6.99
14799 0	LIBERATION DAY	*Andy McNab*	£6.99
77095 7	LONDON IRISH	*Zane Radcliffe*	£6.99
99810 9	THE JUKEBOX QUEEN OF MALTA	*Nicholas Rinaldi*	£6.99
15043 6	TRAITOR'S KISS	*Gerald Seymour*	£6.99
14391 X	A SIMPLE PLAN	*Scott Smith*	£5.99
99864 8	A DESERT IN BOHEMIA	*Jill Paton Walsh*	£6.99
99948 2	HENDERSON'S SPEAR	*Ronald Wright*	£6.99